The Heroine

Eaton Stannard Barrett

Table of Contents

INTRODUCTION

'In Glamorganshire, of a rapid decline, occasioned by the bursting of a blood-vessel, Eaton Stannard Barrett, esq., a native of Ireland, and a student of the Middle Temple. He published "All the Talents", a Poem, 8vo. 1817.—"The Comet", a mock newspaper, 8vo. 1803.—A very pleasing poem intituled "Woman", 8vo. 1810.— "The Heroine, or Adventures of Cherubina", 3 vols. 12mo, 2d. edit. 1814. This volume is said to abound in wit and humour.'

Very little can now be added to this obituary notice, which appeared in the *Gentleman's Magazine* for April, 1820. The young Irishman whose death it records was born at Cork in 1786, received his education chiefly in London, addicted himself to the law, and was early diverted into the profession of letters, which he practised with great energy and versatility. Besides the works mentioned above, he wrote a serio-comic romance called *The Rising Sun*, and a farcical comedy, full of noise and bustle, called *My Wife, What Wife?* The choice of this last phrase (sacred, if any words in poetry are sacred) for the title of a rollicking farce indicates a certain bluntness of sensibility in the author. He was young, and fell head over ears in love with cleverness; he was a law-student, and took to political satire as a duck takes to the rain; he was an Irishman, and found himself the master of a happy Irish wit, clean, quick, and dainty, but no ways searching or profound. At the back of all his satire there lies a simple social creed, which he accepts from the middle-class code of his own time, and does not question. The two of his works which achieved something like fame, *Woman, a Poem*, and *The Heroine*, here reprinted, set forth that creed, describing the ideal heroine in verse, and warning her, in prose, against the extravagances that so easily beset her. The mode in female character has somewhat changed since George was king, and the pensive coyness set up as a model in the poem seems to a modern reader almost as affected as the vagaries described in the novel. Yet the poem has all the interest and brilliancy of an old fashion-plate. Here is woman as she wished to be in the days of the Regency, or perhaps as man wished her to be, for it is impossible to say which began it. Both gloried in the contrast of their habits. If man, in that age of the prize-ring and the press-gang, was pre-eminently a drinking, swearing, fighting animal, his indelicacy was redeemed by the shrinking graces of his mate.

For woman is not undevelopt man,

But diverse:

as the poet of the later nineteenth century sings. But Tennyson was anticipated in this discovery by Mr. Barrett:

Yes, heaven a contrast not unmeet, designed

Between the bearded and the blushing kind.

Those who often see the bearded kind clad in overcoats, carrying umbrellas, and timorous of social greetings, may have some difficulty in recognizing the essential truth of the following lines, which describe man in his grandeur, as his blushing consort loves to think of him:

Man, from those moments, when his infant age

Cried for the moon, ambitious aims engage,

One world subdued, more worlds he wishes given,

He piles his impious tower to clamber heaven;

Scoops cities under earth; erects his home

On mountains of wild surges, vales of foam;

Soars air, and high above the thunder runs,

Now flaked with sleet, now reddened under suns.

Even in his pastime man his soul reveals;

Raised with carousing shout, his goblet reels.

Now from his chase imperial lions fly,

And now he stakes a princedom on a die.

What would he more? The consecrated game

Of murder must transmit his epic name,

Some empire tempts him; at his stern command,

An armed cloud hails iron o'er the land.

Earth thunders underneath the pondrous tread,

Son slaughters sire, the dying stab the dead.

The vallies roar, that loved a warbling mood,
Their mutilated lilies float on blood;
And corpses sicken streams, and towns expire,
And colour the nocturnal clouds with fire.
Last, vultures pounce upon the finished strife,
And dabble in the plash of human life.

Such is man, all magnificence and terror. And now a softly trilling note ushers in the partner of his cares:

But the meek female far from war removes,
Girt with the Graces and endearing Loves.
To rear the life we destine to destroy,
To bind the wound we plant, is her employ.
Her rapine is to press from healing bud,
Or healthful herb, the vegetable blood;
Her answer, at the martial blast abhorred,
Harmonic noise along the warbling chord.
To her belong light roundelay and reel,
To her the crackling hearth and humming wheel;
(Sounds of content!) to her the milky kine,
And Peace, O Woman, gentle Peace is thine.

Their studies are as dissimilar as their tastes. Nothing less than a comet will excite the curiosity of man; for woman the flower-garden is science enough:

Prone o'er abstruse research, let man expound
Dark causes; what abyss our planet drowned;
And where the fiery star its hundred years
Of absence travels, ere it re-appears.
To Woman, whose best books are human hearts,
Wise heaven a genius less profound imparts.
His awful, her's is lovely; his should tell
How thunderbolts, and her's how roses fell.

Here is the genesis of the Early Victorian ideal of female beauty. The author describes, with heart-felt sentiment, its graces and charms,

The beautiful rebuke that looks surprise,
The gentle vengeance of averted eyes;

—which last line so pleased him that it occurs again in *The Farewell* (Letter XXV of *The Heroine*). The shorter poem, like the longer, has the indescribable old-world charm of a pressed rose-leaf, an elegant tarnished mirror, a faded silken fan, a vanished mode. The secret of this sentimental type of beauty perhaps lies here, that the simplicity and shyness and ardour of youth are reduced, not by a conscious science, but by the timid rules of propriety and modesty, to the service of an all-prevailing coquetry. Ovid, as expounded by Mrs. Chapone or Miss Hannah More, gains something in the delicacy of his methods, and loses nothing of his empire:

Ut quondam iuvenes, ita nunc, mea turba, puellae
Inscribant spoliis: Naso magister erat.

It must be said, however, that the author of *Woman, a Poem* does not confine himself to the alluring graces. His best known and most quoted lines are written in praise of courage and fidelity:

Not she denied her God with recreant tongue,
Not she with traitrous kisses round him clung;
She, while Apostles shrank, could danger brave,
Last at his cross and earliest at his grave.

If he were to survive in a single quotation, it is probably by these lines that the author, who spent much labour on the revision and polishing of his poem, would wish to be remembered.

It may seem strange that the author of this romantic poem on Woman should have been so ready to parody the new school of prose romance. Miss Cherry Wilkinson, when she took the name of Cherubina, and commenced heroine, might certainly have found some useful hints for her behaviour in this earlier treatise. But the fact is that no parodist is successful who has not at some time fallen deeply under the spell of the literature that he parodies. Parody is, for the most part, a weak and clinging kind of tribute to the force of its original. Very perfect parodies, which catch the soul, as well as the form, of the models that they imitate, almost lose their identity and become a part of that which they were meant to ridicule. Feeble parodies, where poor matter, not strong enough to speak for itself, claims notice by the aid of a notorious tune, are even more conspicuously dependent on the vogue of their original. The art of a tailor is seen in the cut of a coat; to make a mechanical copy of it, substituting tartan or fustian for velvet, is what any Chinese slave can do. It is form in literature which is difficult to invent. When a poem or a story, by the individuality and novelty of its form, has caught the public taste, there are always some among its victims who are nothing if not critical. They cannot forget it, yet it does not content them. They think it narrow and partial in its conception; it does not mirror Nature exactly as they see her; in short, they have ideas of their own. These ideas perhaps have not vitality enough to create their own definite form, so when a form is presented to them they seize on it for their purpose. Hence every new and original kind in literature produces a tribe of imitators, some of them contented imitators, who undersell the first author with colourable copies; others discontented imitators, or parodists, who offer their own substitute for the author's wares, yet stamp it with his brand. The compliment is the same in either case; and the effect is not much different, for nothing so quickly exhausts the popularity of a work of art as its power of multiplying its kind. Some congenital weakness, it is fair to say, there must have been in the original, when the form designed for a single purpose serves so many others. The weakness is not always easy to detect; but it is always there. It may be the weakness of excess; an ample and loose-folded robe like Walt Whitman's is characteristic of its wearer, but can soon be adapted to a borrower. Or it may be the weakness of defect; the music and solemnity of the *Psalm of Life* are a world too wide for the shrunken body of the thought that they conceal. A perfect conception expressing itself inevitably in the form that has grown with its growth defies imitators. The great things of Virgil and of Dante suffer no parody. And this is what is meant by a classic.

Yet lesser books have their day; and young authors, or old authors trying a new kind of work, often begin by imitation. They discover their genius by their failure. The famous parodies (so to call them) are not parodies at all; their freedom from the servility of parody is what has given them their place in literature. Cervantes may have thought that he could criticize and banter the romances of chivalry by telling the adventures of a poor and high-minded gentleman travelling on the roads of Spain; but once the new situation was created it called for a new treatment. Fielding doubtless intended to parody Richardson by a tale of the chastity of a serving-man; and it is easy to see how a mere wit would have carried out the design. But Fielding, like Cervantes, was too rich in ideas, and too brave in purpose, to be another man's mocking servitor. First Mrs. Slipslop incommodes the framework by her intrusion, and then Parson Adams enters to complete the disaster. The breakdown of these pretended parodies is always due to the same cause—the appearance on an artificially designed scene of real character. Character, where it is fully conceived, will not take its orders from the scene-shifter; it reacts in surprising ways to slight accidental provocations; it will not play the part or speak the words assigned to it; it is consistent with nothing but itself; from self-revelation it soon passes to self-assertion, and subdues the world to its will, disordering all the puppet-show.

It cannot be claimed for Eaton Stannard Barrett that he proved superior to the task which he undertook. There is little or no real character in *The Heroine*. Perhaps Jerry Sullivan, the faithful Irish servitor, with his ready speech and bold resourcefulness, comes nearest to the life, but even he is drawn, like Lever's comic Irishmen, not intimately. A few touches of verisimilitude are sufficient to portray a servant, whose business is to come when he is called and to help others in their necessities. The heroine herself has no breath in her; she is inconceivably credulous, impossibly ignorant, and even while she talks the author often forgets her very existence and speaks in her stead, so that she seems to be quizzing her own fatuity. Perhaps this incompetent portraiture was to be expected from the author of *Woman, a Poem*, but it takes some of the edge off the fun of the book. Cherubina is not a girl, with silly, flighty notions in her head, such as romance engenders, but a pedantic female lawyer, determined to order her life, down to the smallest detail, on precedents borrowed from her favourite reading. Miss Austen's girls, in *Northanger Abbey*, talk like girls; Cherubina talks like a book. Nevertheless, Miss Austen herself read *The Heroine*, and confessed to the pleasure she had from it. It enjoyed a high and brief reputation. The first edition appeared in 1813; the second followed it in the space of a year; and in 1816 the author, before he was thirty years old, may have read a notice of himself in the *Biographical Dictionary of the Living Authors of Great Britain and Ireland* concluding with the following eulogy: 'This work (*The Heroine*) has been pronounced not inferior in wit and humour to Tristram Shandy, and in point of plot and interest infinitely beyond Don Quixote.'

Let us save what remnants we can of this monstrous pronouncement. Of character, as has been said, there is next to none in *The Heroine*; so that only those who can read *Don Quixote* and *Tristram Shandy*, careless of the characters portrayed, might possibly be able to return a verdict on the comparison. There are many readers of

6

books who grudge labour spent on character-drawing; the long colloquies between Don Quixote and Sancho or between my Uncle Toby and Corporal Trim they would be glad to see abbreviated, so they might get back to the confusion and bustle of life. Why all this dissection of the heart, while there are crowns to be broke? What the soldier said is not evidence; it is what he did that they desire to hear. For readers of this temper there is abundance of entertainment in *The Heroine*, if once they can bring themselves to accept the perilously slender illusion. The scenes described are as full of movement as a harlequinade. No Irish fair is richer in incident. And there is such a flow of high spirits; the author carries the whole business through with such unflagging zest, that the farce, though it hardly ever touches on the confines of comedy, is pleasant farce, instinct with good nature and good fellowship. Those who like a book that saves them from the more exacting companionship of their own thoughts might do worse than read *The Heroine*.

This is lukewarm praise; but the book has a stronger claim than this on the interest of the reader; it marks a crisis in literary history. The author was a well-read man, and all the fashionable literature of his day is reflected in his pages. He was familiar with the essayists and moralists of the eighteenth century; indeed, he often falls into their attitude in his opposition to the extravagances of the Romantic movement. His parody of Johnson's later style is one of the very best of the multitude of Johnsonian imitations. Boswell, writing before 1791, was able to enumerate a distinguished array of disciples and copyists, among them Hugh Blair, Professor of Rhetoric at Edinburgh, George Colman the elder, Robertson the historian, Gibbon, Miss Burney, Mrs. Barbauld, Henry Mackenzie, Vicesimus Knox, and last, John Young, Professor of Greek at Glasgow, whose *Criticism on the Elegy written in a Country Church-yard, being a continuation of Dr. Johnson's Criticism on the Poems of Gray* (1783) is rightly praised by Boswell as the most perfect of all professed imitations of Johnson's style. It is only half a parody; Johnson's method in criticism has been so thoroughly assimilated by the author, that some of Johnson's strong sense filters in here and there as if by oversight. Horace Walpole said of it, acutely enough, that the author seemed to wish to be taken by Gray's admirers for a ridiculer of Johnson, and by Johnson's admirers for a censurer of Gray. But if this is the best imitation of Johnson's critical manner, his biographical style and his light occasional verse have never been so happily mimicked as in the *Memoirs of James Higginson, by Himself*, which occur in Letter X of *The Heroine*. Johnson continued to be the most influential teacher of English prose until Macaulay, by introducing a more glittering kind of antithesis and a freer use of the weapons of offence in criticism, usurped his supremacy.

A more voluminous and easier literature had enthralled the popular taste for some thirty or forty years before the author of *The Heroine* delivered his attack. Only a few are now remembered even by name of that horde of romances which issued from the cheap presses, in the train of Mrs. Radcliffe. It is reasonable to suppose that many of them, which had not the help of that great preservative of a bad book, good binding, have perished from off the face of the earth. They are not yet old enough to be precious, as Elizabethan trash is precious, and doubtless the surviving copies of some of them are even now being cast out from lumber-rooms and remote country libraries, to suffer their fate by fire. Their names are scattered plentifully up and down the *Bibliotheca Britannica* and other monumental compilations, where books that go under in their fight against time have Christian burial and a little headstone reserved for them. In *The Heroine* only the chief of them are referred to by name. The romances of Mrs. Radcliffe—*The Mysteries of Udolpho*, *The Italian*, and *The Bravo of Venice*— are praised as being 'often captivating and seldom detrimental'. The rivals of Mrs. Radcliffe who wrote those enormously popular works, *The Children of the Abbey* and *Caroline of Lichtfield*, receive a less respectful treatment. At the close of his book the author of *The Heroine* summarizes his indictment against these and their kind: 'They present us with incidents and characters which we can never meet in the world; and act upon the mind like intoxicating stimulants; first elevate, and then enervate it. They teach us to revel in ideal scenes of transport and distraction; and harden our hearts against living misery, by making us so refined as to feel disgust at its unpoetical accompaniments.' Throughout the book he keeps up a running fire of criticism. When Cherubina visits Westminster Abbey, 'It is the first,' she says, 'that I have ever seen, though I had read of thousands.' She apologizes for using the vulgar word 'home'—'you know that a mere home is my horror'. She confesses that she is very inadequately armed with religion—'I knew nothing of religion except from novels; and in these, though the devotion of heroines is sentimental and graceful to a degree, it never influences their acts, or appears connected with their moral duties. It is so speculative and generalized, that it would answer the Greek or the Persian church, as well as the Christian; and none but the picturesque and enthusiastic part is presented; such as kissing a cross, chanting a vesper with elevated eyes, or composing a well-worded prayer.'

The notable thing is that this attack on the novels of the day was not an isolated protest; it expressed the general mind and echoed the current opinion. Miss Austen, with more suavity and art, had long before said the same thing. The romance was declining; it had become a cheap mechanical thing; and the mind of the nation was turning away from it to reinstate those teachers of moral prudence whose influence had been impaired by the flood, but not destroyed. If any one had been rash enough, in the year 1814, to prophesy the future of literature, he would have been justified in saying that, to all appearances, the prose romance was dead. It had fallen into its dotage, and the hand of Eaton Stannard Barrett had killed it. *The Heroine* seemed to mark the end of an age of romance, and the beginning of a new era of sententious prose.

Such a prophet would have been approved by *The Edinburgh Review* and all the best judges of the time. He would have been wrong, for he could not foresee the accident of genius. Walter Scott, like Cherubina (whose adventures he read and applauded), had fallen a victim to the fascinations of the writers of romance, yet, unlike her, had not allowed them to deprive him of all acquaintance with 'a more useful class of composition' and the toils of active life. Romance was what he cared for, and he brought the sobriety and learning of a judge to the task of vindicating his affection. He proved that the old romantic stories are convincing enough if only the blood of life flows through them. His great panoramas of history are exhibited in the frame-work of a love-plot. In place of the feeble comic interest of the earlier romances he supplied a rich and various tissue of national character and manners. Ancient legend and song, fable and superstition, live again in his work. And, as if Cherubina's unhappy experiences had all been in vain, there is always a heroine. The readers who had been laughed into scepticism by the wit of the enemy were within a few years won back to poetry and romance; Cherubina was deposed, and in her place there reigned the Bride of Lammermoor.

WALTER RALEIGH.

Oxford,
Christmas, 1908.

THE
HEROINE,
OR
ADVENTURES OF A FAIR ROMANCE READER,
BY
EATON STANNARD BARRETT, ESQ.

"L'Histoire d'une femme est toujours un Roman."

IN THREE VOLUMES.
VOL. I.

LONDON:
PRINTED FOR HENRY COLBURN,
PUBLIC LIBRARY, CONDUIT-STREET, HANOVER-SQUARE;
AND SOLD BY GEORGE GOLDIE, EDINBURGH,
AND JOHN CUMMING, DUBLIN.

1813.

TO THE
RIGHT HONORABLE
GEORGE CANNING
&c. &c. &c.

Sir,

It was the happiness of Sterne to have dedicated his volumes to a Pitt. It is my ambition to inscribe this work to you. My wishes would be complete, could I resemble the writer as you do the statesman.

I have the honor to be,

Sir,

Your most sincere, and most humble servant,

E. S. BARRETT.

Attend, gentle and intelligent reader; for I am not the fictitious personage whose memoirs you will peruse in 'The Heroine;' but I am a corporeal being, and an inhabitant of another world.

Know, that the moment a mortal manuscript is written out in a legible hand, and the word End or Finis annexed thereto, whatever characters happen to be sketched in it (whether imaginary, biographical, or historical), acquire the quality of creating and effusing a sentient soul or spirit, which instantly takes flight, and ascends through the regions of air, till it arrives at the moon; where it is then embodied, and becomes a living creature; the precise counterpart, in mind and person, of its literary prototype.

Know farther, that all the towns, villages, rivers, hills, and vallies of the moon, owe their origin, in a similar manner, to the descriptions given by writers of those on earth; and that all the lunar trades and manufactures, fleets and coins, stays for men, and boots for ladies, receive form and substance here, from terrestrial books on war and commerce, pamphlets on bullion, and fashionable magazines.

Works consisting of abstract argument, ethics, metaphysics, polemics, &c. which, from their very nature, cannot become tangible essences, send up their ideas, in whispers, to the moon; where the tribe of talking birds receive, and repeat them for the Lunarians. So that it is not unusual to hear a mitred parrot screaming a political sermon, or a fashionable jay twittering unfigurative canzonets. These birds then are our philosophers; and so great is their value, that they sell for as much as your patriots.

The moment, however, that a book becomes obsolete on earth, the personages, countries, manners, and things recorded in it, lose, by the law of sympathy, their existence in the moon.

This, most grave reader, is but a short and imperfect sketch of the way we Moonites live and die. I shall now give you some account of what has happened to me since my coming hither.

It is something more than three lunar hours; or, in other words, about three terrestrial days ago, that, owing to the kindness of some human gentleman or other (to whom I take this opportunity of returning my grateful thanks), I became conscious of existence. Like the Miltonic Eve, almost the first thing I did was to peep into the water, and admire my face;—a very pretty one, I assure you, dear reader. I then perceived advancing a lank and grimly figure in armour, who introduced himself as Don Quixote; and we soon found each other kindred souls.

We walked, hand in hand, through a beautiful tract of country called Terra Fertilitatis; for your Selenographers, Langrenus, Florentius, Grimaldus, Ricciolus, and Hevelius of Dantzic, have given proper names to the various portions of our hemisphere.

As I proceeded, I met the Radcliffian, Rochian, and other heroines; but they tossed their heads, and told me pertly that I was a slur on the sisterhood; while some went so far as to say I had a design upon their lives. They likewise shunned the Edgeworthian heroines, whom they thought too comic, moral, and natural.

I met the Lady of the Lake, and shook hands with her; but her hand felt rather hard from the frequent use of the oar; and I spoke to the Widow Dido, but she had her old trick of turning on her heel, without answering a civil question.

I found the Homeric Achilles broiling his own beefsteaks, as usual; the Homeric Princesses drawing water, and washing linen; the Virgilian Trojans eating their tables, and the Livian Hannibal melting mountains with the patent vinegar of an advertisement.

The little boy in the Æneid had introduced the amusement of whipping tops; and Musidora had turned bathing-woman at a halfpenny a dip.

A Cæsar, an Alexander, and an Alfred, were talking politics, and quaffing the Horatian Falernian, at the Garter Inn of Shakespeare. A Catiline was holding forth on Reform, and a Hanno was advising the recall of a victorious army.

As I walked along, a parcel of Moonites, fresh from your newspapers, just popped up their heads, nodded, and died. About twenty statesmen come to us in this way almost every day; and though some of them are of the same name, and drawn from the same original, they are often as unlike each other as so many clouds. The Buonapartes, thus sent, are, in general, hideous fellows. However, your Parliamentary Reports sometimes agreeably surprise us with most respectable characters of that name.

On my way, I could observe numbers of patients dying, according as the books that had created them were sinking into oblivion. The Foxian James was paraded about in a sedan chair, and considered just gone; and a set of politicians, entitled All the Talents, who had once made a terrible noise among us, lay sprawling in their last agonies. But the most extensive mortality ever known here was caused by the burning of the Alexandrian Library. This forms quite an æra in the Lunar Annals; and it is called The great Conflagration.

I had attempted to pluck an apple from a tree that grew near the road; but, to my surprise, grasped a vacuum; and while Don Quixote was explaining to me that this phænomenon arose from the Berkeleian system of immaterialism; and that this apple was only a globular idea, I heard a squeaking voice just beside me cry:

'I must remark, Madam, that the writer who sent you among us had far too much to say, and too little to do.'

I looked round, but saw nobody.

"Tis Junius,' observed Don Quixote. 'He was invisible on earth, and therefore must be so here. Do not mind his bitter sayings.'

'An author,' continued the satirist, 'who has judgment enough to write wit, should have judgment enough to prevent him from writing it.'

'Sir,' said Don Quixote, 'if, by his works of wit, he can attain popularity, he will ensure a future attention to his works of judgment. So here is at thee, caitiff!' and closing his visor, he ran atilt at pure space.

'Nay,' cried Junius, 'let us not quarrel, though we differ. Mind unopposed by mind, fashions false opinions of its own, and degenerates from its original rectitude. The stagnant pool resolves into putridity. It is the conflict of the waters which keeps them pure.'

'Except in dropsical cases, I presume,' said Tristram Shandy, who just then came up, with his Uncle Toby. 'How goes it, heroine? How goes it?—By the man in the moon, the moment I heard of your arrival here, I gave three exulting flourishes of my hand, thus 1 2 3 then applying my middle finger to my thumb, and compressing them, by means of the flexory muscles, I shot them asunder transversely; so that the finger coming plump upon the aponeurosis—

In short,—for I don't much like the manner in which I am getting on with the description—I snapped my fingers.

'Now, Madam, I will bet the whole of Kristmanus's, Capuanus's, Schihardus's, Phocylides's, and Hanzelius's estates,—which are the best on our disk,—to as much landed property as could be shovelled into your shoe— that you will get miserably mauled by their reverences, the Scotch Reviewers. My life for it, these lads will say that your character is a mere daub drawn in distemper—the colouring too rich—the hair too golden—an eyelash too much—then, that the book itself has too little of the rational and argumentative;—that the fellow merely wrote it to make the world laugh,—which, an' please your reverences, is the gravest occupation an author can chuse;—that some of its incidents are plastered as thick as butter on the bread of Mamma's darling; others so diluted, that they wash down the bread and butter most unpalatably, and the rest unconducive to the plot, moral, and peripeteia. In short, Madam, it will appear that the work has every fault which must convict it Aristotellically and Edinburgo—reviewically, in the eyes of ninety-nine barbati; but which will leave it not the ninety-ninth part of a gry the worse in the eyes of fifteen millions of honest Englishmen; besides several very respectable ladies and gentlemen yet unborn, and nations yet undiscovered, who will read translations of it in languages yet unspoken. Bless me, what hacking they will have at you! Small sword and broad sword—staff and stiletto—flankonnade and cannonade—hurry-scurry—right wing and left wing——'

But Tristram paused short in consternation; for his animated description of a fight had roused the military spirits of Don Quixote and Captain Shandy, who were already at hard knocks; the one with his spear, and the other with his crutch. I therefore took this occasion of escaping.

And now day begins to decline; and your globe, which never sets to us, will soon shed her pale earthshine over the landscape. O how serene, how lovely these regions! Here are no hurricanes, or clouds, or vapours. Here heroines cannot sigh; for here there is no air to sigh withal. Here, in our great pits, poetically called vallies, we retire from all moonly cares; or range through the meads of Cysatus or Gruemberget, and luxuriate in the coolness of the Conical Penumbra.

I trust you will feel, dear reader, that you now owe more to my discoveries than to those of Endymion, Copernicus, Tycho Brahe, Galileus, and Newton. I pray you, therefore, to reward my services with a long and happy life; though much I fear I shall not obtain it. For, I am told, that two little shining specks, called England and Ireland (which we can just see with our glasses on your globe), are the places that I must depend upon for my health and prosperity. Now, if they fall, I must fall with them; and I fancy they have seen the best of their days already. A parrot informs me, that they are at daggers drawn with a prodigious blotch just beside them; and that their most approved patriots daily indite pamphlets to shew how they cannot hold out ten years longer. The Sternian Starling assured me just now that these patriots write the triumphs of their country in the most commiserating language; and portray her distresses with exultation. Of course, therefore, they conceive that her glories would undo her, and that nothing can save her but her calamities. So, since she is conquering away at a great rate, I may fairly infer that she is on her last legs.

Before I conclude, I must inform you of how I shall have this letter conveyed to your world. Laplace, and other philosophers, have already proved, that a stone projected by a volcano, from the moon, and with the velocity of a mile and a half per second, would be thrown beyond the sphere of the moon's attraction, and enter into the confines of the earth's. Now, hundreds have attested on oath, that they have seen luminous meteors moving through the sky; and that these have fallen on the earth, in stony or semi-metallic masses. Therefore, say the philosophers, these masses came all the way from the moon. And they say perfectly right. Believe it piously, dear reader, and quote me as your authority.

It is by means of one of these stones that I shall contrive to send you this letter. I have written it on asbestus, in liquid gold (as both these substances are inconsumable by fire); and I will fasten it to the top of a volcanic mountain, which is expected to explode in another hour.

Alas, alas, short-sighted mortals! how little ye foresee the havoc that will happen hereafter, from the pelting of these pitiless stones. For, about the time of the millenium, the doctrine of projectiles will be so prodigiously improved, that while there is universal peace upon earth, the planets will go to war with each other. Then shall we Lunarians, like true satellites, turn upon our benefactors, and instead of merely trying our small shot (as at present), we will fire off whole mountains; while you, from your superior attraction, will find it difficult to hit us at all. The consequence must be, our losing so much weight, that we shall approach, by degrees, nearer and nearer to you; 'till at last, both globes will come slap together, flatten each other out, like the pancakes of Glasse's Cookery, and rush headlong into primeval chaos.

Such will be the consummation of all things.

Adieu.

THE HEROINE

LETTER I

My venerable Governess, guardian of my youth, must I then behold you no more? No more, at breakfast, find your melancholy features shrouded in an umbrageous cap, a novel in one hand, a cup in the other, and tears springing from your eyes, at the tale too tender, or at the tea too hot? Must I no longer wander with you through painted meadows, and by purling rivulets? Motherless, am I to be bereft of my more than mother, at the sensitive age of fifteen? What though papa caught the Butler kissing you in the pantry? What though he turned you by the shoulder out of his house? I am persuaded that the kiss was maternal, not amorous, and that the interesting Butler is your son.

Perhaps you married early in life, and without the knowledge of your parents. A gipsy stole the pretty pledge of your love; and at length, you have recognized him by the scar on his cheek. Happy, happy mother!

Happy too, perhaps, in being cast upon the world, unprotected and defamed; while I am doomed to endure the security of a home, and the dullness of an unimpeached reputation. For me, there is no hope whatever of being reduced to despair. I am condemned to waste my health, bloom, and youth, in a series of uninterrupted prosperity.

It is not, my friend, that I wish for ultimate unhappiness, but that I am anxious to suffer present sorrow, in order to secure future felicity: an improvement, you will own, on the system of other girls, who, to enjoy the passing moment, run the risk of being wretched for ever after. Have not all persons their favorite pursuits in life, and do not all brave fatigue, vexation, and calumny, for the purpose of accomplishing them? One woman aspires to be a beauty, another a title, a third a belle esprit; and to effect these objects, health is sacrificed, reputation tainted, and peace of mind destroyed. Now my ambition is to be a Heroine, and how can I hope to succeed in my vocation, unless I, too, suffer privations and inconveniences? Besides, have I not far greater merit in getting a husband by sentiment, adventure, and melancholy, than by dressing, gadding, dancing, and singing? For heroines are just as much on the alert to get husbands, as other young ladies; and to say the truth, I would never voluntarily subject myself to misfortunes, were I not certain that matrimony would be the last of them. But even misery itself has its consolations and advantages. It makes one, at least, look interesting, and affords an opportunity for ornamental murmurs. Besides, it is the mark of a refined mind. Only fools, children, and savages, are happy.

With these sentiments, no wonder I should feel discontented at my present mode of life. Such an insipid routine, always, always, always the same. Rising with no better prospect than to make breakfast for papa. Then 'tis, 'Good morrow, Cherry,' or 'is the paper come, Cherry?' or 'more cream, Cherry,' or 'what shall we have to dinner, Cherry?' At dinner, nobody but a farmer or the Parson; and nothing talked but politics and turnips. After tea I am made sing some fal lal la of a ditty, and am sent to bed with a 'Good night, pretty miss,' or 'sweet dear.' The clowns!

Now, instead of this, just conceive me a child of misery, in a castle, a convent, or a cottage; becoming acquainted with the hero by his saving my life—I in beautiful confusion—'Good Heaven, what an angel!' cries he—then sudden love on both sides—in two days he kisses my hand. Embarrassments—my character suspected—a quarrel—a reconciliation—fresh embarrassments.—O Biddy, what an irreparable loss to the public, that a victim of thrilling sensibility, like me, should be thus idling her precious time over the common occupations of life!—prepared as I am, too, by a five years' course of novels (and you can bear witness that I have read little else), to embody and ensoul those enchanting reveries, which I am accustomed to indulge in bed and bower, and which really constitute almost the whole happiness of my life.

That I am not deficient in the qualities requisite for a heroine, is indisputable. All the world says I am handsome, and it would be melancholy were all the world in error. My form is tall and aërial, my face Grecian, my tresses flaxen, my eyes blue and sleepy. But the great point is, that I have a remarkable mole just over my left temple. Then, not only peaches, roses, and Aurora, but snow, lilies, and alabaster, may, with perfect propriety, be adopted in a description of my skin. I confess I differ from other heroines in one point. They, you may remark, are always unconscious of their charms; whereas, I am, I fear, convinced of mine, beyond all hope of retraction.

There is but one serious flaw in my title to Heroine—the mediocrity of my lineage. My father is descended from nothing better than a decent and respectable family. He began life with a thousand pounds, purchased a farm, and by his honest and disgusting industry, has realized fifty thousand. Were even my legitimacy suspected, it would be some comfort; since, in that case, I should assuredly start forth, at one time or other, the daughter of some plaintive nobleman, who lives retired, and slaps his forehead.

One more subject perplexes me. It is my name; and what a name—Cherry! It reminds one so much of plumpness and ruddy health. Cherry—better be called Pine-apple at once. There is a green and yellow melancholy in Pine-apple, that is infinitely preferable. I wonder whether Cherry could possibly be an abbreviation of Cherubina. 'Tis only changing y into ubina, and the name becomes quite classic. Celestina, Angelina, Seraphina, are all of the same family. But Cherubina sounds so empyrean, so something or other beyond mortality; and besides I have just a face for it. Yes, Cherubina I am resolved to be called, now and for ever.

But you must naturally wish to learn what has happened here, since your departure. I was in my boudoir, reading the Delicate Distress, when I heard a sudden bustle below, and 'Out of the house, this moment,' vociferated by my father. The next minute he was in my room with a face like fire.

'There!' cried he, 'I knew what your famous romances would do for us at last.'

'Pray, Sir, what?' asked I, with the calm dignity of injured innocence.

'Only a kissing match between the Governess and the Butler,' answered he. 'I caught them at the sport in the pantry.'

I was petrified. 'Dear Sir,' said I, 'you must surely mistake.'

'No such thing,' cried he. 'The kiss was too much of a smacker for that:—it rang through the pantry. But please the fates, she shall never darken my doors again. I have just discharged both herself and her swain; and what is better, I have ordered all the novels in the house to be burnt, by way of purification. As they love to talk of flames, I suppose they will like to feel them.' He spoke, and ran raging out of the room.

Adieu, then, ye dear romances, adieu for ever. No more shall I sympathize with your heroines, while they faint, and blush, and weep, through four half-bound octavos. Adieu ye Edwins, Edgars, and Edmunds; ye Selinas, Evelinas, Malvinas; ye inas all adieu! The flames will consume you all. The melody of Emily, the prattle of Annette, and the hoarseness of Ugo, all will be confounded in one indiscriminate crackle. The Casa and Castello will blaze with equal fury; nor will the virtue of Pamela aught avail to save; nor Wolmar delighting to see his wife in a swoon; nor Werter shelling peas and reading Homer, nor Charlotte cutting bread and butter for the children.

You, too, my loved governess, I regret extremely.

Adieu.

Cherubina.

It was not till this morning, that a thought of the most interesting nature flashed across my mind. Pondering on the cruel conduct of my reputed father, in having burnt my novels, and discharged you, without even allowing us to take a hysterical farewell, I was struck with the sudden notion that the man is not my father at all. In short, I began with wishing this the case, and have ended with believing it. My reasons are irresistible, and deduced from strong and stubborn facts. For, first, there is no likeness between this Wilkinson and me. 'Tis true, he has blue eyes, like myself, but has he my pouting lip and dimple? He has the flaxen hair, but can he execute the rosy smile? Next, is it possible, that I, who was born a heroine, and who must therefore have sprung from an idle and illustrious family, should be the daughter of a farmer, a thrifty, substantial, honest farmer? The thing is absurd on the face of it, and never will I tamely submit to such an indignity.

Full of this idea, I dressed myself in haste, resolving to question Wilkinson, to pierce into his inmost soul, to speak daggers to him; and if he should not unfold the mystery of my birth, to fly from his house for ever. With a palpitating heart, I descended the stairs, rushed into the breakfast-room, and in a moment was at the feet of my persecutor. My hands were folded across my bosom, and my blue eyes raised to his face.

'Heyday, Cherry,' said he, laughing, 'this is a new flourish. There, child, now fancy yourself stabbed, and come to breakfast.'

'Hear me,' cried I.

'Why,' said he, 'you keep your countenance as stiff and steady as the face on our rapper.'

'A countenance,' cried I, 'is worth keeping, when the features are a proof of the descent, and vindicate the noble birth from the baseness of the adoption.'

'Come, come,' said he, 'your cup is full all this time.'

'And so is my heart,' cried I, pressing it expressively.

'What is the meaning of this mummery?' said he.

'Hear me, Wilkinson,' cried I, rising with dignified tranquillity. 'Candor is at once the most amiable and the most difficult of virtues; and there is more magnanimity in confessing an error, than in never committing one.'

'Confound your written sentences,' cried he, 'can't you come to the point?'

'Then, Sir,' said I, 'to be plain and explicit, learn, that I have discovered a mystery in my birth, and that you—you, Wilkinson, are not—my real Father!'

I pronounced these words with a measured emphasis, and one of my ineffable looks. Wilkinson coloured like scarlet and stared steadily in my face.

'Would you scandalize the mother that bore you?' cried he, fiercely.

'No, Wilkinson,' answered I, 'but you would, by calling yourself my father.'

'And if I am not,' said he, 'what the mischief must *you* be?'

'An illustrious heiress,' cried I, 'snatched from my parents in her infancy;—snatched by thee, vile agent of the diabolical conspiracy!'

He looked aghast.

'Tell me then,' continued I, 'miserable man, tell me where my dear, my distracted father lingers out the remnant of his wretched days? My mother too—or say, am I indeed an orphan?'

Still he remained mute, and gazed on me with a searching intensity. I raised my voice:

'Expiate thy dire offences, restore an outcast to her birthright, make atonement, or *tremble at retribution*!'

I thought the farmer would have sunk into the ground.

'Nay,' continued I, lowering my voice, 'think not I thirst for vengeance. I myself will intercede for thee, and stay the sword of Justice. Poor wretch! I want not thy blood.'

The culprit had now reached the climax of agony, and writhed through every limb and feature.

'What!' cried I, 'can nothing move thee to confess thy crimes? Then hear me. Ere Aurora with rosy fingers shall unbar the eastern gate——'

'My child, my child, my dear darling daughter!' exclaimed this accomplished crocodile, bursting into tears, and snatching me to his bosom, 'what have they done to you? What phantom, what horrid disorder is distracting my treasure?'

'Unhand me, guileful adulator,' cried I, 'and try thy powers of tragedy elsewhere, for—*I know thee*!' I spoke, and extricated myself from his embrace.

'Dreadful, dreadful!' muttered he. 'Her sweet senses are lost.' Then turning to me: 'My love, my life, do not speak thus to your poor old father.'

'Father!' exclaimed I, accomplishing with much accuracy that hysterical laugh, which (gratefully let me own) I owe to your instruction; 'Father!'

The fat farmer covered his face with his hands, and rushed out of the room.

I relate the several conversations, in a dramatic manner, and word for word, as well as I can recollect them, since I remark that all heroines do the same. Indeed I cannot enough admire the fortitude of these charming creatures, who, while they are in momentary expectation of losing their lives, or their honours, or both, sit down with the utmost unconcern, and indite the wittiest letters in the world. They have even sufficient presence of mind to copy the vulgar dialect, uncouth phraseology, and bad grammar, of the villains whom they dread; and all this in the neatest and liveliest style imaginable.

Adieu.

LETTER III

Soon after my last letter, I was summoned to dinner. What heroine in distress but loaths her food? so I sent a message that I was unwell, and then solaced myself with a volume of the Mysteries of Udolpho, which had escaped the conflagration. At ten, I flung myself on my bed, in hopes to have dreams portentous of my future fate; for heroines are remarkably subject to a certain prophetic sort of night-mare. You remember the story that Ludovico read, of a spectre who beckons a baron from his castle in the dead of night, and leading him into a forest, points to his own corpse, and bids him bury it. Well, owing, I suppose, to my having just read this episode, and to my having fasted so long, I had the following dreams.

Methought a delicious odour of viands attracted me to the kitchen, where I found an iron pot upon the fire simmering in unison with my sighs. As I looked at it with a longing eye, the lid began to rise, and I beheld a half-boiled turkey stalk majestically forth. It beckoned me with its claw. I followed. It led me into the yard, and pointed to its own head and feathers, which were lying in a corner. I felt infinitely affected.

Straight the scene changed. I found myself seated at a dinner-table; and while I was expecting the repast, lo, the Genius of Dinner appeared. He had a mantle laced with silver eels, and his locks were dropping with costly soups. A crown of golden fishes was on his head, and pheasants' wings at his shoulders. A flight of little tartlets fluttered around him, and the sky rained down hock, comfits, and Tokay. As I gazed on him, he vanished, in a sigh, that was strongly impregnated with the fumes of brandy. What vulgar, what disgusting visions, when I ought to have dreamt of nothing but coffins and ladies in black.

At breakfast, this morning, Wilkinson affected the most tender solicitude for my health; and as I now watched his words, I could discover in almost all that he said, something to confirm my surmise of his not being my father.

After breakfast a letter was handed to him, which he read, and then gave to me. It was as follows:

London.

In accepting your invitation to Sylvan Lodge, my respected friend, I am sure I shall confer a far greater favor on myself, than, as you kindly tell me, I shall on you. After an absence of seven years, spent in the seclusion of a college, and the fatigues of a military life, how delightful to revisit the scene of my childhood, and those who contribute to render its memory so dear! I left you while you were my guardian; I return to you with the assurances of finding you a friend. Let me but find you what I left you, and you shall take what title you please.

Yet, much as I flatter myself with your retaining all your former feelings towards me, I must expect a serious alteration in those of my friend Cherry. Will she again make me her playmate? Again climb my shoulders, and gallop me round the lawn? Are we to renew all our little quarrels, then kiss and be friends? Shall we even recognize each other's features, through their change from childhood to maturity? There is, at least, one feature of our early days, that, I trust, has undergone no alteration—our mutual affection and friendship.

I fear I cannot manage matters so as to be with you before ten to-morrow night: remember I bespeak my old room.

Ever affectionately your's,

Robert Stuart.

To Gregory Wilkinson, Esq.

'There,' cries the farmer, 'if I have deprived you of an old woman, I have got you a young man. Large estates, you know;—handsome, fashionable;—come, pluck up a heart, my girl; ay, egad, and steal one too.'

I rose, gave him one of my ineffable looks, and retired to my chamber.

'So,' said I, locking my door, and flinging myself on the bed, 'this is something like misery. Here is a precious project against my peace. I am to be forced into marriage, am I? And with whom? A man whose legitimacy is unimpeached, and whose friends would certainly consent. His name Robert too:—master Bobby, as the servants used to call him. A fellow that mewed like a cat, when he was whipt. O my Bob! what a pretty monosyllable for a girl like me to pronounce. Now, indeed, my wretchedness is complete; the cup is full, even to overflowing. An orphan, or at least an outcast; immured in the prison of a proud oppressor—threatened with a husband of decent birth, parentage and education—my governess gone, my novels burnt, what is left to me but flight? Yes, I will roam through the wide world in search of my parents; I will ransack all the sliding pannels and tapestries in Italy; I will explore Il Castello Di Udolpho, and will then enter the convent of Ursulines, or Carmelites, or Santa della Pieta, or the Abbey of La Trappe. Here I meet with nothing better than smiling faces and honest hearts; or at best, with but sneaking villains. No precious scoundrels are here, no horrors, or atrocities, worth mentioning. But abroad I shall encounter banditti, monks, daggers, racks—O ye celebrated terrors, when shall I taste of you?'

I then lay planning an elopement, till I was called to dinner.

Adieu.

LETTER IV

O my friend, such a discovery!—a parchment and a picture. But you shall hear.

After dinner I stole into Wilkinson's study, in hopes of finding, before my flight, some record or relic, that might aid me in unravelling the mystery of my birth. As heroines are privileged to ransack private drawers, and read whatever they find there, I opened Wilkinson's scrutoire, without ceremony. But what were my sensations, when I discovered in a corner of it, an antique piece of tattered parchment, scrawled all over, in uncouth characters, with this frightful fragment.

This Indenture
For and in consideration of
Doth grant, bargain, release
Possession, and to his heirs and assigns
Lands of Sylvan Lodge, in the
Trees, stones, quarries.
Reasonable amends and satisfaction
This demise
Molestation of him the said Gregory Wilkinson
The natural life of
Cherry Wilkinson only daughter of
De Willoughby eldest son of Thomas
Lady Gwyn of Gwyn Castle.

O Biddy, does not your blood run cold at this horrible scrawl? for already you must have decyphered its terrific import. The part lost may be guessed from the part left. In short, it is a written covenant between this Gregory Wilkinson, and the miscreant (whom my being an heiress had prevented from enjoying the title and estate that would devolve to him at my death), stipulating to give Wilkinson 'Sylvan Lodge,' together with 'trees, stones, quarries, &c.' as 'reasonable amends and satisfaction,' for being the instrument of my 'Demise:' and declaring that there shall be 'no molestation of him the said Gregory Wilkinson,' for taking away 'the natural life of Cherry Wilkinson'—'only daughter of——' something—'De Willoughby, eldest son of Thomas'—What an unfortunate chasm! Then follows, 'Lady Gwyn of Gwyn Castle.' So that it is evident I am at least a De Willoughby, and if not noble myself, related to nobility. For what confirms me in this supposition of my relationship to Lady Gwyn, is an old portrait which I found a few minutes after, in one of Wilkinson's drawers, representing a young and beautiful female dressed in a superb style, and underneath it, in large letters, the name of, 'Nell Gwyn.'

Distraction! what shall I do? Whither turn? To sleep another night under the same roof with a wretch, who has bound himself to assassinate me, would be little short of madness. My plan, therefore, is already arranged for flight, and this very evening I mean to begin my pilgrimage.

15

The picture and parchment I will hide in my bosom during my journey; and I will also carry with me a small bandbox, containing my satin slip, a pair of silk stockings, my spangled muslin, and all my jewels. For as some benevolent duchess may possibly take me into her family, and her son persecute me, I might just as well look decent, you know.

On mature deliberation, I have resolved to take but five guineas with me, since more would make me too comfortable, and tempt me, in some critical moment, to extricate myself from distress.

I shall leave the following billet on my toilet.

To Gregory Wilkinson, Farmer.

Sir,

When this letter meets your eye, the wretched writer will be far removed from your machinations. She will be wandering the convex earth in pursuit of those parents, from whose dear embraces you have torn her. She will be flying from a Stuart, for whose detestable embraces you have designed her.

Your motive for this hopeful match I can guess. As you obtained one property by undertaking my death, you are probably promised another for effecting my marriage. Learn that the latter fate has more terrors for me than the former. But I have escaped both. As for the ten thousand pounds willed to me by your deceased wife, I suppose it will revert to you, as soon as I prove that I am not your daughter. Silly man! you might at this moment obtain that legacy, by restoring me to my real parents.

Alas! Sir, you are indeed very wicked. Yet remember, that repentance is never too late, and that virtue alone is true nobility.

The much injured Cherubina.

All is prepared, and in ten minutes I commence my interesting expedition. London being the grand emporium of adventure, and the most likely place for obtaining information on the subject of my birth, I mean to bend my steps thither; and as Stuart is to be here at ten to-night, and as he must come the London road, I shall probably meet him. Should I recognize him, what a scene we shall have! but he cannot possibly recognize me, since I was only eight years old when we last parted.

Adieu.

LETTER V

The rain rattled and the wind whistled, as I tied on my bonnet for my journey. With the bandbox in my hand, I descended the stairs, and paused in the hall to listen. I heard a distant door shut, and steps advancing. Not a moment was to be lost, so I sprang forward, opened the hall door, and ran down the shrubbery.

'O peaceful shades!' exclaimed I, 'why must I leave you? In your retreats I should still find "pleasure and repose!"'

I then hastened into the London road, and pressed forward with a hurried step, while a violent tempest beat full against my face. Being in such distress, I thought it incumbent on me to compose a sonnet; which I copy for you.

SONNET

Bereft by wretches of endearing home,
And all the joys of parent and of friend,
Unsheltered midst the shattering storm I roam,
On mangled feet, and soon my life must end.
So the young lark, whom sire and mother tend,
Some fowler robs of sire and mother dear.
All day dejected in its nest it lies;
No food, no song, no sheltering pinion near.
Night comes instead, and tempests round it rise,
At morn, with gasping beak, and upward breast: it dies.

Four long and toilsome miles had I now walked with a dignified air; till, finding myself fatigued, and despairing of an interview with Stuart, I resolved to rest awhile, in the lone and uninhabited house which lies, you may recollect, on the grey common, about a hundred paces from the road. Besides, I was in duty bound to explore it, as a ruined pile.

I approached it. The wind moaned through the broken windows, and the rank grass rustled in the court. I entered. All was dark within; the boards creaked as I trod, the shutters flapped, and an ominous owl was hooting in the chimney. I groped my way along the hall, thence into a parlour—up stairs and down—not a horror to be found. No dead hand met my left hand, firmly grasping it, and drawing me forcibly forward; no huge eye-ball glared at me through a crevice. How disheartening!

The cold was now creeping through me; my teeth chattered, and my whole frame shook. I had seated myself on the stairs, and was weeping piteously, wishing myself safe at home, and in bed; and deploring the dire necessity which had compelled me to this frightful undertaking, when on a sudden I heard the sound of approaching steps. I sprang upon my feet with renovated spirits. Presently several persons entered the hall, and a vulgar accent cried:

'Jem, run down to the cellar and strike a light.'

'What can you want of me, now that you have robbed me?' said the voice of a gentleman.

'Why, young man,' answered a ruffian, 'we want you to write home for a hundred pounds, or some such trifle, which we will have the honour of spending for you. You must manufacture some confounded good lie about where you are, and why you send for the money; and one of us will carry the letter.'

'I assure you,' said the youth, 'I shall forge no such falsehood.'

'As you please, master,' replied the ruffian, 'but, the money or your life we must have, and that soon.'

'Will you trust my solemn promise to send you a hundred pounds?' said the other. 'My name is Stuart: I am on my way to Mr. Wilkinson, of Sylvan Lodge, so you may depend upon my sending you, by his assistance, the sum that you require, and I will promise not to betray you.'

'No, curse me if I trust,' cried the robber.

'Then curse me if I write,' said Stuart.

'Look you, Squire,' cried the robber. 'We cannot stand parlying with you now; we have other matters on hands. But we will lock you safe in the cellar, with pen, ink, and paper, and a lantern; and if you have not a fine bouncing lie of a letter, ready written when we come back, you are a dead man—that is all.'

'I am almost a dead man already,' said Stuart, 'for the cut you gave me is bleeding torrents.'

They now carried him down to the cellar, and remained there a few minutes, then returned, and locked the door outside.

'Leave the key in it,' says one, 'for we do not know which of us may come back first.' They then went away.

Now was the fate of my bitter enemy, the wily, the wicked Stuart, in my power; I could either liberate him, or leave him to perish. It struck me, that to miss such a promising interview, would be stupid in the extreme; and I felt a sort of glow at the idea of saying to him, live! besides, the fellow had answered the robbers with some spirit, so I descended the steps, unlocked the door, and bursting into the cellar, stood in an unparalleled attitude before him. He was sitting on the ground, and fastening a handkerchief about his wounded leg, but at my entrance, he sprang upon his feet.

'Away, save thyself!' cried I. 'She who restores thee to freedom flies herself from captivity. Look on these features—Thou wouldest have wrung them with despair. Look on this form—Thou wouldest have prest it in depravity. Hence, unhappy sinner, and learn, that innocence is ever victorious and ever merciful.'

'I am all amazement!' exclaimed he. 'Who are you? Whence come you? Why speak so angrily, yet act so kindly?'

I smiled disdain, and turned to depart.

'One moment more,' cried he. 'Here is some mistake; for I never even saw you before.'

'Often!' exclaimed I, and was again going.

'So you will leave me, my sweet girl,' said he, smiling. 'Now you have all this time prevented me from binding my wound, and you owe me some compensation for loss of blood.'

I paused.

'I would ask you to assist me,' continued he, 'but in binding one wound, I fear you would inflict another.'

Mere curiosity made me return two steps.

'I think, however, there would be healing in the touch of so fair a hand,' and he took mine as he spoke.

At this moment, my humanity conquered my reserve, and kneeling down, I began to fasten the bandage; but resolved on not uttering another word.

'What kindness!' cried he. 'And pray to whom am I indebted for it?'

No reply.

'At least, may I learn whether I can, in any manner, repay it?'

No reply.

'You said, I think, that you had just escaped from confinement?'

No reply.

'You will stain your beautiful locks,' said he: 'my blood should flow to defend, but shall not flow to disfigure them. Permit me to collect those charming tresses.'

'Oh! dear, thank you, Sir!' stammered I.

'And thank you, ten thousand times,' said he, as I finished my disagreeable task; 'and now never will I quit you till I see you safe to your friends.'

'You!' exclaimed I. 'Ah, traitor!'

He gazed at me with a look of pity. 'Farewell then, my kind preserver,' said he; "tis a long way to the next habitation, and should my wound open afresh and should I faint from loss of blood——'

'Dear me,' said I, 'let me assist you.'

He smiled. 'We will assist each other,' answered he; 'and now let us not lose a moment, for the robbers may return.'

He took the lantern to search the cellar for his watch and money. However, we saw nothing there but a couple of portmanteaus, some rusty pistols, and a small barrel, half full of gunpowder. We then left the house; but had hardly proceeded twenty yards, when he began to totter.

'I can go no farther,' said he, sinking down. 'I have lost so much blood, that my strength is entirely exhausted.'

'Pray Sir,' said I, 'exert yourself, and lean on me.'

'Impossible,' answered he; 'but fly and save your own life.'

'I will run for assistance,' said I, and flew towards the road, where I had just heard the sound of an approaching carriage. But on a sudden it stopped, voices began disputing, and soon after a pistol was fired. I paused in great terror, for I judged that these were the robbers again. What was I to do? When a heroine is reduced to extremities, she always does one of two things, either faints on the spot, or exhibits energies almost superhuman.

Faint I could not, so nothing remained for me, but energies almost superhuman. I pondered a moment, and a grand thought struck me. Recollecting the gunpowder in the cellar, I flew for it back to the ruin, carried it up to the hall, threw most of it on the floor, and with the remainder, strewed a train, as I walked towards Stuart.

When I was within a few paces of him, I heard quick steps; and a hoarse voice vociferating, 'Who goes yonder with the light?' for I had brought the lantern with me.

'Fly!' cried Stuart, 'or you are lost.'

I snatched the candle from the lantern, applied it to the train, and the next moment dropped to the ground at the shock of the tremendous explosion that followed. A noise of falling timbers resounded through the ruin, and the robbers were heard scampering off in all directions.

'There!' whispered I, after a pause; 'there is an original horror for you; and all of my own contrivance. The villains have fled, the neighbours will flock to the spot, and you will obtain assistance.'

By this time we heard the people of the carriage running towards us.

'Stuart!' cried I, in an awful voice.

'My name indeed!' said he. 'This is completely inexplicable.'

'Stuart,' cried I, 'hear my parting words. *Never again*', (quoting his own letter,) '*will I make you my playmate; never again climb your shoulders, and gallop you round the lawn!* Ten o'clock is past. Go not to Sylvan Lodge to-night. She departed two hours ago. Look to your steps.'

I spoke this portentous warning, and fled across the common. Miss Wilkinson! Miss Wilkinson! sounded on the blast; but the wretch had discovered me too late. I ran about half a mile, and then looking behind me, beheld the ruin in a blaze. Renovated by the sight of this horror, I walked another hour, without once stopping; till, to my surprise and dismay, I found myself utterly unable to proceed a step farther. This was the more provoking, because heroines often perform journeys on foot that would founder fifty horses.

I now knocked at a farm-house, on the side of the road; but the people would not admit me. Soon after, I perceived a boy watching sheep in a field, and begged earnestly that he would direct me to some romantic cottage, shaded with vines and acacias, and inhabited by a lovely little Arcadian family.

'There is no family of that name in these here parts,' said he.

18

These here! cried I, 'Ah, my friend, that is not pastoral language. I see you will never pipe madrigals to a Chloris or a Daphne.'

'And what sort of nasty language is that?' cried he. 'Get along with you, do: I warrant you are a bad one.' And he began pelting me with tufts of grass.

At last, I contrived to shelter myself under a haycock, where I remained till day began to dawn. Then, stiff and chilled, I proceeded on my journey; and in a short time, met a little girl with a pail of milk, who consented to let me change my dress at her cottage, and conducted me thither.

It was a family of frights, flat noses and thick lips without mercy. No Annettes and Lubins, or Amorets and Phyllidas, or Florimels and Florellas; no little Cherubin and Seraphim amongst them. However, I slipped on (for *slipping on* is the heroic mode of dressing) my spangled muslin, and joined their uglinesses at breakfast, resolving to bear patiently with their features. They tell me that a public coach to London will shortly pass this way, so I shall take a place in it.

On the whole, I see much reason to be pleased with what has happened hitherto. How fortunate that I went to the house on the common! I see plainly, that if adventure does not come to me, I must go to adventure. And indeed, I am authorized in doing so by the example of my sister heroines; who, with a noble disinterestedness, are ever the chief artificers of their own misfortunes; for, in nine cases out of ten, were they to manage matters like mere common mortals, they would avoid all those charming mischiefs which adorn their memoirs.

As for this Stuart, I know not what to think of him. I will, however, do him the justice to say, that he has a pleasing countenance; and although he neither kissed my hand, nor knelt to me, yet he had the decency to talk of 'wounds,' and my 'charming tresses.' Perhaps, if he had saved my life, instead of my having saved his; and if his name had consisted of three syllables ending in i or o; and, in fine, were he not an unprincipled profligate, the man might have made a tolerable hero. At all events, I heartily hate him; and his smooth words went for nothing.

The coach is in sight.

Adieu.

LETTER VI

'I shall find in the coach,' said I, approaching it, 'some emaciated Adelaide, or sister Olivia. We will interchange congenial looks—she will sigh, so will I—and we shall commence a vigorous friendship on the spot.'

Yes, I did sigh; but it was at the huge and hideous Adelaide that presented herself, as I got into the coach. In describing her, our wittiest novelists would say, that her nose lay modestly retired between her cheeks; that her eyes, which pointed inwards, seemed looking for it, and that her teeth were

'Like angels' visits; short and far between.'

She first eyed me with a supercilious sneer, and then addressed a diminutive old gentleman opposite, in whose face Time had ploughed furrows, and Luxury sown pimples.

'And so, Sir, as I was telling you, when my poor man died, I so bemoaned myself, that between swoons and hysterics, I got nervous all over, and was obliged to go through a regiment.'

I stared in astonishment. 'What!' thought I, 'a woman of her magnitude and vulgarity, faint, and have nerves? Impossible!'

'Howsomdever,' continued she, 'my Bible and my daughter Moll are great consolations to me. Moll is the dearest little thing in the world; as straight as a popular; then such dimples; and her eyes are the very squintessence of perfection. She has all her catechism by heart, and moreover, her mind is uncontaminated by romances and novels, and such abominations.'

'Pray, Ma'am,' said I, civilly, 'may I presume to ask how romances and novels contaminate the mind?'

'Why, Mem,' answered she tartly, and after another survey: 'by teaching little misses to go gadding, Mem, and to be fond of the men, Mem, and of spangled muslin, Mem.'

'Ma'am,' said I, reddening, 'I wear spangled muslin because I have no other dress: and you should be ashamed of yourself for saying that I am fond of the men.'

'The cap fits you then,' cried she.

'Were it a fool's cap,' said I, 'perhaps I might return the compliment.'

I thought it expedient, at my first outset in life, to practise apt repartee, and emulate the infatuating sauciness, and elegant vituperation of Amanda, the Beggar Girl, and other heroines; who, when irritated, disdain to speak below an epigram.

'Pray, Sir,' said she, to our fellow traveller, 'what is your opinion of novels? Ant they all love and nonsense, and the most unpossible lies possible?'

'They are fictions, certainly,' said he.

'Surely, Sir,' exclaimed I, 'you do not mean to call them fictions.'

'Why no,' replied he, 'not absolute fictions.'

'But,' cried the big lady, 'you don't pretend to call them true.'

'Why no,' said he, 'not absolutely true.'

'Then,' cried I, 'you are on both sides of the question at once.'

He trod on my foot.

'Ay, that you are,' said the big lady.

He trod on her foot.

'I am too much of a courtier,' said he, 'to differ from the ladies,' and he trod on both our feet.

'A courtier!' cried I: 'I should rather have imagined you a musician.'

'Pray why?' said he.

'Because,' answered I, 'you are playing the pedal harp on this lady's foot and mine.'

'I wished to produce harmony,' said he, with a submitting bow.

'At least,' said I, 'novels must be much more true than histories, because historians often contradict each other, but novelists never do.'

'Yet do not novelists contradict themselves?' said he.

'Certainly,' replied I, 'and there lies the surest proof of their veracity. For as human actions are always contradicting themselves, so those books which faithfully relate them, must do the same.'

'Admirable!' exclaimed he. 'And yet what proof have we that such personages as Schedoni, Vivaldi, Camilla, or Cecilia ever existed?'

'And what proof have we,' cried I, 'that such personages as Alfred the Great, Henry the Fifth, Elfrida, or Mary Queen of Scots, ever existed? I wonder at a man of sense like you. Why, Sir, at this rate you might just as well question the truth of Guy Faux's attempt to blow up the Parliament-House, or of my having blown up a house last night.'

'You blow up a house!' exclaimed the big lady with amazement.

'Madam,' said I, modestly, 'I scorn ostentation, but on my word and honour, 'tis fact.'

'Of course you did it accidentally,' said the gentleman.

'You wrong me, Sir,' replied I; 'I did it by design.'

'You will swing for it, however,' cried the big lady.

'Swing for it!' said I; 'a heroine swing? Excellent! I presume, Madam, you are unacquainted with the common law of romance.'

'Just,' said she, 'as you seem to be with the common law of England.'

'I despise the common law of England,' cried I.

'Then I fancy,' said she, 'it would not be much amiss if you were hanged.'

'And I fancy,' retorted I, nodding at her big figure, 'it would not be much amiss if you were quartered.'

Instantly she took out a prayer-book, and began muttering over it with the most violent piety and indignation.

Meantime the gentleman coincided in every syllable that I said, praised my parts and knowledge, and discovered evident symptoms of a discriminating mind, and an amiable heart. That I am right in my good opinion of him is most certain; for he himself assured me that it would be quite impossible to deceive me, I am so penetrating. In short, I have set him down as the benevolent guardian, whom my memoirs will hereafter celebrate, for having saved me from destruction.

Indeed he has already done so. For, when our journey was almost over, he told me, that my having set fire to the ruin might prove a most fatal affair; and whispered that the big lady would probably inform against me. On my pleading the prescriptive immunities of heroines, and asserting that the law could never lay its fangs on so ethereal a name as Cherubina, he solemnly swore to me, that he once knew a golden-haired, azure-eyed heroine, called Angelica Angela Angelina, who was hanged at the Old Bailey for stealing a broken lute out of a haunted chamber; and while my blood was running cold at the recital, he pressed me so cordially to take refuge in his house, that at length, I threw myself on the protection of the best of men.

I now write from his mansion in Grosvenor Square, where we have just dined. His name is Betterton; he has no family, and is possessed of a splendid independence. Multitudes of liveried menials watch his nod; and he does me the honour to call me cousin. My chamber too is charming. The curtains hang quite in a new style, but I do not like the pattern of the drapery.

To-morrow I mean to go shopping; and I may, at the same time, pick up some adventures on my way; for business must be minded.

Adieu.

LETTER VII

Soon after my last letter, I was summoned to supper. Betterton appeared much interested in my destiny, and I took good care to inspire him with a due sense of my forlorn and unprotected state. I told him that I had not a friend in the wide world, related to him my lamentable tale, and as a proof of my veracity shewed him the parchment, the picture, and the mole.

To my great surprise, he said that he considered my high birth improbable; and then began advising me to descend from my romantic flights, as he called them, and to seek after happiness instead of misery.

'In this town,' continued he, after a long preamble, 'your charms would be despotic, if unchained by legal constraints. But for ever distant from you be that cold and languid tie which erroneous policy invented. For you be the sacred community of souls, the mystic union, whose tie of bondage is the sway of passion, the wish, the licence, and impulse the law.'

'Pretty expressions enough,' said I, 'only I cannot comprehend them.'

'Charming girl!' cried he, while he conjured up a fiend of a smile, and drew a brilliant from his finger, 'accept this ring, and the signature of the hand that has worn it, securing to you five hundred a-year, while you remain under my protection.'

'Ha, monster!' exclaimed I, 'and is this thy vile design?'

So saying, I flung the ruffian from me, then rushed down stairs, opened the door, and quick as lightning darted along the streets.

At last, panting for breath, I paused underneath a portico. It was now midnight. Not a wheel, not a hoof fatigued the pavement, or disturbed the slumbering mud of the metropolis. But soon steps and soft voices broke the silence, and a youth, encircling a maiden's waist with his arm, and modulating the most mellifluent phraseology, passed by me. Another couple succeeded, and another, and another. The town seemed swarming with heroes and heroines. 'Fortunate pairs!' ejaculated I, 'at length ye enjoy the reward of your incomparable constancy and virtue. Here, after a long separation, meeting by chance, and in extreme distress, ye pour forth the pure effusions of your souls. O blissful termination of unexampled miseries!'

I now perceived, on the steps of a house, a fair and slender form, robed in white. She was sitting with her elbow in her lap, and her head leaning on one side, within her hand.

'She seems a sister in misfortune,' said I; 'so, should she but have a Madona face, and a name ending in a, we will live, we will die together.'

I then approached, and discovered a countenance so pale, so pensive, so Roman, that I could almost have knelt and worshipped it.

'Fair unfortunate,' said I, taking her hand and pressing it; 'interesting unknown, say by what name am I to address so gentle a sister in misery.'

'Eh? What?' cried she, in a tone somewhat coarser than I was prepared to expect.

'May I presume on my sudden predilection,' said I, 'and inquire your name?'

'Maria,' replied she, rising from her seat; 'and now I must be gone.'

'And where are you going, Maria?' said I.

'To the Devil,' said she.

'Alas! my love,' whispered I, 'sorrow hath bewildered thee. Impart to me the cause of thy distress, and perhaps I can alleviate, if not relieve it. I am myself a miserable orphan; but happy, thrice happy, could I clasp a sympathetic bosom, in this frightful wilderness of houses and faces, where, alas! I know not a human being.'

'Then you are a stranger here?' said she quickly.

'I have been here but a few hours,' answered I.

'Have you money?' she demanded.

'Only four guineas and a half,' replied I, taking out my purse. 'Perhaps you are in distress—perhaps—forgive this officiousness—not for worlds would I wound your delicacy, but if you want assistance——'

'I have only this old sixpence upon earth,' interrupted she, 'and there 'tis for you, Miss.'

So saying, she put sixpence into my purse, which I had opened while I was speaking.

'Generous angel!' cried I.

'Now we are in partnership, a'nt we?' said she.

'Yes, sweet innocent,' answered I, 'we are partners in grief.'

'And as grief is dry,' cried she, 'we will go moisten it.'

'And where shall we moisten it, Maria?' said I.

'In a pothouse,' cried she. 'It will do us good.'

'O my Maria!' said I, 'never, never!'

'Why then give me back my sixpence,' cried she, snatching at my purse; but I held it fast, and, springing from her, ran away.

'Stop thief, stop thief!' vociferated she.

In an instant, I heard a sort of rattling noise from several quarters, and an old fellow, called a watchman, came running out of a wooden box, and seized me by the shoulder.

'She has robbed me of my purse,' exclaimed the wily wanton. ''Tis a green one, and has four guineas and a half in it, besides a curious old sixpence.'

The watchman took it from me, and examined it.

''Tis my purse,' cried I, 'and I can swear it.'

'You lie!' said the little wretch; 'you know well that you snatched it out of my hand, when I was going to give you sixpence, out of charity.'

Horror and astonishment struck me dumb; and when I told my tale, the watchman declared that both of us must remain in custody, till next morning; and then be carried before the magistrate. Accordingly, he escorted us to the watchhouse, a room filled with smoke and culprits; where we stayed all night, in the midst of swearing, snoring, laughing and crying.

In the morning we were carried before a magistrate; and with step superb, arms folded, and neck erect, I entered the room.

'Pert enough,' said the magistrate; and turning from me, continued his examination of two men who stood near him.

It appeared that one of them (whose name was Jerry Sullivan) had assaulted the other, on the following occasion. A joint sum of money had been deposited in Sullivan's hands, by this other, and a third man, his partner, which sum Sullivan had consented to keep for them, and had bound himself to return, whenever both should go together to him, and demand it. Sometime afterwards, one of them went to him, and told him that the other being ill, and therefore unable to come for the money, had empowered him to get it. Sullivan, believing him, gave the money, and when he next met the other, mentioned the circumstance. The other denied having authorized what had been done, and demanded his own share of the deposit from Sullivan, who refused it. Words ensued, and Sullivan having knocked him down, was brought before the magistrate, to be committed for an assault.

'Have you any defence?' said the magistrate to him.

'None that I know of,' answered he, 'only I would knock him down again, if he touched my honour again.'

'And is this your defence?' said the magistrate.

'It is so,' replied Sullivan, 'and I hope your worship likes it, as well as I like your worship.'

'So well,' said the magistrate, 'that I now mean to do you a signal service.'

'Why then,' cried Sullivan, 'may the heavens smile on you.'

'And that service,' continued the magistrate, 'is to commit you immediately.'

'Why then,' cried Sullivan, 'may the Devil inconvenience you!'

'By your insolence, you should be an Irishman,' said the magistrate.

'I was an Irishman forty years ago,' replied Sullivan, 'and I don't suppose I am anything else now. Though I have left my country, I scorn to change my birth-place.'

'Commit him,' said the magistrate.

Just then, a device struck me, which I thought might extricate the poor fellow; so, having received permission, I went across, and whispered it to him.

'The heavens smile on you,' cried he, and then addressed his accuser: 'If I can prove to you that I have not broken our agreement about the money, will you promise not to prosecute me for this assault?'

'With all my heart,' answered he; 'for if you have not broken our agreement, you must have the money still, which is all I want.'

'And will your worship,' said Sullivan, 'permit this compromise, and stand umpire between us?'

'I have not the least objection,' answered the magistrate; 'for I would rather be the means of your fulfilling an agreement, than of your suffering a punishment; and would rather recompense your accuser with money than with revenge.'

'Well then,' said Jerry to his accuser; 'was not our agreement, that I should return the money to yourself and your partner, whenever you came together to me, and asked for it?'

'Certainly,' said the man.

'And did you both ever come together to me, and ask for it?'

'Never,' said the man.

'Then I have not broken our agreement,' cried Sullivan.

'But you cannot keep it,' said the other; 'for you have given away the money.'

'No matter for that,' cried Sullivan, 'provided I have it when both of you come to demand it. But I believe that will be never, for the fellow who ran off will not much like to shew his face again. So now will your worship please to decide.'

The magistrate, after complimenting me upon my ingenuity, confessed, he said, with much unwillingness, that Sullivan had made out his case clearly. The poor accuser was therefore obliged to abide by his promise, and Sullivan was dismissed, snapping his fingers, and offering to treat the whole world with a tankard.

My cause came after, and the treacherous Maria was ordered to state her evidence.

But what think you, Biddy, of my keeping you in suspense, till my next letter? The practice of keeping in suspense is quite common among novelists. Nay, there is a lady in the Romance of the Highlands, who terminates, not her letter, but her life, much in the same style. For when dying, she was about to disclose the circumstances of a horrid murder, and would have done so too, had she not unfortunately expended her last breath in a beautiful description of the verdant hills, rising sun, all nature smiling, and a few streaks of purple in the east.

Adieu.

LETTER VIII

Maria being ordered to state her evidence, 'That I will,' said she, 'only I am so ashamed of having been out late at night—but I must tell your worship how that happened.'

'You need not,' said the magistrate.

'Well then,' she continued, 'I was walking innocently home, with my poor eyes fixed upon the ground, for fear of the fellors, when what should I see, but this girl, talking on some steps, with a pickpocket, I fancy, for he looked pretty decent. So I ran past them, for I was so ashamed you can't think; and this girl runs after me, and says, says she, "The fellor wouldn't give me a little shilling," says she, "so by Jingo, you must," says she.'

'By Jingo! I say by Jingo?' cried I. 'St. Catherine guard me! Indeed, your Excellenza, my only oath is Santa Maria.'

'She swore at me like a trooper,' continued the little imp, 'so I pulled out my purse in a fright, and she snatched it from me, and ran away, and I after her, calling stop thief; and this is the whole truth 'pon my honour and word, and as I hope to be married.'

The watchman declared that he had caught me running away, that he had found the purse in my hand, and that Maria had described it, and the money contained in it, accurately.

'And will your worship,' said Maria, 'ask the girl to describe the sixpence that is in it?'

The magistrate turned to me.

'Really,' said I, 'as I never even saw it, I cannot possibly pretend to describe it.'

'Then I can,' cried she. ''Tis bent in two places, and stamped on one of its sides with a D and an H.'

The sixpence was examined, and answered her description of it.

'The case is clear enough,' said the magistrate, 'and now, Miss, try whether you can advocate your own cause as well as Jerry Sullivan's.'

Jerry, who still remained in the room, came behind me, and whispered, 'Troth, Miss, I have no brains, but I have a bit of an oath, if that is of any use to you. I would sell my soul out of gratitude, at any time.'

'Alas! your Excellenza,' said I to the magistrate, 'frail is the tenure of that character, which has Innocence for its friend, and Infamy for its foe. Life is a chequered scene of light and shade; life is a jest, a stage——'

'Talking of life is not the way to save it,' said the magistrate. 'Less sentiment and more point, if you please.'

I was silent, but looked anxiously towards the door.

'Are you meditating an escape?' asked he.

'No,' said I, 'but just wait a little, and you shall see what an interesting turn affairs will take.'

'Come,' cried he, 'proceed at once, or say you will not.'

'Ah, now,' said I, 'can't you stop one moment, and not spoil everything by your impatience. I am only watching for the tall, elegant young stranger, with an oval face, who is to enter just at this crisis, and snatch me from perdition.'

'Did he promise to come?' said the magistrate.

'Not at all,' answered I, 'for I have never seen the man in my life. But whoever rescues me now, you know, is destined to marry me hereafter. That is the rule.'

'You are an impudent minx,' said the magistrate, 'and shall pay dear for your jocularity. Have you parents?'

'I cannot tell.'

'Friends?'

'None.'

'Where do you live?'

'No where.'

'At least 'tis plain where you will die. What is your name?'

'Cherubina.'

'Cherubina what?'

'I know not.'

'Not know? I protest this is the most hardened profligate I have ever met. Commit her instantly.'

I now saw that something must be done; so summoning all my most assuasive airs, I related the whole adventure, just as it had occurred.

Not a syllable obtained belief. The fatal sixpence carried all before it. I recollected the fate of Angelica Angela Angelina, and shuddered. What should I do? One desperate experiment remained.

'There were four guineas and half a guinea in the purse,' said I to the girl.

'To be sure there were,' cried she. 'How cunning you are to tell me my own news.'

'Now,' said I, 'answer me at once, and without hesitation, whether it is the half guinea or one of the guineas that is notched in three places, like the teeth of a saw?'

She paused a little, and then said; 'I have a long story to tell about those same notches. I wanted a silk handkerchief yesterday, so I went into a shop to buy one, and an impudent ugly young fellor was behind the counter. Well, he began ogling me so, I was quite ashamed; and says he to me, there is the change of your two pound note, says he, a guinea and a half in gold, says he, and you are vastly handsome, says he. And there are three notches in one of the coins, says he; guess which, says he, but it will pass all the same, says he, and you are prodigious pretty, says he. So indeed, I was so ashamed, that though I looked at the money, and saw the three notches, I have quite forgotten which they were in—guinea or half guinea; for my sight spread so, with shame at his compliments, that the half guinea looked as big as the guinea. Well, out I ran, blushing like a poor, terrified little thing, and sure enough, a horrid accident was near happening me in my hurry. For I was just running under the wheel of a carriage, when a gentleman catches me in his arms, and says he, you are prodigious pretty, says he; and I frowned so, you can't think; and I am sure, I never remembered to look at the money since; and this is the whole truth, I pledge you my credit and honour, and *by the immaculate Wenus*, as the gentlemen say.'

The accusing witness who insulted the magistrate's bench with the oath, leered as she gave it in; and the recording clerk, as he wrote it down, drew a line under the words, and pointed them out for ever.

'Then you saw the three notches?' said I.

'As plain as I see you now,' replied she, 'and a guilty poor thing you look.'

24

'And yet,' said I, 'if his Excellenza examines, he will find that there is not a single notch in any one of the coins.'

''Tis the case indeed,' said the magistrate, after looking at them.

He then questioned both of us more minutely, and turning to me, said, 'Your conduct, young woman, is unaccountable: but as your accuser has certainly belied herself, she has probably belied you. The money, by her own account, cannot be her's, but as it was found in your possession, it may be your's. I therefore feel fully justified in restoring it to you, and in acquitting you of the crime laid to your charge.'

Jerry Sullivan uttered a shout of joy. I received the purse with silent dignity, gave Maria back her sixpence, and hurried out of the room.

Jerry followed me.

'Why then,' cried he, shaking me heartily by the hand, as we walked along, 'only tell me how I can serve you, and 'tis I am the man that will do it; though, to be sure, you must be the greatest little scapegrace (bless your heart!) in the three kingdoms.'

'Alas!' said I, 'you mistake my character. I am heiress to an immense territory, and a heroine—the proudest title that can adorn a woman.'

'I never heard of that title before,' said Jerry, 'but I warrant 'tis no better than it should be.'

'You shall judge for yourself,' said I. 'A heroine is a young lady, rather taller than usual, and often an orphan; at all events, possessed of the finest eyes in the world. Though her frame is so fragile, that a breath of wind might scatter it like chaff, it is sometimes stouter than a statue of cast iron. She blushes to the tips of her fingers, and when other girls would laugh, she faints. Besides, she has tears, sighs, and half sighs, at command; lives a month on a mouthful, and is addicted to the pale consumption.'

'Why then, much good may it do her,' cried Jerry; 'but in my mind, a phthisicky girl is no great treasure; and as for the fashion of living a month on a mouthful, let me have a potatoe and chop for my dinner, and a herring on Saturday nights, and I would not give a farthing for all the starvation you could offer me. So when I finish my bit of herring, my wife says to me, winking, a fish loves water, says she, and immediately she fetches me a dram.'

'These are the delights of vulgar life,' said I. 'But to be thin, innocent, and lyrical; to bind and unbind her hair; in a word, to be the most miserable creature that ever augmented a brook with tears, these, my friend, are the glories of a heroine.'

'Famous glories, by dad!' cried Jerry; 'but as I am a poor man, and not particular, I can contrive to make shift with health and happiness, and to rub through life without binding my hair.—Bind it? by the powers, 'tis seldom I even comb it.'

As I was all this time without my bonnet (for in my hurry from Betterton's I had left it behind me), I determined to purchase one. So I went into a shop, with Jerry, and asked the woman of it for an interesting and melancholy turn of bonnet.

She looked at me with some surprise, but produced several; and I fixed on one which resembled a bonnet that I had once seen in a picture of a wood nymph. So I put it on me, wished the woman good morning, and was walking away.

'You have forgotten to pay me, Miss,' said she.

'True,' replied I, 'but 'tis no great matter. Adieu.'

'You shall pay me, however,' cried she, ringing a bell, and a man entered instantly from an inner room.

'Here is a hussey,' exclaimed she, 'who refuses to pay me for a bonnet.'

'My sweet friend,' said I to her, 'a distressed heroine, which I am, I assure you, runs in debt every where. Besides, as I like your face, I mean to implicate you in my plot, and make you one of the *dramatis personæ* in the history of my life. Probably you will turn out to be my mother's nurse's daughter. At all events, I give you my word, I will pay you at the *denouement*, when the other characters come to be provided for; and meantime, to secure your acquaintance, I must insist on owing you money.'

'By dad,' said Jerry, 'that is the first of all ways to lose an acquaintance.'

'The bonnet or the money!' cried the man, stepping between me and the door.

'Neither the one nor the other,' answered I. 'No, Sir, to run in debt is part of my plan, and by what right dare you interfere to save me from ruin? Pretty, indeed, that a girl at my time of life cannot select her own misfortunes! Sir, your conduct astonishes, shocks, disgusts me.'

To such a reasonable appeal the man could not reply, so he snatched at my bonnet. Jerry jumped forward, and arrested his arm.

'Hands off, bully!' cried the shopman.

'No, in troth,' said Jerry; 'and the more you bid me, the more I won't let you go. If her ladyship has set her heart on a robbery, I am not the man to balk her fancy. Sure, did not she save me from a gaol? And sure, would not I help her to a bonnet? A bonnet? 'Pon my conscience, she shall have half a dozen. 'Tis I that would not much mind being hanged for her!'

So saying, he snatched a parcel of bonnets from the counter, and was instantly knocked down by the shopman. He rose, and both began a furious conflict. In the midst of it, I was attempting to rush from the shop, when I found my spangled muslin barbarously seized by the woman, who tore it to pieces in the struggle; and pulling off the bonnet, gave me a horrid slap in the face. I would have cuffed her nicely in return, only that she was more than my match; but I stamped at her with my feet. At first I was shocked at having made this unheroic gesture; till I luckily recollected, that Amanda once stamped at an amorous footman.

Meantime Jerry had stunned his adversary with a blow; so taking this opportunity of escape, he dragged me with him from the shop, and hurried me through several streets, without uttering a word.

At length I was so much exhausted, that we stopped; and strange figures we were: Jerry's face smeared with blood, nothing on my head, my long hair hanging loose about me, and my poor spangled muslin all in rags.

'Here,' said Jerry to an old woman who was selling apples at the corner of the street, 'take care of this young body, while I fetch her a coach.' And off he ran.

The woman looked at me with a suspicious eye, so I resolved to gain her good opinion. It struck me that I might extract pathos from an apple, and taking one from her stall, 'An apple, my charming old friend,' said I, 'is the symbol of discord. Eve lost Paradise by tasting it, Paris exasperated Juno by throwing it.'—A loud burst of laughter made me turn round, and I perceived a crowd already at my elbow.

'Who tore her gown?' said one.

'Ask her spangles,' said another.

'Or her hair,' cried a third.

"Tis long enough to hang her,' cried a fourth.

'The king's hemp will do that job for her,' added a fifth.

A pull at my muslin assailed me on the one side, and when I turned about, my hair was thrown over my face on the other.

'Good people,' said I, 'you know not whom you thus insult. I am descended from illustrious, and perhaps Italian parents——'

A butcher's boy advanced, and putting half a hat under his arm; 'Will your ladyship,' said he, 'permit me to hand you into that there shop?'

I bowed assent, and he led me, nothing loath. Peals of laughter followed us.

'Now,' said I, as I stood at the door, 'I will reward your gallantry with half a guinea.'

As I drew forth my money, I saw his face reddening, his cheeks swelling, and his mouth pursing up.

'What delicate sensibility!' said I, 'but positively you must not refuse this trifle.'

He took it, and then, just think, the brute laughed in my face!

'I will give this guinea,' cried I, quite enraged, 'to the first who knocks that ungrateful down.'

Hardly had I spoken, when he was laid prostrate. He fell against the stall, upset it, and instantly the street was strewn with apples, nuts, and cakes. He rose. The battle raged. Some sided with him, some against him. The furious stall-woman pelted both parties with her own apples; while the only discreet person there, was a ragged little girl, who stood laughing at a distance, and eating one of the cakes.

In the midst of the fray, Jerry returned with a coach. I sprang into it, and he after me.

'The guinea, the guinea!' cried twenty voices at once. At once twenty apples came rattling against the glasses.

'Pay me for my apples!' cried the woman.

'Pay me for my windows!' cried the coachman.

'Drive like a devil,' cried Jerry, 'and I will pay you like an emperor!'

'Much the same sort of persons, now-a-days,' said the coachman, and away we flew. The guinea, the guinea! died along the sky. I thought I should have dropt with laughter.

My dear friend, do you not sympathize with my sorrows? Desolate, destitute, and dependent on strangers, what is to become of me? I declare I am extremely unhappy.

I write from Jerry's house, where I have taken refuge for the present; and as soon as I am settled elsewhere, you shall hear from me again.

Adieu.

Jerry Sullivan is a petty woollendraper in St. Giles's, and occupies the ground-floor of a small house. At first his wife and daughter eyed me with some suspicion; but when he told them how I had saved him from ruin, and that I was somehow or other a great lady in disguise, they became very civil, and gave me a tolerable breakfast. Then fatigued and sleepy, I threw myself on a bed, and slept till two.

I woke with pains in all my limbs; but anxious to forward the adventures of my life, I rose, and called mother and daughter to a consultation on my dress. They furnished me with their best habiliments, for which I agreed to give them two guineas; and I then began equipping myself.

While thus employed, I heard the voices of husband and wife in the next room, rising gradually to the matrimonial key. At last the wife exclaims,

'A Heroine? I will take my corporal oath, there is no such title in all England; and if she has the four guineas, she never came honestly by them; so the sooner she parts with them the better; and not a step shall she stir in our cloathes till she launches forth three of them. So that's that, and mine's my own, and how do you like my manners, Ignoramus?'

'How dare you call me Ignoramus?' cried Jerry. 'Blackguard if you like, but no ignoramus, I believe. I know what I could call you, though.'

'Well,' cried she, 'saving a drunkard and a scold, what else can you call me?'

'I won't speak another word to you,' said Jerry; 'I would not speak to you, if you were lying dead in the kennel.'

'Then you're an ugly unnatural beast, so you are,' cried she, 'and your Miss is no better than a bad one; and I warrant you understand one another well.'

This last insinuation was sufficient for me. What! remain in a house where suspicion attached to my character? What! act so diametrically, so outrageously contrary to the principle of aspersed heroines, who are sure on such occasions to pin up a bundle, and set off? I spurned the mean idea, and resolved to decamp instantly. So having hastened my toilette, I threw three guineas on the table, and then looked for a pen and ink, to write a sonnet on gratitude. I could find nothing, however, but a small bit of chalk, and with this substitute, I scratched the following lines on the wall.

SONNET ON GRATITUDE

Addressed to Jerry Sullivan

As some deputed angel, from the spheres

Of empyrean day, with nectar dewed,

Through firmamental wildernesses steers,

To starless tracts of black infinitude—

Here the chalk failed me, and just at the critical moment for my simile had also failed me, nor could I have ever gotten beyond infinitude. I got to the street door, however, and without fear of being overheard; to such an altitude of tone had words arisen between husband and wife, who were now contesting a most delicate point— which of them had beaten the other last.

'I know,' cried Jerry, 'that I gave the last blow.'

'Then take the first now,' cried his wife, as I shut the door.

Anticipating the probability that I should have occasion for Jerry's services again, I marked the number of the house, and then hastened along the street. It was swarming and humming like a hive of bees, and I felt as if I could never escape alive out of it. Here a carriage almost ran over me; there a waggoner's whip almost blinded me. Now a sweep brushed against me. 'Beauty!' cried a man like a monkey, and chucked my chin, while a fellow with a trunk shoved me aside.

I now turned into a street called Bond Street, where a long procession of carriages was passing. I remarked that the coachmen (they could not be gentlemen, I am sure) appeared to stand in great estimation; for the ladies of one carriage used to nod most familiarly to the driver of another. Indeed, I had often heard it said, that ladies and coachmen are sometimes particularly intimate; but till now I could never believe it.

The shops next attracted my attention, and I stopped to look at some of them. You cannot conceive any thing more charming: Turkish turbans, Indian shawls, pearls, diamonds, fans, feathers, laces; all shewn for nothing at the windows. I had but one guinea remaining!

At length feeling tired and hungry, and my feet being quite foundered, I determined to lose no farther time in taking lodgings. Perceiving 'Apartments to let,' written on a door, I rapped, and a servant girl opened it.

'Pray,' said I to her, 'are your northern apartments uninhabited?'

She replied that there were two rooms on the second floor disengaged, and comfortably furnished.

'I do not want them comfortable,' said I; 'but are they furnished with tapestry and old pictures? That is the point.'

'There is only master's face over the chimney,' said she.

'Do the doors creak on their hinges?' asked I.

'That they don't,' said she, 'for I oiled 'em all only yesterday.'

'Then you shewed a depraved taste,' cried I. 'At least, are the apartments haunted?'

'Lauk, no!' said she, half shutting the door.

'Well then, my good girl, tell me candidly whether your mistress is like the landladies one reads of. Is she a fat, bustling little woman, who would treat me to tea, cakes, and plenty of gossip, and at the end of a week, say to me, "out, hussy, tramp this moment;" or is she a pale, placid matron, worn to a thread-paper, and whose story is interwoven with mine?'

'Deuce take your impudence!' cried she, slapping the door in my face.

I tried other houses with no better success; and even when I merely asked for common lodgings, without stipulating for spectres or tapestry, the people would not accommodate me, unless I could procure some recommendation besides my own.

As I had no friend to give me a character, it became necessary to make a friend; so I began to look about for a fit subject. Passing a shop where eggs and butter were sold, and lodgings to be let, I perceived a pretty woman sitting behind the counter, and a fine infant playing upon it. I thought that all this bore an auspicious appearance; so I tottered into the shop, and placing myself opposite to the woman, I gazed at her with an engaging and gentle intelligence. She demanded my business.

'Interesting creature!' whispered I, pressing her hand as it rested on the counter. 'O may that little rosy fatling——'

Unfortunately there was an egg in the hand that I took, which I crushed by the compression, and the yolk came oozing between her fingers.

'Reptile!' cried she, as she threw the fragments in my face.

'Savage!' cried I, as I ran out of the shop, and wiped off the eggy dishonours.

At length I reached an immense edifice, which appeared to me the castle of some brow-knitting baron. Ponderous columns supported it, and statues stood in the niches. The portal lay open. I glided into the hall. As I looked anxiously around, I beheld a cavalier descending a flight of steps. He paused, muttered some words, laid his hand upon his heart, dropped it, shook his head, and proceeded.

I felt instantly interested in his fate; and as he came nearer, perceived, that surely never lighted on this orb, which he hardly seemed to touch, a more delightful vision. His form was tall, his face oval, and his nose aquiline. Seducing sweetness dwelled in his smile, and as he pleased, his expressive eyes could sparkle with rapture, or beam with sensibility. Once more he paused, frowned, and waving his arm, exclaimed, with an elegant energy of enunciation!

'To watch the minutes of this night, that if again this apparition come, he may approve our eyes, and speak to it!'

That moment a pang, poignant, but delicious, transfixed my bosom. Too well I felt and confessed it the dart of love. In sooth, too well I knew that my heart was lost to me for ever. Silly maiden! But fate had decreed it.

I rushed forward, and sank at the feet of the stranger.

'Pity and protect a destitute orphan!' cried I. 'Here, in this hospitable castle, I may hope for repose and protection. Oh, Signor, conduct me to your respected mother, the Baroness, and let me pour into her ear my simple and pathetic tale.'

'O ho! simple and pathetic!' cried he. 'Come, my dear, let me hear it.'

I seated myself on the steps, and told him my whole story. During the recital, the noble youth betrayed extreme sensibility. Sometimes he turned his head aside to conceal his emotion; and sometimes stifled a hysterical laugh of agony.

When I had ended, he begged to know whether I was quite certain that I had ten thousand pounds in my power. I replied, that as Wilkinson's daughter, I certainly had; but that the property must devolve to some one else, as soon as I should be proved a nobleman's daughter.

He then made still more accurate inquiries about it; and after having satisfied himself:

'Beshrew my heart!' exclaimed he; 'but I will avenge your injuries; and ere long you shall be proclaimed and acknowledged the Lady Cherubina De Willoughby. Meantime, as it will be prudent for you to lie concealed from the search of your enemies, hear the project which I have formed. I lodge at present in Drury-lane, an obscure street; and as one apartment in the house is unoccupied, you can hire it, and remain there, a beautiful recluse, till fortune and my poor efforts shall rescue from oppression the most enchanting of her sex.'

He spoke, and seizing my hand, carried it to his lips.

'What!' cried I, 'do you not live in this castle, and are you not its noble heir?'

'This is no castle,' said he, 'but Covent Garden Theatre.'

'And you?' asked I with anxiety.

'Am an actor,' answered he.

'And your name?'

'Is Abraham Grundy.'

'Then, Mr. Abraham Grundy,' said I, 'allow me to have the satisfaction of wishing you a very good evening.'

'Stay!' cried he, detaining me, 'and you shall know the whole truth. My birth is illustrious, and my real name Lord Altamont Mortimer Montmorenci. But like you, I am enveloped in a cloud of mysteries, and compelled to the temporary resource of acting. Hereafter I will acquaint you with the most secret particulars of my life; but at present, you must trust to my good faith, and accept of my protection.'

'Generous Montmorenci!' exclaimed I, giving him my hand, which he pressed upon his heart.

'Now,' said he, 'you must pass at these lodgings as my near relation, or they will not admit you.'

At first, I hesitated at deviating from veracity; but soon consented, on recollecting, that though heroines begin with praising truth, necessity makes them end with being the greatest story-tellers in the world. Nay, Clarissa Harlowe, when she had a choice, often preferred falsehood to fact.

During our walk to the lodgings, Montmorenci instructed me how to play my part, and on our arrival, introduced me to the landlady, who was about fifty, and who looked as if the goddess of fasting had bespoken her for a hand-maid.

With an amiable effrontery, and a fine easy flow of falsehood, he told her, as we had concerted, that I was his second cousin, and an orphan; my name Miss Donald (Amanda's assumed name), and that I had come to Town for the purpose of procuring by his interest, an appointment at the Theatre.

The landlady said she would move heaven and earth, and her own bed, for so good a gentleman; and then consented to give me her sleeping-room on the ground-floor, at some trifle or other,—I forget what. I have also the use of a parlour adjoining it. There is, however, nothing mysterious in these chambers, but a dark closet belonging to the parlour, whither I may fly for refuge, when pursued by my persecutors.

Thus, my friend, the plot of my history begins to take a more interesting shape, and a fairer order of misfortune smiles upon me. Trust me, there is a taste in distress as well as in millinery. Far be from me the loss of eyes or limbs, such publicity as the pillory affords, or the grossness of a jail-fever. I would be sacrificed to the lawless, not to the laws, dungeoned in the holy Inquisition, not clapped into Bridewell, recorded in a novel, not in the Newgate Calender. Were I inelegantly unhappy, I should be wretched indeed.

Yes, my Biddy, sensations hitherto unknown now heave my white bosom, vary the carnation of my cheeks, and irradiate my azure eyes. I sigh, gaze on vacancy, start from a reverie; now bite, now moisten my coral lip, and pace my chamber with unequal steps. Too sure I am deeply, distractedly in love, and Altamont Mortimer Montmorenci is the first of men.

Adieu.

LETTER X

The landlady, his lordship, and another lodger, are accustomed to dine in common; and his lordship easily persuaded me to join the party. Accordingly, just as I had finished my last letter, dinner was announced, so having braided my tresses, I tripped up stairs, and glided into the room. You must know I have practised tripping, gliding, flitting, and tottering, with great success. Of these, tottering ranks first, as it is the approved movement of heroic distress.

'I wonder where our mad poet can be?' said the hostess; and as she spoke, an uncouth figure entered, muttering in emphatic accents,

'The hounds around bound on the sounding ground.'

29

He started on seeing me, and when introduced by his lordship, as Mr. Higginson, his fellow lodger, and a celebrated poet, he made an unfathomable bow, rubbed his hands, and reddened to the roots of his hair.

This personage is tall, gaunt, and muscular; with a cadaverous countenance, and black hair in strings on his forehead. I find him one of those men who spend their lives in learning how the Greeks and Romans lived; how they spoke, dressed, ate; what were their coins and houses, &c.; but neglect acquainting themselves with the manners and customs of their own times. Montmorenci tells me that his brain is affected by excessive study; but that his manners are harmless.

At dinner, Montmorenci looked all, said all, did all, which conscious nobility, united with ardent attachment, could inspire in a form unrivalled, and a face unexcelled. I perceived that the landlady regarded him with eyes of tender attention, and languishing allurement, but in vain. I was his magnet and his Cynosure.

As to Higginson, he did not utter a word during dinner, except asking for a bit of *lambkin*; but he preserved a perpetuity of gravity in his face, and stared at me, the whole time, with a stupid and reverential fixedness. When I spoke, he stopped in whatever attitude he happened to be; whether with a glass at his mouth, or a fork half lifted to it.

After dinner, I proposed that each of us should relate the history of our lives; an useful custom established by heroines, who seldom fail of finding their account in it; as they are almost always sure to discover, by such means, either a grandmother or a murder. Thus too, the confession of a monk, the prattle of an old woman, a diamond cross on a child's neck, or a parchment, are the certain forerunners of virtue vindicated, vice punished, rights restored, and matrimony made easy.

The landlady was asked to begin.

'I have nothing to tell of myself,' said she, 'but that my mother left me this house, and desired me to look out for a good husband, Mr. Grundy; and I am not as old as I look; for I have had my griefs, as well as other folks, and every tear adds a year, as they say; and 'pon my veracity, Mr. Grundy, I was but thirty-two last month. And my bitterest enemies never impeached my character, that is what they did'nt, nor could'nt; they dare'nt to my face. I am a perfect snowdrop for purity. Who presumes to go for to say that a lord left me an annuity or the like? Who, I ask? But I got a prize in the lottery. So this is all I can think to tell of myself; and, Mr. Grundy, your health, and a good wife to you, Sir.'

After this eloquent piece of biography, we requested of Higginson to recount his adventures; and he read a short sketch, which was to have accompanied a volume of poems, had not the booksellers refused to publish them. I copy it for you.

MEMOIRS OF JAMES HIGGINSON

BY HIMSELF:

'Of the lives of poets, collected from posthumous record, and oral tradition, as little is known with certainty, much must be left to conjecture. He therefore, who presents his own memoirs to the public, may surely merit the reasonable applause of all, whose minds are emancipated from the petulance of envy, the fastidiousness of hypercriticism, and the exacerbation of party.

'I was born in the year 1771, at 24, Swallow Street; and should the curious reader wish to examine the mansion, he has every thing to hope from the alert urbanity of its present landlord, and the civil obsequiousness of his notable lady. He who gives civility, gives what costs him little, while remuneration may be multiplied in an indefinite ratio.

'My parents were reputable tobacconists, and kept me behind the counter, to negociate the titillating dust, and the tranquillizing quid. Of genius the first spark which I elicited, was reading a ballad in the shop, while the woman who sold it to me was stealing a canister of snuff. This specimen of mental abstraction (a quality which I still preserve), shewed that I would never make a good tradesman; but it also shewed, that I would make an excellent scholar. A tutor was accordingly appointed for me; and during a triennial course of study, I had passed from the insipidity of the incipient *hic, hæc, hoc*, to the music of a Virgil, and the thunder of a Demosthenes.

'Debarred by my secluded life from copying the polished converse of high society, I have at least endeavoured to avoid the vulgar phraseology of low; and to discuss the very weather with a sententious association of polysyllabical ratiocination.

'With illustrations of my juvenile character, recollection but ill supplies me. That I have always disliked the diurnal ceremony of ablution, and a hasty succession of linen, is a truth which he who has a sensitive texture of skin will easily credit; which he who will not credit, may, if he pleases, deny; and may, if he can, controvert. But I assert the fact, and I expect to be believed, because I assert it. Life, among its quiet blessings, can boast of few things more comfortable than indifference to dress.

'To honey with my bread, and to apple-sauce with my goose, I have ever felt a romantic attachment, resulting from the classical allusions which they inspire. That man is little to be envied, whose honey would not remind him of the Hyblean honey, and whose apple-sauce would not suggest to him the golden apple.

'But notwithstanding my cupidity for such dainties, I have that happy adaptation of taste which can banquet, with delight, upon hesternal offals; can nibble ignominious radishes, or masticate superannuated mutton.

'My first series of teeth I cut at the customary time, and the second succeeded them with sufficient punctuality. This fact I had from my mother.

'My first poetical attempt was an epitaph on the death of my tutor, and it was produced at the precocious age of ten.

EPITAPH

Here lies the body of John Tomkins, who Departed this life, aged fifty-two; After a long and painful illness, that He bore with Christian fortitude, though fat. He died lamented deeply by this poem, And all who had the happiness to know him.

'This composition my father did not long survive; and my mother, to the management of the business feeling quite unequal, relinquished it altogether, and retired with the respectable accumulation of a thousand pounds.

'I still pursued my studies, and from time to time accommodated confectionaries and band-boxes with printed sheets, which the world might have read, had it pleased, and might have been pleased with, had it read. For some years past, however, the booksellers have declined to publish my productions at all. Envious enemies poison their minds against me, and persuade them that my brain is disordered. For, like Rousseau, I am the victim of implacable foes; but my genius, like an arch, becomes stronger the more it is opprest.

'On a pretty little maid of my mother's, I made my next poetical effort, which I present to the reader.

TO DOROTHY PULVERTAFT

If Black-sea, White-sea, Red-sea ran

One tide of ink to Ispahan;

If all the geese in Lincoln fens,

Produc'd spontaneous, well-made pens;

If Holland old or Holland new,

One wond'rous sheet of paper grew;

Could I, by stenographic power,

Write twenty libraries an hour;

And should I sing but half the grace

Of half a freckle on thy face;

Each syllable I wrote, should reach

From Inverness to Bognor's beach;

Each hairstroke be a river Rhine,

Each verse an equinoctial line.

'Of the girl, an immediate dismission ensued; but for what reason, let the sedulous researches of future biographers decide.

'At length, having resolved on writing a volume of Eclogues, I undertook an excursion into the country to learn pastoral manners, and write in comfort, far from my tailor. An amputated loaf, and a contracted Theocritus, constituted my companions. Not a cloud blotted the blue concave, not a breeze superinduced undulation over the verdant tresses of the trees.

'In vain I questioned the youths and maidens about their Damons and Delias; their Dryads and Hamadryads; their Amabœan contentions and their amorous incantations. When I talked of Pan, they asked me if it was a pan of milk; when I requested to see the pastoral pipe, they shewed me a pipe of tobacco; when I spoke of satyrs with horns, they bade me go to the husbands; and when I spoke of fawns with cloven heel, they bade me go to the Devil. While charmed with a thatched and shaded cottage, its slimy pond or smoking dunghill disgusted me; and when I recumbed on a bank of cowslips and primroses, my features were transpierced by wasps and ants and nettles. I fell asleep under sunshine, and awoke under a torrent of rain. Dripping and disconsolate, I returned to my mother, drank some whey; and since that misadventurous perambulation have never ruralized again. To him who subjects himself to a recurrence of disaster, the praise of boldness may possibly be accorded, but the praise of prudence must certainly be denied.

'A satirical eclogue, however, was the fruit of this expedition. It is called Antique Amours, and is designed to shew, that passions which are adapted to one time of life, appear ridiculous in another. The reader shall have it.

ANTIQUE AMOUR

AN ECLOGUE

'Tis eve. The sun his ardent axle cools
In ocean. Dripping geese shake off the pools.
An elm men's shadows measure; red and dun,
The shattered leaves are rustling as they run;
While an aged bachelor and ancient maid,
Sit amorous under an old oak decayed.
He (for blue vapours damp the scanty grass)
Strews fodder underneath the hoary lass;
Then thus,—O matchless piece of season'd clay,
'Tis Autumn, all things shrivel and decay.
Yet as in withered Autumn, charms we see,
Say, faded maiden, may we not in thee?
What tho' thy cheek have furrows? ne'er deplore;
For wrinkles are the dimples of threescore:
Tho' from those azure lips the crimson flies,
It fondly circles round those roseate eyes;
And while thy nostrils snuff the fingered grain,
The tinct thy locks have lost, thy lips obtain.
Come then, age urges, hours have winged feet,
Ah! press the wedding ere the winding sheet.
To clasp that waist compact in stiffened fold,
Of woof purpureal, flowered with radiant gold;
Then, after stately kisses, to repair
That architectural edifice of hair,
These, these are blessings.—O my grey delight,
O venerable nymph, O painted blight,
Give me to taste of these. By Heaven above,
I tremble less with palsy than with love;
And tho' my husky murmurs creak uncouth,
My words flow unobstructed by a tooth.
Come then, age urges, hours have winged feet,
Ah! press the wedding ere the winding sheet.
Come, thou wilt ne'er provoke crimconic law,
Nor lie, maternal, on the pale-eyed straw.
Come, and in formal frolic intertwine,
The braided silver of thy hair with mine.
Then sing some bibulous and reeling glee,
And drink crusht juices of the grape with me.
Sing, for the wine no water shall dilute;
'Tis drinking water makes the fishes mute.
Come then, age urges, hours have winged feet;
Ah! press the wedding, ere the winding sheet.
So spoke the slim and elderly remains
Of once a youth. A staff his frame sustains;
And aids his aching limbs, from knee to heel,

32

Thin as the spectre of a famished eel.
Sharpening the blunted glances of her eyes,
The virgin a decrepid simper tries,
Then stretches rigid smiles, which shew him plain,
Her passion, and the teeth that still remain.
Innocent pair! But now the rain begins,
So both knot kerchiefs underneath their chins.
And homeward haste. Such loves the Poet wrote,
In the patch'd poverty of half a coat;
Then diadem'd with quills his brow sublime,
Magnanimously mad in mighty rhime.

'With my venerable parent, I now pass a harmless life. As we have no society, we have no scandal; ourselves, therefore, we make our favourite topic, and ourselves we are unwilling to dispraise.

'Whether the public will admire my works, as well as my mother does, far be from me to determine. If they cannot boast of wit and judgment, to the praise of truth and modesty they may at least lay claim. To be unassuming in an age of impudence, and veracious in an age of mendacity, is to combat with a sword of glass against a sword of steel; the transparency of the one may be more beautiful than the opacity of the other; yet let it be recollected, that the transparency is accompanied with brittleness, and the opacity with consolidation.'

I listened with much compassion to this written evidence of a perverted intellect. O my friend, what a frightful disorder is madness!

My turn came next, and I repeated the fictitious tale that Montmorenci had taught me. He confirmed it; and on being asked to relate his own life, gave us, with great taste, such a natural narrative of a man living on his wits, that any one who knew not his noble origin must have believed it.

Soon afterwards, he retired to dress for the theatre; and when he returned, I beheld a perfect hero. He was habited in an Italian costume; his hair hung in ringlets, and mustachios embellished his lip.

He then departed in a coach, and as soon as he had left us:

'I declare,' said the landlady to me, 'I do not like your cousin's style of beauty at all; particularly his pencilled eyebrows and curled locks, they look so womanish.'

'What!' said I, 'not admire Hesperian, Hyacinthine, clustering curls? Surely you would not have a hero with overhanging brows and lank hair? These are worn by none but the villains and assassins.'

I perceived poor Higginson colouring, and twisting his fingers; and I then recollected that his brows and hair have precisely the faults which I reprobated.

'Dear, dear, dear!' muttered he, and made a precipitate retreat from the room.

I retired soon after; and I now hasten to throw myself on my bed, dream of love and Montmorenci, and wake unrefreshed, from short and distracted slumbers.

Adieu.

LETTER XI

This morning, soon after breakfast, I heard a gentle knocking at my door, and, to my great astonishment, a figure, cased in shining armour, entered. Oh! ye conscious blushes, it was my Montmorenci! A plume of white feathers nodded on his helmet, and neither spear nor shield were wanting.

'I come,' cried he, bending on one knee, and pressing my hand to his lips, 'I come in the ancient armour of my family, to perform my promise of recounting to you the melancholy memoirs of my life.'

'My lord,' said I, 'rise and be seated. Cherubina knows how to appreciate the honour that Montmorenci confers.'

He bowed; and having laid by his spear, shield, and helmet, he placed himself beside me on the sofa, and began his heart-rending history.

'All was dark. The hurricane howled, the hail rattled, and the thunder rolled. Nature was convulsed, and the traveller inconvenienced.

'In the province of Languedoc stood the Gothic Castle of Montmorenci. Before it ran the Garonne, and behind it rose the Pyrenees, whose summits exhibiting awful forms, seen and lost again, as the partial vapours rolled along, were sometimes barren, and gleamed through the blue tinge of air, and sometimes frowned with forests of gloomy fir, that swept downward to their base.

'My lads, are your carbines charged, and your daggers sharpened?' whispered Rinaldo, with his plume of black feathers, to the banditti, in their long cloaks.

'If they an't,' said Bernardo, 'by St. Jago, we might load our carbines with the hail, and sharpen our daggers against this confounded north-wind.'

'The wind is east-south-east,' said Ugo.

'At this moment the bell of Montmorenci Castle tolled one. The sound vibrated through the long corridors, the spiral staircases, the suites of tapestried apartments, and the ears of the personage who has the honour to address you. Much alarmed, I started from my couch, which was of exquisite workmanship; the coverlet of flowered gold, and the canopy of white velvet painted over with jonquils and butterflies, by Michael Angelo. But conceive my horror when I beheld my chamber filled with banditti!

'Snatching my sword, I flew to a corner, where my coat of mail lay heapt. The bravos rushed upon me; but I fought and dressed, and dressed and fought, till I had perfectly completed my unpleasing toilette.

'I then stood alone, firm, dignified, collected, and only fifteen years of age.

Alack! there lies more peril in thine eye,
Than twenty of their swords.——

'To describe the horror of the contest that followed, were beyond the pen of an Anacreon. In short, I fought till my silver skin was laced with my golden blood; while the bullets flew round me, thick as hail,

And whistled as they went for want of thought.

'At length my sword broke, so I set sail for England.

'As I first touched foot on her chalky beach; Hail! exclaimed I, happy land, thrice hail! Take to thy fostering bosom the destitute Montmorenci—Montmorenci, once the first and richest of the Gallic nobility—Montmorenci, whom wretches drove from his hereditary territories, for loyalty to his monarch, and opposition to the atrocities of exterminators and revolutionists.

'Nine days and nights I wandered through the country, the rivulet my beverage, and the berry my repast: the turf my couch, and the sky my canopy.'

'Ah!' interrupted I, 'how much you must have missed the canopy of white velvet painted over with jonquils and butterflies!'

'Extremely,' said he, 'for during sixteen long years, I had not a roof over my head.—I was an itinerant beggar!

'One summer's day, the cattle lay panting under the broad umbrage; the sun had burst into an immoderate fit of splendour, and the struggling brook chided the matted grass for obstructing it. I sat under a hedge, and began eating wild strawberries; when lo! a form, flexile as the flame ascending from a censer, and undulating with the sighs of a dying vestal, flitted inaudible by me, nor crushed the daisies as it trod. What a divinity! she was fresh as the Anadyomene of Apelles, and beautiful as the Gnidus of Praxitiles, or the Helen of Zeuxis. Her eyes dipt in Heaven's own hue.'——

'Sir,' said I, 'you need not mind her eyes: I dare say they were blue enough. But pray who was this immortal doll of your's?'

'Who!' cried he. 'Why who but—shall I speak it? Who but—the Lady Cherubina De Willoughby!!!'

'I!'

'You!'

'Ah! Montmorenci!'

'Ah! Cherubina! I followed you with cautious steps,' continued he, 'till I traced you into your—you had a garden, had you not?'

'Yes.'

'Into your garden. I thought ten thousand flowerets would have leapt from their beds to offer you a nosegay. But the age of gallantry is past, that of merchants, placemen, and fortune-hunters has succeeded, and the glory of Cupid is extinguished for ever!

'You disappeared, I uttered incoherent sentences, and next morning resumed my station at a corner of the garden.'

'At which corner?' asked I.

'Why really,' said he, 'I cannot explain; for the place was then new to me, and the ground was covered with snow.'

'With snow!' cried I. 'Why I thought you were eating wild strawberries only the day before.'

'I!' said he. 'Sure you mistake.'

'I declare most solemnly you told me so,' cried I.

'Why then,' said he, 'curse me if I did.'

'Sir,' said I. 'I must remark that your manners——'

'Bless me!' cried he, 'yes, I did say so, sure enough, and I did eat wild strawberries too; but they were *preserved* wild strawberries. I had got a small crock of them from an oyster woman, who was opening oysters in a meadow, for a hysterical butcher; and her knife having snapt in two, I lent her my sword; so, out of gratitude, she made me a present of the preserves. By the bye, they were mouldy.

'One morning, as I sat at the side of the road, asking alms, some provincial players passed by me. I accosted them, and offered my services. In short, they took me with them; I performed, was applauded; and at length my fame reached London, where I have now been acting some years, with much success; anxious as I am, to realize a little money, that I may return, in disguise, to my native country, and petition Napoleon to restore my forfeited estates.

'Such, fair lady, such is my round, unvarnished tale.

'But wherefore,' cried he, starting from his seat; 'wherefore talk of the past? Oh! let me tell you of the present and of the future. Oh! let me tell you, how dearly, how devotedly I love you!'

'Love me!' cried I, giving such a start as the nature of the case required. 'My lord, this is so—really now so——'

'Pardon this abrupt avowal of my unhappy passion,' said he, flinging himself at my feet. 'Fain would I have let concealment, like a worm in the bud, feed on my damask cheek; but, oh! who could resist the maddening sight of so much beauty?'

I remained silent, and with the elegant embarrassment of modesty, cast my blue eyes to the ground. I never looked so lovely.

'But I go!' cried he, springing on his feet. 'I fly from you for ever! No more shall Cherubina be persecuted with my hopeless love. But Cherubina, the hills and the vallies shall echo, and the songsters of the grove shall articulate Cherubina. I will shake the leaves of the forest with my sighs, and make the stream so briny with my tears, that the turbot shall swim into it, and the sea-weed grow upon its banks!'

'Ah, do not!' said I, with a look of unutterable anguish.

'I will!' exclaimed he, pacing the chamber with long strides, and slapping his heart, 'and I call all the stars of respectability to witness the vow. Then, Lady Cherubina,' continued he, stopping short before me; 'then, when maddened and emaciated, I shall pillow my haggard head on a hard rock, and lulled by the hurricanes of Heaven, shall sink into the sleep of the grave.'——

'Dear Montmorenci!' said I, quite overcome, 'live for my sake—as you value my—friendship,—live.'

'Friendship!' echoed he. 'Oh! Cherubina, Oh! my soul's precious treasure, say not that icy word. Say hatred, disgust, horror; any thing but friendship.'

'What shall I say?' cried I, ineffably affected, 'or what shall I do?'

'What you please,' muttered he, looking wild and pressing his forehead. 'My brain is on fire. Hark! chains are clanking—The furies are whipping me with their serpents—What smiling cherub arrests yon bloody hand? Ha! 'tis Cherubina. And now she frowns at me—she darts at me—she pierces my heart with an arrow of ice!'

He threw himself on the floor, groaned grievously, and tore his hair. I was horror-struck.

'I declare,' said I, 'I would say any thing on earth to relieve you;—only tell me what.'

'Angel of light!' exclaimed he, springing upon his feet, and beaming on me a smile that might liquefy marble. 'Have I then hope? Dare I say it? Dare I pronounce the divine words, she loves me?'

'I am thine and thou art mine!' murmured I, while the room swam before me.

He took both my hands in his own, pressed them to his forehead and lips, and leaned his burning cheek upon them.

'My sight is confused,' said he, 'my breathing is opprest; I hear nothing, my veins swell, a palpitation seizes my heart, and I scarcely know where I am, or whether I exist!'

Then softly encircling my waist with his arm, he pressed me to his heart. With what modesty I tried to extricate myself from his embrace; yet with what willing weakness I trembled on his bosom. It was Cherubina's hand that fell on his shoulder, it was Cherubina's tress that played on his cheek, it was Cherubina's sigh that breathed on his lip.

'Moment of a pure and exquisite emotion!' cried he. 'In the life of man you are known but once; yet once known, can you ever be forgotten? Now to die would be to die most blest!'

Suddenly he caught me under the chin, and kissed me. I struggled from him, and sprang to the other end of the room, while my neck and face were suffused with a glow of indignation.

'Really,' said I, panting with passion, 'this is so unprovoked, so presuming.'

He cast himself at my feet, execrated his folly, and swore that he had merely fulfilled an etiquette indispensible among lovers in his own country.

"Tis not usual here, my lord,' said I; 'and I have no notion of submitting to any freedom that is not sanctioned by the precedent of those exalted models whom I have the honour to imitate.

'I fancy, my lord, you will find, that, as far as a kiss on the hand, or an arm round the waist, they have no particular objection. But a salute on the lip is considered inaccurate. My lord, on condition that you never repeat the liberty, here is my hand.'

He snatched it with ardor, and strained it to his throbbing bosom.

'And now,' cried he, 'make my happiness complete, by making this hand mine for ever.'

On a sudden an air of dignified grandeur involved my form. My mind, for the first time, was called upon to reveal its full force. It felt the solemnity of the appeal, and triumphed in its conscious ability.

'What!' cried I, 'knowest thou not the fatal, the inscrutable, the mysterious destiny, which must ever prevent our union?'

'Speak, I conjure you,' cried he, 'or I expire on the spot.'

'Alas!' exclaimed I, 'can'st thou suppose the poor orphan Cherubina so destitute of principle and of pride, as to intrude herself unknown, unowned, unfriended; mysterious in her birth, and degraded in her situation, on the ancient and illustrious House of Montmorenci?

'Here then I most solemnly vow, never to wed, till the horrible mystery which hangs over my birth be developed.'

You know, Biddy, that a heroine ought always to snatch at an opportunity of making a fatal vow. When things are going on too smooth, and interest drooping, a fatal vow does wonders. I remember reading in some romance, of a lady, who having vowed never to divulge a certain secret, kept it twenty years; and with such inviolability, that she lived to see it the death of all her children, several of her friends, and a fine old aunt.

As soon as I had made this fatal vow, his lordship fell into the most afflicting agonies and attitudes.

'Oh!' cried he, 'to be by your side, to see you, touch you, talk to you, love you, adore you, and yet find you lost to me for ever. Oh! 'tis too much, too much.'

'The milliner is here, Miss,' said the maid, tapping at the door.

'Bid her call again,' said I.

'Beloved of my soul!' murmured his lordship.

'Ma'am,' interrupted the maid, opening the door, 'she cannot call again, as she must go from this to Kensington.'

'Then let her come in,' said I, and she entered with a charming assortment of bonnets and dresses.

'We will finish the scene another time,' whispered I to his lordship.

His lordship swore that he would drop dead that instant.

The milliner declared that she had brought me the newest patterns.

'On my honour,' said I to his lordship, 'you shall finish this scene to-morrow morning, if you wish it.'

'You may go and be—— Heigho!' said he, suddenly checking himself. What he was about to say, I know not; something mysterious, I should think, by the knitting of his brows. However, he snatched his spear, shield, and helmet, made a low bow, laid his hand on his heart, and stalked out of the chamber. Interesting youth!

I then ran in debt for some millinery, drank hartshorn, and chafed my temples.

I think I was right about the kiss. I confess I am not one of those girls who try to attract men through the medium of the touch; and who thus excite passion at the expence of respect. Lips are better employed in sentiment, than in kissing. Indeed, had I not been fortified by the precedent of other heroines, I should have felt, and I fear, did actually feel, even the classical embrace of Montmorenci too great a freedom. But remember I am still in my noviciate. After a little practice, I shall probably think it rather a pleasure to be strained, and prest, and folded to the heart. Yet of this I am certain, that I shall never attain sufficient hardihood to ravish a

36

kiss from a man's mouth; as the divine Heloise did; who once ran at St. Preux, and astonished him with the most balmy and remarkable kiss upon record. Poor fellow! he was never the same after it.

I must say too, that Montmorenci did not shew much judgment in urging me to marry him, before I had undergone adventures for four volumes. Because, though the heroic etiquette allowed me to fall in love at first sight, and confess it at second sight, yet it would not authorize me to marry myself off quite so smoothly. A heroine is never to be got without agony and adventure. Even the ground must be lacerated, before it will bring forth fruits, and often we cannot reach the lovely violet, till we have torn our hands with brambles.

I did not see his lordship again until dinner time; and we had almost finished our repast, before the poet made his appearance and his bow. His bow was as usual, but his appearance was strangely changed. His hair stood in stiff ringlets on his forehead, and he had pruned his bushy eyebrows, till hardly one bristle remained; while a pair of white gloves, small enough for myself, were forced upon his hands. He glanced at us with a conscious eye, and hurried to his seat at table.

'Ovid's Metamorphoses, by Jupiter!' exclaimed Montmorenci. 'Why, Higginson, how shameful for the mice to have nibbled your eyebrows, while Apollo Belvidere was curling your hair!'

The poet blushed, and ate with great assiduity.

'My dear fellow,' continued his lordship, 'we can dispense with those milk-white gloves during dinner. Tell me, are they mamma's, dear mamma's?'

'I will tell my mother of you!' cried the poet, half rising from his chair.

Now his mother is an old bed-ridden lady in one of the garrets. I then interfered in his behalf, and peace was restored.

After dinner, I took an opportunity, when the landlady had left the room, to request ten pounds from his lordship, for the purpose of paying the milliner. Never was regret so finely pictured in a face as in his, while he swore that he had not a penny upon earth. Indeed so graceful was his lamentation, so interesting his penury, that though the poet stole out of the room for ten pounds, which he slipped into my hand, I preferred the refusal of the one to the donation of the other.

Yes, this amiable young nobleman increases in my estimation every moment. Never can you catch him out of a picturesque position. He would exhaust in an hour all the attitudes of all the statues; when he talks tenderness, his eyes glow with a moist fire, and he always brings in his heart with peculiar happiness. Then too, his oaths are at once well conceived and elegantly expressed. Thunderbolts and the fixed stars are ever at his elbow, and no man can sink himself to perdition with so fine a grace.

But I could write of him, talk of him, think of him, hour after hour, minute after minute; even now, while the shadows of night are blackening the blushes of the rose, till dawn shall stain with her ruddy fire, the snows of the naked Apennine; till the dusky streams shall be pierced with darts of light, and the sun shall quaff his dewy beverage from the cup of the tulip, and the chalice of the lily. That is pretty painting.

Adieu.

LETTER XII

'It is my lady, O it is my love!' exclaimed Lord Altamont Mortimer Montmorenci, as he flew, like a winged mercury, into my apartment this morning. A loud rap at the door checked his eloquence, and spoiled a most promising posture.

'Is Miss Wilkinson within?' said a voice in the hall.

'No such person lives here,' replied the maid, who was accustomed to hear me called Miss Donald.

'But there does, and on the ground-floor too, and I will find her out, I warrant,' cried the same voice.

My door was then thrown open, and who should waddle into the room, but fat Wilkinson!

My first feeling (could you believe it) was of gladness at seeing him; nor had I presence of mind enough, either to repulse his embrace, or utter a piercing shriek. Happily my recollection soon returned, and I flung him from me.

'Cherry,' said he, 'dear Cherry, what have I done to you, that you should use me thus? Was there ever a wish of your heart that I left ungratified? And now to desert me in my old age! Only come home with me, my child, only come home with me, and I will forgive you all.'

'Wilkinson,' said I, 'this interview must be short, pointed, and decisive. As to calling yourself my father, that is a stale trick, and will not pass; and as to personating (what I perceive you aspire to) the grand villain of my plot, your corpulency, pardon me, puts that out of the question for ever. I should be just as happy to employ you as any other man I know, but excuse me if I say, that you rather overrate your talents and qualifications. Have you the gaunt ferocity of famine in your countenance? Can you darken the midnight of a scowl? Have you the quivering lip and the Schedoniac contour? And while the lower part of your face is hidden in black drapery, can your eyes glare from under the edge of a cowl? In a word, are you a picturesque villain, full of plot, and horror, and magnificent wickedness? Ah, no, Sir, you are only a sleek, good-humoured, chuckle-headed gentleman. Continue then what nature made you; return to your plough, mow, reap, fatten your pigs and the parson; but never again attempt to get yourself thrust into the pages of a romance.'

Disappointment and dismay forced more meaning into his features than I thought them possessed of. The fact is, he had never imagined that my notions of what villains ought to be were so refined; and that I have formed my taste in these matters upon the purest models.

As a last effort of despair, the silly man flung himself on his knees before me, and grasping my hands, looked up in my face, with such an imploring wretchedness of expression, while the tears rolled silently down his cheeks, that I confess I was a little moved; and for the moment fancied him sincere.

'Now goodness bless thee,' said he, at length, 'goodness bless thee, for those sweet tears of thine, my daughter!'

'Tears!' cried I, quite shocked.

'Yes, darling,' said he, 'and now with this kiss of peace and love, we will blot out all the past.'

I shrieked, started from my seat, and rushed into the expanding arms of Montmorenci.

'And pray, Sir,' cried Wilkinson, advancing fiercely, 'who are you?'

'A lodger in this house, Sir,' answered his lordship, 'and your best friend, as I trust you will acknowledge hereafter. I became acquainted with this lady at the table of our hostess, and learned from her, that she had left your house in disgust. Yesterday morning, on entering her apartment, to make my respects, I found an old gentleman there, one Doctor Merrick, whom I recognized as a wretch of infamous character; tried twice for shoplifting, and once for having swindled the Spanish ambassador out of a golden snuff-box. I, though an humble individual, yet being well acquainted with this young lady's high respectability, presumed to warn her against such a dangerous companion; when I found, to my great concern, that she had already promised him her hand in marriage.'

Wilkinson groaned: I stared.

'On being apprised of his character,' continued Montmorenci, 'the young lady was willing enough to drop the connection, but unfortunately, the ruffian had previously procured a written promise of marriage from her, which he now refuses to surrender; and at the moment you came, I was consulting with your daughter what was best to be done.'

'Lead me to him!' cried Wilkinson, 'lead me to the villain this instant, and I will shew you what is best to be done!'

'I have appointed an interview with him, about this time,' said his lordship, 'and as your feelings might probably prompt you to too much warmth, perhaps you had better not accompany me; but should I fail in persuading him to deliver up the fatal paper, you shall then see him yourself.'

'You are a fine fellow!' cried the farmer, shaking his hand, 'and have bound me to you for ever.'

'I will hasten to him now,' said his lordship, and casting a significant glance at me, departed; leaving me quite astonished, both at his story, and his motive for fabricating it. It was, however, my business to support the deception.

Wilkinson then told me that he discovered my place of residence in London, from the discharged Butler, who, it seems, is not your son, but your lover; and to whom you have shewn all my letters. He went to Wilkinson, and made the disclosure for forty guineas. Sordid wretch! and Wilkinson says that he wants to marry you, merely for the sake of your annuity. Biddy, Biddy! had you known as much of the world as I do now, a fortune hunter would not have imposed upon you.

As to your shewing him my letters, I cannot well blame you for a breach of trust, which has answered the purpose of involving my life in a more complicated labyrinth of entanglements.

But to return. In the midst of our conversation, the maid brought me a note. It was from Montmorenci, and as follows:

'Will my soul's idol forgive the tale I told Wilkinson, since it was devised in order to save her from his fangs? This Doctor Merrick, whom I mentioned to him, instead of being a swindler, is a mad-doctor; and keeps a private madhouse. I have just seen him, and have informed him that I am about to put a lunatic gentleman, my honoured uncle, under his care. I told him, that this dear uncle (who, you may well suppose is Wilkinson) has lucid intervals; that his madness arose from grief at an unfortunate amour of his daughter's, and shews itself in his fancying that every man he sees wants to marry her, and has her written promise of marriage.

'I have already advanced the necessary fees, and now is your time to wheedle Wilkinson out of money, by pretending that you will return home with him. A true heroine, my sweet friend, ever shines in deception.

Good now, play one scene

Of excellent dissembling.—Shakespeare.

'Ever, ever, ever,

'Your faithful

'Montmorenci.

'P.S. Excuse tender language, as I am in haste.'

This dear letter I placed in my bosom: and when I begged of the farmer to let me have a little money, he took out his pocket-book.

'Here, my darling,' said he, 'here are notes to the tune of a hundred pounds, that you may pay all you owe, and purchase whatever baubles and finery you like. This is what you get for discarding that swindler, and promising to return home with old dad.'

Soon afterwards, our hero came back, and told us that his interview had proved unsuccessful. It was therefore determined that we should all repair to the Doctor's (for Wilkinson would not go without me), and off we set in a hired coach. On our arrival, we were shewn into a parlour, and after some minutes of anxious suspense, the Doctor, a thin little figure, with a shrivelled face and bushy wig, came humming into the room.

Wilkinson being introduced, the Doctor commenced operations, by trying the state of his brain.

'Any news to-day, Mr. Wilkinson?' said he.

'Very bad news for me, Sir,' replied Wilkinson, sullenly.

'I mean public news,' said the Doctor.

'A private grievance ought to be considered of public moment,' said Wilkinson.

'Well remarked, Sir,' cried the Doctor, 'a clear-headed observation as possible. Sir, I give you credit. There is a neatness in the turn of it that argues a collected intellect.'

'Sir,' said Wilkinson, 'I hope that some other observations which I am about to offer will please you as well.'

'I hope so for your own sake,' answered the Doctor; 'I shall certainly listen to them with a favourable ear.'

'Thank you, Sir,' said the farmer: 'and such being the case, I make no doubt that all will go well; for men seldom disagree, when they wish to coincide.'

'Good again,' cried the Doctor. 'Apt and good. Sir, if you continue to talk so rationally, I promise you that you will not remain long in my house.'

'I am sorry,' replied Wilkinson, 'that talking rationally is the way to get turned out of your house, because I have come for the purpose of talking rationally.'

'And while such is your resolution,' said the Doctor, 'nothing shall be left undone to make my house agreeable. You have only to hint your wishes, and they shall be gratified.'

'Sir, Sir,' cried Wilkinson, grasping his hand, 'your kindness is overpowering, because it is unexpected. However, I do not mean to trespass any farther on your kindness than just to request, that you will do me the favour of returning to my daughter the silly paper written by her, containing her promise to marry you; and if you could conveniently lay your hand on it now, you would add to the obligation, as I mean to leave Town in an hour.'

'Mr. Wilkinson,' said the Doctor, 'I shall deal candidly with you. Probably you will not leave Town these ten years. And pardon me, if I give you fair warning, that should you persist in asking for the paper, a severe horse-whipping will be the consequence.'

'A horse-whipping!' repeated Wilkinson, as if he could not believe his ears.

'You shall be cut from shoulder to flank,' said the Doctor. ''Tis my usual way of beginning.'

'Any thing more, my fine fellow?' cried the farmer.

'Only that if you continue refractory,' said the Doctor, 'you shall be lashed to the bed-post, and shall live on bread and water for a month.'

'Here is a proper ruffian for you!' cried Wilkinson. 'Now, by the mother that bore me, I have a good mind to flay you within an inch of your life!'

'Make haste then,' said the Doctor, ringing the bell; 'for you will be handcuffed in half a minute.'

'Why you little creature,' cried Wilkinson, 'do you hope to frighten me? Not ask for the paper, truly! Ay, ten thousand times over and over. Give me the paper, give me the paper; give me the paper, the paper, the paper! What say you to that, old Hector?'

'The handcuffs!' cried the Doctor to the servant.

'Ay, first handcuff me, and then pick my pockets,' cried Wilkinson. 'You see I have found you out, sirrah! yes I have discovered that you are a common shoplifter, tried five times for your life—and the very fellow that swindled the Spanish ambassador out of a diamond snuff-box.'

'A good deal deranged, indeed,' whispered the Doctor to his lordship.

'But how the deuce the girl could bring herself to fancy you,' cried Wilkinson, 'that is what shocks me most. A fellow, by all that is horrid, as ugly as if he were bespoke—an old fellow, too, and twice as disgusting, and not half so interesting, as a monkey in a consumption.'

'Perfectly distracted, 'pon my conscience!' muttered the Doctor; 'the maddest scoundrel, confound him, that ever bellowed in Bedlam!'

Two servants entered with handcuffs.

'Look you,' cried Wilkinson, shaking his cane; 'dare to bring your bullies here, and if I don't cudgel their carcases out of shape, and your's into shape, may I be shot.'

'Secure his hands,' said the Doctor.

Wilkinson instantly darted at the Doctor, and knocked him down. The servants collared Wilkinson, who called to Montmorenci for assistance; but in vain; and after a furious scuffle, the farmer was handcuffed.

'Dear uncle, calm these transports!' said his lordship. 'Your dutiful and affectionate nephew beseeches you to compose yourself.'

'Uncle!—nephew!' cried the farmer. 'What do you mean, fellow? Who the devil is this villain?'

'Are you so far gone, as not to know your own nephew?' said the Doctor, grinning with anger.

'Never set eyes on the poltron till an hour ago!' cried Wilkinson.

'Merciful powers!' exclaimed Montmorenci. 'And when I was a baby, he dandled me; and when I was a child, he gave me whippings and sugar-plums; and when I came to man's estate, he cherished me in his bosom, and was unto me as a father!' Here his lordship applied a handkerchief to his face.

'The man is crazed!' cried Wilkinson.

'No, dear uncle,' said Montmorenci, ''tis you who are crazed; and to be candid with you, this is a madhouse, and this gentleman is the mad-doctor, and with him you must now remain, till you recover from your complaint—the most afflicting instance of insanity, that, perhaps, was ever witnessed.'

'Insanity!' faltered the farmer, turning deadly pale. 'Mercy, mercy on my sinful soul, for I am a gone man!'

'Nay,' said his lordship, 'do not despair. The Doctor is the first in his profession, and will probably cure you in the course of a few years.'

'A few years? That bread and water business will dispatch me in a week! Mad? I mad? I vow to my conscience, Doctor, I was always reckoned the quietest, easiest, sweetest—sure every one knows honest Gregory Wilkinson. Don't they, Cherry? Dear child, answer for your father. Am I mad? Am I, Cherry?'

'As butter in May,' said Montmorenci.

'You lie like a thief!' vociferated the farmer, struggling and kicking. 'You lie, you sneering, hook-nosed reprobate!'

'Why, my dear uncle,' said Montmorenci, 'do you not recollect the night you began jumping like a grasshopper, and scolding the full-moon in my deer-park?'

'Your deer-park? I warrant you are not worth a cabbage-garden! But now I see through the whole plot. Ay, I am to be kept a prisoner here, while my daughter marries that old knave before my face. It would kill me, Cherry; I tell you I should die on the spot. Oh, my unfortunate girl, are you too conspiring against me? Are you, Cherry? Dear Cherry, speak. Only say you are not!'

'Indeed, my friend,' said I, 'you shall be treated with mildness. Doctor, I beg you will not act harshly towards him. With all his faults, the man is goodnatured and well tempered, and to do him justice, he has always used me kindly.'

'Have I not?' cried he. 'Sweet Cherry, beautiful Cherry, blessings on you for that!'

'Come away,' said Montmorenci hastily. 'You know 'tis near dinner time.'

'Farewell, Doctor,' said I. 'Adieu, poor Wilkinson.'

'What, leaving me?' cried he, 'leaving your old father a prisoner in this vile house? Oh, cruel, cruel!'

'Come,' said Montmorenci, taking my hand: 'I have particular business elsewhere.'

'For pity's sake, stay five minutes!' cried Wilkinson, struggling with the servants.

'Come, my love!' said Montmorenci.

'Only one minute—one short minute!' cried the other.

'Well,' said I, stopping, 'one minute then.'

'Not one moment!' cried his lordship, and was hurrying me away.

'My child, my child!' cried Wilkinson, with a tone of such indescribable agony, as made the blood curdle in my veins.

'Dear Sir,' said I, returning; 'indeed I am your friend. But you know, you know well, I am not your child.'

'You are!' cried he, 'by all that is just and good, you are my own child!'

'By all that is just and good,' exclaimed Montmorenci, 'you shall come away this instant, or remain here for ever.' And he dragged me out of the room.

'Now then,' said the poor prisoner, as the door was closing, 'now do what you please with me, for my heart is quite broken!'

On our way home, his lordship enjoined the strictest secrecy with regard to this adventure. I shewed him the hundred pounds, and reimbursed him for what he had paid the Doctor; and on our arrival, I discharged my debt to the poet.

Adieu.

LETTER XIII

Soon after I had got into these lodgings, I sent the servant to Grosvenor Square, with a message for Betterton, requesting him to let me have back the bandbox, which I left at his house the night I fled from him. In a short time she returned with it, and I found every article safe.

To my amazement and dismay, who should enter my apartment this morning but Betterton himself! I dropped my book. He bowed to the dust.

'Your business, Sir?' said I, rising with a dignity, which, from my being under the repeated necessity of assuming it, has now become natural to me.

'To make a personal apology,' replied he, 'for the disrespectful and inhospitable treatment which the loveliest of her sex experienced at my house.'

'An apology for one insult,' said I, 'must seem insincere, when the mode adopted for making it is another insult.'

'The retort is exquisitely elegant,' answered he, 'but I trust, not true. For, granting, my dear Madam, that I offer a second insult by my intrusion, still I may lessen the first insult so much by my apology that the sum of both may be less than the first, as it originally stood.'

'Really,' said I, 'you have blended politeness and arithmetic so happily together; you have clothed multiplication and subtraction in such polished phraseology——'

'Good!' cried he, 'that is real wit.'

'You have added so much algebra to so much sentiment,' continued I.

'Good, good!' interrupted he again.

'In short, you have apologized so gracefully by the rule of three, that I know not which has assisted you the most—Chesterfield or Cocker.'

'Inimitable,' exclaimed he. 'Really your retorting powers are superior to those of any heroine on record.'

In short, my friend, I was so delighted with my repartee, that I could not, for my life, continue vexed with the object of it; and before he left me, I said the best things in nature, found him the most agreeable old man in the world, shook hands with him at parting, and gave him permission to visit me again.

On calm consideration, I do not disapprove of my having allowed him this liberty. Were he merely a good kind of good for nothing old gentleman, it would only be losing time to cultivate an acquaintance with him. But as the man is a reprobate, I may find account in enlisting him amongst the other characters; particularly, since I am at present miserably off for villains. Indeed, I augur auspiciously of his powers, from the fact (which he confessed), of his having discovered my place of abode, by following the maid, when she was returning with my bandbox.

But I have to inform you of another rencontre.

Last night, the landlady, Higginson, and myself, went to see his lordship perform in the new Spectacle. The first piece was called a melodrama; a compound of horror and drollery, where scenery, dresses, and decorations, prevailed over nature, genius, and moral. As to the plot, I could make nothing of it; only that the hero and heroine were in very great trouble about trifles, and quite at their ease in real distress. For instance, when the heroine had arrived at the height of her misery, she began to sing. Then the hero, resolving to revenge her wrongs, falls upon one knee, turns up his eyes, and calls on the sacred majesty of God to assist him. This invocation to the Divinity might, perhaps, prove the hero's piety, but I am afraid it shewed the poet's want of any. Certainly, however, it produced a powerful effect on my feelings. I heard the glory of God made subservient to a theatrical clap-trap, and my blood ran cold. So, I fancy, did the blood of six or seven sweet little children behind the scenes, for they were presently sent upon the stage, to warm themselves with a dance. After dancing, came murder, and the hero gracefully advanced with a bullet in his head. He falls; and many well-meaning persons suppose that the curtain will fall with him. No such thing: Hector had a funeral, and so must Kemble. Accordingly the corpse appears, handsomely dished up on an escutcheoned coffin; while certain virgins of the sun (who, I am told, support that character better than their own), chaunt a holy requiem round it. When horror was exhausted, the poet tried disgust.

After this piece came another, full of bannered processions, gilded pillars, paper snows, and living horses, that were really far better actors than the men who rode them. It concluded with a grand battle, in which twenty men on horseback, and twenty on foot, beat each other indiscriminately, and with the utmost good humour. Armour clashed, sabres struck fire, a castle was burnt to the ground, horses fell dead, the audience rose shouting and clapping, and a man just below me in the pit, cried out in an ecstasy, 'I made their saddles! I made their saddles!'

As to Montmorenci's performance, nothing could equal it; for though his character was the meanest in the piece, he contrived to make it the most prominent. He had an emphasis for every word, an attitude for every emphasis, and a look for every attitude. The people, indeed, hissed him repeatedly, because they knew not, as I did, that his acting a broken soldier in the style of a dethroned monarch, proceeded from his native nobility of soul, not his want of talent.

After the performance, we were pressing through the crowd in the lobby, when I saw, as I thought, Stuart (Bob Stuart!), at a short distance from me, looking anxiously about him. On nearer inspection, I found I was right, and it occurred to me, that I might extract a most interesting scene from him, besides laying a foundation for future incident. I therefore separated myself (like Evelina at the Opera) from my party, and contrived to cross his path. At first he did not recognize me, but I continued by his side till he did.

'Miss Wilkinson!' exclaimed he, 'how rejoiced I am to see you! Where is your father?'

'Let us leave this place,' said I, 'they are searching for me, I know they are.'

'Who?' said he.

'Hush!' whispered I. 'Conduct me in silence from the theatre.'

He put my hand under his arm, and hurried me away. When we had gained the street:

'You may perceive by my lameness,' said he, 'that I am not yet well of the wound I received the night I met you on the Common. But I could not refrain from accompanying your father to Town, in search of you; and as I heard nothing of him since he went to your lodgings yesterday, I called there myself this evening, and was told that you had gone to the theatre. They could give me no information about your father, but of course, you have seen him since he came to Town.'

'I have not, I assure you,' said I, an evasive, yet conscientious answer, because Wilkinson is not my real father.

'That is most extraordinary,' cried he, 'for he left the hotel yesterday, to call on you. But tell me candidly, Miss Wilkinson, what tempted you to leave home? How are you situated at present? with whom? and what is your object?'

'Alas!' said I, 'a horrible mystery hangs over me, which I dare not now develop. It is enough, that in flying from one misfortune, I have plunged into a thousand others, that peace has fled from my heart, and that I am ruined.'

'Ruined!' exclaimed he, with a look of horror.

'Past redemption,' said I, hiding my face in my hands.

'This will be dreadful news for your poor father,' said he. 'But I beg of you to tell me the particulars.'

'Then to be brief,' answered I, 'the first night I came to Town, a gentleman decoyed me into his house, and treated me extremely ill.'

'The villain!' muttered Stuart.

'Afterwards I left him,' continued I, 'and walked the streets, till I was taken up for a robbery, and put into the watchhouse.'

'Is this fact?' asked Stuart, 'or are you merely sporting with my feelings?'

"Tis fact, on my honour,' said I, 'and to conclude my short, but pathetic tale, a gentleman, a mysterious and amiable youth, met me by mere accident, after my release; and I am, at present, under his protection.'

'A shocking account indeed!' said he. 'But have you never considered the consequences of continuing this abandoned course of life?'

'Now here is a pretty insinuation!' cried I; 'but such is always the fate of us poor heroines. No, never can we get through an innocent adventure in peace and quietness, without having our virtue called in question. 'Tis always our virtue, our virtue. If we are caught coming out of a young man's bed-room,—'tis our virtue. If we remain a whole night in the streets,—'tis our virtue. If we make a nocturnal assignation,—Oh! 'tis our virtue, our virtue. Such a rout as they make.'

'I regret,' said Stuart, 'to see you treat the subject so lightly, but I do beseech of you to recollect, that your wretched parent——'

"Tis a fine night, Sir.'

'That your wretched parent——'

'Sir,' said I, 'when spleen takes the form of remonstrance, a lecture is only a scolding put into good language. This is my house, Sir.' And I stopped at the door.

'At least,' said he, 'will you do me the favour of being at home for me to-morrow morning?'

'Perhaps I may,' replied I. 'So good night, master Bobby!'

The poet and the landlady did not return for half an hour. They told me that their delay was occasioned by their search for me; but I refused all explanation as to what happened after I had lost them.

Adieu.

LETTER XIV

Just as I had finished my last letter, his lordship entered my room, but saluted me coldly.

'I am informed,' said he, 'that you strayed from your party last night, and refused, afterwards, to give an account of yourself to the landlady. May I hope, that to me, who feel a personal interest in all your actions, you will be more communicative?'

'I regret,' said I, 'that circumstances put it out of my power to gratify your wishes. I foresee that you, like an Orville, or a Mortimer, will suspect and asperse your mistress. But the Sun shall return, the mist disperse, and the landscape laugh again.'

'Confound your metaphors! 'cried he, discarding attitude and elegance in an instant. 'Do you hope to hide your cunning under mists and laughing landscapes? But I am not to be gulled; I am not to be done. No going it upon me, I say. Tell me directly, madam, where you were, and with whom; or by the devil of devils, you shall repent it finely.'

I was thunderstruck. 'Sir,' said I, 'you have agitated the gentle air with the concussion of inelegant oaths and idioms, uttered in the most ungraceful manner. Sir, your vulgarity is unpardonable, and we now part for ever.'

'For ever!' exclaimed he, reverting into attitude, and interlacing his knuckles in a clasp of agony. 'Hear me, Cherubina. By the shades of my ancestors, my vulgarity was assumed!'

'Assumed, Sir?' said I, 'and pray, for what possible purpose?'

'Alas!' cried he, 'I must not, dare not tell. It is a sad story, and enveloped in a mysterious veil. Oh! fatal vow! Oh! cruel Marchesa!' Shocking were his contortions as he spoke.

'No!' cried I. 'No vow could ever have produced so dreadful an effect on your language.'

'Well, 'said he, after a painful pause, 'sooner than incur the odium of falsehood, I must disclose to you the horrid secret.

'The young Count Di Narcissini was my friend. Educated together, we became competitors in our studies and accomplishments; and in none of them could either of us be said to excel the other; till, on our introduction at Court, it was remarked by the Queen, that I surpassed the Count in shaking hands. 'Narcissini,' said her Majesty, 'has judgment enough in knowing when to present a single finger, or perhaps two; but, for the positive pressure, or the negligent hand with a drooping wrist; or the cordial, honest, dislocating shake, give me Montmorenci. I cannot deny that the former has great taste in this accomplishment; but then the latter has more genius—more execution—more, as it were, of the *magnifique* and *aimable*.'

'His mother the Marchesa overheard this critique, turned as pale as ashes, and left the levee.

'That night, hardly had I fallen into one of those gentle slumbers, which ever attends the virtuous, when a sudden noise roused me; and on opening my eyes, I beheld the detested Marchesa, with an Italian assassin, standing over me.'

'Montmorenci!' cried she, 'thou art the bane of my repose. Thou hast surpassed my son in the graces. Now listen. Either pledge thyself, by an irrevocable vow, henceforth to sprinkle thy conversation with uncouth phrases, and colloquial barbarisms, or prepare to die!'

'Terrible alternative! What could I do? The dagger gleamed before my face. I shuddered, and took the fatal vow of vulgarity.

'The Marchesa then put into my hand the Blackguard's Dictionary, which I studied night and day with much success; and I have now the misfortune to state, that I can be, so far as language goes, the greatest blackguard in England.'

'Unhappy youth!' cried I. 'This, indeed, accounts for what had often made me uneasy. But say, can nothing absolve you from this hateful vow?'

'There is one way,' he replied. 'The Marchesa permitted me to resume my natural elegance, as soon as my marrying should put an end to competition between her son and me. Oh! then, my Cherubina, you, you alone can restore me to hope, to happiness, and to grammar!'

'Ah! my lord,' cried I, 'recollect my own fatal vow. Never, never can I be your's!'

'Drive me not mad!' he cried. 'You are mine, you shall be mine. This, this is the bitterest moment of my life. You do not, cannot love me. No, Cherubina, no, you cannot love me.'

I fixed my eyes in a wild gaze, rose hastily from my chair, paced the room with quick steps; and often sighing deeply, clasped my hands and shuddered.

He led me to the sofa, kissed the drapery of my cambric handkerchief, and concealed his face in its folds. Then raising his head.

'Do you love me?' said he, with a voice dropping manna.

A smile, bashful in its archness, played round my rich and trembling lip; and with an air of bewitching insinuation, I placed my hand on his shoulder, shook my head, and looked up in his face, with an expression half reproachful, half tender.

He snatched me in a transport to his heart; and that trembling pressure, which virtue consecrated, and love understood, conveyed to each of us an unspeakable sensation; as if a beam from Heaven had passed through both our frames, and left some of its divine warmth behind it.

What followed, angels might have attested.

A ringlet had escaped from the bandage of my bodkin. He clipped it off with my scissors, and fixed it next his heart; while I prettily struggled to prevent him, with arch anger, and a pouting playfulness. A thousand saucy triumphs were basking in his eyes, when the door opened, and who should make his appearance, but—Master Bobby!

I could have boxed him.

'I avail myself,' said he, 'of the permission you gave me last night, to call on you this morning.'

Montmorenci looked from the one to the other with amazement.

'And as I am anxious,' continued Stuart, 'to speak with you in private——'

'Sir,' said I, 'any thing which you have to communicate, this gentleman, my particular friend, may hear.'

'Yes, Sir,' cried his lordship, in a haughty tone, 'for I have the honour to boast myself the protector of this lady.'

'If you mean her protector from injury and insult,' said Stuart, 'I hope, Sir, you are not on this occasion, as on others, an actor?'

'You know me then?' said his lordship.

'I saw you perform last night,' answered Stuart, 'but, to say the truth, I do not recollect your name.'

'My name is Norval on the Grampian Hills,' cried his lordship.

'Sir,' said Stuart, 'though we sometimes laugh at you, even in your grave characters, the part you have now chosen seems much too serious for drollery. Allow me to ask, Sir, by what right you feel entitled to call yourself the protector of this lady?'

'First inform me,' said Montmorenci, 'by what right you feel entitled to put that question?'

'By the right of friendship,' answered Stuart.

'No, but enmity,' cried I, 'unprovoked, unprincipled, inexorable enmity. This is the Stuart whom you have often heard me mention, as my persecutor; and I hope you will now make him repent of his temerity.'

'Sir,' said his lordship, 'I desire you to leave the house.'

'Not till you favour me with your company,' replied Stuart; 'for I find I must have some serious conversation with you.'

'Beshrew my heart!' cried Lord Altamont Mortimer Montmorenci, 'if you want satisfaction, follow me this moment. I am none of your slovenly, slobbering shots. Damme, I scorn to pistol a gentleman about the ankles. I can teach the young idea how to shoot, damme.'

He spoke, and strode out of the room.

Stuart smiled and followed him. You must know, I speculate upon a duel.

In short, my plot is entangling itself admirably; and such characters as Betterton and Stuart will not fail to keep the wheels of it going. Betterton is probably planning to carry me off by force; Stuart and our hero are coming to a misunderstanding about me; the latter will, perhaps, return with his arm in an interesting sling, and another parting-forever interview cannot be far distant.

Such is the promising aspect of affairs.

Adieu.

LETTER XV

While I was sitting in the most painful suspense, a knock came to the door, and Stuart entered.

'You terrify, shock, amaze me!' cried I. 'What dreadful blow awaits me? Speak!'

'Pray,' said he, laughing, 'what was your fancy for telling me that you were ruined?'

'And so I am,' answered I.

'At least, not in the way you wished me to suppose,' said he.

'I repeat, Sir,' cried I, 'that I am ruined: no matter in what manner; but ruined I am.'

'Your friend, the player, tells me that you are not,' said he.

'My friend, the player, is very meddling,' answered I. 'This is the way that whatever plot I lay down for my memoirs is always frustrated. Sir, I say I am ruined.'

'Well,' cried he, 'I will not dispute the point. I wish only to guard you against being ruined again. I mistrust this Grundy much. From his conversation, after we left you, I can perceive that he has a matrimonial design upon you. Pray beware of the fellow.'

'The fellow!' cried I. 'Alas! you know him not. His large and piercing eye is but the index of a soul fraught with every human virtue.'

'Ah! my friend,' said he, 'you stand on the very verge of a precipice, and I must endeavour, even at the risk of your displeasure, to snatch you from it.'

He then began a long lecture on my conduct, and asserted that my romantic turn is a sort of infatuation, amounting to little less than madness, and likely to terminate in ruin. He painted, in language pretty enough, the distraction of Wilkinson, after I had fled from his house; and, at last, contrived to extract from me (what, I remark, I can never obtain when I want them)—tears.

Seeing me thus affected, he turned the conversation to desultory topics. We talked of old times, of our juvenal sports and quarrels, when we were playfellows; what happened after our separation; his life at college and in the army; my studies and accomplishments. Thence we made a natural transition to the fine arts. In short, it was the first time in my life that I had a rational conversation (as it is called) with a well-informed young man, and I confess I felt gratified. Besides, even his serious remonstrances were so happily interspersed with humour and delicate irony, that I could not bring myself to be displeased with him.

He remained more than two hours, and at parting took my hand.

'I have hitherto been scolding you,' said he, with a smile, 'and I must now praise you, that I may be better entitled to scold you again. You have the elements of every thing amiable and endearing in your mind, and an admirable understanding to direct them. But you want some one to direct that understanding. Your father and I have already had a serious consultation on the subject; but till he comes, nothing can be done. Indeed, I am much alarmed at his absence. Meantime, will you permit me to legislate in his stead, and to begin by chusing more eligible lodgings for you. I confess I dread the machinations of that actor.'

As he spoke, a rap came to the door.

'Do me the favour to take tea with me this evening,' said I, 'and we will talk the matter over.'

He promised, and took his leave.

Montmorenci then made his appearance, and in visible perturbation, at having found Stuart here again. If I can constitute a jealousy between them it will add to the animation of several scenes. I therefore praised Stuart to the skies, and mentioned my having asked him to tea. His lordship flew into a violent rage, and swore that the villain wanted to unheroinize me, in order to gain me himself. He then renewed his entreaties that I would consent to an immediate marriage; but now the benefits of my fatal vow shone forth in their full lustre, and its irrevocability gave rise to some of the finest agonies that his lordship ever exhibited.

At length we separated to dress for dinner.

At my toilette I recollected with exactness every particular of his late conversation; his sentiments so congenial with mine; his manners so engaging; his countenance so noble and ingenuous.

'I shall see him no more,' said I.

A sigh that followed, told me more of my heart than I wished to know.

No, my Biddy, never, never can he be mine. I must banish his dear image from my mind; and to speak in the simple and unsophisticated language of the heroine in the Forest of Montalbo:

'Indeed, surely, I think, we ought, under existing circumstances, dearest, dearest madam, to avoid, where we can, every allusion, to this, I fear, alas! our, indeed, hopeless attachment.'

Adieu.

LETTER XVI

When Stuart came, he found his lordship, the landlady, the poet, and myself sitting round the tea-table. At first the conversation was general, and on the topics of the day. These Stuart discussed with much animation and volubility, while his lordship sat silent and contemptuous. I fancy that his illustrious tongue disdained to trifle.

Meantime Higginson, in a new coat and waistcoat, sat anglicising the Latinity of his face, and copying the manners and attitudes of Montmorenci, whom the poor man, I verily believe, is endeavouring to rival. At length the word poetry caught his ear; he gave the graces to the winds, and listened.

'Therefore,' continued Stuart to me, 'satirical poetry must be much more useful than encomiastic.'

'Sir,' said Higginson, drawing back his head and lowering his voice, as if he dreaded nothing so much as being heard, 'I must beg leave, in all humility, to coincide with your exprest proposition; but to suggest a doubt whether it be decorous to violate the repose of noble blood.'

'If the great deserve exposure as much as the mean,' said Stuart, 'their rank is rather a reason why they should be censured sooner; because their bad example is more conspicuous, and, therefore, more detrimental.' 'But,' said I, 'though satirizing the vicious may be beneficial to the community, is it always advantageous to the satirist?'

'Johnson observes,' answered Stuart, 'that *it is no less a proof of eminence to have many enemies than many friends*; and, indeed, without the one we seldom have the other. On the whole, however, I would advise a writer not to drop the olive-branch in grasping at the rod; though those whom he finds privately endeavouring to vilify his own character, self-defence entitles him to expose without mercy.'

'That satire is salutary to society, I am convinced,' said I. 'It becomes mischievous only when it is aimed at the worthy heart.'

'And yet,' said Stuart, 'those that are loudest in declaiming against the satirist, are often fondest of disseminating the satire. Now he who slanders with his tongue, is just as culpable as he who defames with his pen; for, if the one weapon be not as extensive, in its effects, as the other, the motives of those who use it are equally vile. Hume, in one of his essays, says, that *a whisper may fly as quick, and be as pernicious, as a pamphlet*.'

'And I think,' said I, 'that those who never allow people faults, are just as injurious to the community as those who never allow them virtues.'

'True,' said Stuart; 'and a late publication (which equals in sentiment, diction, and pictures of character, any work of the kind in our language) thus concludes a description of them: *These, assuming the name of Good-nature, say, that for their part, they wish to avoid making enemies, and when they cannot speak well of people, they make it a rule not to speak of them at all. Now this is an admirable system, for thus, permitting vice, they sanction it, and by not opposing, assist its progress.*'

'So you see,' said Higginson, 'that next to laws and religion, which correct the serious derelictions, writing, which chastises the smaller foibles, is the most useful instrument in a state.'

'Observe,' whispered I to Stuart, 'how the ruling passion breaks forth.'

'And, therefore,' continued Higginson, 'next to the legislator and divine, the poet is the most exalted member of the community.'

'Pardon me there,' said I. 'The most exalted members are not legislators, or divines, or poets, who prescribe, but heroes and heroines, who perform.'

'If you mean the heroes and heroines of romance,' said Stuart, 'their performances are useful in teaching us what we should shun, not what we should imitate. The heroine, in particular, quits a comfortable home, turns out to be the best pedestrian in the world; and, after weeping tears enough to float her work-basket, weds some captious, passionate, and kneeling hero.'

'Better,' cried I, 'than to remain a domesticated rosy little Miss, who romps with the squire, plays an old tune on an old piano, and reads prayers for the good family—servants and all. At last, marrying some honest gentleman, who lives on his saddle, she degenerates into a dangler of keys and whipper of children; trots up and down stairs, educates the poultry, and superintends the architecture of pies.'

'Now for my part,' said Stuart, 'I would have a young lady neither a mere homely drudge, nor a sky-rocket heroine, let off into the clouds. I would educate her heart and head, as well as her fingers and feet. She should be at once the ornament of the social group, and the delight of the domestic circle; abroad attractive, at home endearing; the enchantress to whom levity would apply for mirth, and wisdom for admonition; and her mirth should be graceful, and her admonition fascinating. If she happened to be solitary, she should have the power of contemplation, and if her needle broke, she should be capable of finding resource in a book. In a word, she should present a proof, that wit is not inconsistent with good-nature, nor liveliness with good-sense, and that to make the virtues attractive, they ought to be adorned with the graces.'

'And pray, to whom would you marry this charmer?' asked his lordship, winking at me.

'Why,' replied he, 'when she wishes to settle in life, I would have her consult her parents, and make a prudent match.'

'A prudent match!' cried I. 'Just conceive—a prudent match! Oh, Stuart, I declare I am quite ashamed of you.'

"Pon honour,' said his lordship, 'you are too severe. I will bet five to four he means well.'

'No doubt,' said I. 'And to be candid, I think him a mighty good sort of a man.'

'A proper behaved young person,' said his lordship.

'An honest *bon diable*!' added I.

'A worthy soul!' said he.

'A respectable character!' cried I.

'A decent creature!' said he.

'A humane and pious christian,' cried I.

This last hit was irresistible, and both of us burst out laughing, while Stuart sat silent, and even affected to smile.

'Now is your time,' whispered I, to his lordship. 'A few more sarcasms, and he crouches to you for ever.'

'I fancy, young gentleman,' said his lordship, turning full upon Stuart, and laughing so long, that I thought he would never finish the sentence; 'I fancy, my tight fellow, you may now knock under.'

'I am not always inclined to do so,' replied Stuart; 'neither am I easily provoked to knock down.'

'Knock down whom?' demanded his lordship, with the most complete frown I had ever beheld.

'A puppy,' said Stuart coolly.

'You lie!' vociferated our hero.

'Leave the room, Sir,' cried Stuart, starting from his seat.

Montmorenci rose, retreated to the door;—stopped—went on—stopped again—moved—stopped—

'Vanish!' cried Stuart, advancing.

His lordship vanished.

I ran, snatched a pen, and wrote on a scrap of paper

'Vindicate your honour, or never appear in my presence!'

I then rang the bell for the maid, and slipping some silver into her hand, begged that she would deliver the paper to his lordship.

Higginson then started from his chair.

'After a deliberate consideration of the subject,' said he, 'I am more and more convinced, that a poet is the first character in society.'

During a whole hour, I remained in a state of the most distracting suspense, for he never returned! Meantime, Stuart was privately pressing me to leave my lodgings, and remain at his father's, till Wilkinson should be found. Indignant at the cowardly conduct of his lordship, I was almost consenting; when on a sudden, the door flew open, and with a slow step and dignified deportment, Lord Altamont Mortimer Montmorenci entered. All eyes were rivetted on him. He walked towards Stuart, and fell upon one knee before him:

'I come, Sir,' said he, 'to retract that abuse which I gave you just now. I submit to whatever punishment you please; nor shall I think my honour re-established till my fault is repaired. Then grant me the pardon that I beg, on whatever conditions you think proper.'

'For shame!' exclaimed I, with an indignation that I could not suppress. 'You a hero?'

His lordship instantly snatched a book from his pocket, and opening a passage, presented it to me. The book was *La Nouvelle Heloise*.

'You see there,' said he, 'how Lord B., after having given St. Preux the lie, begs forgiveness on his knees, and in the precise words which I have just used. Will Cherubina condemn the conduct that Heloise applauded?'

'Ever excellent, ever exalted mortal!' cried I. 'O thou art indeed all that is just, dignified, magnanimous.'

I gave him my hand, and he bowed over it. Supper was announced. Mirth ruled the night. The landlady sat gazing on his lordship; his lordship on me. Stuart uttered a thousand witticisms; and even the poet determined to be heard; for, in the midst of our merriment, I saw him, with his mouth open, and his neck stretched forward, watching for the first moment of silence. It came.

'This is the fun,

Equalled by none;

So never, never, never have done!'

cried the happy creature, and protruded such an exorbitant laugh as made ample amends for the gravity of his whole life.

At length Stuart took leave; and the rest of us separated to our several apartments.

That coxcomb, I see, has no notion of sentiment, and no taste for admiring those who have. There he sits, calm, unconcerned, and never once fixes his eyes on me with a speaking gaze. Oh, no; nothing but wit or wisdom for him. Not only is the fellow far from a pathetic turn himself, but he has also an odd faculty of detaching even me from my miseries, and of reducing me to horrid hilarity. It would vex a saint to see how he makes me laugh, though I am predetermined not to give him a single smile. But Montmorenci, the sentimental Montmorenci, timely interposes the fine melancholy of his features;—he looks, he sighs, he speaks; and in a moment I am recalled to the soft emotions, and a due sense of my deplorable destiny.

Adieu.

LETTER XVII

Clouds are impending, and I know not whether they will clash together, and elicit lightning, or mingle into one, and descend in refreshing showers.

This morning, Montmorenci, the hostess, and myself, breakfasted early, and then went shopping. I purchased a charming scarf, a bonnet, two dresses, a diamond cross, and a pair of pearl ear-rings. His lordship borrowed a guinea from me, and then bought a small casket, which he presented to me in the handsomest manner.

We next visited Westminster Abbey; the first that I have ever seen, though I had read of thousands. To my great disappointment, I found in it no cowled monks with scapulars, and no veiled nuns with rosaries. Nothing but statues of statesmen and warriors, in stone wigs and marble regimentals.

Soon after we had returned home, Higginson entered my room, stealing, and with a look of terror.

'My mother presents her respectful compliments,' said he in a whisper, 'and begs you will honour her with your presence, that she may do herself the pleasure of saving you from destruction.'

'Tell me,' said I, with a look that pierced into his soul, 'which character do *you* mean to support on this occasion? that of my friend, or of an accomplice in the plot against me?'

Higginson looked aghast.

'As to your being a principal,' continued I, 'that is not likely; but I must ascertain if your object is to be— excuse me—an understrapping ruffian. Never fear, speak your mind candidly.'

'And I was writing verses on you all the morning, and it was for you that I clipped my eyebrows, and it was for you that I—dear me, dear me!' cried the poor man, and began whimpering like a child.

'Nay,' said I, 'if it is not your taste, that is another affair; but though I cannot countenance you as a villain, I will at least respect you as an honest man. I will, I assure you; so now lead me to your mother.'

We proceeded up stairs, and entered a garret; where his mother, a corpulent old lady, was lying in a fit of the gout.

Higginson having introduced us: 'Miss,' said she, 'I sent for you to tell you that I have just overheard your hostess, and an old gentleman (Betterton, I think she called him), planning something against you. They were in the next room, and thought I could not hear; but this I know, that he offered her fifty pounds, if she would assist him in obtaining you. And so, Miss, from all my son says of you, and sure enough he raves of you like mad, I thought you would wish to be saved from ruin.'

'Certainly, Madam,' answered I. 'At the same time, I must beg permission to remark, that you have destroyed half the interest of this intrigue against me, by forewarning me of it.'

'May be so, Miss,' said she. 'I have done my duty as a Christian, however.'

'Nay,' said I, 'do not suppose I resent your conduct, old lady. I am sure you meant all for the best, and I sincerely wish you health and happiness. Farewell.'

On returning to my room, I found Betterton there before me. He came to request that I would accept of a ticket for the masquerade, at the Pantheon: and he gave another to the landlady; who, he said, must accompany me thither: so 'tis clear that he means to decoy me from it. Unhappy girl! But how can I refuse going? A heroine, you know, never misses a masquerade: it is always the scene of her best adventure; and to say the truth, I cannot resist the temptation of so delightful an amusement. Now to consult about my character.

LETTER XVIII

At dinner, yesterday, I bespoke his lordship as an escort to the masquerade; and we then held a council of dress. It was resolved, that I should appear in the character of Sterne's Maria, and his lordship as Corporal Trim.

This morning, just as I had finished reading the closet-scene, in the Children of the Abbey, Betterton and the landlady came into my room; and in a short time, I perceived the purport of their visit; as they began requesting that I would not take either Stuart or Montmorenci with me to the masquerade.

'The fact is, Miss,' said the landlady, 'that I have heard your real story. Mr. Grundy is not your cousin at all, and your name is Wilkinson, not Donald. Howsomever, as I believe you meant no harm, in this deception, I am willing, at the solicitations of this excellent gentleman, to let you remain in my house, provided you promise not to receive any more visits from that Stuart, who is the greatest villain unhanged; or from Mr. Grundy, who has certainly bad designs on you; though he made proposals of marriage to myself, no longer ago than yesterday.'

A tapping at my door prevented me from expressing my total disbelief in her latter assertion. It struck me that should the person prove to be his lordship, I might make her look extremely foolish, by letting her overhear his declarations of attachment to me. 'Conceal yourselves in this closet,' whispered I to my visitors. 'I have particular reasons.' They looked at each other, and hesitated.

'In, in!' said I; 'for I suspect that this visit is from a villain, and I wish you to hear what passes.'

Both then went into the closet. I opened the door of my chamber, and, to my great disappointment, the poet appeared at it, with his eyes rolling, and his mouth ajar.

'What is the matter?' asked I.

He gaped still wider, but said nothing.

'Ah,' cried I, 'that is an awkward attempt at expressing horror. If you have any hideous news to communicate, why do you not rush into the room, tossing your hands on high, and exclaiming, "Fly, fair lady, all is lost!"'

'Indeed, Miss,' said he, 'I was never in the way of learning good breeding. But don't go to the masquerade, Miss, Oh, don't! My mother overheard old Betterton just now planning with the landlady, to carry you from it by force. But, Miss, I have a fine sword, above stairs, three feet and a half long, and I will rub off the rust, and——'

A knock at the street-door interrupted him. I was in a hiding mood. Already the scene promised wonders; and I resolved not to damp its rising spirit; so made the simple Higginson get underneath the sofa.

The next moment my door opened, and Vixen, Montmorenci's terrier, came bounding towards me.

'Go, dear Vixen,' cried I, snatching her to my bosom; 'carry back to your master all that nourishes his remembrance. Go, dear Vixen, guard him by night, and accompany him by day, serve him with zeal, and love him with fidelity!'

I turned round, and perceived—Montmorenci! The poor timid girl bent her eyes to the ground.

'Yes, dear Vixen,' said he, 'you have now indeed a claim to my regard; and with the fondest gratitude will I cherish you!'

He then flew to me, and poured forth, at my feet, the most passionate acknowledgments, and tender protestations.

I tried to break from him.

'No, loveliest Cherubina!' said he, detaining me. 'Not thus must we part.'

'We must part for ever!' exclaimed I. 'After that rash soliloquy which you have just heard, never can I bear you in my sight. Besides, Sir, you are betrothed, at this moment, to another.'

'I? Ridiculous! But to whom?'

'Our hostess—a most charming woman.'

'Our hostess! Yes, a charming woman indeed. She has roses in her cheek, and lilies in her skin; but they are white roses, and orange lilies. Our hostess! Beshrew my heart, I would let cobwebs grow on my lips before I would kiss her.'

Another knock came to the door.

'Me miserable!' exclaimed I. 'If this be the person I suspect, we are both undone—separated for ever!'

'Who? what? where shall I hide?' cried his lordship.

'Yon dark closet,' said I, pointing. 'Fly.'

His lordship sprang into the closet, and closed the door.

'I can hear no tidings of your father,' said Stuart, entering the room. 'I have searched every hotel in Town, and I really fear that some accident——'

'Mercy upon me! who's here?' cried his lordship from the closet. 'As I hope to be saved, the place is full of people. Let me go; whoever the devil you are, let me go!'

'Take that—and that—and that:—you poor, pitiful, fortune-hunting play-actor!' vociferated the landlady, buffetting him about.

That unhappy young nobleman bolted from the closet, with his face running blood, and the landlady fast at his heels.

'Yes, you dog!' exclaimed she; 'I have discovered your treacherousness at last. As for your love-letters and trinkets, to me, villain—I never valued 'em a pin's point; but that you should go for to try to ruin this sweet innocent young creature, that is what distresses me, so it is.' And she burst out crying.

'Love-letters and trinkets to you!' exclaimed I. 'Surely he was not so base, Madam.'

'But he was so base, Madam,' said she with a bitter look; 'and if you fancy that 'tis yourself he loves, why look there; read the letter he sent me yesterday, just after I had asked him to pay me for six months' diet and lodging.'

I read:

'Accept, my lovely hostess, the pair of bracelets which accompanies this note, and rest assured that I will discharge my bill, in the course of another month.

'My motive for having brought Miss Wilkinson into your house, as my cousin, was simply to restore her to her friends. Your jealousy, though most unfounded, is most flattering.

'Ah, how little do you know your Grundy!—If I pay the silly girl a few slight attentions, it is only to cloak that tenderness for you, which preys upon my heart, and consumes my vitals;—that tenderness, which I yesterday so solemnly vowed to evince (as soon as my affairs are arranged) at the altar.

'Your own, own, own,

'Abraham Grundy.'

It was as much as my dignity could do to suppress my indignation at this letter; but the heroine prevailed, and I cast on his lordship my famous compound expression of pity, contempt, and surprise, which I tinged with just fascination enough to remind him of what a jewel he had lost.

Meantime he stood wiping his face, and did not utter a word.

'And now,' cried I, 'now for the grand developement. James Higginson, come forth!'

In a moment the poet was seen, creeping, like a huge tortoise, from under the sofa.

'Mr. Higginson,' said I, 'did not your mother tell you, that this lady here—this amiable lady,' (and I curtsied low to her, and she curtsied still lower to me), 'that this first and best of women,' (and again we exchanged rival curtsies), 'is plotting with a Mr. Betterton to betray me into his hands at the masquerade?'

'Madam,' answered the poet, with a firm demeanour, 'I do solemnly certify and asseverate, that so my mother told me.'

'Then your mother told a confounded falsehood!' cried Betterton, popping out of the closet.

Higginson walked up to him, and knocked him down with the greatest gravity imaginable. The hostess ran at Higginson, and fastened her fangs in his face. Montmorenci laid hold of the hostess, and off came her cap. Stuart dropped into a chair with laughter. I too forgot all my dignity, and clapped my hands, and danced with delight, while they kicked and scratched each other without mercy.

At length Stuart interfered, and separated the combatants. The landlady retired to repair her dismantled head; and his lordship and Higginson to wash their wounds. Betterton too was about to take his departure.

'Sir,' said Stuart, 'I must beg leave to detain you for a few moments.'

Betterton bowed and returned.

'Your name is Betterton, I believe.'

'It is, Sir.'

'After Mr. Higginson's accusation of you,' said Stuart, 'I feel myself called upon, as the friend of this lady's father, to insist on your apologizing for the designs which you have dared to harbour against her; and to demand an unequivocal renunciation of those views for the future.'

'You are an honest fellow,' said Betterton, 'and I respect your spirit. Most sincerely, most humbly, Miss Wilkinson, do I solicit your forgiveness; and I beg you will believe, that nothing but a misrepresentation of your real character and history tempted me to treat you with such undeserved insult. I now declare, that you have nothing further to fear from me.'

'But before I can feel perfectly satisfied,' said Stuart, 'I must stipulate for the discontinuance of your visits to Miss Wilkinson, as a proof that you have relinquished all improper projects against her.'

'I had formed that resolution before you spoke,' answered Betterton, 'though many a bitter pang it will cost me. Now then we are all friends. I may have my faults, but upon my soul, I am a man of honour;—I am, upon my soul. As for you, Mr. Stuart, without flattery, you have evinced more discretion and coolness, throughout this affair, than I have ever seen in so young a man. Sir, you are an honour to the human race, and I wish you would dine with me this evening at the Crown and Anchor. Some friends of us meet there to discuss a radical reform. Do, my dear fellow. We want nothing but men of respectability like you; for our sentiments "are the finest in the world."'

'You will excuse me,' said Stuart, 'though I am told that your wines are as fine and as foreign as your sentiments.'

'Well, adieu, good people,' said Betterton. 'Think of me with kindness. Faults I may have, but my heart——' (tapping at it with his forefinger), 'all is right here.'

After he had left us, I reprimanded Stuart so severely, for his officiousness in having interfered about Betterton, that he went away quite offended; and, I much fear, will never return. If he does not, he will use me basely, to leave me here in this unprotected state, after all his anxieties about me—anxieties too, which (I cannot tell why) have pleased me beyond expression. I confess, I feel a regard for the man, and should be sorry to have hurt his feelings seriously. Would Sir Charles Bingley have deserted me so, I ask? No. But Stuart has no notion of being a plain, useful, unsuccessful lover, like him. Well, I must say, I hate to see a man more ready to fall out with one, than to fall in love with one.

But Montmorenci—what shall I say of him? How can he possibly exculpate himself from his treacherous intrigue with the landlady? I confess I am predisposed to credit any feasible excuse which he can assign, rather than find myself deceived, outrivalled, and deprived of a lover, not alone dear to me, but indispensible to the progress of my memoirs.

Then, that closet-scene, from which I had a right to expect the true pathetic, what a bear-garden it became! In short, I feel at this moment disgusted with the world. I half wish I were at home again. Now too, that Stuart has reminded me of our early days, I cannot avoid sometimes picturing to myself the familiar fireside, the walks, frolics, occupations of our childhood; and well I remember how he used to humour my whims. Oh, these times are past, and now he opposes me in every thing.

But whither am I wandering? Pardon these vulgar sentiments. They have escaped my pen. You know that a mere home is my horror. Forgive them.

Adieu.

Determined to support my dignity, I dined alone in my room, after the closet-scene; and during this evening, letters of the most heart-rending nature passed between his lordship and me.

To be brief, he has convinced me, that the letter written in his name, to the landlady, was a forgery of her own. The circumventing wretch! I am of opinion, that it ought to be made a hanging matter.

The following is an extract from his and my correspondence. After a most satisfactory disquisition on the various circumstances tending to prove the forgery, he writes thus:

'I have begun twenty letters to you, and have torn them all. I write to you on my knees, and the paper is blistered with my tears; but I have dried it with my sighs.

'Sun, moon, and stars may rise and set as they will. I know not whether it be day, or whether it be night.

'When the girl came with your last note, the idea that your eyes had just been dwelling on her features, on her cap, ribbon, and apron, made her and them so interesting, so dear to me, that, though her features are snubbed, her cap tattered, her ribbon bottle-green (which I hate), and her apron dirty, I should certainly have taken her in my arms, if I had not been the most bashful of men.

'Though that note stung me to the heart, the words were hosts of angels to me, and the small paper the interminable regions of bliss. Any thing from you!

'How my heart beats, and my blood boils in my veins, when by chance our feet meet under the table. The diapason of my heart-strings vibrates to the touch. How often I call to mind the sweet reproof you once gave me at dinner, when I trod on your toe in a transport of passion.

'"If you love me, tell me so," said you, smiling; "but do not hurt my foot."

'Another little incident is always recurring to me. As we parted from each other, the night before last, you held out your hand and said, "Good-night, my dear Montmorenci." It was the first time you had ever called me *dear*. The sound sank deep into my heart. I have repeated it a hundred times since, and when I went to bed, I said, good night, my dear Montmorenci. I recollected myself and laughed. The fatal kiss that I once dared to snatch from you has undone me for ever. The moisture on your lip was like a suppuration of rubies. O immortal remembrance of that illusive, frantic, and enchanting moment!'

BILLET FROM CHERUBINA.

He who could be capable of the letter, could be capable of calling it a forgery.

BILLET FROM MONTMORENCI.

Misery with you, were better than happiness without you.

BILLET FROM CHERUBINA.

Hatred and certainty were better than love and suspicion.

BILLET FROM MONTMORENCI.

Love is heaven and heaven is love.

BILLET FROM CHERUBINA.

If heaven be love, I fear that heaven is not eternal.

BILLET FROM MONTMORENCI.

If my mind be kept in suspense, my body shall be suspended too.

BILLET FROM CHERUBINA.

Foolish youth! If my life be dear to thee, attempt not thine own.

BILLET FROM MONTMORENCI.

It were easier to kill myself than to fly from Cherubina.

BILLET FROM CHERUBINA.

Live. I restore you to favour.

BILLET FROM MONTMORENCI.

Angelic girl! But how can I live without the means? My landlady threatens me with an arrest. Heloise lent money to St. Preux.

BILLET FROM CHERUBINA.

In enclosing to you half of all I have, I feel, alas! that I am but half as liberal of my purse as of my heart.

BILLET FROM MONTMORENCI.

I promise to pay Lady Cherubina de Willoughby, or order, on demand, the sum of twenty-five pounds sterling, value received.

Montmorenci.

In a few minutes after I had received this last billet, his lordship came in person to perfect the reconciliation. Never was so tender, so excruciating a scene.

We then consulted about the masquerade; and he brought me down his dress for it. The Montero cap and tarnished regimentals (which he procured at the theatre) are admirable.

Soon after his departure, a letter was brought to me by the maid; who said, that a tall man, wrapped in a dark cloak, put it into her hand, and then fled with great swiftness.

Conceive my sensations on reading this note, written in an antiquated hand.

To Lady Cherubina de Willoughby.

These, greeting.

Most fayre Ladie

An aunciente and loyall Vassall that erewhyles appertained unto y^e ryhgte noble Auncestrie, in y$_e$ qualitie of Seneschal, hath, by chaunce, discovered y^{er} place of hiding, and doth crave y$_e$ boon that you will not fayle to goe unto y$_e$ Masquerade at y$_e$ Pantheon; where, anon he will joyn you, and unravell divers mysterys touching your pedigree.

Lette nonne disswaid you from to goe, and eke lette nonne, save a Matron, goe with you; els I dare not holde parle with you.

Myne honoured Ladie, if you heede not this counsell, you will work yourselfe woefull ruth.

Judge if I can sleep a wink after such a mysterious communication. Excellent old man! I mean to make him my steward.

Adieu.

LETTER XX

I believe I mentioned, in a former letter, that my bed-chamber was on the ground floor, and looking into the yard at the back of the house. Soon after I went to bed, last night, I heard a whispering and rustling outside of the window, and while I was awaiting with anxiety the result, sleep surprised me.

I awoke earlier, as I thought, than usual, this morning; for not a ray penetrated my curtainless window. I then tried to compose myself to sleep again, but in vain; so there I lay turning and tumbling about, for eight or nine hours, at the very least. At last I became alarmed. What can be the matter? thought I. Is the sun quenched or eclipsed? or has the globe ceased rolling? or am I struck stone blind?

In the midst of my conjectures, a sudden cry of fire! fire! reverberated through the house. I sprang out of bed, and huddled on me whatever cloaths came to hand. I then groped for my casket of jewels, and having secured it, rushed into the outer room, where my eyes were instantly dazzled by the sudden glare of light.

However, I had presence of mind enough to snatch up Corporal Trim's coat, which still remained on a chair; and to slip it on me. For, in the first place, I had no gown underneath; and in the next, I recollected, that Harriot Byron, at a moment of distress, went wild about the country, in masquerade.

Hurrying into the hall, I saw the street door wide open, Stuart and Montmorenci struggling with each other near it, the landlady dragging a trunk down stairs, and looking like the ghost of a mad housemaid; and the poet just behind her, with his corpulent mother, bed and all, upon his back; while she kept exclaiming, that we should all be in heaven in five minutes, and he crying out, Heaven forbid! Heaven forbid!

I darted past Stuart, just as he had got Montmorenci down; thence out of the house, and had fled twenty paces, before I discovered, that, so far from being night, it was broad, bright, incontrovertible day!

I had no time to reflect on this mystery, as I heard steps pursuing me, and my name called. I fled the faster, for I dreaded I knew not what. The portentous darkness of my room, the false alarm of fire, all betokened some diabolical conspiracy against my life; so I rushed along the street, to the horror and astonishment of all who saw me. For conceive me drest in a long-skirted, red coat, stiff with tarnished lace; a satin petticoat, satin shoes, no stockings, and my flaxen hair streaming like a meteor behind me!

Stop her, stop her! was now shouted on all sides. Hundreds seemed in pursuit. Panting and almost exhausted, I still continued my flight. They gained on me. What should I do? I saw the door of a carriage just opened, and two ladies, dressed for dinner, stepping into it. I sprang in after them, crying, save me, save me! The footman endeavoured to drag me out; the mob gathered round shouting; the horses took fright, and set off in full gallop; I, meantime, on one knee, with my meek eyes raised, and my hands folded across my bosom, awaited my fate; while the ladies gazed on me in dismay, and supported one unbroken scream.

At last, the carriage dashed against a post, and was upset. Several persons ran forward, and, I being uppermost, took me out the first. Again I began running, and again a mob was at my heels. I felt certain they would tear me in pieces. My head became bewildered; and all the horrid sights I had ever read of rose in array before me. Bacchantes, animated with Orphean fury, slinging their serpents in the air, and uttering dithyrambics, appeared to surround me on every side. On I flew. Knock it down! cried several voices.

A footman was just entering a house. I rushed past him, and into a parlour, where a large party were sitting at dinner.

Save me! exclaimed I, and sank on my knees before them. All arose:—some, in springing to seize me, fell; and others began dragging me away. I grasped the table-cloth, in my confusion, and the next instant, the whole dinner was strewn about the floor. Those who had fallen down, rose in piteous plight; one bathed in soup, another crowned with vegetables, and the face of a third all over harico.

They held me fast, and questioned me; then called me mad, and turned me into the street. The mob were still waiting for me there, and they cheered me as I came out; so seeing a shop at hand, I darted through it, and ran up stairs, into the drawing-room.

There I found a mother in the cruel act of whipping her child. Ever a victim to thrilling sensibility, I snatched the rod from her hand; she shrieked and alarmed the house; and again I was turned out of doors. Again, my friend the mob received me with a shout; again I took to flight; rushed through another shop, was turned out— through another, was turned out. In short, I threaded a dozen different houses, and witnessed a dozen different domestic scenes. In this, they were singing, in that scolding:—here, I caught an old man kissing the maid, there, I found a young man reading the Bible. Entering another, I heard ladies laughing and dancing in the drawing-room. I hurried past them to the garrets, and saw their aged servant dying.

Shocked by the sight, I paused at his half-opened door. Not a soul was in the room with him; and vials and basons strewed the table.

'Is that my daughter?' said he feebly. 'Will no one go for my daughter? To desert me thus, after first breaking my heart! Well then, I will find her out myself.'

He made a sudden effort to rise, but it was fatal. His head and arms dropped down motionless, and hung out of the bed. He gave a hollow sob, and expired.

Horrorstruck, I rushed into an adjoining garret, and burst into tears. I felt guilty of I knew not what; and the picture of Wilkinson, dying in the madhouse, and calling on his daughter, shot across me for a moment.

The noise of people searching the rooms below, and ascending the stairs, put an end to my disagreeable reflections; and I thought but of escape. Running to the window of the garret, I found that it opened upon the roof of a neighbouring house; and recollecting that robbers often escape by similar means, I sprang out of the window, closed it after me, and ran along a whole row of roofs.

At last I came to a house higher than the rest, with a small window, similar to that by which I had just got out, and happily lying open. On looking into the garret, I found that nobody was there, so I scrambled into it, and fastened the window after me. A servant's bed, a chair, a table, and an immense chest, constituted all the furniture. The chest had nothing but a little linen in it; and I determined to make it my place of refuge, in case of an alarm.

Having sat a few minutes, to compose my spirits, after the shock they had just experienced, I resolved on exploring the several apartments; for I felt a secret presentiment that this house was, some way or other, connected with my fate—a most natural idea.

I first traversed the garrets, but found nothing in them worthy of horror; so I stole, with cautious steps, down the first flight of stairs, and found the door of the front room open. Hearing no noise inside, I ventured to put in my head, and perceived a large table, with lighted candles on it, and covered over with half-finished dresses of various descriptions, besides bonnets, feathers, caps, and ribbons in profusion; whence I concluded that the people of the house were milliners.

Here I sat some time, admiring the dresses, and trying at a mirror how the caps became me, till I was interrupted by steps on the stairs. I ran behind a window-curtain; and immediately three young milliners came into the room.

They sat down at the table, and began working.

'I wonder,' said one, 'whether our lodger has returned from dinner.'

'What a sly eye the fellow casts at me,' says another.

'And how he smiles at me,' says the first.

'And how he teases me about my being pretty,' says the second.

'And me too,' says the first; 'and he presses my hand into the bargain.'

'Presses!' says the second; 'why, he *squeezes* mine; and just think, he tries to kiss me too.'

'I know,' says the third, who was the only pretty girl of the three, 'that he never lays a finger on me, nor speaks a word to me, good or bad—never: and yesterday he lent me the Mysteries of Udolpho with a very bad grace; and when I told him that I wanted it to copy the description of the Tuscan girl's dress, as a lady had ordered me to make up a dress like it, for the masquerade to-night, he handed me the book, and said, that if I went there myself, the people would take my face for a mask.'

Judge of my horror, when I recollected, that this was, indeed, the night of the masquerade; and that I was pent behind a curtain, without even a dress for it!

That Tuscan costume, thought I, would just answer. Perhaps I could purchase it from the milliner. Perhaps— — But in the midst of my perhaps's, the first and second milliner set off with some Indian robes, which they had finished for the masquerade, while the pretty one still remained to complete the Tuscan dress.

While I was just resolving to issue from my retreat, and persuade her to sell me the dress, I heard a step stealing up the stairs; and presently perceived a young gentleman peeping into the room. He nodded familiarly to the milliner; and said, in a whisper, that he had seen her companions depart, and was now come to know how soon she would go, that he might meet her at their old corner. She replied, that she would soon be ready; and he then stole back again.

I had now no time to lose in accomplishing my plan, so I drew aside the curtain, and stood, in a commanding attitude before her.

The poor girl looked up, started, made a miserable imitation of the heroic scream, and ran down stairs.

I ran after her, as far as the landing-place; and on looking over the balusters, into the hall, I saw the young man who had just been with her, listening to her account of the transaction. 'I will call the watch,' said she, 'and do you keep guard at the door.'

She then hastened into the street, and he stood in such a manner, that it was impossible for me to pass him.

'What is the matter?' cried the mistress of the house, coming out of the parlour.

'A mad woman that is above stairs,' answered the young man. 'Miss Jane has just seen her; dressed half like a man, half like a woman, and with hair down to the ground!'

'What is all this?' cried a maid, running out of the kitchen.

'Oh! Molly,' said the mistress, 'Miss Jane is just frightened to death by a monster above stairs, half man, half woman, and all over covered with hair!'

Another servant now made her appearance.

'Oh! Betty,' cried Molly, 'Miss Jane is just killed by a huge monster above stairs, half man, half beast, all over covered with black hair, and I don't know what other devilments besides!'

'I will run and drive it down,' cried Betty, and began ascending the stairs. Whither could I hide? I luckily recollected the large chest; so I flew up to the garret. It was now quite dark; but I found the chest, sprang into it, and having closed the lid, flung some of the linen over me. I then heard the girl enter the next room, and in a few moments, she came into mine, with another person.

'Here is the trunk, Tom,' said she, 'and I must lock it on you till the search is over. You see, Tom, what risks I am running on your account; for there is Miss Jane, killed by it, and lying in bits, all about the floor.'

The man had now jumped into the chest; the girl locked it in an instant, took out the key, and ran down.

Almost prest to death, I made a sudden effort to get from under him.

'What's this! Oh! mercy, what's this?' cried he, feeling about.

I gathered myself up; but did not speak.

'Help!' vociferated he. "Tis the monster—here is the hair! help, help!'

'Hush!' said I, 'or you will betray both of us. I am no monster, but a woman.'

'Wasn't? it you that murdered the milliner?' said he, still trembling.

'No, really,' replied I, 'but now not a word; for I hear people coming.'

As I spoke, several persons entered the room. We lay still. They searched about; and one of them, approaching the chest, tried to lift the lid.

'That is locked this month past,' said the voice of the maid who had hidden the man in it, 'so you need not look there.'

They then searched the remaining garrets; and I heard them say, as they were going down stairs, that I must have jumped out of a window.

'And now, Madam,' said the man, 'will you have the goodness to tell me who you are?'

'A young and innocent maiden,' answered I, 'who, flying from my persecutors, took refuge here.'

'Young and innocent!' cried he, 'good ingredients, faith. Come then, my dear; I will protect you.'

So saying, he caught me round the waist, and attempted to kiss me.

I begged, reasoned, menaced—all would not do. I had read of a heroine, whose virtue was saved by a timely brain-fever; so, as I could not command one at that instant, I determined on affecting one.

'I murdered her famously!' exclaimed I; and then commenced singing and moaning by turns.

He stopped, and lay quiet, as if uncertain what to make of me. I scratched the chest with my nails, and laughed, and shrieked. He began to mutter curses and prayers with great rapidity; till, as I was gabbling over the finest passage in Ossian, 'Oh! merciful!' ejaculated he, rolling himself into a ball; "tis a Bedlamite broke loose!'

By this time, between my terror, and the heat of the chest, I was gasping for breath; and my companion appeared on the very point of suffocation; when, at this critical juncture, some one fortunately came into the room. The man called for help, the chest was unlocked, opened; and the maid with a candle appeared before us.

The man darted out like an arrow; she remained motionless with astonishment at seeing me, while I lay there, almost exhausted; though, as usual, not worth a swoon. I do believe, that the five fingers I am writing with would leave me, sooner than my five senses.

'She has confessed to the murder!' cried the man; while the maid held by his arm, and shrunk back, as I rose from the chest with an air of dignity.

'Be not frightened, my friends,' said I smiling, 'for I assure you that I am no murderess; and that the milliner is alive and well, at this moment. Is she not, young woman?'

'Yes, sure,' answered she, somewhat recovering from her terror.

'How I came into this extraordinary situation,' continued I, 'it were needless to relate; but I must have your assistance to get out of it. If you, my good girl, will supply me with a decent gown, bonnet, and pair of stockings, I will promise not to tell the family that you had a lover secreted in the house, and I will give you two guineas for your kindness.'

So saying, I took the casket from the pocket of my regimental coat, and displayed the jewels and money that were in it.

'Mercy me!' cried the maid; 'how could they dare for to say that so rich a lady murdered the girl?'

'Ay, or so handsome a lady,' added the man, bowing.

In a word, after some explanations and compliments, I gave the maid four guineas, and the man the regimental coat; and was supplied with a gown, bonnet, and pair of stockings.

As soon as I had dressed myself, we determined that I should steal down stairs, and out of the house; and that, if discovered in my passage, I should not betray the maid.

Accordingly, with much trepidation, I began to descend the stairs. Not a soul seemed stirring. But as I passed by the milliner's room, I perceived the door half open, and heard some one humming a tune inside. I peeped through the chink, and saw the pretty milliner again seated there, and still busied about the Tuscan dress. I resolved to make another effort for it; and as I had gained my point with the maid, by having discovered her intrigue, it struck me that I might succeed with the milliner in a similar manner.

I therefore glided into the room, and seated myself just opposite to her.

'Your business, Ma'am?' said she, looking surprised.

'To purchase that dress,' answered I.

"Tis already purchased,' said she.

'Do you remember the mad woman with the long hair?' said I, as I took off my bonnet, and let down my tresses, with all the grandeur of virtue victorious over vice.

She started and turned pale.

'You are the very person, I believe,' faltered she. 'What upon earth shall I do?'

'Do?' cried I. 'Why, sell me the Tuscan dress of course. The fact is—but let it go no farther—I am a heroine; I am, I give you my word and honour. So, you know, the lady being wronged of the dress, (inasmuch as she is but an individual), is as nothing compared with the wrong that the community will sustain, if they lose the pleasure of finding that I get it from you. Sure the whole scene, since I came to this house, was contrived for the express purpose of my procuring that individual costume; and just conceive what pretty confusion must take place, if, after all, you prevent me! My dear girl, we must do poetical justice. We must not disappoint the reader.

'You will tell me, perhaps, that selling the dress is improper? Granted. But, recollect, what improper things are constantly done, in novels, to bring about a pre-determined event. Your amour with the gentleman, for instance; which I shall certainly tell your employer, if you refuse to sell me the dress.

'As you value your own peace of mind, therefore, and in the name of all that is just, generous, and honourable, I conjure you to reflect for a moment, and you must see the matter in its rational light. What can you answer to these arguments?'

'That the person who could use them,' said she, 'will never listen to reason. I see what is the matter with you, and that I have no resource but to humour you, or be ruined.' And she began crying.

To conclude, after a little farther persuasion, I got the dress, gave her ten guineas, and, tripping down stairs, effected a safe escape out of the house.

I then called a coach, and drove to Jerry Sullivan's; for I would not return to my lodgings, lest the conspirators there should prevent me from going to the masquerade.

The poor fellow jumped with joy when he saw me; but I found him in great distress. His creditors had threatened his little shop with immediate ruin, unless he would discharge his debts. He had now provided the whole sum due, except forty pounds; but this he could not procure, and the creditors were expected every minute.

'I have only twelve guineas in the world,' said I, opening my casket, 'but they are at your service.' And I put them into his hand.

'Dear Lady!' cried the wife, 'what a mortal sight of jewels you have got! Do you know, now, I could borrow thirty pounds at least on them, at the pawnbroker's; and that sum would just answer.'

'Nay,' said I, 'I cannot consent to part with them; though, had I thirty pounds, I would sooner give it to you, than buy jewels with it.'

'Sure then,' cried she, 'by the same rule, you would sooner sell your jewels, than let me want thirty pounds.'

'Not at all,' answered I, 'for I am fond of my jewels, and I do not care about money. Besides, have I not already given you twelve guineas?'

'You have,' answered she, 'and that is what vexes me. If you had given me nothing at all, I would not have minded, because you were a stranger. But first to make yourself our friend, by giving us twelve guineas, and then to refuse us the remainder—'tis so unnatural!'

'Ungrateful woman!' cried I. 'Had I ten thousand pounds, you should not touch a farthing of it.'

The arrival of the creditors interrupted us, and a touching scene ensued. The wife and daughter flung themselves on their knees, and wrung their hands, and begged for mercy; but the wretches were inexorable.

How could I remain unmoved? In short, I slipped the casket into the wife's hand; out she ran with it, and in a few minutes returned with forty pounds. The creditors received the money due, passed receipts, and departed, and Jerry returned me the twelve guineas, saying: 'Bless your sweet face, for 'tis that is the finger-post to heaven, though, to be sure, I can't look strait in it, after all you have done for me. Och! 'tis a murder to be under an obligation: so if just a little bit of mischief would happen you, and I to relieve you, as you did me, why that would make me *aisy*.'

I am writing to you, from his house, while his daughter is finishing the sleeve of my Tuscan dress; and in a short time I shall be ready for the masquerade.

I confess I am not at all reconciled to the means I used in obtaining that dress. I took advantage of the milliner's indiscretion in one instance, to make her do wrong in another. But doubtless my biographer will find excuses for me, which I cannot discover myself. Besides, the code of moral law that heroines acknowledge is often quite opposite from those maxims which govern other conditions of life. And, indeed, if we view the various ranks and departments of society, we shall see, that what is considered vicious in some of them, is not esteemed so in others. Thus: it is deemed dishonest in a servant to cheat his master of his wines, but it is thought perfectly fair for his master to defraud the King of the revenue from those wines. In the same way, what is called wantonness in a little minx with a flat face, is called only susceptibility in a heroine with an oval one. We weep at the letters of Heloise; but were they written by an alderman's fat wife, we should laugh at them. The heroine may permit an amorous arm round her waist, fly in the face of her parents, and make assignations in dark groves, yet still be described as the most prudent of human creatures; but the mere Miss has no business to attempt any mode of conduct beyond modesty, decorum, and filial obedience. In a word, as different classes have distinct privileges, it appears to me, from what I have read of the law national, and the law romantic, that the heroine's prerogative is similar to the King's, and that she, like him, can do no wrong.

Adieu.

LETTER XXI

O Biddy, I have ascertained my genealogy. I am—but I must not anticipate. Take the particulars.

Having secured a comfortable bed at Jerry's, and eaten something (for I had fasted all day), I went with him in a coach to the Pantheon, where he promised to remain, and escort me back.

But I must first describe my Tuscan dress. It was a short petticoat of pale green, with a bodice of white silk; the sleeves loose, and tied up at the shoulders with ribbons and bunches of flowers. My hair, which fell in ringlets on my neck, was also ornamented with flowers and a straw hat. I wore no mask, heroines so seldom do.

Palpitating with expectation, I entered the assembly. Such a multitude of grotesque groups as presented themselves! Clowns, harlequins, nuns, devils; all talking and none listening. The clowns happy to be called fools, the harlequins as awkward as clowns, the nuns impudent, and the devils well-conducted. But as there is a description of a masquerade in almost every novel, you will excuse me from entering into farther particulars.

Too much agitated to support my character with spirit, I retired to a recess, and there anxiously awaited the arrival of the ancient vassal.

Hardly had I been seated five minutes, when an infirm and reverend old man approached, and sat down beside me. His feeble form was propt upon a long staff, a palsy shook his white locks, and his garments had all the quaintness of antiquity.

During some minutes, he gazed on me with earnestness, through a black mask; at length, heaving a heavy sigh, he thus broke forth in tremulous accents:

'Well-a-day! how the scalding tears do run adown my furrowed cheeks; for well I wis, thou beest herself—the Lady Cherubina De Willoughby, the long-lost daughter of mine honoured mistress!'

'Speak, I beseech you!' cried I. 'Are you, indeed, the ancient and loyal vassal?'

'Now by my truly, 'tis even so,' said he.

I could have hugged the dear old man to my heart.

'Welcome, thrice welcome, much respected menial!' cried I, grasping his hand. 'But keep me not in suspense. Unfold to me the heart-harrowing mysteries of my unhappy house!'

'Now by my fay,' said he, 'I will say forth my say. My name is Whylome Eftsoones, and I was accounted comely when a younker. But what boots that now? Beauty is like unto a flower of the field.—Good my lady, pardon a garrulous old man. So as I was saying, the damozels were once wont to leer at me right waggishly; but time changeth all things, as the proverb saith; and time hath changed my face, from that of a blithesome Ganymede to one of those heads which Guido has often painted; mild, pale, penetrating. Good my lady, I must tell thee a right pleasant and quaint saying of a certain nun, touching my face.'

'For pity's sake,' cried I, 'and as you value the preservation of my senses, continue your story without these digressions.'

'Certes, my lady,' said he. 'Well, I was first taken, as a bonny page, into the service of thy great great grandfader's fader's brother; and I was in at the death of these four generations, till at last, I became seneschal to thine honoured fader, Lord De Willoughby. His lordship married the Lady Hysterica Belamour, and thou wast the sole offspring of that ill-fated union.

'Soon after thy birth, thy noble father died of an apparition; or, as some will have it, of stewed lampreys. Returning, impierced with mickle dolour, from his funeral, which took place at midnight, I was stopped on a common, by a tall figure, with a mirksome cloak, and a flapped hat. I shook grievously, ne in that ghastly dreriment wist how myself to bear.'

'I do not comprehend your expressions,' interrupted I.

'I mean,' said he, 'I was in such a fright I did not know what to do. Anon, he threw aside his disguise, and I beheld—Lord Gwyn!'

'Lord Gwyn!' cried I.

'Yea,' said he. 'Lord Gwyn, who was ywedded unto Lord De Willoughby's sister, the Lady Eleanor.'

'Then Lady Eleanor Gwyn is my aunt!' cried I.

'Thou sayest truly,' replied he. '"My good Eftsoones," whispered Lord Gwyn to me, "know you not that my wife, Lady Eleanor Gwyn, will enjoy all the extensive estates of her brother, Lord De Willoughby, if that brother's infant, the little Cherubina, were no more?"

'"I trow, ween, and wote, 'tis as your lordship saith," answered I.

'His lordship then put into mine hand a stiletto.

'"Eftsoones," said he, with a hollow voice, "if this dagger be planted in a child's heart, it will grow, and bear a golden flower!"

'He spake, and incontinently took to striding away from me, in such wise, that maulgre and albe, I gan make effort after him, nathlesse and algates did child Gwyn forthwith flee from mine eyne.'

'I protest most solemnly,' said I, 'I do not understand five words in the whole of that last sentence!'

'And yet, my lady,' replied he, "tis the pure well of English undefiled, and such as was yspoken in mine youth.'

'But what can you mean by *child* Gwyn?' said I. 'Surely his lordship was no suckling at this time.'

'Child,' said Eftsoones, 'signified a noble youth, some centuries ago; and it is coming into fashion again. For instance, there is Childe Harold.'

'Then,' said I, 'there is "second childishness;" and I fancy there will be "mere oblivion" too. But if possible, finish your tale in the corrupt tongue.'

'I will endeavour,' said he. 'Tempted by this implied promise of a reward, I took an opportunity of conveying you away from your mother, and of secreting you at the house of a peasant, whom I bribed to bring you up as his own daughter. I told Lord Gwyn that I had dispatched you, and he gave me three and fourpence halfpenny for my trouble.

'When the dear lady, your mother, missed you, she went through the most elegant extravagancies; till, having plucked the last hair from her head, she ran wild into the woods, and has never been heard of since.'

'Dear sainted sufferer!' exclaimed I.

'A few days ago,' continued Eftsoones, 'a messenger out of breath came to tell me, that the peasant to whom I had consigned you was dying, and wished to see me. I went. Such a scene! He confessed to me that he had sold you, body and bones, as he inelegantly expressed it, to one farmer Wilkinson, about thirteen years before; for that this farmer, having discovered your illustrious birth, speculated on a handsome consideration from Lord Gwyn, for keeping the secret. Now I am told there is a certain parchment——'

'Which I have!' cried I.

'And a certain portrait of Nell Gwyn——'

'Which I have!'

'And a mole just above your left temple——'

'Which I have!' exclaimed I, in an ecstasy.

'Then your title is made out, as clear as the sun,' said he; 'and I bow, in contrition, before Lady Cherubina de Willoughby, rightful heiress of all the territory now appertaining, or that may hereafter appertain, to the House of De Willoughby.'

'Oh, dear, how delightful!' cried I. 'But my good friend, how am I to set about proving my title?'

'Nothing easier,' answered he. 'Lady Gwyn (for his lordship is dead) resides at this moment on your estate, which lies about thirty miles from Town; so to-morrow morning you shall set off to see her ladyship, and make your claims known to her. I will send a trusty servant with you, and will myself proceed before you, to prepare her for your arrival. You will therefore find me there.'

While we were in the act of arranging affairs more accurately, who should make his appearance, but Stuart in a domino!

The moment he addressed me, old Eftsoones slunk away; nor could I catch another glimpse of him during that night.

Stuart told me that he had come to the masquerade, on the chance of finding me there, as I seemed so determined on going, the last time he was with me. He likewise explained the mystery of the darkened chamber, and the false alarm of fire.

It appears, that as soon as he had discovered the views of Betterton, he hired a lodging at the opposite side of the street, and had two police officers there, for the purpose of watching Betterton's movements, and frustrating his attempts. He knocked several times in the course of yesterday, but was always answered that I had walked out. Knowing that I had not, he began to suspect foul play, and determined on gaining admittance to me. He therefore knocked once more, and then rushed into the house crying fire. This manœuvre had the desired effect, for an universal panic took place; and in the midst of it, he saw me issuing forth, and effect my escape. After having pursued me till he lost all traces of my route, he returned to my lodgings, and was informed by the poet, that Betterton had persuaded the landlady to fasten a carpet at the outside of my window, in order to make me remain in bed, till the time for the masquerade should arrive; and thus prevent me from having an interview with Stuart.

We then walked up and down the room, while I gave him an account of the ancient and loyal vassal, and of all that I had heard respecting my family. He was silent on the subject; and only begged of me to point out Eftsoones, as soon as I should see him; but that interesting old man never appeared. However, I was in great hopes of another adventure; for a domino now began hovering about us so much, that Stuart at last addressed it; but it glided away. He said he knew it was Betterton.

In about an hour, I became tired of the scene; for no one took notice of my dress. We therefore bade Jerry, who was in waiting, call a coach; and we proceeded in it to his house.

On our way, I mentioned my determination of setting off to Lady Gwyn's the very next morning, as Eftsoones had promised to meet me there. Stuart, for a wonder, applauded my resolution; and even offered to accompany me himself.

'For,' said he, 'I think I know this old Eftsoones; and if so, I fancy you will find me useful in unravelling part of the mystery. Besides, I would assist, with all my soul, in any plan tending to withdraw you from the metropolis.'

I snatched at his offer with joy; and it was then fixed that we should take a chaise the next morning, and go together.

On our arrival at the lodging, Stuart begged a bed of Jerry, that he might be ready for the journey in time; and the good-natured Irishman, finding him my friend, agreed to make up a pallet for him in the parlour.

Matters were soon arranged, and we have just separated for the night.

Well, Biddy, what say you now? Have I not made a glorious expedition of it? A young, rich, beautiful titled heiress already—think of that, Biddy.

As soon as I can decently turn Lady Gwyn out of doors, I mean to set up a most magnificent establishment. But I will treat the poor woman (who perhaps is innocent of her husband's crime) with extreme delicacy. She shall never want a bed or a plate. By the by, I must purchase silver plate. My livery shall be white and crimson. Biddy, depend upon my patronage. How the parson and music-master will boast of having known me. Then our village will swarm so, *to hear tell as how* Miss Cherry has grown a great lady. Old mother Muggins, at the bottom of the hill, will make a good week's gossip out of it. However, I mean to condescend excessively, for there is nothing I hate so much as pride.

Yet do not suppose that I am speculating upon an easy life. Though the chief obstacle to my marriage will soon be removed, by the confirmation of my noble birth, still I am not ignorant enough to imagine that no other impediments will interfere. Besides, to confess the fact, I do not feel my mind quite prepared to marry Montmorenci at so short a notice. Hitherto I have thought of him but as a lover, not as a husband—very different characters, in general.

Ah, no, my friend; be well assured, that adversity will not desert me quite so quickly. A present good is often the prognostic of an approaching evil; and when prosperity points its sunshine in our faces, misfortune, like our shadows, is sure to be behind.

Adieu.

LETTER XXII

After having breakfasted, and remunerated our entertainers, Stuart and I set out in a post-chaise, while Jerry ran at our side half way down the street, heaping me with blessings; and bidding me come to him if ever I should be ruined. After we had advanced a few miles into the country, Stuart began to look frequently through the back window, and appeared uneasy. At length he stopped the carriage, and desired the driver to turn round. As soon as the man had done so, another carriage, which, it seems, had followed us from London, passed us, and immediately turned after us.

"Tis as I thought!' cried Stuart, and stopping the chaise again, jumped out of it.

The chaise behind us also stopped; and a gentleman alighted from it and approached. But imagine my surprise, when I found that this gentleman was old Betterton! I could almost have embraced him, his villainous face looked so promising, and so pregnant with mischief.

'Sir,' said he to Stuart, 'as you have perceived me following your carriage, I find myself compelled, however unwillingly, to declare my motives for doing so. Last night I happened to be at the Pantheon, in a domino, and saw you there escorting this lady. I confess I had long before suspected your intentions towards her, and seeing you now together at a masquerade, and without a matron, I did not feel my suspicions lessened. I therefore had you both traced home, and I found, to my great horror, that you stopped at a wretched, and, as I am informed, infamous house in St. Giles's, where you remained during the night. I found too, that a chaise was at the door of it this morning: whence concluding, as I well might, that an elopement was in agitation, I determined, if possible, to prevent so dreadful a catastrophe, by hiring a carriage and pursuing you.

'Sir, you undertook to lecture me, when last I saw you; and plausibly enough you performed your part. It is now my duty to return the obligation. Mr. Stuart, Mr. Stuart, is it not a shame for you, Mr. Stuart? Is this the way to treat the daughter of your friend, Mr. Stuart? Go, silly boy, return to your home; and bless that heaven which hath sent me to the rescue of this fair unfortunate.'

'By all that is comical,' cried Stuart, laughing immoderately, 'this is too ludicrous even to be angry at! Miss Wilkinson, allow me to introduce you to Mr. Whylome Eftsoones, an ancient and loyal vassal of the De Willoughbys;—a mere modern in his principles, I am afraid; but addicted, I wis, to antiquated language.'

Betterton, I thought, looked rather blank, as he said, 'Really, Sir, I do not understand——'

'But really, Sir,' cried Stuart, 'I *do* understand. I understand, that if you would take less trouble in protecting this lady's honour, you would have a better chance of preserving your own.'

'Sir,' answered Betterton, 'I will have you to know, that I would sacrifice my life in defence of my honour.'

'Well, then,' said Stuart, 'though your life has but little of the saint, it will, at least, have something of the martyr.'

Betterton scowled at him askance, and grinned a thousand devils.

'Hear me, gentlemen,' cried I. 'If either of you again say any thing disrespectful or insulting to the other, I declare, on my honour, he shall leave me instantly. At present, I should be happy if both would do me the favour of escorting me to Lady Gwyn's, as I may meet with treatment there that will render the support of friends indispensible.'

It was now Stuart's turn to look downcast, and Betterton's to smile triumphant. The fact is, I wished to shew this admirable villain how grateful I felt for his meritorious conduct in not having deserted me.

'I will accept of your invitation with pleasure,' said he, 'for my seat lies within a few miles of her ladyship, and I wish to visit my tenantry.'

It was now noon. A few fleecy clouds floated in the blue depths of ether. The breeze brought coolness on its wings, and an inviting valley, watered by a rivulet, lay on the left; here whitened with sheep, and there dotted with little encampments of hay.

Exhilarated by the scene, after so long a confinement in the smoke and stir of London, I proposed to my companions the rural exercise of walking, as preferable to proceeding cooped up in a carriage. Each, whatever was his motive, caught at the proposal with delight, and we dismissed our chaises.

I now hastened to luxuriate in Arcadian beatitude. The pastoral habit of Tuscany was favourable; nothing remained but to rival an Ida, or a Glorvina, in simple touches of nature; and to trip along the lawns, like a Daphne or a Hamadryad.

In an instant, I sprang across a hedge, and fled towards the little valley, light as a wood-nymph flying from a satyr. I then took up a most picturesque position. It was beside of the streamlet, under a weeping willow, and on a grassy bank. Close behind me lay one of the most romantic cottages that I had ever seen, and at its back was a small garden, encompassed by green paling. The stream, bordered with wild-flowers, prattled prettily; save here and there, where a jutting stone shattered its crystal, and made its music hoarse. It purled and murmured a little too, but no where could it be said either to tinkle or gurgle, to chide or brawl.

Flinging off my bonnet, I shook my narcissine locks over my shoulders, and began braiding them in the manner of a simple shepherdess.

Stuart came up the first. I plucked a daisy that was half dipt into the brook; and instead of shaking off its moisture, I quaffed the liquid fragrance with my lip, and then held the flower to him.

'What am I to do with it?' said he.

'To pledge me,' replied I. 'To drink Nature's nectar, that trembles on the leaves which my lip has consecrated.'

He laughed and kissed the flower. That moment a lambkin began its pretty bleat.

'Now,' said I, 'make me a simple tripping little ditty on a lambkin.'

'You shall have it,' answered he, 'and such as an attorney's clerk would read to a milliner's apprentice.'

Dear sensibility, O la!

I heard a little lamb cry, ba;

Says I, so you have lost mamma?

Ah!

The little lamb, as I said so,

Frisking about the field did go,

And frisking, trod upon my toe.

Oh!

'Neat enough,' said I, 'only that it wants the word love in it.'

'True,' cried Stuart; 'for all modern poems of the kind abound in the word, though they seldom have much of the feeling.'

'And pray, my good friend,' asked I archly, as I bound up my golden ringlets—'What is love?'

'Nay,' said he, 'they say that talking of love is making it.'

Plucking a thistle that sprang from the bank, I blew away its down with my balmy breath, merely to hide my confusion.

Surely I am the most sensitive of all created beings!

Betterton had now reached us, out of breath after his race, and utterly unable to articulate.

'Betterton,' cried I, 'what is love?'

"Tis,' said he, gasping, "tis—'tis——'

'The gentleman,' cried Stuart, 'gives as good a description of it as most of our modern poets; who make its chief ingredients panting and broken murmurs.'

'Now in my opinion,' said I, 'love is a mystical sympathy, which unfolds itself in the glance that seeks the soul,—the sentiment that the soul embodies—the tender gaiety—the more delicious sadness—the stifled sigh—the soft and malicious smile—the thrill, the hope, the fear—each in itself a little bliss. In a word, it is the swoon of the soul, the delirium of the heart, the elegant inebriety of unsophisticated sentiment.'

'If such be love,' said Stuart, 'I fear I shall never bring myself to make it.'

'And pray,' said I, 'how would you make love?'

'There are many modes,' answered he, 'and the way to succeed with one girl is often the way to fail with another. Girls may be divided into the conversable and inconversable. He who can talk the best, has therefore the best chance of the former; but would a man make a conquest of one of the beautiful Inutilities, who sits in sweet stupidity, plays off the small simpers, and founds her prospects in life on the shape of her face, he has little more to do than call her a goddess and make himself a monkey. Or if that should fail, as he cannot apply to her understanding, he must have recourse to her feeling, and try what the touch can do for him. The touch has a thousand virtues. Only let him establish a lodgment on the first joint of her little finger, he may soon set out on his travels, and make the grand tour of her waist. This is, indeed, to have wit at his fingers' ends; and this, I can assure you, is the best and shortest way to gain the hearts of those demure misses, who think that all modesty consists in silence, that to be insipid is to be innocent, and that because they have not a word for a young man in public, they may have a kiss for him in private.'

'Come,' said I, 'let us talk of love in poetry, not prose. I want some pretty verses to fill up my memoirs; so, Betterton, now for an amorous ode to your mistress.'

Betterton bowed and began:

TO FANNY

Say, Fanny, why has bounteous heaven,

In every end benign and wise,

Perfection to your features given?

Enchantment to your witching eyes?

Was it that mortal man might view

Thy charms at distance, and adore?

Ah, no! the man who would not woo,

Were less than mortal, or were more.

The mossy rose that scents the sky,

By bee, by butterfly caress'd,

We leave not on the stalk to die,

But fondly snatch it to the breast

There, unsurpassed in sweets, it dwells;—

Unless the breast be Fanny's own:

There blooming, every bloom excels;—
Except of Fanny's blush alone.
O Fanny, life is on the wing,
And years, like rivers, glide away:
To-morrow may misfortune bring,
Then, gentle girl, enjoy to-day
And while a lingering kiss I sip,
Ah, start not from these ardent arms;
Nor think the printure of my lip
Will rob your own of any charms.
For see, we crush not, though we tread,
The cup and primrose. Fanny smiled.
Come then and press the cup, she said,
Come then and press the primrose wild.

'Now,' cried Stuart, 'I can give you a poem, with just as much love in it, and twice as much kissing.'
'That,' said I, 'would be a treasure indeed.'
He then began thus:

TO SALLY
Dawn with stains of ruddy light,
Streaks her grey and fragrant fingers,
While the Ethiop foot of night,
Envious of my Sally, lingers.
Upward poplars, downward willows,
Rustle round us; zephyrs sprinkle
Leaves of daffodillies, lilies,
Pennyroyal, periwinkle.
Rosy, balmy, honied, humid,
Biting, burning, murmuring kisses,
Sally, I will snatch from you, mid
Looks demure that tempt to blisses.
If your cheek grow cold, my dear,
I will kiss it, till it flushes,
Or if warm, my raptured tear,
Shall extinguish all its blushes.
Yes, that dimple is a valley,
Where sports many a little true love,
And that glance you dart, my Sally,
Might melt diamonds into dew love.
But while idle thus I chat,
I the war of lips am missing.
This, this, this, and that, that, that,
These make kissing, kissing, kissing.

The style of this poem reminded me of Montmorenci, and at the same moment I heard a rustling sound behind me. I started. ''Tis Montmorenci!' cried I.

Agitated in the extreme, I turned to see.—It was only a cock-sparrow.

'I deserve the disappointment,' said I to myself, 'for I have never once thought of that amiable youth since I last beheld him. 'Sweetest and noblest of men,' exclaimed I, aloud, 'say, dost thou mourn my mysterious absence? Perhaps the draught of air that I now inhale is the same which thou hast breathed forth, in a sigh for the far distant Cherubina!'

'That cannot well be,' interrupted Stuart, 'or at least the sigh of this unknown must have been packed up in a case, and hermetically sealed, to have come to you without being dispersed on the way.'

'There you happen to be mistaken,' answered I. 'For in the Hermit of the Rock, the heroine, while sitting on the coast of Sardinia, seemed to think it highly probable, that the billow at her feet might be the identical billow which had swallowed up her lover, about a year before, off the coast of Martinique.'

'That was not at all more improbable than Valancourt's theory,' said Stuart.

'What was it?' asked I.

'Why,' said he, 'that the sun sets, in different longitudes, at the same moment. For when his Emily was going to Italy, while he remained in France, he begged of her to watch the setting of the sun every evening, that both their eyes might be fixed upon the same object at once. Now, as the sun would set, where she was in Italy, much earlier than where he was in France, he certainly took the best of all possible methods to prevent their looking at it together.'

'But, Sir,' said Betterton, 'heroes and heroines are not bound to understand astronomy.'

'And yet,' answered Stuart, 'they are greater star-gazers than the ancient Egyptians. To form an attachment for the moon, and write a sonnet on it, is the principal test of being a heroine.'

As he spoke, a painted butterfly came fluttering about me. To pursue it was a classical amusement, for Caroline of Lichfield made a butterfly-hunt her pastime; so springing on my feet, I began the chace. The nimble insect eluded me for a long time, and at last got over the paling, into the little garden. I followed it through a small gate, and caught it; but alas! bruised it in the capture, and broke one of its wings. The poor thing sought refuge in a lily, where it lay struggling a few moments, and then its little spirit fled for ever.

What an opportunity for a sonnet! I determined to compose one under the willow. A beautiful rose-bush was blushing near the lily, and reminded me how pastoral I should look, could I recline on roses, during my poetical ecstasy. But would it be proper to pick them? Surely a few could do no harm. I glanced round—Nobody was in sight—I picked a few. But what signified a few for what I wanted? I picked a few more. The more I picked, the more I longed to pick—'Tis human nature; and was not Eve herself tempted in a garden? So from roses I went to lilies, from lilies to carnations, thence to jessamine, honey-suckle, eglantine, sweet-pea; till, in short, I had filled my bonnet, and almost emptied the beds. I then hurried to the willow with my prize; sentenced Stuart and Betterton to fifty yards banishment, and constructed a charming couch of flowers, which I damasked and inlaid with daisies, butter-flowers, and moss.

Enraptured with my paradisaical carpet, I flung myself upon it, and my recumbent form, as it pressed the perfumes, was indeed that of Mahomet's Houri. Exercise and agitation had heightened the glow of my cheeks, and the wind had blown my yellow hair about my face, like withered leaves round a ripened peach. I never looked so lovely.

In a short time I was able to repeat this sonnet aloud.

SONNET

Where the blue stream reflected flowerets pale,
A fluttering butterfly, with many a freak,
Dipped into dancing bells, and spread its sail
Of azure pinions, edged with jetty streak.
I snatched it passing; but a pinion frail,
Ingrained with mealy gold, I chanced to break.
The mangled insect, ill deserving bane,
Falls in the hollow of a lily new.
My tears drop after it, but drop in vain.
The cup, embalmed with azure airs and dew,
And flowery dust and grains of fragrant seed,
Can ne'er revive it from the fatal deed.
So guileless nymphs attract some traiterous eye,
So by the spoiler crushed, reject all joy and die.

Now that the pomp of composition was over, I began to think I had treated the owner of the garden extremely ill. I felt myself guilty of little less than theft, and was deliberating on what I ought to do, when an old, grey-headed peasant came running towards me from the garden.

64

'Miss!' cried he, 'have you seen any body pass this way with a parcel of flowers; for some confounded thief has just robbed me of all I had?'

I raised myself a little to reply, and he perceived the flowers underneath.

'Odd's life!' cried he, 'so you are the thief, are you? How dare you, hussey, commit such a robbery?'

'I am no hussey, and 'tis no robbery,' cried I: 'and trust me, you shall neither have apology nor compensation. Hussey, indeed! Sir, it was all your own fault for leaving that uncouth gate of your's open. I am afraid, Sir, that you are a shockingly ignorant old man.'

The peasant was just about to seize me, when Stuart ran up, and prevented him. They had then some private conversation together, and I saw Stuart give him a guinea. The talismanic touch of gold struck instant peace, and a compact of amity followed. Indeed, I have ever found, that even my face, though a heroine's, and with all its dimples, blushes, and glances, could never do half so much for me as the royal face on a bit of gold.

The peasant was now very civil, and invited us to rest in his cottage. Thither we repaired, and found his daughter, a beautiful young woman, just preparing the dinner. I felt instantly interested in her fate. I likewise felt hungry; so calling her aside, I told her that I would be happy to have a dinner, and, if possible, a bed, at the cottage; and that I would recompense her liberally for them, as I was a lady of rank, but at present in great affliction.

She said she would be very glad to accommodate me, if her father would permit her; and she then went to consult him. After a private conference between them and Stuart, she told me that her father was willing to let me remain. So we soon agreed upon the terms, and a village was at hand, where Stuart and Betterton might dine and sleep.

Before they left me, they made me give a solemn promise not to quit the cottage, till both of them should return, the next morning.

Stuart took an opportunity of asking me, whether he could speak to me in private, that evening.

'At ten o'clock to-night,' answered I, 'I will be sitting at the casement of my chamber. Trill a lamenting canzonet beneath it, as a signal, and I will admit you to a stolen interview.'

Betterton and he then departed, but not in company with each other.

Dinner is announced.

Adieu

LETTER XXIII

At dinner, a young farmer joined us; and I soon perceived that he and the peasant's daughter, Mary, were born for each other. They betrayed their mutual tenderness by a thousand little innocent stratagems, that passed, as they thought, unobserved.

After dinner, when Mary was about accompanying me to walk, the youth stole after us, and just as I had got into the garden, he drew her back, and I heard him kiss her. She came to me with her face a little flushed, and her ripe lips ruddier than before.

'Well, Mary,' said I, 'what was he doing to you?'

'Doing, Ma'am? Nothing, I am sure.'

'Nothing, Mary?'

'Why, Ma'am, he only wanted to be a little rude, and kiss me, I believe.'

'And you would not allow him, Mary?'

'Why should I tell a falsehood about it, Ma'am?' said she. 'To be sure I did not hinder him; for he is my sweetheart, and we are to be married next week.'

'And do you love him, Mary?'

'Better than my life, Ma'am. There never was such a good lad; he has not a fault in the wide world, and all the girls are dying of envy that I have got him.'

'Well, Mary,' said I, 'I foresee we shall spend a most delicious evening. We will take a rural repast down to the brook, and tell our loves. The contrast will be beautiful;—mine, the refined, sentimental, pathetic story; your's the pretty, simple, little, artless tale. Come, my friend; let us return, and prepare the rustic banquet. No souchong, or bohea; (blessed names these!) no hot or cold cakes—Oh! no, but creams, berries, and fruits; goat's milk, figs, and honey—Arcadian, pastoral, primeval dainties!'

We then went back to the cottage, but could get nothing better than currants, gooseberries, and a maple bowl of cream. Mary, indeed, cut a large slice of bread and butter for her private amusement; and with these we returned to the streamlet. I then threw myself on my flowery couch, and my companion sat beside me.

We helped ourselves. I took rivulet to my cream, and scooped the brook with my rosy palm. Innocent nymph! ah, why couldst thou not sit down in the lap of content here, and dance, and sing, and say thy prayers, and go to heaven with this nut-brown maid?

I picked up a languishing rose, and sighed as I inhaled its perfume, and gazed on its decay.

'Such, Mary,' said I, 'such will be the fate of you and me. How soft, how serene this evening. It is a landscape for a Claud. But how much more charming is an Italian or a French than an English landscape. O! to saunter over hillocks, covered with lavender, wild thyme, juniper and tamarise, while shrubs fringe the summits of the rocks, or patches of meagre vegetation tint their recesses! Plantations of almonds, cypresses, palms, olives, and dates stretch along; nor are the larch and ilex, the masses of granite, and dark forests of fir wanting; while the majestic Garonne wanders, descending from the Pyrenees, and winding its blue waves towards the Bay of Biscay.

'Is not all this exquisite, Mary?'

'It must, Ma'am, since you say so,' replied she.

'Then,' continued I, 'though your own cottage is tolerable, yet is it, as in Italy, covered with vine leaves, fig-trees, jessamine, and clusters of grapes? Is it tufted with myrtle, or shaded with a grove of lemon, orange, and bergamot?'

'But Ma'am,' said Mary, ''tis shaded by some fine old elms.'

'True,' cried I, with the smile of approaching triumph. 'But do the flowers of the spreading agnus castus mingle with the pomegranate of Shemlek? Does the Asiatic andrachne rear its red trunk? Are the rose-coloured nerit, and verdant alia marina imbost upon the rocks? And do the golden clusters of Eastern spartium gleam amidst the fragrant foliage of the cedrat, the most elegant shrub of the Levant? Do they, Mary?'

'I believe not, Ma'am,' answered she. 'But then our fields are all over daisies, butterflowers, clover-blossoms, and daffodowndillies.'

'Daffodowndillies!' cried I. 'Ah, Mary, Mary, you may be a very good girl, but you do not shine in description. Now I leave it to your own taste, which sounds better,—Asiatic andrachne, or daffodowndillies? If you knew any thing of novels, you would describe for the ear, not for the eye. Oh, my young friend, never, while you live, say daffodowndillies.'

'Never, if I can help it, Ma'am,' said Mary. 'And I hope you are not offended with me, or think the worse of me, on account of my having said it now; for I could safely make oath that I never heard, till this instant, of its being a naughty word.'

'I am satisfied,' said I. 'So now let us tell our loves, and you shall begin.'

'Indeed, Ma'am,' said she, 'I have nothing to tell.'

'Impossible,' cried I. 'Did William never save your life?'

'Never, Ma'am.'

'Well then, he had a quarrel with you?'

'Never, in all his born days, Ma'am.'

'Shocking! Why how long have you known him?'

'About six months, Ma'am. He took a small farm near us; and he liked me from the first, and I liked him, and both families wished for the match; and when he asked me to marry him, I said I would; and so we shall be married next week; and that is the whole history, Ma'am.'

'A melancholy history, indeed!' said I. 'What a pity that an interesting pair, like you, who, without flattery, seem born for one of Marmontel's tales, should be so cruelly sacrificed.'

I then began to consider whether any thing could yet be done in their behalf, or whether the matter was indeed past redemption. I reflected that it would be but an act of common charity,—hardly deserving praise—to snatch them awhile from the dogged and headlong way they were setting about matrimony, and introduce them to a few of the sensibilities. Surely with very little ingenuity, I might get up an incident or two between them;—a week or a fortnight's torture, perhaps;—and afterwards enjoy the luxury of reuniting them.

Full of this laudable intention, I sat meditating awhile; and at length hit upon an admirable plan. It was no less than to make Mary (without her own knowledge) write a letter to William, dismissing him for ever! This appears impossible, but attend.

'My story,' said I, to the unsuspecting girl, 'is long and lamentable, and I fear, I have not spirits to relate it. I shall merely tell you, that I yesterday eloped with the younger of the gentlemen who were here this morning, and married him. I was induced to take this step, in consequence of my parents having insisted that I should marry my first cousin; who, by the by, is a namesake of your William's. Now, Mary, I have a favour to beg of you. My cousin William must be made acquainted with my marriage; though I mean to keep it a secret from my family, and as I do not wish to tell him such unhappy tidings in my own hand-writing—and in high life, my fair rustic, young ladies must not write to young gentlemen, your taking the trouble to write out the letter for me, would bind me to you for ever.'

'That I will, and welcome,' said the simple girl; 'only Ma'am, I fear I shall disgrace a lady like you, with my bad writing. I am, out and out, the worst scribbler in our family; and William says to me but yesterday, ah, Mary, says he, if your tongue talked as your pen writes, you might die an old maid for me. Ah, William, says I, I would bite off my tongue sooner than die an old maid. So, to be sure, Willy laughed very hearty.'

We then returned home, and retired to my chamber, where I dictated, and Mary wrote as follows:

'Dear William,

'Prepare your mind for receiving a great and unexpected shock. To keep you no longer in suspense, learn that I am married.

'Before I had become acquainted with you, I was attached to another man, whose name I must beg leave to conceal. About a year since, circumstances compelled him to go abroad, and before his departure, he procured a written promise from me, to marry him on the first day of his return. You then came, and succeeded in rivalling him.

'As he never once wrote, after he had left the country, I concluded that he was dead. Yesterday, however, a letter from him was put into my hand, which announced his return, and appointed a private interview. I went. He had a clergyman in waiting to join our hands. I prayed, entreated, wept—all in vain.

'I became his wife.

'O William, pity, but do not blame me. If you are a man of honour and of feeling, never shew this letter, or tell its contents to one living soul. Do not even speak to myself on the subject of it.

'You see I pay your own feelings the compliment of not signing the name that I now bear.

'Adieu, dear William: adieu for ever.'

We then returned to the sitting-room, and found William there. While we were conversing, I took an opportunity to slip the letter, unperceived, into his hand, and to bid him read it in some other place. He retired with it, and we continued talking. But in about half an hour he hurried into the room, with an agitated countenance; stopped opposite to Mary, and looked at her earnestly.

'William!' cried she, 'William! For shame then, don't frighten one so.'

'No, Mary,' said he, 'I scorn to frighten you, or injure you either. I believe I am above that. But no wonder my last look at you should be frightful. There is your true-lover's knot—there is your hair—there are your letters. So now, Mary, good-bye, and may you be for ever happy, is what I pray Providence, from the bottom of my broken heart!'

With these words, and a piteous glance of anguish, he rushed from the room.

Mary remained motionless a moment; then half rose, sat down, rose again; and grew pale and red by turns.

"Tis so—so laughable,' said she at length, while her quivering lip refused the attempted smile. 'All my presents returned too. Sure—my heavens!—Sure he cannot want to break off with me? Well, I have as good a spirit as he, I believe. The base man; the cruel, cruel man!' and she burst into a passion of tears.

I tried to sooth her, but the more I said, the more she wept. She was sure, she said, she was quite sure that he wanted to leave her; and then she sobbed so piteously, that I was on the point of undeceiving her; when, fortunately, we heard her father returning, and she ran into her own room. He asked about her; I told him that she was not well;—the old excuse of a fretting heroine; so the good man went to her, and with some difficulty gained admittance. They have remained together ever since.

How delicious will be the happy denouement of this pathetic episode, this dear novellette; and how sweetly will it read in my memoirs!

Adieu.

The night was so dark when I repaired to the casement, that I have been trying to compose a description of it for you, in the style of the best romances. But after having summoned to my mind all the black articles of value that I can recollect—ebony, sables, palls, pitch, and even coal, I find I have nothing better to say, than, simply, that it was a dark night.

Having opened the casement, I sat down at it, and repeated these lines aloud.

SONNET

Now while within their wings each feather'd pair,
Hide their hush'd heads, thy visit, moon, renew,
Shake thy pale tresses down, irradiate air,
Earth, and the spicy flowers that scent the dew.
The lonely nightingale shall pipe to thee,
And I will moralize her minstrelsy.
Ten thousand birds the sun resplendent sing,
One only warbles to the milder moon.
Thus for the great, how many wake the string,
Thus for the good, how few the lyre attune.

As soon as I had finished the sonnet, a low and tremulous voice, close to the casement, sung these words:

SONG

Haste, my love, and come away;
What is folly, what is sorrow?
'Tis to turn from, joys to-day,
Tis to wait for cares to-morrow.
O'er the river,
Aspens shiver
Thus I tremble at delay.
Light discovers,
Vowing lovers:
See the stars with sharpened ray,
Gathering thicker,
Glancing quicker;
Haste, my love, and come away.

I sat enraptured, and heaved a sigh.

'Enchanting sigh!' cried the singer, as he sprang through the window; but it was not the voice of Stuart.

I screamed loudly.

'Hush!' cried the mysterious unknown, and advanced towards me; when, to my great relief, the door was thrown open, and the old peasant entered, with Mary behind him, holding a candle.

In the middle of the room, stood a man, clad in a black cloak, with black feathers in his hat, and a black mask on his face.

The peasant, pale as death, ran forward, knocked him to the ground, and seized a pistol and carving-knife, that were stuck in a belt about his waist.

'Unmask him!' cried I.

The peasant, kneeling on his body, tore off the mask, and I beheld—Betterton!

'Alarm the neighbours, Mary!' cried the peasant.

Mary put down the candle, and went out.

'I must appear in an unfavourable light to you, my good man,' said this terrifying character; 'but the young lady will inform you that I came hither at her own request.'

'For shame!' cried I. 'What a falsehood!'

'Falsehood!' said he. 'I have your own letter, desiring me to come.'

'The man is mad,' cried I. 'I never wrote him a letter.'

'I can produce it to your face,' said he, pulling a paper from his pocket, and to my great amazement reading these lines.

'Cherubina begs that Betterton will repair to her window, at ten o'clock to-night, disguised like an Italian assassin, with dagger, cloak, and pistol. The signal is to be his singing an air under the casement, which she will then open, and he may enter her chamber.'

'I will take the most solemn oath,' cried I, 'that I never wrote a line of it. But this unhappy wretch, who is a ruffian of the first pretensions, has a base design upon me, and has followed me from London, for the purpose of effecting it; so I suppose, he wrote the letter himself, as an excuse, in case of discovery.'

'Then he shall march to the magistrate's,' said the peasant, 'and I will indict him for house-breaking!'

A man half so frantic as Betterton I never beheld. He foamed, he grinned, he grinded the remnants of his teeth; and swore that Stuart was at the bottom of the whole plot.

By this time, Mary having returned with two men, we set forward in a body to the magistrate's, and delivered our depositions before him. I swore that I did not write the letter, and that, to the best of my belief, Betterton harboured bad designs against me.

The peasant swore that he had found the culprit, armed with a knife and pistol, in his house.

The magistrate, therefore, notwithstanding all that Betterton could say, committed him to prison without hesitation.

As they were leading him away, he cast a furious look at the magistrate, and said:

'Ay, Sir, I suppose you are one of those pensioned justices, who minister our vague and sanguinary laws, and do dark deeds for our usurping oligarchy, that has assumed a power of making our most innocent actions misdemeanours, of determining points of law without appeal, of imprisoning our persons without trial, and of breaking open our houses with the standing army. But nothing will go right till we have a reform in Parliament—neither peace nor war, commerce nor agriculture——'

'Clocks nor watches, I suppose,' said the magistrate.

'Ay, clocks nor watches,' cried Betterton, in a rage. 'For how can our mechanics make any thing good, while a packed parliament deprives them of money and a mart?'

'So then,' said the magistrate, 'if St. Dunstan's clock is out of order, 'tis owing to the want of a reform in Parliament.'

'I have not the most distant doubt of it,' cried Betterton.

''Tis fair then,' said the magistrate, 'that the reformists should take such a latitude as they do; for, probably, by their encouragement of time-pieces, they will at last discover the longitude.'

'No sneering, Sir,' cried Betterton. 'Now do your duty, as you call it, and abide the consequence.'

This gallant grey Lothario was then led off; and our party returned home.

Adieu.

LETTER XXV

I rose early this morning, and repaired to my favourite willow, to contemplate the placid landscape. Flinging myself on the grass, close to the brook, I began to warble a rustic madrigal. I then let down my length of tresses, and, stooping over the streamlet, laved them in the little urn of the dimpling Naiad.

This, you know, was agreeable enough, but the accident that befel me was not. For, leaning too much over, I lost my balance, and rolled headlong into the middle of the rivulet. As it was shallow, I did not fear being drowned, but as I was a heroine, I hoped to be rescued. Therefore, instead of rising, as I might easily have done, there I lay, shrieking and listening, and now and then lifting up my head, in hopes to see Stuart come flying towards me on the wings of the wind. Oh no! my gentleman thought proper to make himself scarce; so dripping, shivering, and indignant, I scrambled out, and bent my steps towards the cottage.

On turning the corner of the hedge, who should I perceive at the door, but the hopeful youth himself, quite at his ease, and blowing a penny trumpet for a chubby boy.

'What has happened to you?' said he, seeing me so wet.

'Only that I fell into the brook,' answered I, 'and was under the disagreeable necessity of saving my own life, when I expected that you would have condescended to take the trouble off my hands.'

'Expected!' cried he. 'Surely you had no reason for supposing that I was so near to you, as even to have witnessed the disaster.'

'And it is, therefore,' retorted I, 'that you ought to have been so near me as to have witnessed it.'

'You deal in riddles,' said he.

'Not at all,' answered I. 'For the farther off a distrest heroine believes a hero, the nearer he is sure to be. Only let her have good grounds for supposing him at her Antipodes, and nine times out of ten she finds him at her elbow.'

'Well,' said he, laughing, 'though I did not save your life, I will not endanger it, by detaining you in your wet dress. Pray hasten to change it.'

I took his advice, and borrowed some clothes from Mary, while mine were put to the fire. After breakfast, I once more equipped myself in my Tuscan costume, and a carriage being ready for us, I took an affectionate leave of that interesting rustic. Poor girl! Her attempts at cheerfulness all the morning were truly tragical; and, absorbed in another sorrow, she felt but little for my departure.

On our way, Stuart confessed that he was the person who wrote the letter to Betterton in my name; and that he did so for the purpose of entrapping him in such a manner as to prevent him from accompanying me farther. He was at the window during the whole scene; as he meant to have seized Betterton himself, had not the peasant done so.

'You will excuse my thus interfering in your concerns,' added he; 'but gratitude demands of me to protect the daughter of my guardian; and friendship for her improves the duty to a pleasure.'

'Ah!' said I, 'however it has happened, I fear you dislike me strangely.'

'Believe me, you mistake,' answered he. 'With a few foibles (which are themselves as fascinating as foibles can be), you possess many virtues; and, let me add, a thousand attractions. I who tell you blunt truths, may well afford you flattery.'

'Flattery,' said I, pleased by his praises, and willing to please him in return by serious conversation, 'deserves censure only when the motive for using it is mean or vicious.'

'Your remark is a just one,' observed he. 'Flattery is often but the hyperbole of friendship; and even though a compliment itself may not be sincere, our motive for paying it may be good. Flattery, so far from injuring, may sometimes benefit the object of it; for it is possible to create a virtue in others, by persuading them that they possess it.'

'Besides,' said I, 'may we not pay a compliment, without intending that it should be believed; but merely to make ourselves agreeable by an effort of the wit? And since such an effort shews that we consider the person flattered worthy of it, the compliment proves a kind intention at least, and thus tends to cement affection and friendship.'

In this manner Stuart insensibly led me to talk on grave topics; and we continued a delightful conversation the remainder of the day. Sometimes he seemed greatly gratified at my sprightly sallies, or serious remarks; but never could I throw him off his guard, by the dangerous softness of my manner. He now calls me the lovely visionary.

Would you believe that this laughing, careless, unpathetic creature, is a poet, and a poet of feeling, as the following lines will prove. But whether he wrote them on a real or an imaginary being, I cannot, by any art, extract from him.

THE FAREWELL

Go, gentle muse, 'tis near the gloomy day,
Long dreaded; go, and say farewell for me;
A sad farewell to her who deigned thee, say,
For far she hastens hence. Ah, hard decree!

Tell her I feel that at the parting hour,
More than the waves will heave in tumult wild:
More than the skies will threat a gushing shower,
More than the breeze will breathe a murmur mild.

Say that her influence flies not with her form,
That distant she will still engage my mind:
That suns are most remote when most they warm,
That flying Parthians scatter darts behind.

Long will I gaze upon her vacant home,
As the bird lingers near its pilfered nest,
There, will I cry, she turned the studious tome;
There sported, there her envied pet caressed.
There, while she plied accomplished works of art,
I saw her form, inclined with Sapphic grace;
Her radiant eyes, blest emblems of her heart,
And all the living treasures of her face.
The Parian forehead parting clustered hair,
The cheek of peachy tinct, the meaning brow;
The witching archness, and the grace so rare,
So magical, it charmed I knew not how.
Light was her footstep as the silent flakes
Of falling snow; her smile was blithe as morn;
Her dimple, like the print the berry makes,
In some smooth lake, when dropping from the thorn.
To snatch her passing accents as she spoke,
To see her slender hand, (that future prize)
Fling back a ringlet, oft I dared provoke,
The gentle vengeance of averted eyes.
Yet ah, what wonder, if, when shrinking awe
Withheld me from her sight, I broke my chain?
Or when I made a single glance my law,
What wonder if that law were made in vain?
And say, can nought but converse love inspire?
What tho' for me her lips have never moved?
The vale that speaks but with its feathered choir,
When long beheld, eternally is loved.
Go then, my muse, 'tis near the gloomy day
Of parting; go, and say farewell for me;
A sad farewell to her who deigned thee, say,
Whate'er engage her, wheresoe'er she be.
If slumbering, tell her in my dreams she sways,
If speaking, tell her in my words she glows;
If thoughtful, tell her in my thoughts she strays,
If tuneful, tell her in my song she flows.
Tell her that soon my dreams unblest will prove;
That soon my words on absent charms will dwell;
That soon my thoughts remembered hours will love;
That soon my song of vain regrets will tell.
Then, in romantic moments, I will frame,
Some scene ideal, where we meet at last;
Where, by my peril, snatched from wreck or flame,
She smiles reward and talks of all the past.
Now for the lark she flies my wistful lay.
Ah, could the bard some winged warbler be,
Following her form, no longer would he say,
Go, gentle muse, and bid farewell for me.

I write from an inn within a mile of Lady Gwyn's. Another hour and my fate is decided.

Adieu.

LETTER XXVI

At length, with a throbbing heart, I now, for the first time, beheld the mansion of my revered ancestors—the present abode of Lady Gwyn. That unfortunate usurper of my rights was not denied to me; so I alighted; and though Stuart wished much to be present at the interview, I would not permit him; but was ushered by the footman into the sitting-room.

I entered with erect, yet gentle majesty; while my Tuscan habit, which was soiled and shrivelled by the brook, gave me an air of complicated distress.

I found her ladyship at a table, classifying fossils. She was tall and thin, and bore the remains of beauty; but I could not discover the family face.

She looked at me with some surprise; smiled, and begged to know my business.

'It is a business,' said I, 'of the most vital importance to your ladyship's honour and repose; and I lament that an imperious necessity compels me to the invidious task of acquainting you with it. Could anything add to the painful nature of my feelings, it would be to find that I had wounded yours.'

'Your preamble alarms me,' said she. 'Do, pray be explicit.'

'I must begin,' said I, 'with declaring my perfect conviction of your ignorance, that any person is existing, who has a right to the property which your ladyship at present possesses.'

'Assuredly such a notion never entered my head,' said she, 'and indeed, were such a claim made, I should consider it as utterly untenable—in fact, impossible.'

'I regret,' said I, 'that it is undeniable. There are documents extant, and witnesses living, to prove it beyond all refutation.'

Her ladyship, I thought, changed colour, as she said:

'This is strange; but I cannot believe it. Who would have the face to set up such a silly claim?'

'I am so unfortunate as to have that face,' answered I, in a tone of the most touching humility.

'You!' she cried with amazement. 'You!'

'Pardon me the pain I give you,' said I, 'but such is the fact; and grating as this interview must be to the feelings of both parties, I do assure you, that I have sought it, solely to prevent the more disagreeable process of a law-suit.'

'You are welcome to twenty law-suits, if you wish them,' cried she, 'but I fancy they will not deprive me of my property.'

'At least,' said I, 'they may be the means of sullying the character of your deceased lord.'

'I defy the whole world,' cried she, 'to affix the slightest imputation on his character.'

'Surely,' said I, 'you cannot pretend ignorance of the fact, that his lordship had the character of being—I trust, more from misfortune, than from inherent depravity; for your ladyship well knows that man, frail man, in a moment of temptation, perpetrates atrocities, which his better heart afterwards disowns.'

'But his character!' cried she. 'What of his character?'

'Ah!' said I, 'your ladyship will not compel me to mention.'

'You have advanced too far to retreat,' cried she. 'I demand an unequivocal explanation. What of his character?'

'Well, since I must speak plain,' replied I, 'it was that of an—assassin!'

'Merciful powers!' said she, in a faint voice, and reddening violently. 'What does the horrid woman mean?'

'I have at this moment,' cried I, 'a person ready to make oath, that your unhappy husband bribed a servant of my father's to murder me, while yet an infant, in cold blood.'

''Tis a falsehood!' cried she. 'I would stake my life on its being a vile, malicious, diabolical falsehood.'

'Would it were!' said I, 'but oh! Lady Gwyn, the circumstances, the dreadful circumstances—these cannot be contradicted. It was midnight;—the bones of my noble father had just been deposited in the grave;—when a tall figure, wrapt in a dark cloak, and armed with a dagger, stood before the seneschal. *It was the late Lord Gwyn!*'

'Who are you?' cried she, starting up quite pale and horror-struck. 'In the name of all that is dreadful, who can you be?'

'Your own niece!' said I, meekly kneeling to receive her blessing—'Lady Cherubina De Willoughby, the daughter of your ladyship's deceased brother, Lord De Willoughby, and of his much injured wife, the Lady Hysterica Belamour!'

'Never heard of such persons in all my life!' cried she, ringing the bell furiously.

'Pray,' said I, 'be calm. Act with dignity in this affair. Do not disgrace our family. On my honour, I mean to treat you with kindness. Nay, we must positively be on terms of friendship—I make it a point. After all, what is rank? what are riches? How vapid their charms, compared with the heartfelt joys of truth and virtue! O, Lady Gwyn, O, my respected aunt; I conjure you by our common ties of blood, by your brother, who was my father, spurn the perilous toy, fortune, and retire in time, and without exposing your lost lord, into the peaceful bosom of obscurity!'

'Conduct this wretch out of the house,' said her ladyship to the servant who had entered. 'She wants to extort money from me, I believe.'

'A moment more,' cried I. 'Where is old Eftsoones? Where is that worthy character?'

'I know no such person,' said she. 'Begone, impostor!'

At the word impostor, I smiled; drew aside my ringlets with one hand, and pointed to my inestimable mole with the other.

'Am I an impostor now?' cried I. 'But learn, unfortunate woman, that I have a certain parchment too.'——

'And a great deal of insolence too,' said she.

'The resemblance of it, at least,' cried I, 'for I have your ladyship's portrait.'

'My portrait!' said she with a sneer.

'As sure as your name is Nell Gwyn,' cried I; 'for Nell Gwyn is written under it; and let me add, that you would have consulted both your own taste, and the dignity of our house better, had you got it written Eleanor instead of Nell.'

'You little impertinent reprobate!' exclaimed she, feeling the peculiar poignancy of the sarcasm. 'Begone this moment, or I will have you drummed through the village!'

I waved my hand in token of high disdain, and vanished.

'Well,' said Stuart, as I got to the carriage, 'has her ladyship acknowledged your claims?'

'No, truly,' cried I, 'but she has turned me out of my own house—think of that!'

'Then,' said he, springing from the chaise, 'I will try whether I cannot succeed better with her ladyship;' and he went into the house.

I remained in a state of the greatest perturbation till he came back.

'Good news!' cried he. 'Her ladyship wishes to see you, and apologize for her rudeness; and I fancy,' added he, with a significant nod, 'all will go well in a certain affair.'

'Yes, yes,' said I, nodding in return, 'I flatter myself she now finds civility the best of her game.'

I then alighted, and her ladyship ran forward to meet me. She pressed my hand, *my-deared* me twice in a breath, told me that Stuart had given her my little history—that it was delicious—elegant—exotic; and concluded with declaring, that I must remain at her house a few days, to talk over the great object of my visit.

Much as I mistrusted this sudden alteration in her conduct, I consented to spend a short time with her, on the principle, that heroines always contrive to get under the same roof with their bitterest enemies.

Stuart appeared quite delighted at my determination, and after another private interview with her ladyship, set off for London, to make further inquiries about Wilkinson. I am, however, resolved not to release that mischievous farmer, till I have secured my title and estate. You see I am grown quite sharp.

Her ladyship and I had then a long conversation, and she fairly confessed the probability that my claims are just, but denied all knowledge of old Eftsoones. I now begin to think rather better of her. She has the sweetest temper in the world, loves literature and perroquets, scrapes mezzotintos, and spends half her income in buying any thing that is hardly to be had. She led me through her cabinet, which contains the most curious assortment in nature—vases of onyx and sardonyx, cameos and intaglios; subjects in sea-horse teeth, by Fiamingo and Benvenuto Cellini; and antique gems in jadestone, mochoa, coral, amber, and Turkish agate.

She has already presented me with several dresses, and she calls me her lovely *protégée*, and the Lady Cherubina,—a sound that makes my very heart leap within me. Nay, she did me the honour of assuring me, that her curiosity to know a real heroine was one motive for her having asked me on this visit; and that she positively considers an hour with me worth all her curiosities put together. What a delicate compliment! So could I do less, in return, than repeat my assurances, that when I succeed in dispossessing her of the property, she shall never want an asylum in my house.

Adieu.

Think of its having never once struck me, till I had retired for the night, that I might be murdered! How so manifest a danger escaped my recollection, is inconceivable; but so it was, I never thought of it. Lady Gwyn might be (for any thing I could tell to the contrary) just as capable of plotting an assassination as the Marchesa di Vivaldi; and surely her motives were far more urgent.

I therefore searched in my chamber, for some trap-door, or sliding pannel, by which assassins might enter it; but I could find none. I then resolved on exploring the galleries, corridors, and suites of apartments, in this immense mansion; in hopes to discover some place of retreat, or at least some mystery relative to my birth.

Accordingly, at the celebrated hour of midnight, I took up the taper, and unbolting my door, stole softly along the lobby.

I stopped before one of our family pictures. It was of a lady, pale, pensive, and interesting; and whose eyes, which appeared to look at me, were sky-blue, like my own. That was sufficient.

'Gentle image of my departed mother!' ejaculated I, kneeling before it, 'may thy sacred ashes repose in peace!'

I then faintly chaunted a fragment of a hymn, and advanced. No sigh met my listening ear, no moan amidst the pauses of the gust.

With a trembling hand I opened a door, and found myself in a spacious chamber. It was magnificently furnished, and a piano stood in one corner of it. Intending to run my fingers over the keys, I walked forward; till a low rustling in that direction made me pause. But how shall I paint to you my horror, my dismay, when I heard the mysterious instrument on a sudden begin to sound; not loudly, but (more terrible still!) with a hurried murmur; as if all its chords were agitated at once, by the hand of some invisible demon.

I did not faint, I did not shriek; but I stood transfixed to the spot. The music ceased. I recovered courage and advanced. The music began again; and again I paused.

What! should I not lift the simple lid of a mere piano, after Emily's having drawn aside the mysterious veil, and discovered the terrific wax doll underneath it?

Emulation, enthusiasm, curiosity prompted me, and I rushed undaunted to the piano. Louder and more rapid grew the notes—my desperate hand raised the cover, and beneath it, I beheld a sight to me the most hideous and fearful upon earth,—a mouse!

I screamed and dropped the candle, which was instantly extinguished. The mouse ran by me; I flew towards the door, but missed it, and fell against a table; nor was it till after I had made much clamour, that I got out of the room. As I groped my way through the corridor, I heard voices and people in confusion above stairs; and presently lights appeared. The whole house was in a tumult.

'They are coming to murder me at last!' cried I, as I regained my chamber, and began heaping chairs and tables against the door. Presently several persons arrived at it, and called my name. I said not a word. They called louder, but still I was silent; till at length they burst open the door, and Lady Gwyn, with some of her domestics, entered. They found me kneeling in an attitude of supplication.

'Spare, oh, spare me!' cried I.

'My dear,' said her ladyship, 'no harm shall happen you.'

'Alas, then,' exclaimed I, 'what portends this nocturnal visit? this assault on my chamber? all these dreadful faces? Was it not enough, unhappy woman, that thy husband attempted my life, but must thou, too, thirst for my blood?'

Lady Gwyn whispered a servant, who left the room; the rest raised, and put me to bed; while I read her ladyship such a lecture on murder, as absolutely astonished her.

The servant soon after returned with a cup.

'Here, my love,' said her ladyship, 'is a composing draught for you. Drink it, and you will be quite well to-morrow.'

I took it with gladness, for I felt my brain strangely bewildered by the terror that I had just undergone. Indeed I have sometimes experienced the same sensation before, and it is extremely disagreeable.

They then left a candle in my room, and departed.

My mind still remains uneasy; but I have barricaded the door, and am determined on not undressing. I believe, however, I must now throw myself on the bed; for the draught has made me sleepy.

Adieu.

LETTER XXVIII

O Biddy Grimes, I am poisoned! That fatal draught last night—why did I drink it?—I am in dreadful agony. When this reaches you, all will be over.—But I would not die without letting you know.

Farewell for ever, my poor Biddy!

I bequeath you all my ornaments.

LETTER XXIX

Yes, my friend, you may well stare at receiving another letter from me; and at hearing that I have not been poisoned in the least!

I must unfold the mystery. When I woke this morning, after my nocturnal perambulation, I found my limbs so stiff, and such pains in all my bones, that I was almost unable to move. Judge of my horror and despair; for it instantly flashed across my mind, that Lady Gwyn had poisoned me! My whole frame underwent a sudden revulsion; I grew sick, and rang the bell with violence; nor ceased an instant, till half the servants, and Lady Gwyn herself, had burst into my chamber.

'If you have a remnant of mercy left,' cried I, 'send for a doctor!'

'What is the matter, my dear,' said her ladyship.

'Only that you have poisoned me, my dear,' cried I. 'Dear, indeed! I presume your ladyship imagines, that the liberty you have taken with my life, authorizes all other freedoms. Oh, what will become of me!'

'Do, tell me,' said she, 'how are you unwell?'

'I am sick to death,' cried I. 'I have pains in all my limbs, and I shall be a corpse in half an hour. Oh, indeed, you have done the business completely. Lady Eleanor Gwyn, I do here, on my death-bed, and with all my senses about me, accuse you, before your domestics, of having administered a deadly potion to me last night.'

'Go for the physician,' said her ladyship to a servant.

'Well may you feel alarmed,' cried I. 'Your life will pay the forfeit of mine.'

'But you need not feel alarmed,' said her ladyship, 'for really, what I gave you last night, was merely to make you sleep.'

'Yes,' cried I, 'the sleep of the grave! O Lady Gwyn, what have I done to you, to deserve death at your hands? And in such a manner too! Had you even shewn so much regard to custom and common decency, as to have offered me the potion in a bowl or a goblet, there might have been some little palliation. But to add insult to injury;—to trick me out of my life with a paltry tea-cup;—to poison a girl of my pretensions, as vulgarly as you would a rat;—no, no, Madam, this is not to be pardoned!'

Her ladyship again began assuring me that I had taken nothing more than a soporific; but I would not hear her, and at length, I sent her and the domestics out of the chamber, that I might prepare for my approaching end.

How to prepare was the question; for I had never thought of death seriously, heroines so seldom die. Should I follow the beautiful precedent of the dying Heloise, who called her friends about her, got her chamber sprinkled with flowers and perfumes, and then gave up the ghost, in a state of elegant inebriation with home-made wine, which she passed for Spanish? Alas! I had no friends—not even Stuart, at hand; flowers and perfumes I would not condescend to beg from my murderess; and as for wine, I could not abide the thoughts of it in a morning.

But amidst these reflections, a more serious and less agreeable subject intruded itself upon me,—the thoughts of a future state. I strove to banish it, but it would not be repulsed. Yet surely, said I, as a heroine, I am a pattern of perfect virtue; and therefore, I must be happy hereafter. But was virtue sufficient? At church (seldom as I had frequented it, in consequence of its sober ceremonies, so unsuited to my taste,) I remembered to have heard a very different doctrine. There I had heard, that we cannot learn to do right without the Divine aid, and that to propitiate it, we must make ourselves acquainted with those principles of religion, which enable us to prefer duteous prayers, and to place implicit reliance on the power and goodness of the Deity. Alas, I knew nothing of religion, except from novels; and in these, though the devotion of heroines is sentimental and graceful to a degree, it never influences their acts, or appears connected with their moral duties. It is so speculative and generalized, that it would answer the Greek or the Persian church, as well as the christian; and none but the picturesque and enthusiastic part is presented; such as kissing a cross, chanting a vesper with elevated eyes, or composing a well-worded prayer.

The more I thought, the more horrible appeared my situation. I felt a confused idea, that I had led a worthless, if not a criminal life; that I had left myself without a friend in this world, and had not sought to make one in the next. I became more and more agitated. I tried to turn my thoughts back to the plan of expiring with grace, but all in vain. I then wrote the note to you; then endeavoured to pray: nothing could calm or divert my mind. The pains grew worse, I felt sick at heart, my palate was parched, and I now expected that every breath would be my last. My soul recoiled from the thought, and my brain became a confused chaos. Hideous visions of eternity rushed into my mind; I lay shivering, groaning, and abandoned to the most deplorable despair.

In this state the physician found me. O what a joyful relief, when he declared, that my disorder was nothing but a violent rheumatism, contracted, it seems, by my fall into the water the morning before! Never was transport equal to mine; and I assured him that he should have a place in my memoirs.

He prescribed for me; but remarked, that I might remain ill a whole month, or be quite well in a few days.

'Positively,' said her ladyship, 'you must be quite well in four; for then my ball comes on; and I mean to make you the most conspicuous figure at it. I have great plans for you, I assure you.'

I thanked her ladyship, and begged pardon for having been so giddy as to call her a murderess; while she laughed at my mistake, and made quite light of it. Noble woman! But I dare say magnanimity is our family virtue.

No sooner had I ceased to be miserable about leaving the world, than I became almost as much so about losing the ball. To lose it from any cause whatever, was sufficiently provoking; but to lose it by so gross a disorder as a rheumatism, was, indeed, dreadful. Now, had I even some pale, genteel, sofa-reclining illness, curable by hartshorn, I would bless my kind stars, and drink that nauseous cordial, from morning even unto night. For disguise thyself as thou wilt, hartshorn, still thou art a bitter draught; and though heroines in all novels have been made to drink of thee, thou art no less bitter on that account.

Being on this subject, I have to lament, that I am utterly unacquainted with those refined ailments, which every girl that I read of, meets with, as things of course. The consequence is my wanting that beauty, which, touched with the languid delicacy of illness, gains from sentiment what it loses in bloom; so that really this horse's constitution of mine is a terrible disadvantage to me. I know, had I the power of inventing my own indispositions, I would strike out something far beyond even the hectics and head-aches of my fair predecessors. I believe there is not a sigh-fever; but I would fall ill of a scald from a lover's tear, or a classic scratch from the thorn of a rose.

Adieu.

LETTER XXX

This morning I awoke almost free from pain; and towards evening, I was able to appear in the drawing-room. Lady Gwyn had asked several of her friends to tea, so that I passed a delightful afternoon; the charm, admiration, and astonishment of all.

On retiring for the night to my chamber, I found this note on my toilette, and read it with a beating heart.

To the Lady Cherubina.

'Your mother lives! and is confined in one of the subterranean vaults belonging to the villa. At midnight you will hear a tapping at your door. Open it, and two men in masks will appear outside. They will blindfold, and conduct you to her. You will know her by her striking likeness to her picture in the gallery. Be silent, courageous, and circumspect.

'An unknown Friend.'

What a flood of new feelings gushed upon my soul, as I laid down the billet, and lifted my filial eyes to heaven! I was about to behold my mother. Mother—endearing name! I pictured to myself, that unfortunate lady, stretched on a mattrass of straw, her eyes sunken in their sockets, yet still retaining a portion of their wonted fire; her frame emaciated, her voice feeble, her hand damp and chill. Fondly did I depict our meeting—our embrace; she gently pushing me from her, to gaze on all the lineaments of my countenance, and then baring my temple to search for the mole. All, all is convincing; and she calls me the softened image of my noble father!

Two tedious hours I waited in extreme anxiety, till at length the clock struck twelve. My heart beat responsive, and in a few moments after, I heard the promised signal at my door. I unbolted it, and beheld two men in masks and cloaks. They blindfolded me, and each taking an arm, led me along. Not a word passed. We traversed several suites of apartments, ascended flights of stairs, descended others; now went this way, now that; obliquely, circularly, angularly; till I began actually to imagine we were all the time in one spot.

At length my conductors stopped.

'Unlock the postern gate,' whispered one, 'while I light a torch.'

'We are betrayed!' said the other, 'for this is the wrong key.'

'Then thou beest the traitor,' cried the first.

'Thou liest, dost lie, and art lying!' cried the second.

'Take that!' exclaimed the first. A groan followed, and the wretch dropped to the ground.

'You have murdered him!' cried I, sickening with horror.

'I have only hamstrung him, my lady,' said the fellow. 'He will be lame for life.'

'Treason!' shouted the wounded man.

His companion burst open the gate; a sudden current of wind met us, and we fled along with incredible speed, while low moans and smothered shrieks were heard at either side of us.

'Gracious heaven, where are we?' cried I.

'In the cavern of death!' said my conductor, 'famous for rats and banditti.'

On a sudden innumerable footsteps echoed behind us. We ran swifter.

'Fire!' cried a ferocious accent, almost at my ear; and in a moment several pistols were discharged.

I stopped, unable to move, breathe, or speak.

'I am wounded all over, right and left, fore and aft!' cried my conductor.

'Am I bleeding?' said I, feeling myself with my hands.

'No, blessed St. Anthony be praised!' answered he; 'and now all is safe, for we are at the cell, and the banditti have turned into the wrong passage.'

He stopped, and unlocked a door.

'Enter,' said he, 'and behold your unhappy mother!'

He led me forward, took the bandage from my eyes, and retiring, locked the door upon me.

Agitated already by the terrors of my dangerous expedition, I felt additional horror on finding myself in a dismal cell, lighted with a lantern; where, at a small table, sat a woman suffering under a corpulency unparalleled in the memoirs of human monsters. She was clad in sackcloth, her head was swathed in linen, and had grey locks on it, like horses' tails. Hundreds of frogs were leaping about the floor; a piece of mouldy bread, a mug of water, and a manuscript, lay on the table; some straw, strewn with dead snakes and skulls, occupied one corner, and the farther side of the cell was concealed behind a black curtain.

I stood at the door, doubtful, and afraid to advance; while the prodigious prisoner sat examining me from head to foot.

At last I summoned courage to say, 'I fear, Madam, I am an intruder here. I have certainly been shewn into the wrong room.'

'It is, it is my own, my only daughter, my Cherubina!' cried she, with a tremendous voice. 'Come to my maternal arms, thou living picture of the departed Theodore!'

'Why, Ma'am,' said I, 'I would with great pleasure, but I am afraid that—— Oh, Madam, indeed, indeed, I am quite sure you cannot be my mother!'

'For shame!' cried she. 'Why not?'

'Why, Madam,' answered I, 'my mother was of a thin habit; as her picture proves.'

'And so was I once,' said she. 'This deplorable plumpness is owing to want of exercise. You see, however, that I retain all my former paleness.'

'Pardon me,' said I, 'for I must say that your face is a rich scarlet.'

'And is this our tender meeting?' cried she. 'After ten years' imprisonment, to be disowned by my daughter, and taunted with sarcastic insinuations against my face? Here is a pretty joke! Tell me, girl, will you embrace me, or will you not?'

'Indeed, Madam,' answered I, 'I will embrace you presently.'

'Presently!' cried she.

'Yes,' said I, 'depend upon it I will. Only let me get over the first shock.'

'Shock!' vociferated she.

Dreading her violence, and feeling myself bound to do the duties of a daughter, I kneeled at her feet, and said:

'Ever excellent, ever exalted author of my being, I beg thy maternal blessing!'

My mother raised me from the ground, and hugged me to her heart, with such cruel vigour, that almost crushed, I cried out stoutly, and struggled for release.

'And now,' said she, relaxing her grasp, 'let us talk over our wrongs. This manuscript is a faithful narrative of my life, previous to my marriage. It was written by my female confidant, to divert her grief, during the long and alarming illness of her Dutch pug. Take it to your chamber, and blot it with your tears, my love.'

I put the scroll in my bosom.

'Need I shock your gentle feelings,' continued she, 'by relating my subsequent story? Suffice it, that as soon as you were stolen, I went mad about the woods, till I was caught; and on recovering my senses, I found myself in this infernal dungeon. Look at that calendar of small sticks, notched all over with my dismal days and nights. Ten long years I have eaten nothing but bread. Oh, ye favourite pullets, oh ye inimitable apple-pies, shall I never, never, taste you more? Oft too, my reason wanders. Oft I see figures that rise like furies, to torment me. I see them when asleep; I see them now—now!'

She sat in a fixed attitude of horror, while her straining eyes moved slowly round, as if they followed something. I stood shuddering, and hating her more and more every moment.

'Gentle companion of my confinement!' cried she, apostrophizing a huge toad that she pulled out of her bosom; 'dear, spotted fondling; thou, next to my Cherubina, art worthy of my love. Embrace each other, my friends.' And she put the hideous pet into my hand. I screamed and dropped it.

'Oh!' cried I, in a passion of despair, 'what madness possessed me to undertake this execrable enterprize!' and I began beating with my hand against the door.

'Do you want to leave your poor mother?' said she, in a whimpering tone.

'Oh! I am so frightened!' said I.

'You will spend the night here, however,' cried she; 'and probably your whole life too; for no doubt the ruffian who brought you hither was employed by Lady Gwyn to entrap you.'

When I heard this terrible suggestion, my blood ran cold, and I began crying bitterly.

'Come, my love!' said my mother, 'and let me lull thee to repose on my soft bosom. What is the world to us? Here in each other's society, we will enjoy all that affection, all that virtue can confer. Come, my daughter, and let me clasp thee to my heart once more!'

'Ah,' cried I, 'spare me!'

'What!' exclaimed she, 'do you spurn my proffered embrace?'

'Dear, no, Madam,' answered I. 'But—but you squeeze one so!'

My mother made a huge stride towards me; then stood groaning and rolling her eyes.

'Help!' cried I, half frantic; 'help! help!'

I was stopped by a suppressed titter of infernal laughter, as if from many demons; and on looking towards the black curtain, whence the sound came, I saw it agitated; and about twenty terrific faces appeared peeping through slits in it, and making grins of a most diabolical nature. I hid my face in my hands.

''Tis the banditti!' cried my mother.

As she spoke, the door opened, a bandage was flung over my eyes, and I was hurried off, almost senseless, in some one's arms; till at length, I found myself alone in my own chamber.

Such was the detestable adventure of to-night. Oh, Biddy, that I should have lived to meet this mother of mine! How different from the mothers that other heroines contrive to rummage out in northern turrets and ruined chapels! I am out of all patience. Liberate her I will, of course, and make a suitable provision for her, when I get possession of my property, but positively, never will I sleep under the same roof with—(ye powers of filial love forgive me!) such a living mountain of human horror.

Adieu.

LETTER XXXI

While her ladyship is busied in preparing for the ball of to-morrow night, I find time to copy my mother's memoirs for your perusal. Were she herself elegant and interesting, perhaps I might think them so too; and if I dislike them, it must be because I dislike her; for the plot, sentiment, diction, and pictures of nature, differ little from what we find in other novels.

Il Castello di Grimgothico,

OR

MEMOIRS OF LADY HYSTERICA BELAMOUR.

A NOVEL.

By Anna Maria Marianne Matilda Pottingen,
Author of the Bloody Bodkin, Sonnets on most of the Planets, &c. &c. &c.

Oh, Sophonisba, Sophonisba, oh!

Thompson.

CHAPTER I

Blow, blow, thou wintry wind.—Shakespeare.

Blow, breezes, blow.—Moore.

A Storm. — A rustic Repast. — An Alarm. — Uncommon readiness in a Child. — An inundated Stranger. — A Castle out of repair. — An impaired Character.

It was on a nocturnal night in autumnal October; the wet rain fell in liquid quantities, and the thunder rolled in an awful and Ossianly manner. The lowly, but peaceful inhabitants of a small, but decent cottage, were just sitting down to their homely, but wholesome supper, when a loud knocking at the door alarmed them. Bertram armed himself with a ladle. 'Lackadaisy!' cried old Margueritone, and little Billy seized the favourable moment to fill his mouth with meat. Innocent fraud! happy childhood!

The father's lustre and the mother's bloom.—Thompson.

Bertram then opened the door; when lo! pale, breathless, dripping, and with a look that would have shocked the Humane Society, a beautiful female tottered into the room.

'Lackadaisy, Ma'am,' said Margueritone, 'are you wet?'

'Wet!' exclaimed the fair unknown, wringing a rivulet of rain from the corner of her robe; 'O ye gods, wet!'

Margueritone felt the justice, the gentleness of the reproof, and turned the subject, by recommending a glass of spirits.

Spirit of my sainted sire.

The stranger sipped, shook her head, and fainted. Her hair was long and dark, and the bed was ready; so since she seems in distress, we will leave her there awhile; lest we should betray an ignorance of the world, in appearing not to know the proper time for deserting people.

On the rocky summit of a beetling precipice, whose base was lashed by the angry Atlantic, stood a moated, and turreted structure, called Il Castello di Grimgothico.

As the northern tower had remained uninhabited since the death of its late lord, Henriques De Violenci, lights and figures were, *par consequence*, observed in it at midnight. Besides, the black eyebrows of the present baron had a habit of meeting for several years, and *quelquefois*, he paced the picture-gallery with a hurried step. These circumstances combined, there could be no doubt of his having committed murder. Accordingly, all avoided him, except the Count Stiletto, and the hectic, but heavenly Hysterica. The former, he knew, was the most pale-faced, flagitious character in the world. But birds of a plume associate. The latter shall be presented to the reader in the next chapter.

CHAPTER II

'Oh!'—Milton.

'Ah!'—Pope.

A History. — a Mystery. — An original Reflection on Death. — The Heroine described. — The Landscape not described. — An awful Reason given.

One evening, the Baroness De Violenci, having sprained her left leg in the composition of an ecstatic ode, resolved not to go to Lady Penthesilea Rouge's rout. While she was sitting alone, at a plate of prawns, the footman entered with a basket, which had just been left for her.

'Lay it down, John,' said she, touching his forehead with her fork.

That gay-hearted young fellow did as he was desired, and capered out of the room.

Judge of her astonishment, when she found, on opening it, a little cherub of a baby sleeping within.

An oaken cross, with 'Hysterica,' inscribed in chalk, was appended at its neck, and a mark, like a bruised gooseberry, added interest to its elbow.

As she and her lord never had children (at least she could answer for herself), she determined, *sur le champ*, on adopting the pretty Hysterica.

Fifteen years did this worthy woman dedicate to the progress of her little charge; and in that time, taught her every mortal accomplishment. Her sigh, particularly, was esteemed the softest in Europe.

But the stroke of death is inevitable; come it must at last, and neither virtue nor wisdom can avoid it. In a word, the good old Baroness died, and our heroine fell senseless on her body.

O what a fall was there, my countrymen!

But it is now time to describe our heroine. As Milton tells us, that Eve was '*more lovely than Pandora*' (an imaginary lady, who never existed but in the brains of poets), so do we declare, and are ready to stake our lives, that our heroine excelled in her form the Timinitilidi, whom no man ever saw; and, in her voice, the music of the spheres, which no man ever heard. Perhaps her face was not perfect; but it was more—it was interesting—it was oval. Her eyes were of the real, original old blue; and her eyelashes of the best silk. You forget the thickness of her lips, in the casket of pearls which they enshrined; and the roses of York and Lancaster were united in her cheek. A nose of the Grecian order surmounted the whole. Such was Hysterica.

But alas! misfortunes are often gregarious, like sheep. For one night, when our heroine had repaired to the chapel, intending to drop her customary tear on the tomb of her sainted benefactress, she heard on a sudden,

Oh, horrid, horrible, and horridest horror!

the distant organ peal a solemn voluntary. While she was preparing, in much terror and astonishment, to accompany it with her voice, four men in masks rushed from among some tombs, and bore her to a carriage, which instantly drove off with the whole party. In vain she sought to soften them by swoons, tears, and a simple little ballad: they sat counting murders, and not minding her.

As the blinds of the carriage were closed the whole way, we wave a description of the country which they traversed. Besides, the prospect within the carriage will occupy the reader enough; for in one of the villains, Hysterica discovered—Count Stiletto! She fainted.

On the second day, the carriage stopped at an old castle, and she was conveyed into a tapestried apartment, where the delicate creature instantly fell ill of an inverted eyelash, caused by continual weeping. She then drew upon the contemplation of future sorrows, for a supply of that melancholy which her immediate exigencies demanded.

CHAPTER III

Be thou a spirit of health, or goblin damn'd?—Shakespeare.

Fresh Embarrassments. — An Insult from a Spectre. — Grand Discoveries. — A Shriek. — A Tear. — A Sigh. — A Blush. — A Swoon.

It is a remark founded upon the nature of man, and universally credited by the thinking part of the world, that to suffer is an attribute of mortality.

Impressed with a due conviction of this important precept, our heroine but smiled as she heard Stiletto lock her door. It was now midnight, and she took up her lamp to examine the chamber. Rusty daggers, mouldering bones, and ragged palls, lay scattered in all the profusion of feudal plenty.

Several horrors now made their appearance; but the most uncommon was a winged eyeball that fluttered before her face.

Say, little, foolish, fluttering thing?

She began shrieking and adjusting her hair at a mirror, when lo! she beheld the reflection of a ghastly visage peeping over her shoulder! Much disconcerted, the trembling girl approached the bed. An impertinent apparition, with a peculiar nose, stood there, and made faces at her. She felt offended at the freedom, to say nothing of her being half dead with fright.

'Is it not enough,' thought she, 'to be harassed by beings of this world, but those of the next too must think proper to interfere? I am sure,' said she, as she raised her voice in a taunting manner, '*En verité*, I have no desire to meddle with *their* affairs. *Sur ma vie*, I have no taste for brim-stone. So let me just advise a *certain* inhabitant of a *certain* world (not the *best*, I believe,) to think less of *my* concerns, and more of *his own*.'

Having thus asserted her dignity, without being too personal, she walked to the casement in tears, and sang these simple lines, which she graced with intermittent sobs.

SONG

Alas, well-a-day, woe to me,

Singing willow, willow, willow;

My lover is far, far at sea.

On a billow, billow, billow.

Ah, Theodore, would thou could'st be,

On my pillow, pillow, pillow!

Here she heaved a deep sigh, when, to her utter astonishment, a voice, as if from a chamber underneath; took up the tune with these words:

SONG

Alas, well-a-day, woe to me,

Singing sorrow, sorrow, sorrow;

A ducat would soon make me free,

Could I borrow, borrow, borrow;

And then I would pillow with thee,

To-morrow, morrow, morrow!

Was it?—It was!—Yes, it *was* the voice of her love, her life, her long-lost Theodore De Willoughby!!! How should she reach him? Forty times she ran round and round her chamber, with agitated eyes and distracted tresses.

Here we must pause a moment, and express our surprise at the negligence of the sylphs and sylphids, in permitting the ringlets of heroines to be so frequently dishevelled. O ye fat-cheeked little cherubims, who flap your innocent wings, and fly through oceans of air in a minute, without having a hair of your heads discomposed,—no wonder that such stiff ringlets should be made of gold!

At length Hysterica found a sliding pannel. She likewise found a moth-eaten parchment, which she sat down to peruse. But, gentle reader, imagine her emotions, on decyphering these wonderful words.

MANUSCRIPT

—— Six tedious years —— —— and all for what? —— —— —— —— —— No sun, no moon. —— —— Murd —— —— Adul —— —— because I am the wife of Lord Belamour. —— —— then tore me from him, and my little Hysterica —— —— —— —— —— Cruel Stiletto! —— —— He confesses that he put the sleeping babe into a basket —— —— sent her to the Baroness de Violenci —— —— oaken cross —— —— Chalk —— —— bruised gooseberry —— —— —— —— —— I am poisoned —— —— a great pain across my back —— —— i —— j —— k —— —— Oh! —— Ah! —— Oh! —— —— —— ——

Fascinante Peggina Belamour.

This then was the mother of our heroine; and the MS. elucidated, beyond dispute, the mysteries which had hitherto hung over the birth of that unfortunate orphan.

We need not add that she fainted, recovered, passed through the pannel, discovered the dungeon of her Theodore; and having asked him how he did,

'Comment vous portez vous?'

fell into unsophisticated hysterics.

CHAPTER IV

Sure such a pair were never seen,

So justly formed to meet by nature.—Sheridan.

A tender Dialogue. — An interesting Flight. — A mischievous Cloud. — Our Hero hits upon a singular Expedient. — Fails. — Takes a trip to the Metropolis.

'And is this you?' cried the delighted youth, as she revived.

'Indeed, indeed it is,' said she.

'Are you quite, quite sure?' cried he.

'Indeed, indeed I am,' said she.

'Well, how do you do?' cried he.

'Pretty well I thank you,' said she.

They then separated, after fixing to meet again.

One night, as they were indulging each other in innocent endearments, and filling up each finer pause with lemonade, a sudden thought struck Lord Theodore.

'Let us escape,' said he.

'Let us,' said she.

'Gods, what a thought was there!'

They then contrived this ingenious mode of accomplishing their object. In one of the galleries which lay between their chambers, there was a window. Having opened it, they found that they had nothing to do but get out at it. They therefore fled into the neighbouring forest.

Happy, happy, happy pair!—Dryden.

But it is an incontrovertible truism, that *les genres humains* are liable to disaster; for in consequence of a cloud that obscured the moon, Hysterica fell into a snow-pit. What could Theodore do? To save her was impossible; to perish with her would be suicide. In this emergency, he formed a bold project, and ran two miles for assistance. But alas! on his return, not a trace of her could be found. He was quite *au desespoir*; so, having called her long enough, he called a chaise, and set off for London.

CHAPTER V

'Tis she!—Pope.

O Vous!—Telemachus.

All hail!—Macbeth.

An Extraordinary Rencontre. — Pathetic Repartees. — Natural Consequences resulting from an Excess in Spirituous Liquors. — Terrific Nonsense talked by two Maniacs.

One night as Lord Theodore, on his return from the theatre, was passing along a dark alley, he perceived a candle lighting in a small window, on the ground-floor of a deciduous hovel.

An indescribable sensation, an unaccountable something, whispered to him, in still, small accents, 'peep through the pane.' He did so; but what were his emotions, when he beheld—whom? Why the very young lady that he had left for dead in the forest—his Hysterica!!!

She was clearstarching in a dimity bedgown.

He sleeked his eyebrows with his finger, then flung open the sash, and stood before her.

'*Ah, ma belle Amie!*' cried he. 'So I have caught you at last. I really thought you were dead.'

'I am dead to love and to hope!' said she.

'O ye powers!' cried he, making a blow at his forehead.

'There are many kinds of powers,' said she carelessly: 'perhaps you now mean the powers of impudence, Mr.—I beg pardon—Lord Theodore De Willoughby, I believe.'

'I believe so,' retorted he, 'Mrs.—or rather Lady Hys—Hys—Hys.'—

'Hiss away, my lord!' exclaimed the sensitive girl, and fainted.

Lord Theodore rushed at a bottle that stood on the dresser, and poured half a pint of it into her mouth; but perceiving by the colour that it was not water, he put it to his lips;—it was brandy. In a paroxysm of despair he swallowed the contents; and at the same moment Hysterica woke from her fainting-fit, in a high delirium.

'What have you done to me?' stammered she. 'Oh! I am lost.' 'What!' exclaimed the youth, who had also got a brain-fever; 'after my preserving you in brandy?' 'I am happy to hear it,' lisped she; 'and every thing round me seems to be happy, for every thing round me seems to be dancing!'

Both now began singing, with dreadful facetiousness; he, 'fill the bowl,' and she, 'drink to me only.'

At length they sang themselves asleep.

CHAPTER VI

Take him for all in all,

We ne'er shall look upon his like again.—Shakespeare.

Birth, Parentage, and Education of our Hero. — An aspiring Porter. — Eclaircissement.

Lord Theodore De Willoughby was the son of Lord De Willoughby, of De Willoughby Castle. After having graduated at Oxford, he took, not alone a tour of the Orkney Islands, but an opportunity of saving our heroine's life. Hence their mutual attachment. About the same time, Count Stiletto had conceived a design against that poor orphan; and dreading Lord Theodore as a rival, waylaid and imprisoned him.

But to return.

Next morning, the lovers woke in full possession of their faculties, when the happiest *denouement* took place. Hysterica told Theodore that she had extricated herself from the snow, at the risk of her life. In fact, she was obliged to pelt it away in balls, and Theodore now recollected having been hit with one, during his search for her. Fearful of returning to the castle, she walked *à Londres*; and officiated there in the respective capacities of cook, milliner, own woman, and washerwoman. Her honour too, was untarnished, though a hulking porter had paid her the most delicate attentions, and assured her that Theodore was married to cruel Barbara Allen.

Theodore called down several stars to witness his unalterable love; and, as a farther proof of the fact, offered to marry her the next day.

Her former scruples (the mysterious circumstances of her birth) being now removed, she beamed an inflammatory glance, and consented. He deposited a kiss on her cheek, and a blush was the rosy result. He therefore repeated the application.

CHAPTER VII

Sure such a day as this was never seen!—Thomas Thumb.

The day, th' important day!—Addison.

O giorno felice!—Italian.

Rural Scenery. — The Bridal Costume. — Old Friends. — Little Billy greatly grown. — The Marriage. — A Scene of Mortality. — Conclusion.

The morning of the happy day destined to unite our lovers was ushered into the world with a blue sky, and the ringing of bells. Maidens, united in bonds of amity and artificial roses, come dancing to the pipe and tabor; while groups of children and chickens add hilarity to the unison of congenial minds. On the left of the village are seen plantations of tufted turnips; on the right a dilapidated dog-kennel,

With venerable grandeur marks the scene;

while every where the delighted eye catches monstrous mountains and minute daisies. In a word,

All nature wears one universal grin.

The procession now set forward to the church. The bride was habited in white drapery. Ten signs of the Zodiac, worked in spangles, sparkled round its edge, but Virgo was omitted at her own desire; and the bridegroom proposed to dispense with Capricorn. Sweet delicacy! She held a pot of myrtle in her hand, and wore on her head a small lighted torch, emblematical of Hymen. The boys and girls bounded about her, and old Margueritone begged the favour of lighting her pipe at her la'ship's head.

'Aha, I remember you!' said little Billy, pointing his plump and dimpled finger at her. She remarked how tall he was grown, and took him in her arms; while he playfully beat her with an infinitude of small thumps.

The marriage ceremony passed off with great spirit; and the fond bridegroom, as he pressed her to his heart, felt how pure, how delicious are the joys of virtue.

That evening, he gave a *fête champetre* to the peasantry; and, afterwards, a magnificent supper to his friends.

The company consisted of Lord Lilliput, Sir James Brobdignag, little Billy, Anacharsis Clootz, and Joe Miller.

Nothing, they thought, could add to their happiness; but they were miserably mistaken. A messenger, pale as Priam's, rushed into the room, and proclaimed Lord Theodore a peer of Great Britain, as his father had died the night before.

All present congratulated Lord De Willoughby on this prosperous turn of affairs; while himself and his charming bride exchanged a look that spoke volumes.

Little Billy then pledged him in a goblet of Falernian; but he very properly refused, alleging, that as the dear child was in love with Hysterica, he had probably poisoned the wine, in a fit of jealousy. The whole party were in raptures at this mark of his lordship's discretion.

After supper, little Billy rose, and bowing gracefully to the bride, stabbed himself to the heart.

Our readers may now wish to learn what became of the remaining personages in this narrative.

Count Stiletto is dead; Lord Lilliput is no more; Sir James Brobdignag has departed this life; Anacharsis Clootz is in his grave; and Mr. J. Miller is in another, and we trust, a better world.

Old Margueritone expired with the bible in her hand, and the coroner's inquest brought in a verdict of lunacy.

Having thus conducted our lovers to the summit of human happiness, we shall take leave of our readers with this moral reflection:—

THE FALLING OUT OF LOVERS IS THE RENEWAL OF LOVE.

THE END.

I must now leave you to prepare my dress for the ball. The ball-room, which occupies an entire wing of the house, is full of artists and workmen; but her ladyship will not permit me to see it till the night of the dance; as, she says, she means to surprise me with its splendour. Cynics may say what they will against expensive decorations; but in my opinion, whatever tends to promote taste in the fine arts (and a mental is in some degree productive of a moral taste); whatever furnishes artizans with employment, and excites their emulation, must improve the condition of society.

Adieu.

The morning of the ball, I awoke without any remains of my late indisposition, except that captivating paleness, that sprinkling of lilies, which adds to interest without detracting from beauty.

I rose with the sun, and taking a small china vase in my hand, tripped into the parterre, to collect the fresh and fragrant dew that glistened on the blossoms. I filled the piece of painted earth with the nectar of the sky, and returned.

During the day, I took nothing but honey, milk, and dried conserves; a repast the most likely to promote that ethereal character which I purposed adopting at night.

Towards evening, I laved my limbs in a tepid bath; and as soon as the sun had waved his last crimson banner in the west, I began my toilette.

So variable is fashion, that I determined not to dress according to its existing laws; since they might be completely exploded in a month; and, at all events, by the time my life is written, they will have become quite antiquated. For instance, do we not already abhor Evelina's and Harriet Byron's powdered, pomatumed, and frizzled hair? It was, therefore, my plan to dress in imitation of classical models, and to copy the immortal toilette of Greece.

Having first divested myself from head to foot of every habiliment, I took a long piece of the finest cambric, and twice wound it gracefully round my shoulders and bosom, and twice enveloped my form in its folds; which, while they delineated the outline of my shape, veiled the tincture of my skin. I then flung over it a drapery of embroidered gauze, and its unimplicated simplicity gave to my perfect figure the spirit of an antique statue. An apparent tissue of woven air, it fell like a vapour round me. A zone of gold and a clasp prettily imprisoned my waist; and my graceful arms, undegraded by gloves, were bare to the shoulder. Part of my hair was confined by a bodkin, and part floated over my neck in native ringlets. As I could not well wear my leg naked, I drew on it a texture of woven silk; and laced a pair of sandals over my little foot; which resembled that of a youthful Thetis, or of a fugitive Atalanta.

I then bathed my face with the dew which I had gathered in the morning, poured on my hair and bosom the balmy waters of the distilled rose, and sprinkled my drapery with fragrant floods of lavender; so that I might be said to move in an ambient atmosphere of odours.

Behold me now, dressed to a charm, to a criticism. Here was no sloping, or goring, or seaming, or frilling, or flouncing. Detestable mechanism of millinery! No tedious papillotes, or unpoetical pins were here. All was done, in a few minutes, with a clasp, a zone, and a bodkin.

As I surveyed my form in the mirror, I was enraptured at its Sylphic delicacy; but I trembled to reflect, that the fairest flowers are the most fragile. You would imagine that a maiden's sigh could dissipate the drapery; and its aerial effect was as if a fairy were to lift the filmy gossamer on her spear, and lightly fling it over a rose-bud.

Resolving not to make myself visible till all the guests had arrived, I sat down and read Ossian, to store my mind with ideas for conversation. I love Ossian, it is so sublime, so bewildered, so full of a blue and white melancholy; of ghosts, and the four elements. I likewise turned over other books; for, as I had never mixed in fashionable society, I could not talk that nothingness, which is every thing in high life. Nor, indeed, if I could, would I; because, as a heroine, it was my part to converse with point, flowers, and sublimation.

About to appear in a world where all was new to me; ignorant of its forms, inexperienced in its rules; fair, young, and original, I resolved on adopting such manners as should not be subject to place, time, accident, or fashion. In short, to copy universal, generalized, unsophisticated nature, and Grecian statues.

As I had studied elegance of attitude before I knew the world, my graces were original, and all my own creation; so that if I had not the temporary mannerisms of a marchioness, I had, at least, the immortal movements of a seraph. Words may become obsolete, but the language of gesture is universal and eternal.

As for smiles, I felt myself perfect mistress of all that were ever ascribed to heroines;—the fatal smile, the smile such as precedes the dissolution of sainted goodness, the fragment of a broken smile, and the sly smile that creates the little dimple on the left side of the little mouth.

At length the most interesting moment of my life arrived; the moment when I was to burst, like a new planet, on the fashionable hemisphere. I descended the stairs, and pausing at the door, tried to tranquillize my fluttered spirits. I then assumed an air-lifted figure, scarcely touching the ground, and glided into the room.

The company were walking in groups, or sitting.

'That is she;—there she is;—look, look!' was whispered on all sides. Every eye fixed itself upon me, while I felt at once elevated and opprest.

Lady Gwyn advanced, took my hand, and paying me the highest compliments on my appearance, led me to a sofa, at the upper end of the room. A semicircle of astonished admirers, head over head, ranged itself in my front, and a smile of glowing approbation illuminated the faces of all. There I sat, in all the bashful diffidence of a simple and inexperienced recluse, trembling for myself, fearing for others, systematically suppressing my feelings, impulsively betraying them; while, with an expression of sweet wildness, and retiring consciousness, was observable a degree of susceptibility too exquisite to admit of lasting peace.

At last a spruce and puny fop stepped from amidst the group, and seated himself beside me.

'This was a fine day, Ma'am,' said he, as he admired the accurate turn of his ankle.

'Yes,' answered I, 'halcyon was the morn, when I strayed into the garden, to gather flowery dew; and it seemed as if the twins of Latona had met to propitiate their rites. Blushes, like their own roses, coloured the vapours; and rays, pure as their thoughts, silvered the foliage.'

The company murmured applause.

'What a pity,' said he, 'that this evening was wet; as in consequence of it, we have probably lost another beautiful description from you.'

'Ah, my good friend,' cried I, wreathing my favourite smile; and laying the rosy tip of my finger on his arm; 'such is the state of man. His morning rises in sunshine, and his evening sets in rain.'

While the company were again expressing their approbation, I overheard one of them whisper to the fop:

'Come, play the girl off, and let her have your best nonsense.'

The fop winked at him, and then turned to me; while I sat shocked and astonished, but collecting all my powers.

'See,' said he, 'how you have fascinated every eye. Actually you are the queen-bee; with all your swarm about you.'

'And with my drone too,' said I, bowing slightly.

'Happy in being a drone,' said he, 'so he but sips of your honey.'

'Rather say,' cried I, 'that he deserves my sting.'

'Ah,' said he, laying his hand on his heart; 'your eyes have fixed a sting here.'

'Then your tongue,' returned I, 'is rather more innocent; for though it may have the venom of a sting, it wants the point.'

The company laughed, and he coloured.

'Do I tease you?' said he, trying to rally. 'How cruel! Actually I am so abashed, as you may see, that my modesty flies into my face.'

'Then,' said I, 'your modesty must be very hard run for a refuge.'

Here the room echoed with acclamations.

'I am not at a loss for an answer,' said he, looking round him, and forcing a smile. 'I am not indeed.'

'Then pray let me have it,' said I, 'for folly never becomes truly ludicrous till it tries to be pert.'

'Bravo! Bravo!' cried an hundred voices at once, and away the little drone flew from my hive. I tossed back my ringlets with an infantine shake of the head, and sat as if unconscious of my triumph.

The best of it is, that every word he said will one day appear in print. Men who converse with a heroine ought to talk for the press, or they will make but a silly figure in her memoirs.

'I thank you for your spirit, my dear,' said Lady Gwyn, sitting down beside me. 'That little puppy deserves every severity. Think of his always sitting in his dressing-gown, a full hour after he has shaved, that the blood may subside from his face. He protests his surprise how men can find pleasure in running after a nasty fox; cuts out half his own coat at his tailor's; has a smile, and a "pretty!" for every one and every thing; sits silent till one of his four only topics is introduced, and then lisping a descant on the last opera, the last boxing-match, the last race, or the last play, he drains his last idea, and has nothing at your service, for the remainder of the night, but an assenting bow. Such insects should never come out but at butterfly-season; and even then, only in a four-wheeled bandbox, while monkeys strew the way with mignionette. No, I can never forgive him for having gone to Lady Bontein's last rout in preference to mine; though he knew that she gave her's on the same evening purposely to thin my party.'

'And pray,' said I, 'who is Lady Bontein?'

'That tall personage yonder, with sorrel hair,' answered her ladyship; 'and with one shoulder of the gothic order, and the other of the corinthian. She has now been forty years endeavouring to look handsome, and she still thinks, that by diligent perseverance she will succeed at last. See how she freshens her smiles, and labours to look at ease; though she has all the awkwardness of a milkmaid, without any of the simplicity. You must know she has pored over Latin, till her mind has become as dead as the language itself. Then she writes well-bred sonnets about a tear, or a primrose, or a daisy; but nothing larger than a lark; and talks botany with the men, as she thinks that science is a sufficient excuse for indecency. Nay, the meek creature affects the bible too; but it is whispered, that she has often thrown it at her footman's head, without any affectation at all. But the magnificence of to-night will put all competition out of her power; and I have also planned a little *Scena*, classical, appropriate, and almost unique; not alone in order to complete my triumph over her, but to grace your entrance into life, by conferring a peculiar mark of distinction on you.'

'On me!' cried I. 'What mark? I deserve no mark, I am sure.'

'Indeed you do,' said she. 'All the world knows that you are the first heroine in it; and the fact is, I mean to celebrate your merits to-night, by crowning you, just as Corinne was crowned in the capitol.'

'Dear Lady Gwyn,' cried I, panting with joy; 'sure you are not—— Ah, are you serious?'

'Most serious, my love,' answered she, 'and in a short time the ceremony will commence. You may perceive that the young men and girls have left the room. It is to prepare for the procession; and now excuse me, as I must assist them.'

She then hurried out, and I remained half an hour, in an agony of anxious expectation.

At last, I heard a confused murmur at the door, and a gentleman ran forward from it, to clear a passage. A lane was soon formed of the guests; and fancy my feelings, when I beheld the promised procession entering!

First appeared several little children, who came tripping towards me; some with baskets of flowers, and others with vases of odorous waters, or censers of fragrant fire. After them advanced a tall youth of noble port, conspicuous in a scarlet robe, that trailed behind him with graceful dignity. On his head was a plat of palm, in his left hand he held a long wand, and in his right the destined wreath of laurel and myrtle. Behind him came maidens, two by two, and hand in hand. They had each a drapery of white muslin flung negligently round them, and knotted just under the shoulder; while their luxuriant hair floated over their bosoms. The youths came next, habited in flowing vestments of white linen.

The leader approached, and making profound obeisance, took my hand. I rose, bowed, and we proceeded with a slow step out of the room; while the children ran before us, tossing their little censers, scattering pansies, and sprinkling liquid sweets. The nymphs and youths followed in couples, and the company closed the procession. We crossed the hall, ascended the winding staircase, and passed along the corridor, till we reached the ball-room. The folding doors then flew open, as if with wings; and a scene presented itself, which almost baffles description.

It was a spacious apartment, oval in its form, and walled all round with a luxuriant texture of interwoven foliage, kept compact by green lattice-work. Branches of the broad chesnut and arbutus were relieved with lauristinas, acacias, and mountain-ash; while here and there, within the branches, appeared clusters of lamps, that mingled their coloured rays, and poured a flood of lustre on the leaves. The floor was chalked into circular compartments, and each depicted some gentle scene of romance. There I saw Mortimer and his Amanda, Delville and his Cecilia, Valencourt and his Emily. The ceiling was of moss, illuminated with large circles of lamps; and from the centre of each circle, a basket was seen peeping, and half inverted, as if about to shower its ripe fruits and chaplets upon our heads.

At the upper end of the room I beheld a large arbour, elevated on a gradual slope of turf. Its outside was intertwined with jessamines, honeysuckles, and eglantines, tufted with clumps of sunflowers, lilies, hollyhocks, and a thousand other blossoms, and hung with clusters of grapes, and trails of intricate ivy; while all its interior was so studded with innumerable lamps, that it formed a resplendent arch of variegated fire. The seat was a grassy bank, strewn with a profusion of aromatic herbs; and the footstool was a heap of roses. Just from under this footstool, and through the turf, came gushing a little rill, that first tumbled its warbling waters down some rugged stones, and then separating itself to the right and left, ran along a pebbled channel, bordered with flowery banks, till it was lost, at either side, amidst overshadowing branches.

The moment I set foot in the room, a stream of invisible music, as if from above, and softened by distance, came swelling on my enraptured ear. Thrice we circled this enchanted chamber, and trod to the solemn measure. I was amazed, entranced; I felt elevated to the empyrean. I moved with the grandeur of a goddess, and the grace of a vision.

At length my conductor led me across the little rill, into the bower. I sat down, and he stood beside me. The children lay in groups on the grass, while the youths and virgins ranged themselves along the opposite side of the streamlet, and the rest of the company stood behind them.

The master of this august ceremony now waved his wand: the music ceased, all was silent, and he thus began.

'My countrymen and countrywomen.

'Behold your Cherubina; behold the most celebrated woman in our island. Need I recount to you all her accomplishments? Her impassioned sensibility, her exquisite art in depicting the delicate and affecting relations between the beauties of nature, and the deep emotions of the soul? Need I dwell on those elegant adventures, those sorrows, and those horrors, which she has experienced; I might almost say, sought? Oh! no. The whole globe already resounds with them, and their fame will descend to the most remote posterity.

'Need I portray her eloquence, the purity of her style, and the smoothness of her periods? Are not her ancestors illustrious? Are not her manners fascinating? Alas! to this question, some of our hearts beat audible response. Her's is the head of a Sappho, deficient alone in the voluptuous languor, which should characterize the countenance of that enamoured Lesbian.

'To crown her, therefore, as the patroness of arts, the paragon of charms, and the first of heroines, is to gratify our feelings, more than her own; by enabling us to pay a just homage to beauty and to virtue.'

He ceased amidst thunders of applause. I rose;—and in an instant, it was the stillness of death. Then with a timorous, yet ardent air, I thus addressed the assembly.

'My countrymen, my countrywomen!

'I will not thank you, for I cannot. In giving me cause to be grateful, you have taken from me the means of expressing my gratitude, for you have overpowered me.

'How I happen to deserve the beautiful eulogium just pronounced, I am sure I cannot conceive. Till this flattering moment, I never knew that the grove resounds with my praises, that my style is pure, and my head a Sappho's. But unconsciousness of merit is the characteristic of a heroine.

'The gratitude, however, which my words cannot express, my deeds shall evince; and I now pledge myself, that neither rank nor riches (which, from my pursuits, I am peculiarly liable to) shall ever make me unmindful of what I owe to adversity. For, from her, I have acquired all my knowledge of the world, my sympathy, my pensiveness, and my sensibility. Yes, since adversity thus adds to virtue, it must be a virtue to seek adversity.

'England, my friends, is now the depository of all that remains of virtue;—the ark that floats upon the waters of the deluge. But what preserves her virtuous? Her women. And whence arises their purity? From education.

'To you, then, my fair auditory, I would enjoin a diligent cultivation of learning. But oh! beware what books you peruse; for, trust me, some are as injurious as others are salutary. I cannot point out to you the mischievous class, because I have never read them; but indubitably, the most useful are novels and romances. Such as I am, these, these alone have made me. These, by depicting heroines sublimated almost to immateriality, teach the common class of womankind to reach what is uncommon, by striving at what is unattainable; to despise the grovelling follies and idlenesses of the mere worker of samplers, and to contract a taste for that sensibility, whose tear is the dissolution of pearls, whose blush is the sunbeam of the cheek, and whose sigh is more costly than the breeze, that comes laden with oriental frankincense.'

I spoke, and peals of acclamation shook the bower.

The priest of the ceremony now raises the crown on high, then lowers it by slow degrees, and holds it suspended over my head. Letting down my tresses, and folding my hands on my bosom, I throw myself upon my knees, and incline forward to receive it.

I am crowned.

At the same moment, drums, and trumpets, and shouts, burst upon my ear, in a hurricane of triumph. The youths and maidens make obeisance; I rise, press my hand to my heart, and bow deeply. Tears start into my eyes. I feel far above mortality.

Hardly had the tumult subsided when a harp was brought to the bower; and they requested that I would sing and play an improvisatore, like Corinne. What was I to do? for I knew nothing of the harp, but a few chords! In this difficulty, I luckily recollected a heroine, who was educated only by an old steward, and his old wife, in an old castle, with an old lute; and who, notwithstanding, as soon as she stepped into society, played and sang, like angels, by intuition.

I therefore felt quite reassured, and sat to the harp. I struck a few low Lydian notes, and cast a timid glance around me. At first my voice was scarcely louder than a sigh; and my accompaniment was a harmonic chord, swept at intervals. The words came from the moment.

'Where is my blue-eyed chief? said the white-bosomed daughter of Erin, as the wave kissed her foot; and wherefore went he from his weeping maid, to the fight of heroes? She saw a dim form rise before her, like a mist from the valley. Pale grew her cheek, as the blighted leaf in autumn. Your lover, it shrilly shrieked, sleeps among the dead, like a broken thistle amidst dandelions; but his spirit, like the thistly down, has ascended into the skies. The maiden heard; she ran, she flew, she sprang from a rock. The waves closed over her. Peace to the daughter of Erin!'

As I sang 'she ran, she flew,' the workings and tremblings of the minstrel were in unison; while my winged fingers fluttered along the chords, light as a swallow over a little lake, when he touches it with the utmost feather of his pinion. But while I sang, 'peace to the daughter of Erin!' my voice, as it died over the faint vibration of the strings, had all the heart-breaking softness of an Eolian lyre; so woeful was it, so wistful, so wildered. 'Viva! viva!' resounded through the room. At the last cadence, I dropped one arm gently down, and hanging the other on the harp, leaned my languishing head upon it, while my moistened eyes were half closed.

A sudden disturbance at the door roused me from my trance. I looked up, and beheld—what?—Can you imagine what? No, my friend, you could not to the day of judgment. I saw, in short, my great mother come striding towards me, with outspread arms, and calling, 'my daughter, my daughter!' in a voice that might waken the dead.

My heart died within me: down I darted from the bower, and ran for shelter behind Lady Gwyn.

'Give me back my daughter!' vociferated the dreadful woman, advancing close to her ladyship.

'Oh! do no such thing!' whispered I, pulling her ladyship by the sleeve. 'Take half—all my property; but do not be the death of me!'

'What are you muttering there, Miss?' cried my mother, espying me. 'What makes you stand peeping over that wretch's shoulder?'

'Indeed, Ma'am,' stammered I, 'I am—I am taking your part.'

'Who could have presumed to liberate this woman?' cried Lady Gwyn.

'The Condottieri,' said my mother, 'headed by the great Damno Sulphureo Volcanoni.'

'Then you must return to your prison, this moment,' cried Lady Gwyn.

My mother fell on her knees, and began blubbering; while the guests got round, and interceded for her being restored to liberty. I too thought it my duty to say something (my mother all the time sobbing horribly); till, at length, Lady Gwyn consented—for my sake, she said,—to set the poor wretch free; but on this special condition, that there should be no prosecution for false imprisonment.

All matters being amicably adjusted, my mother begged a morsel of meat, as she had not eaten any these ten years. In a few minutes, a small table, furnished with a cold turkey and a decanter of wine, was laid for her in the bower. The moment she perceived it, she ran, and seating herself in the scene of my recent triumph, began devouring with such avidity, that I was thunderstruck. One wing soon went; the second shared the fate of its companion, and now she set about a large slice of the breast.

'What a charming appetite your dear mother has got!' said several of the guests to me. I confessed it, but assured them that inordinate hunger did not run in our family. Her appetite being at last satiated, she next assailed the wine. Glass after glass disappeared with inconceivable rapidity, and every glass went to my heart. 'She will be quite intoxicated!' thought I; while my fears for the hereditary honour of our house overcoming my personal terrors, I had the resolution to steal across, and whisper:

'Mother, if you have any regard for your daughter, and respect for your ancestors, drink no more.'

'No more than this decanter, upon my honour!' said she, applying it to her lips.

At this moment the violins struck up.

'And now,' cried my mother, running down from the bower, 'who is for a dance?'

'I am,' said my friend, the little fop, advancing, and taking her hand.

'Then,' said she, 'we will waltz, if you please.'

Santa Maria!—Waltz!

A circle was cleared, and they began whirling each other round at a frightful rate,—or rather she him; for he was like a plaything in her hands; and had he let go his grasp, I am sure he would have been flung up among the branches, and have stuck there, like King Charles in the oak.

At last, while I was standing, a statue of shame, and wondering how any human being, endowed with a common portion of reason, could act so ridiculous a part, this miserable woman, overcome with wine and waltzing, fell flat upon the floor; and was carried out of the room by four grinning footmen.

I could hold no longer: the character of my family demanded a prompt explanation, and with tears in my eyes, I desired to be heard. Silence was obtained.

'I beseech of this assembly,' said I, 'to acquit me of having hand, act, or part, in the conduct of that unfortunate person. I never even saw her, till I came to this house; and that I may never see her again, I pray heaven. I hate her, I dread her; and I now protest, in the most unequivocal manner, that I do not believe her to be my mother at all. She has no resemblance to the portrait in the gallery; and as she was stark mad, when found in the woods, she perhaps imagined herself my mother; for I am told that mad persons are apt to fancy themselves great people. No, my malignant star ordained us to meet, that she might place me in awkward situations by her vulgarity; just as Mrs. Garnet, the supposed mother of the Beggar Girl, used to place that heroine. I am sure this is the case; nothing can convince me to the contrary; and therefore, I thus publicly renounce, disown, and wash my hands of her, now and for ever.'

The company coincided in my sentiments, and applauded my determination.

Country dancing was then proposed: the men sauntered about the room for partners; the mothers walked their daughters up and down, to shew their paces; and their daughters turned away their heads when they saw their favourites approaching to ask them. Ugliness and diamonds occupied the top of the set; the beauties stood in the centre, and the motley couples came last;—old bachelors with misses of fifteen; and boys, who were glad to be thought men, with antiques, who were sorry to be called maids. Other unfortunates, drest to a pin, yet noticed by nobody, sat protruding the supercilious lip at a distance.

And now the merry maze commenced. But what mutilated steps, what grotesque graces! One girl sprang and sprawled to the terror of every ankle; and with a clear idea of space, shewed that she had no notion of time. Another, not deigning to dance, only moved; while her poor partner was seen helping her in, like a tired jade to the distance post. This bartered elegance for a flicflac; that swam down the set; a third cut her way through it; and a fourth, who, by her longevity, could not be dancing for a husband, appeared, by her earnestness, to be dancing for her life.

All this delighted me highly, for it would shew my graces to the greater advantage. My partner was the gentleman who had crowned me; and now, when our turn to dance down came, a general whisper among the spectators, and their sudden hurry towards me, proved that much was expected from my performance. I would not disappoint them for worlds; besides, it was incumbent on me to stamp a marked dissimilarity between my supposed mother, and myself, in every thing; and to call forth respect and admiration, as much as she had excited derision and contempt.

And now, with my right foot behind, and the point of it but just touching the ground, I leaned forward on my left, and stood as if in act to ascend from this vale of tears to regions of interminable beatitude.

The next moment the music gave the signal, and I began. Despising the figure of the common country-dance, I meandered through all the intricacies of the dance of Ariadne; imitating in my circular and oblique motions the harmonious movement of the spheres; and resembling, in my light and playful form, the Horœ of Bathycles, as they appeared in the Temple of Amycla. Sometimes with a rapid flight, and glowing smile, I darted, like a herald Iris, through the mazes of the set; sometimes assuming the dignity of a young Diana, I floated in a swimming languishment; and sometimes, like a pastoral nymph of Languedoc, capriciously did I bend my head on one side, and dance up insidious. What a Hebe!

I happened not to see my partner from the time I began till I had ended; but when panting and playful, I flew like a lapwing, to my seat, he followed, and requested that I would accept the assurances of his high admiration.

Soon afterwards, waltzing was introduced.

'You have already imitated Ida's dancing,' said he. 'Will you now imitate Charlotte's, and allow me, like Werter, to hold in my arms the most lovely of women; to fly with her, like the wind, and lose sight of every other object?'

I consented; he led me forth, and clasping my waist, began the circuitous exercise of waltzing. Round and round we flew, and swifter and swifter; till my head grew quite giddy. Lamps, trees, dresses, faces, all seemed to be shattered and huddled together, and sent whisking round the room in a vortex.

But, oh, my friend, how shall I find language to describe the calamitous termination of an evening so propitious in its commencement? I blush as I write it, till the reflected crimson dyes my paper. For in the midst of my rotatory motion, while heaven seemed earth, and earth seemed heaven; the zone, on which all my attire depended, and by which it was all confined, on a sudden burst asunder, and in the next whirl, more than half of my dress dropped at my feet! Another revolution and I had acted Diana to fifty Acteons; but I shrieked, and extricating myself from my partner, sank on the floor, amidst the wreck of my drapery. The ladies ran, ranged themselves round me, and cast a mantle over my half-revealed charms. I was too much shocked, and indeed too giddy to move; so they lifted me between them, and bore me, in slow procession, out of the room. It was the funeral of modesty; but the pall was supported by tittering malice.

I hurried into bed, and cried myself asleep.

I cannot think, much less write of this disaster, with common fortitude. I wonder whether Thompson's Musidora could be considered a sufficient precedent, or at least a palliative parallel? If not, and that my biographer records it, I am undone.

Adieu.

89

Yesterday Lady Gwyn took me, at my particular request, to visit Monkton Castle, an old ruin, within three miles of us; and as it forms part of that property which she holds at present, it is mine to all intents and purposes.

The door-way was stopped up with stones, so that I could not take a survey of its interior; but outside it looked desolate enough. I mean, at some future period, to furnish it like Udolpho, and other castles of romance, and to reside there during the howling months.

After dinner her ladyship went to superintend the unpacking of some beautiful china, which had just arrived from London; and I was left alone on the sofa. Evening had already begun to close: a delicious indolence thrilled through my limbs, and I felt all that lassitude and vacuity which the want of incident ever creates.

'Were there even some youth in the house,' thought I, 'who would conceive an unhappy attachment for me;—had her ladyship but a persecuting son, what scenes might happen! Suppose at this moment the door were to be thrown open, and he to enter, with a quick step, and booted and spurred. He starts on seeing me. Never had I looked so lovely. 'Heavens!' murmurs he, "tis a divinity!' then suddenly recollecting himself, he advances with a respectful bow. 'Pardon this intrusion,' says he; 'but I—really I—.' I rise, and colouring violently, mutter, without looking at him: 'I wonder where her ladyship can be?' But as I am about to pass him, he snatches my hand, and leading me back to the sofa, says:—'Suffer me to detain you a moment. This occasion, so long desired, I cannot bring myself to relinquish. Prevented by the jealous care of a too fond mother, from appearing before you, I have sought and found a thousand opportunities, on the stairs—in the garden—in the shrubbery—to behold those charms. Fatal opportunities! for they have robbed me of my peace for ever! Yes, charming Cherubina, you have undone me. That airy, yet dignified form; those mild, yet sparkling eyes; those lips, more delicious than the banquet of the gods——' 'Really, Signor,' says I, in all the pleasing simplicity of maiden embarrassment, 'this language is as improper for me to hear as for you to express.' 'It is, it is improper,' cries he, with animation, 'for it is inadequate.' 'Yes,' says I 'inadequate to the respect I deserve as the guest of your mother.' 'Ah!' exclaims he, 'why should the guest imitate the harshness of the hostess?' 'That she may not,' says I, 'countenance the follies of the son. Signor, I desire you will unhand me.' 'Never!' cries he; 'never, till you say you pity me. O, my Cherubina; O, my soul's idol!' and he drops upon his knee, and grasps my hand; when behold, the door opens, and Lady Gwyn appears at it! Never were astonishment and dismay equal to her's. 'Godfrey, Godfrey,' says she, 'is this the conduct that I requested of you? This, to seek clandestine interviews, where I had prohibited even an open acquaintance? And for thee, fair unfortunate,' turning towards me, with that mild look, which cuts more than a thousand sarcasms; 'for thee, lovely frail one, thou must seek some other asylum.' Her sweet eyes swim in tears. I fling myself at her feet. 'I am innocent,' I cry, 'innocent as the little fawn that frisks itself to repose by the bubbling fountain.' She smiles incredulous. 'Come,' says she, taking my hand, 'let me lead you to your apartment.' 'Stay, in mercy stay!' cries Godfrey, rushing between us and the door. She waves him aside. I reach my room. Nothing can console me. I am all despair. In a few minutes the maid taps at my door, with a slip of paper from Godfrey. 'Oh, Cherubina,' it says, 'how my heart is torn for you! As you value your fame, perhaps your life, meet me to-night, at twelve, in the shrubbery.' After a long struggle, I resolve to meet him. 'Tis twelve, the winds are abroad, the shower descends. I fling on something, and steal into the shrubbery. I find him there before me. He thanks me ten thousand, thousand times for my kindness, my condescension; and by degrees, leads me into the avenue, where I see a chaise in waiting. I shrink back; he prays, implores; and at length, snatching me in his arms, is about to force me into the vehicle, when on a sudden—'Hold, villain!' cries a voice. It is the voice of Stuart! I shriek, and drop to the ground. The clashing of swords resounds over my contested body, and I faint. On recovering, I find myself in a small, but decent chamber, with an old woman and a beautiful girl watching over me. 'St. Catherine be praised,' exclaims the young peasant, 'she comes to herself.' 'Tell me,' I cry, 'is he murdered?' 'The gentleman is dead, sure enough, miss,' says the woman. I laugh frantic, and point my finger. 'Ha! look yonder,' I cry; 'see his mangled corpse, mildly smiling, even in death. See, they fight; he falls.—Barbarous Godfrey! valiant, generous, unfortunate Stuart! And hark, hear you that! 'Tis the bell tolling, tolling, tolling!' During six weeks I continue in this dreadful brain-fever. Slowly I recover. A low melancholy preys upon me, and I am in the last stage of a consumption. But though I lose my bloom, illness touches my features with something more than human. One evening, I had got my chair on the green before the door, and was watching the sun as he set in a blaze of gold. 'And oh!' exclaimed I, 'soon must I set like thee, fair luminary;—when I am interrupted by a stifled sigh, just behind me. I turn. Heaven and earth! who should be leaning over me, with looks of unutterable love, but—Stuart! In an instant, I see him, I shriek, I run, I leap into his arms.——

Unfortunate leap; for it wakened me from a delicious reverie, and I found myself in the arms,—not of Stuart,—but of the old butler! Down we both came, and broke in pieces a superb china vase, which he was just bringing into the room.

'What will my lady say to this?' cried he, rising and collecting the fragments.

'She will smile with ineffable grace,' answered I, 'and make a moral reflection on the instability of sublunary things.'

He shook his head, and went on with his work of affliction; while I hastened to the glass, where I found my face flushed from my reverie, my hair dishevelled, and my long eyelashes wet with tears. I perceived too that my dress had got a terrible rent by my fall.

Hardly had I recomposed myself, when her ladyship returned, and called for tea.

'How did you tear your robe, my love?' said she.

'By a fall that I got just now,' replied I. 'Sure never was such an unfortunate fall!'

'Nay, child,' said she, rallying me, 'though a martyr to the tender sensibilities, you must not be a victim to torn muslin.'

'I am extremely distressed, however,' said I.

'But why so?' cried she. 'It was an accident, and all of us are awkward at times. Life has too many serious miseries to admit of vexation about trifles.'

'There now!' cried I, with delight. 'I declare I told the butler, when I broke the china vase, that you would make a moral reflection.'

'Broke the—— Oh! mercy, have you broken my beautiful china vase?'

'Smashed it to atoms,' answered I, in a tone of the most assuasive sweetness.

'You did?' exclaimed she, in a voice that stunned me. 'And pray, how dared you go near it? How dared you even look at it? You, who are not fit company for crockery, much less china;—a crazed creature, that I brought into my house to divert my guests. You a title? You a beauty?'

'Dear Lady Gwyn,' said I, 'do be calm under this calamity. Trust me life has too many serious miseries to admit of vexation about trifles.'

Her ladyship rose, with her cheeks inflamed, and her eyes glittering.

I ran out of the room, in much terror; then up stairs, and into the nearest bed-chamber. It happened to be her ladyship's; and this circumstance struck me as most providential; for, in her present mood, she would probably compel me to quit the house; so that I could never have another opportunity of ransacking her caskets and cabinets, for memorials of my birth.

I therefore began the search; but in the midst of it was interrupted by hearing a small voice cry, 'get out!'

Much amazed, I looked up, and perceived her ladyship's favourite parrot in its cage.

'Get out!' said the parrot.

'I will let thee out, cost what it will,' cried I.

So with much sensibility, and indeed, very little spleen, I took the bird, and put it out at the window.

After having accurately examined several drawers, I found a casket in one of them; opened it, and beheld within (O delightful sight!) a miniature set round with inestimable diamonds, and bearing a perfect resemblance to the portrait in the gallery,—face, attitude, attire, every thing!

'Relic of my much injured house!' exclaimed I, depositing the picture in my bosom.' Image of my sainted mother, never will I part with thee!'

'What are you doing in my room?' cried Lady Gwyn, as she burst into it. 'How is this? All my dresses about the floor! my drawers, my casket open!—And, as I live, here is the miniature gone! Why you graceless little thing, are you robbing me?'

'Madam,' answered I, 'that miniature belongs to my family; I have recovered it at last; and let me see who will dare take it from me.'

'You are more knave than fool,' said her ladyship: 'give it back this instant, or, on my honour, I will expose you to the servants.'

'What is the use of bullying?' said I. 'Sure you are ruined should this swindling affair come to be known, not that I would, for the world, hang your ladyship;—far from it,—but then your character will be blasted. Ah! Lady Gwyn, where is your hereditary honour? where is your prudence? where is your dignity?'

'Where is my parrot?' shrieked her ladyship.

'Ranging the radiant air!' exclaimed I—'inhaling life, and fragrance, and freedom amidst the clouds! I let it out at the window.'

Her ladyship ran towards me, but I passed her, and made the best of my way down stairs; while she followed, calling, stop thief! Too well I knew and rued the dire expression; nor stopped an instant, but hurried out of the house—through the lawn—down the avenue—into a hay-field;—the servants in hot pursuit. Not a moment was to be lost: a drowning man, you know, will grasp at straws, and I crept for refuge under a heap of hay.

But whether they found me there, or how long I remained, or what has become of me since, or what is likely to become of me hereafter, you shall learn in my next.

Adieu.

LETTER XXXIV

I remained in my disagreeable situation till night had closed, and the pursuit appeared over. I then rose, and walked through the fields, without any settled intention. Terror was now succeeded by bitter indignation at the conduct of Lady Gwyn, who had dared to drive me from my own house, and vilify me as a common thief. Insupportable insult! Unparalleled degradation! Was there no revenge? no remedy?

Like a rapid ray from heaven, a thought at once simple and magnificent shot through my brain, and made my very heart bound with transport. When I name Monkton Castle, need I tell you the rest? Need I tell you that I determined to seize on that antique abode of my ancestors, to fortify it against assaults, to procure domestics and suitable furniture for it, and to reside there, the present rival, and the future victress of the vile Lady Gwyn? Let her dispossess me if she dare, or if she can; for I have heard that possession is a great number of points of the law in one's favour.

As to fitting up the castle, that will be quite an easy matter; for the tradespeople of London willingly give credit for any amount to a personage of rank like me; and therefore I have nothing more to do than make some friend there bespeak furniture in my name.

It appeared to me that Jerry Sullivan was the most eligible person I could select; so now, a light heart making a light foot, I tripped back to the road, and took my way towards Monkton Castle, for the purpose of procuring an asylum in some cottage near it, and writing a letter of instructions to Jerry.

It was starlight, and I had walked almost three miles, when a little girl with a bundle of sticks on her back overtook me, and began asking alms. In the midst of her supplications, we came to the hut where she lived, and I followed her into it, with the hope of getting a night's lodging there, or at least a direction to one.

In a room, comfortless, with walls of smoked mud, I found a wrinkled and decrepit beldame, and two smutty children, holding their hands over a few faded embers. I begged permission to rest myself for a short time; the woman, after looking at me keenly, consented, and I sat down. I then entered into conversation, represented myself as a wandering stranger in distress, and inquired if I had any chance of finding a lodging about the neighbourhood. The woman assured me that I had not, and on perceiving me much disconcerted at the disappointment, coarsely, but cordially, offered me her hut for the night. I saw I had nothing for it but to remain there; so the fire was replenished, some brown bread and sour milk (the last of their store) produced, and while we sat round it, I requested of the poor woman to let me know what had reduced her to such distress.

She told me, with many tears and episodes, that her daughter and son-in-law, who had supported her, died about a month ago, and left these children behind, without any means of subsistence, except what they could procure from the charitable.

All their appearances corroborated this account, for famine had set its meagre finger on their faces. I wished to pity them, but their whining, their dirtiness, and their vulgarity, disgusted more than interested me. I nauseated the brats, and abhorred the haggard hostess. How it happens, I know not, but the misery that looks alluring on paper is almost always repulsed in real life. I turn with distaste from a ragged beggar, or a decayed tradesman, while the recorded sorrows of a Belfield or a Rushbrook draw tears of pity from me as I read.

At length we began to think of rest. The children gave me their pallet: I threw myself upon it without undressing, and they slept on some straw with a blanket over them.

In the morning we presented a most dismal group. Not a morsel had we for breakfast, nor the means of obtaining any. The poor cripple, who had expected some assistance from me, sat grunting in a corner; the children whimpered and shivered; and I, with more elegance, but not less misery, chaunted a matin to the Virgin.

I then began seriously to consider what mode of immediate subsistence I ought to adopt; and at last I hit upon a most pleasing and judicious plan. As some days must elapse between my writing to Jerry Sullivan and his coming down (for I mean to have him here, if possible), and as the cottage is within a short distance from the castle, I have resolved to remain with my hostess till he shall arrive, and to go forth every day in the character of a beggar-girl. Like another Rosa, I will earn my bread by asking alms. My simple and imploring address, my half-suppressed sigh, my cheek yet traced with the recent tear, all will be irresistible. Even the shrivelled palm of age will expand at my supplication, and the youths, offering compliments with eleemosynary silver, will call me the lovely vagabond, or the mendicant angel. Thus my few days of beggary will prove quite delightful; and oh, how sweet, when those are over, to reward and patronize, as Lady of the Castle, those hospitable cottagers who have pitied and sheltered me as the beggar-girl.

My first step was writing to Jerry Sullivan; and I fortunately found the stump of a pen, some thick ink, and coarse paper, in the cottage. This was my letter.

'Honest Jerry,

'Since I saw you last, I have established all my claims, and am now the Lady Cherubina de Willoughby, the true and illustrious mistress of Gwyn Castle, Monkton Castle, and other estates of uncommon extent and value. Now, Jerry, as I am convinced that you feel grateful for the services, however trivial, which I have done you, I know you will be happy at an opportunity of obliging me in return.

'Will you then execute some commissions for me? Meaning to make Monkton Castle (which is uninhabited at present) my residence, I wish to furnish it according to the style of the times it was built in. You must, therefore, bespeak, at the best shops, such articles as I shall now enumerate.

'First. Antique tapestry sufficient to furnish one entire wing.

'Second. Painted glass enriched with armorial bearings.

'Third. Pennons and flags, stained with the best old blood;—Feudal if possible.

'Fourth. Black feathers, and cloaks for my liveries.

'Fifth. An old lute, or lyre, or harp.

'Sixth. Black hangings, curtains, and a velvet pall.

'Seventh. A warder's trumpet.

'Eighth. A bell for the portal.

'Besides these, I shall want antique chairs, tables, beds, and, in a word, all the casts-off of castles that you can lay hands upon.

'You must also get a handsome barouche, and four horses; and by mentioning my name (the Lady Cherubina de Willoughby, of Monkton Castle), and by shewing this letter, no shopkeeper or mechanic will refuse you credit for anything. Tell them I will pass my receipts as soon as the several articles arrive.

'I have now to make a proposal, which, I hope and trust, will meet with your approbation. Your present business does not appear to be prosperous: all the offices in my castle are still unoccupied, and as I have the highest opinion of your discretion and honesty, the situation of warden (a most ostensible one) is at your service. The salary is two hundred a-year: consider of it.

'At all events, I do beseech of you to come down, as soon as you can, on receipt of this letter, and remain a few days, for the purpose of assisting me in my regulations.

'You might travel in the barouche, and bring some of the smaller articles with you. Pray be here in three days at farthest.

'Cherubina de Willoughby.

'*Monkton Castle.*'

I now began to think that I might, and should summon other friends, on this important occasion; and accordingly I wrote a few lines to Higginson.

'Dear Sir,

'Intending to take immediate possession of Monkton Castle, which has devolved to me by right of lineal descent; and wishing, in imitation of ancient times, for a wild and enthusiastic minstrel, as part of my household, I have to acquaint you, that if you should think such an office eligible, I shall be happy to place you in it, and to recompense your poetical services with an annual stipend of two hundred pounds.

'Should this proposal prove acceptable, be so good as to call on my trusty servant, Jerry Sullivan, in St. Giles's, and accompany him down in my barouche.

'Cherubina de Willoughby.

'*Monkton Castle.*'

I then penned a billet to Montmorenci; ah, ask not why, but pity me. Silly Cherubina! and yet, mark how her burning pen can write ice.

'My Lord,

'Pardon the trouble I am about giving you, but as I mean to reside, for the future, in one of my castles (my birth and pretensions having already been acknowledged by Lady Gwyn), I wish to secure the parchment and picture that I left at my former lodgings at Drury Lane.

'Will you, my lord, have the goodness to transmit them, by some trusty hand, to Jerry Sullivan, the woollen-draper in St. Giles's, who will convey them to me at Monkton Castle.

'With sentiments of respect and esteem,

'I have the honour to be,

'My Lord,

'Your lordship's most obedient,

'And most humble servant,

'Cherubina de Willoughby.

'*Monkton Castle.*'

Now this is precisely the formal sort of letter which a heroine sometimes indites to her lover: he cannot, for the soul of him, tell why; so down he comes, all distracted in a postchaise, and makes such a dishevelled entrance, as melts her heart in an instant, and the scene ends with his arm round her waist.

Adieu.

LETTER XXXV

As I was now about to go begging, I thought it necessary to look like a beggar; so I dressed myself in a tattered gown, cap, and cloak, that had belonged to the deceased daughter of my hostess. Then placing my mother's portrait in my bosom, I sallied forth, and took the road to the neighbouring village.

Being Sunday, the rustics looked trim and festive, the nymphs and youths frolicked along, the grandsires sat at their doors, the sun was shining; all things smiled but the miserable Cherubina.

At length I reached the village, and deposited my letters for the post. The church, imbosomed in trees, stood at a little distance. The people were at prayers, and as I judged that they would soon be dismissed, I placed myself at the sacred gate, as an auspicious station for the commencement of my supplicatory career.

In a short time they began to leave the church.

'One penny for the poor starving girl,' said I.

'How are you? How are you? How are you?' was gabbled on all sides.

'One penny,—one penny,—Oh, one penny!' softly faltered I.

It was the cooing of a dove amidst the chattering of magpies.

'And who was that stranger in the next pew?' said one lady.

'One penny for the love of——'

'She seemed to think herself too pretty to pray,' said another.

'One penny for the——'

'Perhaps motion does not become her lips,' said another.

'One penny for the love of charity.'

But they had gotten into their carriages.

'If youth, innocence, and distress can touch your hearts,' said I, following some gentlemen down the road, 'pity the destitute orphan, the hungry vagrant, the most injured and innocent of her sex. Gentlemen, good gentlemen, kind gentlemen——.'

'Go to hell,' said they.

'There is for you, sweetheart,' cried a coarse voice from behind, while a halfpenny jingled at my foot. I turned to thank my benefactor, and found that he was a drunken man in the stocks.

Disgusted and indignant at the failure of my first attempt, I hurried out of the village, and strayed along, addressing all I met, but all appeared too gay to pity misery. Hour after hour I passed in fruitless efforts, now walking, now sitting; till at length day began to close, and fatigue and horrid hunger were enfeebling my limbs.

In a piteous condition, I determined to turn my steps back towards the cottage; for night was already blackening the blue hemisphere, the mountainous clouds hung low, and the winds piped the portentous moan of a coming hurricane. By the little light that still remained, I saw a long avenue on my left, which, I thought, might lead to some hospitable place of shelter; and I began, as well as the gloom of the trees would permit, to grope my way through it.

After much labour and many falls, I came to an opening, and as I saw no house, I still walked straight forward. By this time the storm had burst upon my head with tremendous violence, and it was with difficulty that I could keep my feet.

At last I fancied I could perceive a building in front, and I bent my steps towards it. As I drew nearer, I found my way sometimes obstructed by heaps of stones, or broken columns, and I concluded that I was approaching some prodigious castle, where I should be sure to find shelter, horror, owls, and one of my near relations. I therefore hastened towards it, and soon my extended hands touched the structure. My heart struck a throb of joy, and I began to feel along the wall for some ruined portal or archway.

Hardly had I moved ten paces, when my groping hands plunged into unresisting air: I stopped a moment, then entered through the vacuity, and to my great comfort, found myself under immediate shelter.

This then, I guessed, was the great hall of the castle, and I prepared my mind for the most terrible things.

I had not advanced three yards, when I paused in much terror; for I thought I heard a stir just beside me. Again all was still, and I ventured forward. I now fancied that I heard a gentle breathing; and at the same instant I struck my foot against something, which, with a sudden movement, tripped up my heels, and down I came, shrieking and begging for mercy; while a frightful bustle arose all round me,—such passing and repassing, rustling and rushing, that I gave myself over for lost.

'Oh, gentlemen banditti!' cried I, 'spare my persecuted life, and I will never, never betray you!'

They did not answer a syllable, but retired to some distance, where they held a horrid silence.

In a few minutes, I heard steps outside, and two persons entered the building.

'This shelters us well enough,' said one of them.

'Curse on the storm,' cried the other, 'it will hinder any more of them from coming out to-night. However we have killed four already, and, please goodness, not one will be alive on the estate this day month.'

Oh, Biddy, how my soul sickened at the shocking reflection, that four of a family were already murdered in cold blood, and that the rest were to share the same fate in a month!

Unable to contain myself, I muttered, 'Mercy upon me, mercy upon me!'

'Did you hear that?' whispered one of the men.

'I did,' said the other. 'Off with us this moment!' and off they both ran.

I too determined to quit this nest of horrors, for my very life appeared in danger; so, rising, I began to grope my way towards the door, when I fell over something that lay on the ground, and as I put out my hand, I touched (Oh, horrible!) a dead, cold, damp human face. Instantly the thought struck me that this was one of the four whom the ruffians had murdered, and I flung myself from it, with a shiver of horror; but in doing so, laid my hand on another face; while a faint gleam of lightning that flashed at the moment shewed me two bodies, pale, ghastly, naked, and half covered with straw.

I started up, screaming, and made a desperate effort to reach the door; but just as I was darting out of it, I found my shoulder seized with a ferocious grasp.

'I have caught one of them,' cried the person. 'Fetch the lantern.'

'I am innocent of the murder!' cried I. 'I swear to you that I am. They did not fall by my dagger, I can assure you.'

'Who? what murder?' cried he. 'Hollo, help! here is a murder committed.'

'Not by me!' cried I. 'Not by me, not by me! No, no, no, my hands are unstained with their blood.'

And now a lantern being brought, I perceived several servants in liveries, who first examined my features, and then dragged me back into the building, while they searched there for some poachers, whom they had been way-laying when they found me. The building! And what was the building, think you? Why nothing more than the shell of an unfinished house,—a mere modern morsel of a tasteless temple! And what were the banditti who had knocked me down, think you? Why nothing more than a few harmless sheep, that now lay huddled together in a corner! And what were the two corpses, think you? Why nothing more than two Heathen statues for the little temple!—And the ruffians that talked of their having killed, and having to kill, were only the poachers, who had killed four hares! Here then was the whole mystery developed, and a great deal of good fright gone for nothing.

However, some trouble still remained to me. The servants, swearing that I was either concerned with the poachers, or in some murder, dragged me down a shrubbery, till we reached a large mansion. We then entered a lighted hall: one of them went to call his master, and after a few minutes, an elderly gentleman, with a troop of young men and women at his heels, came out of a parlour.

'Is that the murderess? What a young murderess! I never saw a murderess before!' was whispered about by the ladies.

'What murder is this you were talking of, young woman?' said the gentleman to me.

'I will tell you with pleasure,' answered I. 'You must know that I am a wandering beggar-girl, without home, parents, or friends; and when the storm began, I ran, for shelter, into the Temple of Taste, as your servants called it. So, thinking it a castle, and some sheep which threw me down, banditti, and a couple of statues, corpses, of course it was quite natural for me to suppose, when two men entered, and began to talk of having killed something, that they meant these very corpses. Was it not natural now? And so that is the plain and simple narrative of the whole affair.'

To my great surprise, a general burst of laughter ran round the hall.

'Sheep banditti, and statues corpses. Dear me,—Bless me—Well to be sure!' tittered the misses.

'Young woman,' said the gentleman, 'your incoherent account inclines me to think you concerned in some atrocious transaction, which I must make it my business to discover.'

'I am sure,' said a young lady, 'she carries the gallows in her face.'

''Tis so pretty a gallows,' said a young gentleman, 'that I wish I were hanging upon it.'

'Fie brother,' said the young lady, 'how can you talk so to a murderess?'

'And how can you talk so,' cried I, 'before you know me to be a murderess? It is not just, it is not generous, it is not feminine. Men impelled by love, may deprive our sex of virtue; but we ourselves, actuated by rancorous, not gentle impulses, rob each other of character.'

'Oh! indeed, you have done for yourself now,' said the young lady. 'That sentence of morality has settled you completely.'

'Then I presume you do not admire morality,' said I.

'Not from the lips of a low wretch like you,' said she.

'Know, young woman,' cried I, 'that the current which runs through these veins is registered in hereditary heraldry.'

The company gave a most disgusting laugh.

'It is,' cried I, 'I tell you it is. I tell you I am of the blood noble.'

'Oh blood!' squeaked a young gentleman.

What wonder that I forgot my prudence amidst these indignities? Yes, the proud spirit of my ancestors swelled my heart, all my house stirred within me, and the blood of the De Willoughbys rose into my face, as I drew the magnificent picture from my bosom, pointed a quivering finger at it, and exclaimed:

'Behold the portrait of my titled mother!'

'See, see!' cried the girls crowding round. ''Tis covered all over with diamonds!'

'I flatter myself it is,' said I. 'There is proof irrefragable for you!'

'Proof enough to hang you I fancy!' cried the old gentleman, snatching it out of my hand. 'So now, my lady, you must march to the magistrate.' I wept, knelt, entreated, all was in vain: his son, the young man who had paid my face the compliment, took charge of my person, and accompanied by the servant who had seized me, set off with me to the magistrate's.

During our walk, he tried to discover how I had got possession of the picture, but I was on my guard, and merely replied that time would tell my innocence. On a sudden, he desired the servant to go back for an umbrella, and take it to the magistrate's after him.

The man having left us:

'Now,' said the 'squire, 'whether you are a pilferer of pictures I know not, but this I know, that you are a pilferer of hearts, and that I am determined to keep you in close custody, till you return mine, which you have just stolen. To be plain, I will extricate you from your present difficulty, and conceal you in a cottage just at hand, if you will allow me to support and visit you. You understand me.'

The blood gushed into my cheeks as he spoke; but however indignant I felt at the proposal, I likewise felt that it would be prudent to dissemble; and as other heroines in similar predicaments do not hesitate to hint that they will compromise their honours, I too determined to give my tempter some hope; and thus make him my friend till I could extricate myself from this emergency.

I therefore replied that I trusted he would not find me deficient in gratitude.

'Thank you, love,' said he. 'And now here is the cottage.'

He then tapped at a door: an elderly woman opened it, and within I perceived a young woman, with a bold, but handsome face, hastily adjusting her cap at a glass.

'I have brought a wretched creature,' said he, 'whom I found starving on the road. Pray take care of her, and give her some refreshment. You must also contrive a bed for her.'

The women looked earnestly at me, and then significantly at each other.

'She shall have no bed in my house,' said the elder, 'for I warrant this is the hussey who has been setting you against poor Susan, in order to get you yourself, and telling you lies about Tommy Hicks's visiting here—poor girl!'

'Ay, and Bob Saunders,' cried the daughter.

'Sweet innocent!' cried the mother. 'And the three Hawkins's,' cried the daughter.

'Tender lamb!' cried the mother, 'and a girl too that never looked at mortal man but the 'squire.'

'And John Mullins, and Jacob Jones, and Patrick O'Brien,' cried the daughter.

'Think of that!' cried the mother.

'Yes, think of that!' cried the daughter. 'Patrick O'Brien! the broad-shouldered abominable man! Oh! I will cut my throat—I will—so I will!'

'Alas!' said I, 'behold the fatal effects of licentious love. Here is a girl, whom your money, perhaps, allured from the paths of virtue.'

'Oh! no,' cried Susan, 'it was his honour's handsome face, and his fine words, so bleeding and so sore, and he called me an angel above the heavens!'

'Yes,' said I, 'it is the tenderness of youth, the smile of joy, the blush of innocence, which kindle the flame of the seducer; and yet these are what he would destroy. It is the heart of sensibility which he would engage, and yet in that heart he would plant every rankling pang, every bitter misery. Detestable passion! which accomplishes the worst of purposes, through the medium of the best and sweetest affections. She whose innocent mind ascribes to others the motives that actuate itself, she who confides, because she would not deceive, she who has a tear for real grief, and who melts at the simulated miseries of her lover, she soonest falls a sacrifice to his arts; while the cold vestal, who goes forth into the world callous to feeling, and armed with austerity, repulses his approaches with indignation, and calls her prudence virtue.'

The young man gazed on me with surprise, and the mother had come closer; but Susan was peeping at her face in the glass.

'Look on that beautiful girl before you,' cried I. 'Heaven itself is not brighter than her brow; the tints of the morning cannot rival her blushes.'

Susan held down her head, but cast an under glance at the 'squire.

'Such is she now,' continued I, 'but too soon you may behold her pale, shivering, unsteady of step, and hoarse with nocturnal curses, one of those unhappy thousands, who nightly strew our streets with the premature ruins of dilapidated beauty.'

'Yes, look at her, look at her!' cried the mother, who flushing even through her wrinkles, and quivering in every limb, now rushed towards her daughter, and snatching off her cap, bared her forehead. 'Look at her! she was once my lovely pride, the blessing of my heart; and see what he has now made her for me; while I, miserable as I am, must wink at her guilt, that I may save her from disgrace and ruin!'

'Oh! then,' cried I, turning to the 'squire, 'while still some portion of her fame remains, fly from her, fly for ever!'

'I certainly mean to do so,' replied he, 'so pray make your mind easy. You see, Susan, by this young woman's sentiments, that she cannot be what you suspected her.'

'And I am convinced, Susan,' said I, 'that you feel grateful for the pains I have taken to reclaim the 'squire from a connection so fatal to you both.'

'I am quite sure I do,' sobbed Susan, 'and I will pray for your health and happiness ever while I live. So, dear Miss, since I must lose him, I hope you will coax him to leave me some money first; not that I ever valued him for his money, but you know I could not see my mother go without her tea o'nights.'

'Amiable creature!' cried I. 'Yes, I will intercede for you.'

'My giving you money,' said the 'squire, 'will depend on my finding, when I return to-morrow morning, that you have treated this girl well to-night.'

'I will treat her like a sister,' said Susan.

The 'squire now declared that he must be gone; then taking me aside, 'I shall see you early to-morrow,' whispered he, 'and remove you to a house about a mile hence, and I will tell my father that you ran away. Meantime, continue to talk virtue, and these people will think you a saint.'

He then bade us all good-night, and departed.

Instantly I set my wits at work, and soon hit upon a plan to accomplish my escape. I told the women that I had an old mother, about a mile from the cottage, who was almost starving; and that if I could procure a little silver, and a loaf of bread, I would run to her hut with the relief, and return immediately.

To describe the kind solicitude, the sweet goodnature that mother and daughter manifested, in loading me with victuals and money, were impossible. Suffice it, that they gave me half-a-crown, some bread, tea, and sugar; and Susan herself offered to carry them; but this I declined; and now, with a secret sigh at the probability that I might never see them again, I left their house, and hastened towards the cottage of the poor woman. Having reached it, I made the hungry inhabitants happy once more, while I solaced myself with some tea, and the pleasing reflection, that I had brought comfort to the distressed, and had reclaimed a deluded girl from ruin and infamy.

Adieu,

LETTER XXXVI

After my last letter, I spent two tedious days in employments that I now blush to relate;—no less than doing all the dirty work of the cottage, such as sweeping the room, kindling the fire, cooking the victuals; and trying, by dint of comb and soap, to make cherubs of the children. What bewitched me, I cannot conceive, for the humanity of other heroines is ever clean, elegant, and fit for the reader. They give silver and tears in abundance, but they never descend to the bodily charity of working, like wire-drawers, for withered old women and brats with rosy noses. I can only say, in vindication of myself, that those who sheltered me were poor and helpless themselves, and that they deserved some recompense on my part for their hospitality to me. So you must not condemn me totally; for I do declare to you, that I would much rather have relieved them with my purse, and soothed them with my sympathy, than have fried their herrings and washed their faces.

At the same time, take notice, I was not totally forgetful of my nobler destiny; for I dedicated part of this period to the composition of a poem, which I reserve for my memoirs. My biographer can say that it was suggested by the story of Susan; and even if it should still appear to be somewhat forced into my book, I would rather have this the case, than suffer posterity to go without it altogether. Here it is.

CAROLINE

Beneath a thatch, where gadding woodbine flower'd,
About the lattice and the porch embower'd,
An aged widow lived, whose calm decline,
Clung on one hope, her lovely Caroline.
Her lovely Caroline, in virtue blest,
As morning snow, was spotless and unprest.
Her tresses unadorn'd a braid controll'd,
Her pastoral russet knew no civic gold.
In either cheek an eddying dimple play'd,
And blushes flitted with a rosy shade.
Her airy step seem'd lighting from the sky,
And joy and frolic sparkled in her eye.
Yet would she weep at sorrows not her own,
And love foredoom'd her heart his panting throne.
For her the rustics strove a homely grace,
Clipped their redundant locks, and smooth'd their pace;
Lurk'd near her custom'd path, in trimmest guise,
And talk'd the simple praises of her eyes.
But fatal hour, when she, by swains unmov'd,
Beheld the master of the vale, and loved.

Long had he tempted her reserve in vain,
Till one luxuriant eve that sunn'd the plain;
On the bent herbage, where a gushing brook,
Blue harebells and the tufted violet shook;
Where hung umbrageous branches overhead,
And the rain'd roses lay in fragments red,
He found the slumbering maid. Prophane he press'd
Her virgin lip, then first by man carest.
She starts, and like a ruddy cloud bestrewn,
At brake of morning, o'er the paly moon;
Or as on Alpine cliffs, a wounded doe
Sheds all its purple life upon the snow;
So the maid blushes, while her humble eyes
Fear from a knot of primroses to rise;
And mute she sits, affecting to repair
The discomposed meanders of her hair.
Need I his arts unfold? The accomplish'd guile
That glosses poisonous words with gilded smile?
The tear suborned, the tongue complete to please;
Eyes ecstasied, idolatry of knees?
These and his oaths I pass. Enough to tell,
The virgin listen'd, and believ'd, and fell.
And now from home maternal long decoy'd
She dwells with him midst pleasures unenjoy'd;
Till the sad tidings that her parent dear
To grief had died a victim reach her ear.
Pale with despair, 'At least, at least,' she cries,
'Stretch'd on her ashes, let me close these eyes.
Short shelter need the village now bestow,
Ere by her sacred grave they lay me low.'
Then, without nurture or repose, she hastes
Her journey homeward over rocks and wastes;
Till, as her steps a hill familiar gain,
Bursts on her filling eyes her native plain.
She pants, expands her arms, 'Ah, peaceful scene!'
Exclaiming: 'Ah, dear valley, lovely green,
Still ye remain the same; your hawthorn still,
All your white cottages, the little mill;
Its osiered brook, that prattles thro' the meads,
The plat where oft I danced to piping reeds.
All, all remain unalter'd. 'Tis but thine
To suffer change, weak, wicked Caroline!'
The setting sun now purples hill and lake,
And lengthen'd shadows shadows overtake.
A parting carol larks and throstles sing,
The swains aside their heated sickles fling.
Now dairies all arrang'd, the nymphs renew
The straggling tress, and tighten'd aprons blue;
And fix some hasty floweret, as they run

In a blithe tumult to the pipe begun.
And now, while dance and frolic shake the vale,
Sudden the panting girl, dishevell'd, pale,
Stands in the midst. All pausing gather round,
And gaze amaz'd. The tabors cease to sound.
'Yes, ye may well,' the faltering suppliant cries,
'Well may ye frown with those repulsive eyes.
Yet pity one not vicious but deceiv'd,
Who vows of marriage, ere she fell, believ'd.
Without a mother, sire, or fostering home,
Save, save me, leave me not forlorn to roam.
Not now the gifts ye once so fondly gave,
Not now the verse and rural wreath I crave;
Not now to lead your festive sports along,
Queen of the dance, and despot of the song;
One shed is all, oh, just one wretched shed,
To lay my weary limbs and aching head.
Then will I bless your bounty, then inure
My frame to toil, and earn a pittance poor.
Then, while ye mix in mirth, will I, forlorn,
Beside my murder'd parent sit and mourn.'
She paus'd, expecting answer. None replied.
'And have ye children, have ye hearts?' she cried.
'Save me now, mothers, as from future harms
Ye hope to save the babies in your arms!
See, to you, maids, I bend on abject knee;
Youths, even to you, who bent before to me.
O, my companions, by our happy plays,
By dear remembrance of departed days;
By pity's self, your cruel parents move;
By sacred friendship; Oh! by those ye love!
Oft when ye trespassed, I for pardon pray'd;
Oft on myself your little mischiefs laid.
Did I not always sooth the wounded mind?
Was I not called the generous and the kind?
Still silent? What! no word, no look to cheer?
No gentle gesture? What, not even a tear?
Go then, ye pure! to heights of virtue climb;
Let none plead for me, none forgive my crime.
Go—yet the culprit, by her God forgiven,
May plead for you before the throne of heaven!
Ye simple pleasures of my rural hours,
Ye skies all sunshine, and ye paths all flowers;
Home, where no more a soothing friend I see,
Dear happy home, a last farewell to thee!'
Claspt are her hands, her features strewn with hair,
And her eyes sparkle with a keen despair.
But as she turns, a sudden burst of tears,
And struggles, as of one withheld, she hears.

'Speak!' she conjures, 'ere yet to phrenzy driven,
Tell me who weeps? What angel sent from heaven?'
'I, I your friend!' exclaims, with panting charms,
A rosy girl, and darts into her arms.
'What! will you leave me? Me, your other heart,
Your favourite Ellen? No, we must not part;
No, never! come, and in our cottage live;
Come, for the cruel village shall forgive.
O, my own darling, come, and unreproved,
Here on this heart rest ever, ever lov'd;
Here on this constant heart!' While thus she spoke,
Her furious sire the linkt embraces broke.
Borne in his arms, she wept, entreated, rav'd;
Then fainted, as a mute farewell she wav'd.
But now the wretch, with low and wildered cries,
Round and around revolving vacant eyes:
Slow from the green departs, and pauses now,
And gnaws her tresses and contracts her brow.
Shock'd by the change, the matrons, stern no more,
Pursue her steps and her return implore:
Soon a poor maniac, innocent of ill,
She wanders unconfined, and drinks the rill,
And plucks the simple cress. A hovel near
Her native vale defends her from the year.
With tender feet to flint and thistle bare,
And faded willows weeping in her hair,
She climbs some rock at morn, and all alone,
Chaunts hasty snatches of harmonious moan.
When moons empearl the leafy locks of bowers,
With liquid grain, and light the glistening flowers,
She gathers honeysuckle down the dells,
And tangled eglantine, and slumbering bells;
And with moist finger, painted by the leaves,
A coronet of roses interweaves;
Then steals unheard, and gliding thro' the yews,
The odorous offering on her mother strews.
At morn with tender pause, the nymphs admire,
How recent chaplets still the grave attire;
And matrons nightly tell, how fairies seen,
Danc'd roundelays aslant its cowslipped green.
Even when the whiten'd vale is bleak with snows,
That verdant spot the little Robin knows;
And sure to find the flakes at dawn remov'd,
Alights and chirps upon its turf belov'd.
Such her employ; till now, one wintry day,
Some shepherds hurrying by the haunted clay,
Find the pale ruin, life for ever flown,
With her cheek pillow'd on its dripping stone.
The turf unfinish'd wreaths of ivy strew,

And her lank locks are dim with misty dew.

Poor Ellen hymns her requiem. Willows pine

Around her grave. Fallen, fallen Caroline!

This morning, having resumed my muslins, I repaired to my castle, and seated on the stump of a withered oak, began an accurate survey of its strength, for the purpose of ascertaining whether it could stand a siege, in case Lady Gwyn should attempt to dispossess me of it. I must now describe it to you.

It is situated about a quarter of a mile from the road, on a waste tract of land, where a few decayed trunks of trees are all that remain of a former forest. The castle itself, which I fear is rather too small for long corridors and suites of apartments, forms a square, with a turret at each corner, and with a large gateway, now stopped up with stones, at the southern side. While I surveyed its roofless walls, over-topt with briony, grass, and nettles, and admired the gothic points of the windows, where mantling ivy had supplied the place of glass, long suffering and murder came to my thoughts.

As I sat planning, from romances, the revival of the feudal customs and manners in my castle, and of the feudal system among my tenantry (all so favourable to heroines), I saw a magnificent barouche, turning from the road into the common, and advancing towards me. My heart beat high: the carriage approached, stopt; and who should alight from it, but Higginson and Jerry!

After Higginson, with reverence, and Jerry, with familiarity, had congratulated me on my good fortune, the latter looked hard at the castle.

'The people told us that this was Monkton Castle,' said he; 'but where is the Monkton Castle that your ladyship is to live in?'

'There it is, my friend,' answered I.

'What? there!' cried he.

'Yes, there,' said I.

'What, there, there!'

'Yes, there, there.'

'Oh! murder! murder!'

'How far are we from your ladyship's house?' said the postilion, advancing with his hat off.

'This castle is my house,' answered I.

'Begging your ladyship's pardon,' said he; 'what I mean, is, how far are we from where your ladyship lives?'

'I live in this castle,' answered I.

Jerry began making signs to me over the fellow's shoulder, to hold my tongue.

'What are you grimacing about there, Mr. Sullivan?' said I.

'Nothing at all, Ma'am,' answered he. "Tis a way I have got; but your ladyship, you know, is only come down to this castle on a sort of a country excursion, to see if it wants repairing, you know: you don't mean to live in it, you know.' And he put his finger on his nose, and winked at me.

'But I know I do mean to live in it,' cried I, 'and so I request you will cease your grinning.'

'Oh, murder, murder!' muttered he, swinging round on his heel.

The postilion now stood staring at the venerable edifice, with an expression of the most insolent ridicule.

'And what are *you* looking at?' cried Jerry.

'At the sky through the castle window,' said the fellow, reddening, and shaking with smothered laughter.

'Why then mind your own business,' cried Jerry, 'and that is, to take the horses from the carriage, and set off with yourself as fast as you can.'

'Not till I am paid for their journey down,' said the postilion. 'So will your ladyship have the goodness to pay me?'

'Certainly,' said I. 'Jerry, pay the fellow.'

'Deuce a rap have I,' answered Jerry. 'I laid out my last farthing in little things for your ladyship.'

'Higginson,' said I, 'shall I trouble you to pay him?'

'It irks me to declare,' answered Higginson, 'that in equipments for this expedition;—a nice little desk, a nice little comb, a nice little pocket-glass, a nice little——'

'In short you have no money,' cried I.

'Not a farthing,' answered he.

'Neither have I,' said I; 'so, postilion, you must call another time.'

'Here is a pretty to do!' cried the postilion. 'Damme, this is a shy sort of a business. Not even the price of a feed of oats! Snuff my eyes, I must have the money. I must, blow me.'

''Tis I that will blow you,' cried Jerry, 'if you don't unloose your horses this moment, and pack off.'

The postilion took them from the carriage, in silence; then having mounted one of them, and ridden a few paces from us, he stopped.

'Now you set of vagabonds and swindlers,' cried he, 'without a roof over your heads, or a penny in your pockets, to go diddle an honest man out of his day's labour; wait till master takes you in hand: and if I don't tell the coachmaker what a blockhead he was to give you his barouche on tick, may I be particularly horsewhipt! Ladyship! a rummish sort of a tit for a Ladyship! And that is my Lord, I suppose. And this is the Marquis. Three pickpockets from Fleet-street, I would bet a whip to a wisp. Ladyship! Oh, her Ladyship!' and away he cantered, ladyshipping it, till he was out of hearing.

'That young person deserves a moral lecture,' said Higginson.

'He deserves a confounded drubbing,' cried Jerry. 'But now, 'pon your conscience, does your ladyship intend to live in this old castle?'

'Upon my honour I do,' replied I.

'And is there no decent house on the estate, that one of your tenants could lend you?' said he.

'Why you must know,' replied I, 'that though Lady Gwyn, the person who has withheld my property from me so long, acknowledged my right to it but a few days since, still, as she has not yet yielded up the title deeds, in consequence of a quarrel which obliged me to quit her house, it is improbable that the tenantry would treat me as their mistress. All I can do, is, to seize this uninhabited castle which lies on my own estate. But I can tell you, that a heroine of good taste, and who wishes to rise in her profession, would infinitely prefer the desolation of a castle to the comforts of a villa.'

'Well, of all the wise freaks——' cried Jerry, standing astride, sticking his hands in his ribs, and nodding his head, as he looked up at the castle.

'I tell you what, Mr. Sullivan,' interrupted I, 'if you have the slightest objection to remaining here, you are at perfect liberty to depart this moment.'

'And do you think I would leave you?' cried he. 'Oh then, oh then, 'tis I that wouldn't! And the worse your quandary, the more I would stick by you;—that is Jerry Sullivan. And if it was a gallows itself you were speculating in, I would assist you all the same. One can find friends enough when one is in the right, but give me the fellow that would fight for me right or wrong.'

I shook his honest hand with warmth, and then asked him if he had performed my commissions.

'Your ladyship shall hear,' said he. 'As soon as I got your letter, I went with it in my hand, and shewed it at fifty different shops;—clothiers, and glaziers, and upholsterers, and feather-makers, and trumpet-makers; but neither old tapestry, nor old painted glass, nor old flags stained with old blood, nor old lutes, nor old any thing that you wanted, could I get; and what I could get, I must pay for; and so what I must pay for, I would not get; and the reason why, I had no money; and moreover, as sure as ever I shewed them your letter, so sure they laughed at it.'

'Laughed at it!' cried I.

'All but one,' said Jerry.

'And he?' cried I.

'Was going to knock me down,' answered Jerry. 'So, as I did not wish to come without bringing something or other to you, and as you commanded me to get everything old; egad, I have brought three whole pieces of damaged black cloth out of our own shop, that I thought might answer for the hangings and curtains; and I bought a parcel of old funeral feathers and an old pall, from an undertaker; and I bought an old harp with five strings, that will do any thing but play; and I stole our own parlour bell; and I borrowed a horn from the guard of a mail-coach, which I hope will do for a trumpet; and now here they are all in the barouche, and my bed and trunk; and a box of Mr. Higginson's.'

'But the barouche?' said I; 'how did you get that?'

'By not shewing your letter,' answered Jerry; 'and besides, the coach-maker knew me; and I told him it was for my Lady De Willoughby, as beautiful as an angel—but he did not mind that—and as rich as a Jew;—but he minded that; and so he gave me the barouche, and a shake-hands into the bargain.'

'Well, my friend,' said I, 'you did your best; so as soon as I can raise a sufficient sum, I will furnish my castle in a style of gothic grandeur, which your modern painters and glaziers have no notion of. Meantime, if you and Higginson will pull down those stones that choak the gateway, we will enter the building, and see what can be done with our present materials.'

They commenced operations with such alacrity, that they soon cleared away the rubbish, and in we went. Not a sign of a roof on the whole edifice: the venerable verdure of damp stained the walls, nettles and thistles clothed the ground, and three of the turrets, inaccessible to human feet, were to be come at only by an owl or an angel. However, on examining the fourth, or eastern turret, I found it in somewhat better condition than the rest. A half-decayed ladder, leaning against an aperture in the ceiling above, tempted me to mount, and I got into a room of about eight feet square (the breadth of the turret), overrun with moss and groundsel, and having a small window in one of its sides. From the floor, another ladder reached to another aperture in the ceiling above; and on ascending it, I found myself at the top of the tower, round which ran a broken parapet. This tower, therefore, I determined to fit up and inhabit; and to leave the other three in a state of classical dilapidation, as receptacles for strange noises, horrid sights, and nocturnal Condottieri.

I then descended, and made the minstrel and warden (for they have consented to undertake these offices) draw the barouche within the gateway, and convey the luggage up to the room that I meant for my residence.

The next matter that we set about was hanging the chamber with the black cloth; and this we contrived to do by means of wooden pegs, which the warden cut with his knife, and drove, with a stone, through the drapery, into the crevices of the walls. We found two of the three pieces of black cloth sufficient to cover the sides of the room; and when the hangings were all arranged, I gazed on their sombrous and antique effect with the most heartfelt transport. I then named it the Black Chamber, and gave orders that it should always be called so.

Our next object was to contrive a bed for me. Jerry, therefore, procured some branches of trees, and after much labour, and with no small ingenuity, constructed a bedstead, as crazy as any that ever creaked under a heroine. We then hung it round with curtains of black cloth; and Jerry's own bed being placed upon it, we spread the black pall over that. Never was there a more funereal piece of furniture; and I saw, with pride, that it rivalled the famous bed in the Mysteries of Udolpho.

The minstrel all this time appeared stupified with astonishment, but worked like a horse, puffing and panting, and doing every thing that he was desired, without uttering a word.

Dinner now became our consideration, and I have just dispatched the warden (like Peter, in the Romance of the Forest) to procure provisions. Not a farthing has he to purchase any, since even the half-crown which Susan gave me is already exhausted.

But the light that enters at my window begins to grow grey, and an appropriate gloom thickens through the chamber. The minstrel stands in a corner, muttering poetry; while I write with his pen and ink on a stool that the warden made for me. My knees are my desk.

Adieu.

LETTER XXXVII

Just at the close of evening, Jerry came running towards the castle with a milk-pail on his head.

'See,' cried he, putting it down, 'how nicely I have choused a little milk-maid! There was she, tripping along as tight as her garter. 'Fly for your life,' cries I, striding up to her: 'there is the big bull at my heels that has just killed two children, two sucking pigs, two—— Here! here! let me hold your pail for you!' and I whips it off her head. So, what does she do, but she runs off without it one way; and what does I do, but I runs off with it another way. And besides this, I have got my hat filled with young potatoes, and my pockets stuffed with ears of wheat; and if we can't eat a hearty dinner off these dainties, why that our next may be fried fleas and toasted leather!'

Though I was angry at the means used by Jerry to get the provisions, yet, as dinner just then had more charms for me than moral sentiment, instead of instructing him in the lofty doctrines of the social compact, I bade him pound the grains of wheat between two flat stones. In the mean time, I sent the minstrel to the cottage for a light and some fuel; and on his return, made him stop up the window with grass and fern. He then kindled a fire of wood in the centre of the Black Chamber; for, as the floor was of stone, it ran no risk of being burned. This done, I mixed some milk with the bruised wheat, kneaded a cake, and laid it on the red embers, while Jerry took charge of roasting the potatoes.

As soon as our romantic repast was ready, I drew my stool to the fire: my household sat on large stones, and we made a tolerable meal, they on the potatoes, and I on the cake, which hunger had really rendered palatable.

The warden lifted the pail to my lips, and I took a draught of the rural nectar; while the minstrel remarked, that Nestor himself had not a larger goblet.

I now paid the poor cottagers a visit, and carried the fragments of our dinner to them.

On my return, we resumed our seats, and hung over the decayed embers, that cast a gloomy glare upon the bed and the drapery; while now and then, a flash from the ashes, as they sank, shot a reddened light on the paleness of the minstrel, and brightened the broad features of the warden. The wind had risen: there was a good deal of excellent howling round the turret: we sat silent, and looking for likenesses in the fire.

'Come, warden,' cried I, 'repair these embers with a fresh splinter, and let me hear the memoirs of your life.'

The warden consented, the fire was replenished, and he thus began:

'Once upon a time when pigs were swine——'

'I will trouble you for a more respectable beginning,' said I; 'some striking, genteel little picture, to bespeak attention,—such as, "All was dark;" or, "It was on a gloomy night in the month of November."'

'That would be the devil's own lie,' cried Jerry, 'because I was born in January; and by the same token, I was one of the youngest children that ever was born, for I saw light five months after my mother's marriage. Well, being born, up I grew, and the first word I said was mammy; and my hair was quite yellow at first, though 'tis so brown now; and I promised to be handsome, but the symptom soon left me; and I remember I was as proud as Lucifer when I got trowsers; and——'

'Why now, Jerry, what sort of trash is this?' said I. 'Fie; a warden like you! I hoped to have heard something of interest and adventure from you; that your family was respectable, though poor——'

'Respectable!' cried Jerry. 'Why, I am of the O'Sullivans, who were kings of Ireland, and that is the very reason I have not Mister to my name, seeing as how I am of the blood royal. Oh, if 'tis the wonderful your ladyship wants, by the powers, I am at home thereabouts. Well, I was iddicated in great tenderness and ingenuity, and when I came of age, I went and seized on O'Sullivan Castle, and fortified it, and got a crown and sceptre, and reigned in great peace many years. But as the devil would have it——'

'Jerry,' said I, 'I must insist on hearing no more of these monstrous untruths.'

'Untruths!' cried he. 'Why you might as well give me the lie at once. O murder! to think I would tell a falsehood about the matter!'

'Sir,' said I, "tis a falsehood on the very face of it.'

"Pon my conscience then,' cried he, "tis as like your own story as one pea is like another. And sure I did not contradict you (whatever I might think, and I have my thoughts too, I can tell you,) when you talked so glib of your great estates; though, to be sure, your ladyship is as poor as a rat. Howsomever, since you will have it so, 'tis all a falsehood, sure enough; but now you shall hear the real story; though, for that matter, any body can tell truth, and no thanks to them.

'Well, then, my father was nothing more than a common labourer, and just poor enough to be honest, but not poor enough to be a rogue. Poverty is no great disgrace, provided one comes honestly by it; for one may get poor as well as rich by knavery. So, being poor, father used to make me earn odd pennies, when I was a boy; and at last I got so smart, that he resolved on sending me to sell chickens at the next town. But as I could only speak Irish at that time, by reason we lived up the mountains, he sat down and taught me a little English, in case any gentlefolks should ask me about my chickens. Now, Jerry, says he, in Irish, if any gentleman speaks to you, of course it will be to know the price of your chickens; so you are to say, *three shillings, Sir.* Then to be sure he will be for lowering the price, so you are to say stoutly, *No less, Sir*; and if he shakes his head, or looks angry, 'tis a sign he won't buy unless you bate a little, so you are to say, *I believe I must take two, Sir.*

'Well, I got my lesson pat, and off I set, with my hair cut and my face washed, and thinking it the greatest day of my life; and I had not walked a hundred yards from the house, when I met a gentleman.

'Pray how far is it to the next village?' says he.

'Three shillings, Sir,' says I.

'You are a saucy fellow,' says he.

'No less, Sir,' says I.

'I will give you a box in the face,' says he.

'I believe I must take two, Sir,' says I.

'But, instead of two, egad, I got six, and as many kicks as would match 'em; and home I ran howling.—Well, that was very well, so when I told father that I was beaten for nothing:

'I warrant you were not,' says he; 'and if I had done so by my poor father, he would have broken every bone in my skin,' says he. 'But he was a better father than I am,' says he.

'How dare you say that your father was better than my father,' says I; and upon this, father takes me by the ear, and lugs me out of the house. Just as we got outside, the same gentleman was passing by; and he stopped, and began to complain of me to my father; and then the whole matter came out, and both of them laughed very heartily.

'Well, what do you think? 'Pon my veracity, the gentleman took me home with him to clean the knives and boots. And then he sent me to school, where I learned English; and then I began to tend at table, and at last became a regular servant in the family.

'Well, here I lived several years, and might have lived till now, but that one night, when mistress had company, while bringing in the tray of cake and wine, down I came, and broke all the glasses.

'By this and that,' says mistress; (only to be sure, mistress did'nt swear) 'you are quite drunk,' says she.

'Never tasted a drop all day,' says I; and it was true for me, 'cause I did not begin till evening.

'Who taught you to tell falsehoods?' says she.

'Troth, you did,' says I; 'for you taught me to tell visitors you were not at home, when all the time you are peeping down the bannisters. Fine fashions, indeed! Nobody is ever at home now-a-days, but a snail,' says I. And I would have said more too, but that master kicked me out of the house.

'Well, that was very well; and now my misfortunes were all before me, like a wheelbarrow.

'This happened in the year of the Rebellion; so, being out of service, I lived at alehouses; and there it was that I met gentlemen with rusty superfine on their backs, and with the longest words in the world. They soon persuaded me that old Ireland was going to ruin; I forget how now, but I know I had the whole story pat at that time; and the end of it was, that I became an United Irishman.

'Howsomever, though I would have died for my country, it would be carrying the joke too far to starve for her, and I had now spent all my wages. So, at last, back I went to my old master, and fell on my knees, and begged his pardon for my bad conduct when I lived with him, and prayed of him to take me once more. Well, he did; and it was only two nights after that we heard a great noise outside, and master comes running into the kitchen.

'Jerry,' says he, 'here are the rebels breaking into the house; and as I know you are a faithful fellow, take this sword and pistol, and stand by me.'

'No, but I will stand before you,' says I. So we mustered our men, five in all, and posted ourselves on the head of the stairs; when in burst the rebels into the hall, and we began a parley. 'Why then, is that Barney Delany?' says I to their captain.

'Why then, is that Jerry Sullivan?' says he to me. 'You are one of us,' says he, 'so now turn round and shoot your master,' says he.

'I will cut off both my hands first,' says I.

'Take that then,' says he; and he fires a shot, and I another, and to it we kept, till we beat them all off.

'Well, in a few months afterwards, this same Barney being made prisoner, I was bound over as witness against him. So some of the gentlemen with the long words came to me, and told me how wrong I had acted in fighting for my master, instead of for my country, and that I must make amends by giving evidence in Barney's favour.

'Well, they puzzled me so, that from then till now I never could make out whether I was right or wrong in standing by master. But somehow, I think I was right; for though patriotism (as the gentlemen call it) is a fine thing, yet, after all, there is nothing like gratitude. Why, if the devil himself did me a kind office, I believe I would make shift to do him another, and not act like the clergy, who spend their whole lives in snubbing at him, and calling him all manner of names, though they know, that, but for him, there would not be a clergyman or a fat living in the kingdom.

'Howsomever, I was persuaded to do the genteel thing by Barney Delany; so, when the day for the trial came, I drank myself pretty unintelligible; and I swore point blank, before judge and jury, that I did not know Barney good or bad, and that all I knew of him was good; and I bothered the lawyers, and they turned me from the table, and threatened to indite me for perjury. But it was the people that did praise me, and call it iligant swearing, mighty pretty evidence; and I was the great man of the day; and they took me to the fair that was hard by, where we tippled a little more, and then we sallied forth ripe for fun.

'Well, as we were running through the fair, what should I see but a man's bald head sticking out of a hole in one of the tents—to cool, I suppose,—so I just lifted up my cudgel, and just laid it down again; when, in a moment, out came a whole set of fellows from the tent, and the man asks which of us had broken his head.

'It was myself,' says I, 'but curse me if I could help it, that skull of your's looked so inviting.

'Accordingly both parties began a battle, and then others, who had nothing better to do, came and joined; they did not know why, but no matter for that. Any one may fight when there is an occasion; but the beauty of it is, to fight when there is no occasion at all.

'Howsomever, in the midst of it up came the military to spoil sport as usual; and they dispersed us, and made some of us prisoners, I among the rest, and we were put into Bridewell. Well, that was very well. So at night we contrived to break it open, beat the keepers, and make our escape. Then what to do with myself was the question. It would go hard with me if I were caught again; so I skulked about the country several days, till happening to meet some lads going beyond seas to reap the English harvest, they persuaded me to buy a reaping-hook, and go with them.

'But to be sure, to be sure, such a hurricane as we had at sea, and such tumbling and tossing; and then we were driven to the world's end, or the Land's End, or some end; but I know I thought I was come to my own end. In short, such wonderful adventures never were known.'

'What adventures, my friend?' cried I. 'I love to hear wonderful adventures.'

'Why,' said he, 'we had an adventure every moment, for every moment we were near going to the bottom.'

'And was that all?' cried I.

'Then,' said he, 'there was such pulling of ropes, and reefing and rigging; and we went over so many seas and channels; the Irish Channel, and the British Channel, and the Bristol Channel, and the Baltic Sea, and the Atlantic Sea, and—— Oh dear, as good as forty more.'

'Forty more!' cried I. 'And pray what were their names?'

'Bad luck to me if I can remember,' said he.

'Probably you were in the Red Sea,' said I.

'To be sure I was.'

'And in the Black Sea?'

'No doubt of it.'

'And in the White Sea, and the Pacific Ocean?'

'In every mother's soul of them.'

'And pray what kind of seas are they?' asked I.

'Why,' said he, 'the Red Sea is as red as blood, and the Black Sea is as black as ink, and the White Sea is the colour of new milk, or nearer butter-milk; and the Pacifi-ifi—What's that word?'

'Pacific,' said I.

'And what is the meaning of Pacific?' said he.

'It means peaceful or calm,' answered I.

'Gad, I thought so,' said he, 'for the devil a wave that same ocean had on it high or low. 'Pon my conscience, it was as smooth as the palm of my hand.'

'Take care, Jerry,' said I, laughing; 'I am afraid——'

'Why then,' cried he, 'that I may never——'

'Hush!' said I. 'No swearing.'

'By dad,' cried he, 'you had better tell my story yourself; for you seem resolved to have it all your own way. May be you won't believe me neither, when I tell you that I landed?'

'As you are not at sea now,' said I, 'I will believe you.'

'Well then,' said he, 'I suppose you will believe that I made a little money by reaping, and then trudged to London to try my fortune.'

'I make no doubt of the fact,' said I. 'But pray how did you contrive to subsist in London at first?'

'By spitting through my teeth,' said Jerry.

'Take care,' cried I. 'This I suspect is another——'

'If you mean lie,' said he, 'I have caught you at last; for 'tis as true as true can be, and I will tell you all about it. You must know that 'tis now the fashion for gentlemen to be their own coachmen; and not only to drive like coachmen, but to talk, walk, dress, drink, swear, and even spit like coachmen. Well, two days after my arrival in London, as I was standing in the street, and looking about, I happened to spit through my teeth, to the envy and admiration of a gentleman that was just driving his own carriage by me. For he stopped, and called me to him, and swore I should get half-a-crown if I would teach him to *pickle a wig*,—that was the word. So when he gave me plain English for it, I closed with him, and went to his house, and taught him to spit so well, that my fame spread through the town, and all the fashionable bloods came to me for instruction; till at last I had a good mind to set up a Spitting Academy.

'Well, I had now spit myself into such affluence, that I refused a coachman's seat with forty pounds a year (for, as I said, even a curate had more than that); and may be, instead of a seat on the box, I might at last have risen to a seat in the Parliament (for many a man has got there by dirtier tricks than mine), but that my profession, which was of a nature to dry up my mouth, forced me to frequent porterhouses; where, as the devil would have it, I met other gentlemen, such as I had met before, and with just the same set of long words.

'In a short time, all of us agreed that our country was ruined, and that something must be done. So we made ourselves into a club, for the purpose of writing ballads about the war, and the taxes, and a thousand lashes that a soldier got. And we used to set ten or twelve ballad-singers round a table in our club-room, each with her pint of beer; and one of our club would teach them the tune with a little kit, while I was in a cock-loft overhead composing the words. And they reckoned me the best poet of them all; and they told me that my writings would descend to posterity; and sometimes the thoughts came so quick on me, that I was obliged to chalk them down on the back of the bellows. But whenever I wanted an idea, I read the Weekly Register; and then between the Register and the liquor, I got worked up to such a pitch of poetry, that my blood used to run cold in the morning, at the thoughts of what I would have done at night.

'Well, one evening, the ballad-singers were round the table, sipping and singing to the little kit, and I had just popt down my head through the trap-door of the cock-loft, to ask the chairman the rhime for *Reform*:

'Confound you,' says he, 'didn't I tell you twenty times 'tis *a storm*;' when in bursts the door, and a parcel of peace-officers seize him, and the whole set, for holding seditious meetings, and publishing inflammatory songs. Think of that! when I protest to you our only object was, by causing disunion, and convincing our enemies that we could not carry on the war, to procure a speedy and honorable peace.

'Howsomever, I got out of the scrape by being concealed in the cock-loft; and I remember well it was on that very night I first saw my wife.'

'Ah,' said I, 'give me the particulars of that event, the first meeting of lovers is always so interesting!'

'Why,' said he, 'going home sorrowful enough after the ruin of our club, I resolved to drown care in a noggin; and accordingly turned into a gin-shop, where I found three fruit-women from Covent Garden, bound on the same errand.'

'What dram shall we drink?' says they.

'Brandy,' says one.

'Gin,' says another.

'Anniseed-water,' says another. And so they fell to and drank.

'I am happy that I ever came to this City of Lunnun; for my fortune is made,' says Brandy.

'If my father had lived, I would be brought up to good iddication,' says Gin.

'If my mother had lived, I would be brought up at a boarding-school,' says Anniseed-water.

'Why, curse you,' says Gin, 'what was your mother but an old apple-woman?'

'And curse you,' says Anniseed-water, 'what was your father but a gallows-bird of a bum-bailiff?'

'And then they fell a fighting and scratching; and Anniseed-water (the present Mrs. Jerry Sullivan) was getting well cuffed, when I came to her assistance. So that was our first meeting.'

'You may boast of it,' said I. 'Now then for your courtship.'

'You shall hear,' said he. 'She was so much obliged to me, that she asked me home to tea, and I went. I found her a buxom widow, and at that time she was as fine a doorful, as tight a wench over a washing-tub, as you would wish to see. And there was her daughter, and a great deal of good company;—the tailor's wife, and the barber's wife, and the pawnbroker's wife; and none so grand as they. And they told as many lies over the first dish of tea as a parcel of porters would over twenty barrels of strong beer. And a young valet, who I could see was courting the widow, swore that it was as good to be out of the world as out of the fashion, and then he whispered to her that she looked killing genteel. But I only pinched her elbow, and I thought she liked that better.'

'It was very vulgar, however,' observed I. 'The first process is to kiss the hand.'

'Ogh!' cried Jerry, 'that is a slobbering trick, to be mumbling knuckles just as a pup niggles at a bone. I am the man to take at once, and fluster a woman, and reckon her ribs for her. No creeping up, and up, and up; and then down, and down, and down, for me—Why, as I hope to be saved, I gave that same widow a thundering kiss on three days acquaintance.'

'Poor thing!' exclaimed I. 'Well, and what did she say?'

'Say? why she said, "Be quiet now, though I know you can't." So, of course, I kissed her still more; while she changed colour in a minute as often as a blackberry in a month. "Ha done, do;" says she, "or I will call out, only there is nobody at home;"—when, at the moment, in pops the valet, and catches us lip to lip.

'Now he was a conceited sort of a chap, who used to set himself off with great airs, shew his white hands—that, I verily believe, he washed every day of his life;—curse and swear just like a gentleman, keep a toothbrush, and make both his heels meet when he bowed.

'Well, I had nothing upon earth to oppose to all this but a bit of a quarrel;—that was *my* strong point;—and sure enough, I gave him such a beating for catching us, that the widow thought me main stout, and married me in a week.

'With her money I set up shop; and I did not much mind her being ten years older than myself, since she was ten times richer. I only copied my own father there; for he once happened to be divided between two girls, one of them with a single cow for her portion, and the other with two cows; so he consulted his landlord which of them he should marry, and his landlord bade him by all means marry the girl with the two cows; "for," says he, "there is not a cow difference between any two women."

'So now that is my history.'

'If I am to collect from it,' said I, 'the character of your countrymen in your own class of life, I must conclude that they are frank, generous, and noble; but neglected in their morals and education, and oppressed by their superiors.'

'Ay, there is the matter,' said Jerry. 'By way of keeping us quiet they keep us down. Now that is just the way to prevent our keeping quiet, for it is natural that men who are kept down should try to rise up.'

'And why do they keep you down?' asked I.

'Because,' answered he, 'we are of one religion, and they of another; and they say our religion is so bad, that it would make us keep them down, if they did not keep us down.'

'Then,' said I, 'you ought to be greatly obliged to them for keeping you down; because that is doing what they condemn, lest you should do it. Now it is the highest possible test of good-nature, to become criminal ourselves, in order to keep our friends virtuous.'

'A wise legislator,' said the minstrel, 'ought not to forget the eighteenth century, in his retrospection to the sixteenth, nor in his anticipation of the twentieth.'

'I know nothing of anticskippation,' said Jerry, 'but I will tell you a bit of a story. When I first went to London, and was poor, I used to dine in a cellar, with other Irishmen, where the knives and forks were chained to the table, for fear we should steal them; though in my mind, the surest way to make a rogue, is to let him know that you think him one. Well, when we began to grow rich, we got a spirit, and broke the chains, and paid for them; and broke them again, and paid for them again, and so on. At last the master began to see that the same spirit which made us break the chains would prevent us from stealing the knives and forks; so he took off the chains, and then his table was no disgrace, and we brought more company to it, and he made his fortune.'

The minstrel and warden now retired to their allotted place of rest—the barouche. Each was to keep watch in turn at the castle gate, and to toll the hour on the bell.

The wind still moaned round the turret; and now the fire, ghastly in decay, but just tinged the projecting folds of the hangings. Dismal looked the bed as I drew near; and while I lifted the velvet pall to creep beneath, I shivered, and almost expected to behold the apparition of a human face, starting from under it. When I lay down, I kept my eyes quite closed, for fear of seeing something; nor was it till the third bell had tolled that I fell asleep.

Adieu.

LETTER XXXVIII

I rose early this morning, and summoned Jerry to the Black Chamber, for my head was teeming with the most important projects.

'My friend,' said I, 'though Lady Gwyn has already acknowledged me as the rightful owner, not alone of this castle, but of the house that she herself inhabits, yet I cannot apply to my tenantry for rent, or even raise a sum of money sufficient to purchase my breakfast, till she surrenders up those deeds and parchments which would give me a legal claim. Now as I fear I shall find it a hard matter to make her do so, I have resolved on proposing a compromise, and on waving all title to the house and demesne that she now occupies, provided she will consent to put me in formal possession of this castle, and all the land appertaining to it.

'I have therefore determined to pay her ladyship a visit for this purpose; but as I was driven from her house with disgrace once before, I mean to return thither now with such a train of domestics as shall put it out of her power to offer me insult, or detain my person.

'Now, Warden, if I could but hire a set of servants, who would consent to live in my castle and defend it, I would, on my part, give each of them a lot of ground, and consider them as feudal vassals; and they could accompany me to Lady Gwyn's. I have therefore to request that you will instantly set off, and endeavour to procure them for me, as no time is to be lost.'

'Begging your ladyship's pardon,' said Jerry, 'you are sending me of a fool's errand: for who but madmen would hire as servants in such a castle as this? Would you have them build swallows' nests for themselves under the windows, and live on suction like the snipes?'

'Mr. Sullivan,' said I, 'cast no sarcasms, but go and do as you are desired.'

'Well, from this moment out, I say nothing,' cried Jerry. 'Nothing at all, at all: but like the old woman's crow, I will be the devil for thinking.'

'Another sarcasm?' said I.

'May be 'tis better for me to go at once, before I get into a scrape,' cried he. 'So now, your ladyship, how many of these same feudal vessels, as you call 'em; these vessels that are to have no drink——'

'Jerry!——'

'Well, well, give me my directions quick, and there is my hand on my mouth till I am out of the castle.'

'You may hire about fifteen or twenty of them,' said I. 'But remember, I will have no dapper footmen, with smirking faces. I must have a clan such as we read of in the middle ages; fellows with Norman noses, and all sorts of frowns—men of iron, fit to live in comets.'

'Better live in comets, than——' But he clapped his hand on his mouth in time, and then ran down the steps.

During his absence, I paid a visit to the poor cottagers, and after having sat with them awhile, and promised them assistance before evening, I returned towards the castle.

On approaching it, I perceived, to my great surprise, Jerry also advancing at the head of about twenty strange looking men, all armed with bludgeons.

'Here are the boys!' cried Jerry. 'Here are the true sort. Few Norman noses, I believe, but all honest hearts; and though they never lived in comets, egad they lived in Ireland, and that is worth fifty comets. Look at 'em. Hold up your heads, you dogs. They came over only to save the hay, and reap the harvest; but when they found their countryman and a woman in distress, they volunteered their services; and now here they are, ready for that same Lady Gwyn, or any lady in the land.'

'Welcome, my friends,' said I; 'and be well assured that I will reward you munificently.'

'Three cheers!' cried Jerry.

They gave three cheers.

My heart dilated with exultation at beholding this assemblage of feudal vassals at my command; and in a moment I had arranged my project. As it was expedient to inspire Lady Gwyn with respect and awe, I resolved on making the best possible display of my power, taste, and feudal magnificence. Of course, I meant to visit her in my barouche; and since I had no horses for it, my plan was to make some of my domestics draw it in a triumphal manner, while the rest should follow in procession. To let them escort me in their own ragged and unclassical dresses was impossible; but I think you will give me credit for my ingenuity in supplying them with others. I determined to divide the black cloth into large pieces, which they should wear as cloaks, and to stick a black feather in each of their hats, a costume that would give them the pleasing appearance of Udolphian Condottieri.

We now set about making the cloaks, but as we had not sufficient cloth remaining, we were obliged to strip the Black Chamber of part of its hangings.

I had appropriated a large portion of the cloth to make flowing drapery for Higginson, whom I meant to take in the barouche with me; but as minstrels never wear hats, and have always bald heads, I was at a loss how to manage about his, since he still cherished and curled his locks, with a spruceness most unmeet for minstrelsy. At last, after repeated assurances how much better he would look, I persuaded him to let Jerry shave the crown of his head.

Accordingly, Jerry performed the tonsorial operation in the Black Chamber, while I remained below, fixing the feathers and cloaks on my domestics. These poor fellows, who, I suppose, had never read even an alphabet, much less a romance, in their lives, stood gaping at each other in silent wonder, though some of them attempted unmeaning, and, I must say, troublesome jests on what was going forward.

When drest, a more formidable and picturesque group than they presented you never beheld, and while I was still admiring them, forth from the turret issued the minstrel. But such a spectacle! Half his huge head was shorn of its hair: his black garments, knotted just under his bare neck, gave a new ghastliness to his face, while his eyes, as he rivetted them upon me, were starting out of their sockets with anxiety and agitation. He looked preternatural. To contain was impossible: I began laughing, and the Irishman uttered a shout of derision.

The poor man looked round him, turned as pale as ashes; his face began to work and quiver, and at last he burst into a piteous fit of crying. Then suddenly lifting a prodigious stone, he whirled it at Jerry's head, who ducked for his life, and saved it.

'And what did I do to you?' cried Jerry.

'You shaved my head because you knew it would spoil my looks,' cried the minstrel. 'And you are endeavouring to outdo me with my mistress, and she likes you better than me;—but it cannot be holpen. Oh, dear, dear!'

I tried to sooth him: nothing would do, nor could I persuade him to accompany me; so now, all being ready, I posted two sentinels on the top of the turret, and then got into my barouche. Six vassals were deputed to draw it, the rest followed with their oaken saplings under their cloaks, and Jerry headed the whole. Never was a more august procession; and I will venture to say, that this country, at least, never saw any thing like it.

As we proceeded along the road, the people ran out of their houses to gaze on us. Some said that we were strolling players, and others swore that we were going to a funeral; while a rabble of boys and girls capered at our heels, and gathered as we went.

It was not till about five o'clock that we reached Lady Gwyn's avenue. We paused there a moment, while I made my attendants shake the dust from their cloaks, and wipe the barouche; and now, with a beating heart, I found myself at her door.

Jerry then pealed an authoritative rap. The door opened. The servant stared.

'Inform the Lady Gwyn,' said I, 'that her niece, the Lady Cherubina de Willoughby, desires the honour of a conference with her.'

The fellow grinned, and vanished; and, in a few minutes, out came her ladyship, accompanied by several guests, some of whose faces I remembered having seen there before. I therefore felt doubly delighted that I had come in such feudal and chivalric pomp.

They greeted me with great kindness and respect.

Carelessly bowing to Lady Gwyn, as I sat half reclined in the barouche, I thus addressed her:

'I now come to your ladyship with a proposal, which it is as generous in me to offer, as it will be politic in you to accept. And first, learn, that I am at this moment in actual possession of Monkton Castle, the noble seat of my ancestors. To that castle, and to this house, your ladyship has already acknowledged my just right; and to both, of course, I can establish my claim by a judiciary process.

'As, however, I prefer a more amicable mode of adjustment, and am willing to spare the effusion of money, I now declare my readiness to make over this house and demesne to your ladyship, and to your heirs for ever, on condition that you, on your part, will surrender to me, without delay or reservation, the title deeds of Monkton Castle, and all the Monkton estate. This is a generous proposal. What say you? Yes or no?'

'Lady Cherubina,' returned her ladyship, 'I cannot think of entering into terms with you, till you restore the portrait that you purloined from this house. But, in the mean time, as a proof of my desire to settle matters amicably, I request the honour of your company at dinner to-day.'

'Your ladyship must excuse me,' said I, with a noble air. 'During our present dispute respecting this house, I should deem it derogatory to my honour and my dignity, were I to enter it in the capacity of guest.'

'Why then, death and 'ounds!' cried Jerry, 'is it to refuse so good an offer, after starving all the morning!'

'Starving!' cried Lady Gwyn.

'We have not put a morsel inside our mouths this blessed day,' said Jerry; 'and even yesterday we dined on potatoes and milk, and a sort of a contrivance of a cake that your ladyship would'nt throw to your cat.'

I thought I should drop at this exposure of our poverty, and I commanded him to be silent.

'Time enough for silence when one has spoken,' cried he. 'But sure, would'nt it vex a saint to hear you talking about honour and dignity, when all the time you are in a starving state!'

'Sensibly remarked,' said Lady Gwyn. 'And pray, my good fellow, who are you?'

'My warden,' answered I quickly, lest he should speak. 'And these are my feudal vassals; and I have left my minstrel, and the rest of my faithful people, on the battlements of the eastern tower, just over the Black Chamber, to guard my castle.'

'And for all this fine talk,' cried Jerry, 'we have not so much as a rap farthing amongst the whole set of us. So pray, your ladyship, do make her stay dinner—Do. Or may be,' (said he, getting closer and whispering Lady

Gwyn), 'may be you would just lend her half-a-crown or so; and, 'pon my soul, I will pay you myself in ten days.'

'Silence, traitor!' cried I, rising in the barouche, and dignifying my manner. 'I do not want a dinner: I would not accept of a dinner; but above all, of a dinner in this house, till I am mistress of it!'

'And is it true,' cried Jerry to Lady Gwyn, 'that she is the real mistress of this house?'

'Oh! certainly, certainly,' said her ladyship.

'Oh! certainly, certainly,' said the guests.

'Well, bad luck to me, if ever I believed it, till this moment,' cried Jerry. 'And why then won't your ladyship give it up to her?'

'Because,' answered she, 'the quiet surrender of an estate was never yet read of in romances.'

''Tis the only rational excuse you can assign,' said I.

'Dinner is on the table,' said the butler coming to the door.

'And so,' cried Jerry to me, 'you won't dine in this house till you are mistress of it?'

'Never, as I hope to see heaven!' answered I.

'And so,' cried he to Lady Gwyn, 'you won't make her mistress of it?'

'Never, as I hope to see heaven!' answered she.

'Why then,' cried Jerry, 'since one refuses to dine in it till she is mistress of it, and since the other owns that she ought to be mistress of it, and yet won't make her mistress of it; by the powers, I will make her mistress of it in two minutes!'

So saying, he shouted some words in an uncouth jargon (Irish, I suppose) to my vassals, several of whom instantly darted into the house, others brandished their sticks in the faces of the guests; Jerry himself ran, lifted me from the barouche, and bore me into the hall; while the rest brought up the rear, and beat back the gentlemen who were attempting to rush between us and the door.

Jerry set me down in the hall, where I stood motionless, while some of my domestics scudded, with merry uproar, through kitchen, parlour, drawing-room, garret; and drove footman, maid, valet, cook, scullion, and lap-dog, all out of the house.

'Now then,' cried Jerry, shutting the hall-door, 'your ladyship is in quiet possession for ever and ever.'

'Jerry,' said I, 'there is no knowing how this will end. But come into that parlour, for some of my people are making a sad riot there.'

In we went; it was the dining-room, and to my great astonishment, I found about a dozen of my domestics already round the table, eating and drinking as if nothing had happened. In vain Jerry and I desired them to desist; they did not even seem to hear us. They laughed and capered, and tore whole joints with their hands, and swallowed the richest wines from the decanters. The rest soon flocked in, and then such a scene of confusion arose as struck me with utter dismay. And now, having glutted themselves, they ran to the windows, and exhibited the mangled meat and diminished wine to the dismayed eyes of poor Lady Gwyn. There she stood in the midst of her friends, looking like a bedlamite; and as soon as I appeared, she beckoned me, with the most frantic gesticulations, to open the window.

I called the warden to my side, and flung up the sash.

'Let us in, let us in!' cried she. 'My house will be destroyed by these diabolical miscreants! Oh! let us in, let us in!'

'Lady Gwyn,' said I, 'these outrages are on my house, not on your's. But be well assured that whatever injury your personal property may sustain, it is contrary to my wishes, and will by me be amply compensated.'

'Gracious powers!' exclaimed she. 'My precious cabinet, and all my furniture will be demolished! Won't you save my house? won't you? dear ma'am, won't you?'

'*Your* house?' cried Jerry. 'Why I had your own word for it just now that it was my own lady's house. So, if you told a lie, take the consequence. But we have got possession, and let me see who will dare drive us out.'

'Here they are that will soon drive you out!' cried a servant.

'Here they are, here they are!' echoed every one.

All eyes were now directed down the avenue, and, to my horror, I perceived a large party of soldiers, in full march towards the house.

'We shall have a bloody battle of it,' whispered Jerry. 'But never fear, my lady, we will fight to the last gasp. Hollo, lads, here is a battle for you!'

At that magic word, all the Irishmen clubbed their sticks, and ran forward.

'We must surrender,' said I. 'Never could I bear the dreadful contest.'

'By the mother that bore me,' cried Jerry, 'I will defend the house in spite of you!'

'Then I will walk out of it,' said I.

'Well, surrender away!' cried Jerry, 'and may all the—— Oh! murder, murder, to give up your own house without a bit of a battle!'

By this time the soldiers had arrived, and the magistrate who was at their head, advanced, and desired me to have the door opened instantly.

'Provided you pledge yourself that none of my brave fellows shall be punished,' answered I.

'You shall all be punished with the utmost rigour of the law,' said the magistrate.

'Since that is the case then,' cried I, 'and since I cannot keep possession of my house, I am resolved that no one else shall. Know, Sir, I have, at this instant, six of my domestics, each with a lighted brand, stationed in different apartments; and the moment you order your men to advance, that moment I give the signal, and the house bursts into a blaze.'

'If you dare,' cried the magistrate.

'Dare!' cried Lady Gwyn. 'The creature would dare any thing. Dare! why she burned a house once before. She did, I protest to you; so pray, make some conditions with her, or she will burn this now. I tell you the girl is quite——' and she whispered something in the magistrate's ear.

'Well,' said the magistrate to me, 'will you promise never to come here again, provided I now let you and your gang pass without detention or punishment?'

'I will,' answered I. 'But I must make some conditions too. In the first place, will your ladyship give me back my cloaths and the money that I left behind me, when I was here last?'

'I will,' answered her ladyship.

'In the next place,' said I, 'will your ladyship promise not to prevent me from inhabiting Monkton Castle, till such time as the law shall determine which of us has a right to the contested estates?'

'Undoubtedly,' replied her ladyship.

'And now,' said I, 'I must have the distinct and solemn declaration of every individual present, that neither myself nor my people shall suffer any molestation in consequence of what we have done.'

All present pledged their honours.

'Now then,' said I, 'we will open the door.'

Accordingly, the warden opened it, and I issued forth with a majestic demeanour, while my awful band marched after their triumphant mistress.

Lady Gwyn and her guests hastened into the house, without even wishing me good evening, and the soldiers drew up before the door.

In a few minutes, a servant came out with my dresses and the money. Having received them, I got into my barouche, and, drawn by my vassals, proceeded homeward. We were silent for some time, but at length I called Jerry to the side of the carriage.

'Well, my friend,' cried I, quite cheerful, 'I think we have come off famously.'

'Yes,' said Jerry.

'I flatter myself,' added I, 'we have made a good day's work of it.'

'Yes,' said Jerry.

'Nothing but yes!' said I. 'Why now, do you not think we have obtained the most decisive advantages? Was it not a glorious affair?'

'Since I must speak out,' cried Jerry, 'I think it was the bluest business that ever was botched by poltroons.'

'It was all your own doing, however,' said I. 'So now you may walk on, Sir.'

Jerry tossed his hat at one side, and strutted forward.

'Come back, Jerry,' cried I. 'Here is my hand. You are a faithful fellow, and would have died for me.'

'Ah, bless you!' cried he. 'You quarrel like a cat, but you make up like an angel!'

It was night before we reached the castle; and as I had not tasted a morsel all day, I dispatched Jerry to the village for provisions, and other matters. I then divided six guineas among my domestics, and desired them to return next morning, as I should want them to repair the fortifications, dig a mote, and excavate subterranean passages.

They gave three cheers, and departed.

In about an hour Jerry returned with a cart containing an abundant stock of provisions;—bread, meat, potatoes, tea, sugar, &c. besides, a kettle, plates, cups and saucers, &c.

After having unloaded and dismissed the cart, we made a fire in the Black Chamber, and supped. I then took a solitary walk, and carried some victuals to the poor cottagers. They received the donation with gratitude, and I left them to the comforts of a hearty meal.

It is now probable that I may reside some time at my castle; and as to my villa, I wish Lady Gwyn joy of it; for in my opinion it is a fright. Conceive the difference between the two. The villa mere lath and plaster; with its pretty little stucco-work, and its pretty little paintings, and its pretty little bronzes. Nice, new, sweet, and charming, are the only epithets that one can apply to it; while antique, sublime, terrible, picturesque, and Gothic, are the adjectives appropriate to my castello. What signify laced footmen, Chinese vases, Grecian tripods, and Turkish sofas, in comparison with feudal vassals, ruined towers, black hangings, dampness, and ivy? And to a person of real taste, a single stone of this edifice is worth a whole cart-load of such stones as the onyx, and sardonyx, and the other barbarous baubles belonging to Lady Gwyn. But nothing diverts me more than the idea that poor Lady Gwyn is twice as old as the house she lives in. I have got a famous simile on the subject. What think you of a decayed nut in an unripe shell? The woman is sixty if she is a day.

Adieu.

LETTER XXXIX

The moist shadows of night had fled, dawn shook the dew from his purple ringlets, and the sun, that well-known gilder of eastern turrets, arose with his usual punctuality. I too rose, and having now recovered my wardrobe, enjoyed the luxury of changing my dress; for I had worn the same cloaths several days, and consequently was become a perfect slattern. How other heroines manage, I cannot imagine; for I have read of some of them who were thrown among mountains, or into cells, and desolate chambers, and caverns; full of slime, mud, vermin, dust, and cobwebs, where they remained whole months without clean linen, soap, brush, towel, or comb; and, at last, when rescued from captivity, forth they walked, glittering like the morning star, as fragrant as a lily, and as fresh as an oyster.

We breakfasted on the top of the tower; and after our repast, the minstrel told me that he had employed the day before in composing a Metrical Romance, called 'Monkton Castle;' which, with my permission, he would now repeat.

I was delighted; and to give it every advantage, I placed him at the harp, flung his black garments over him, and making him sit on the battlements, endeavoured to fix him in the fine attitude of old Allan Bane; but his limbs were so muscular and impracticable, that I could make nothing of them. With an emphatic enunciation, he thus began.

MONKTON CASTLE

A METRICAL ROMANCE

Awake, my harp, sweet plaintiff, wake once more,
Now while bedight in shadowy amice dim,
Eve bathes the mountains in her radiant gore,
And edges ocean with a fiery rim.
And while I touch, with nails ypared anew,
Thy parallel and quadrupedal strings,
May fairies brush away the vesper dew,
That else mote moist the chorded chitterlings.
And ah! full oft the learned tribe, I trow,
With baleful dews of cavil damp thy strain.
But morning shall return, the sun shall glow,
The baleful dews shall fly, the harp shall sound again.
It was a castle of turrets grey,
All nettles and chickweed inside;
Where the wind did howl the livelong day,
And the livelong night beside.

It had no windows or roof, I am sure,
Or parlour for Bell-accoyle;
Where a Belamay and a Belamoure,
In daynt Bellgards mote moyl.

'That same parlour,' said Jerry, 'has bells enough to bother the rookery of Thomastown, and that is the largest in Ireland.'

Nathlesse, to stablish her rights, I ween,
Came to that castle fair Cherubine.

Nor the wind day and night could her astound,
Nor the nettles and chickweed that grew on the ground.

She was of the house of De Willoughby,
And her story was long and melancholie;
But her beauty never could rivalled be.

Glittered her tresses like beams of sun,
And snake-like over her neck did run.

Her cheek, where dimples made beauteous breach,
Lovelily smiled, and the down on each
Was soft as fur of unfingered peach.

While thro' her marble a blush did gleam,
Like ruddy berries, all crushed in cream.

The minstrel to the castle hied,
His mother's hope, his mother's pride.
Gramercy, how that mother cried!

He was a gentle man of thought,
And grave, but not ungracious aught.
His face with thinking lines was wrought.

And though his head was bald a space,
Than he who shore it will get grace.

'Now that is a slap at me!' cried Jerry.

Yet, though he sold full half his books,
To lay out money on his looks;
The lady had such deep disdain;

That the poor minstrel, in his pain,
From the hour that is natal,
To the hour that is fatal,
Mote sing these words, and sing in vain.

SONG

The birds are all singing,
The bells are all ringing,
And tidings are bringing,
Of peace and of joy.
Then let us, my treasure,
In love without measure,
And tenderest pleasure,
Our moments employ.

'Eh! what? what's all that?' cried Jerry. 'Why sure—body o'me, sure you ant—Oh, confound me, but 'tis making love to the mistress you are!'

The minstrel blushed, and more pointedly repeated;
But her favourite warden, could he but sing,

115

He not unlistened, would touch the string,

Tho' he was a man with unchisseled face;

From eye to eye too little a space;

A jester withouten one attic joke,

And the greatest liar that ever spoke.

'Bad luck to you, what do you mean by that?' cried Jerry, running towards him. 'I will box you for a shilling!'

'You are not worth one,' exclaimed the minstrel, starting up.

'I will leave your carcase not worth one,' cried Jerry.

'That would be more than your's is worth now,' returned the minstrel.

'For shame, my friends!' cried I. 'Mr. Higginson, I declare your conduct is that of a child.'

'Because you treat me like one,' said he. 'And you treat him like a man.'

'But you should treat him like a gentleman,' said I.

'Well, well, well,' cried the minstrel; 'there is my hand for you, Mr. Sullivan.'

'And there is mine for you,' said Jerry. 'Hand in hand is better than fist to fist at any time.'

'I will defer hearing the remainder of your poem,' said I, 'till you have altered it. But my good friend, do not forget to tell that I inhabit the *eastern* turret, and to give a full description of it. You might begin thus:

He who would view that east turret aright,

Must go at rosy-finger'd morning bright.'

'Rosy-fingered morning!' cried Jerry. 'Why, how can the morning have rosy fingers?'

'It has not,' answered I. 'The poets only say so by way of ornament.'

'And yet,' cried Jerry, 'if I had said, when I was telling you my history, that I saw a set of red fingers and thumbs rising in the east every morning, I warrant you would have called me a liar, just as you did about that business of the Pacific Ocean.'

'Why,' said the minstrel, 'we poets are permitted a peculiar latitude of language, which enables us to tell Homeric falsehoods, without fear of the society for discountenancing vice. Thus, when we speak of

The lightning of her angel smile,

we do not expect one to believe that fire comes out of her mouth, whenever it laughs.'

'Not unless her teeth were flints,' said Jerry. 'But if you said that fire came out of her eyes, one would believe you sooner; for this I know, that many and many a time Molly has struck fire out of mine.'

'A heroine's eye,' said I, 'gives a greater scope to the poet than any thing in the world. It is all fire and water. If it is not beaming, or sparkling, it is sure to be drowned or swimming——'

'In the Pacific Ocean, I hope,' cried Jerry.

'No, but in tears,' said the minstrel. 'And of these there is an infinite variety. There is the big tear, and the bitter tear, and the salt tear, and the scalding tear.'

'And, ah!' cried I, 'how delightful, when two lovers lay cheek to cheek, and mingle these tears; or when the tender youth kisses them from his mistress's cheek!'

'Troth, then, that must be no small compliment,' said Jerry, 'since they are so brackish and scalding as you say. Water itself is maukish at any time, but salt water is the devil. Well, if I took such a dose of a snivelling chit's tears, I would season it with a dram, or my name is not Jerry.'

'And, by the by, I wish Jerry were not your name,' said I. ''Tis so vulgar for a warden. Indeed, I have often thought of altering it to *Jeronymo*; which, I fancy, is the Italian of *Jerry*. For, in my opinion, nothing can equal Italian names ending in O.'

'Except Irish names beginning with O,' cried Jerry.

'Nay,' said I, 'what can be finer than Montalto, Stefano, Morano, Rinaldo, Ubaldo, Utaldo?'

'I will tell you,' said Jerry. 'O'Brien, O'Leary, O'Flaherty, O'Flanigan, O'Guggerty, O'Shaugnassy——'

'Oh, ecstasy!' exclaimed a voice just beneath the turret. I looked down, and beheld—Montmorenci himself, clad in armour, and gazing up at me with an attitude that mocked mortal pencil.

I waved my hand, and smiled.

'What? whom do I behold?' cried he. 'Ah, 'tis but a dream! Yet I spoke to her, I am sure I spoke to her; and she beckoned me. Merciful powers! Why this terror? Is it not Cherubina, and would Cherubina hurt her Montmorenci?'

'Jerry, Jerry,' said I; 'run down to the Black Chamber, and clean it out quick. Sweep the ashes into a corner, hide the pipkin and kettle, pin up the cloaks against the walls; put the leg of mutton under the bed. Run, run.— My lord, the Lady Cherubina hastes to receive your lordship at her ever-open portal.'

I then descended, and met him beneath the gateway. His greeting was frantic, but decorous; mine endearing, but reserved. Several very elegant things were said on both sides. Of course, he snatched my hand, and fed upon it.

At last, when I supposed that Jerry had regulated the room above, I conducted his lordship up the steps; while I anticipated his delight at beholding so legendary, fatal, and inconvenient a chamber.

His astonishment was, indeed, excessive. He stared round and round, admired the black hangings, the bed, the bell, and the horn.

'I see,' said he, advancing to the ashes, 'that you are even classical enough to burn a fire of wood. But ha! (and he started,) what do mine eyes behold beneath these embers? A bone, by all that is horrible! Perhaps part of the skeleton of some hysterical innocent, or some pathetic count, who was murdered centuries ago in the haunted apartment of this mysterious castle. Interesting relic! Speak, Lady Cherubina. Is it as I suspect?'

'Why,' said I, 'I believe—that is to say—for aught I can tell——'

"Pon my conscience,' cried Jerry, 'her ladyship knows just as well as I do that 'tis nothing but the blade-bone of mutton which she got broiled for her supper last night.'

'Impossible, Sir!' exclaimed his lordship. 'A heroine never eats of a four-footed animal. 'Tis always the leg of a lark, or the wing of a chicken.' And so saying, he began divesting himself of his spear, shield, and helmet.

'Pray, Mr. Blunderer,' whispered I to Jerry, 'did I not desire you to clean out the room?'

'You did not say a word about the blade-bone,' said Jerry.

'But did I not bid you clean out the room?' repeated I.

'Don't I tell you——' cried Jerry.

'Can't you speak low?' said I.

'Don't I tell you that not one syllable about the blade-bone ever came outside your lips?'

'Grant me patience!' said I. 'Answer me yes or no. Did I, or did I not, order you to clean out the room?'

'Now bad luck to me,' said he, 'if you ant all this time confounding the blade-bone of mutton with the leg of mutton that you bade me put under the bed. And accordingly——'

'Gracious goodness!' said I, 'can't you speak within your breath?'

'And accordingly,' whispered he, 'I put it under the velvet pall, because I thought it might be seen under the bed.'

'Well, that shewed *some* discretion,' said I.

'Though after all my pains,' said Jerry, 'there is the man in the tin cloaths has just stripped down that same pall, and discovered the mutton, and the parsnips, and the bag of salt, and the pewter spoons, and——'

'Oh, Jerry, Jerry!' said I, dropping my arms lifeless at my sides; 'after that, I give you up!'

I then called to his lordship, and drew off his attention, by beginning an account of all that had happened since our parting. He listened with great eagerness; and, after my recital, begged of the warden to retire with him, that they might consult on the best line of policy to be adopted in the present state of my affairs.

They descended the steps; I remained alone. Montmorenci had left his helmet, shield, and spear behind. I pressed each of them to my heart, heaved several sighs, and paced the chamber. Still I felt that I was not half fervent or tender enough; something was still wanting, and I had just asked myself if that something could be love, when I heard a sudden disturbance below; his lordship crying out, 'Oh, what shall I do?' and Jerry bidding him 'grin and bear it.'

Down I hastened, and beheld Jerry belabouring him without mercy.

'Wretch,' cried I, rushing between them: 'forbear.'

'Not till I beat him to a paste,' cried Jerry. 'The villain, to go and offer me a bribe if I would help him in forcing you to marry him.'

"Tis false as hell!' cried his lordship.

'I would stake my life that it is,' said I. 'So now, Mr. Sullivan, down on your knees this moment, and ask pardon, or quit my service.'

'But can that restore the teeth he has knocked out?' exclaimed his lordship, with a finger in his mouth.

'Teeth!' cried I, shuddering.

'Two teeth,' said he.

117

'Two teeth!' exclaimed I, faintly.

'Two front teeth,' said he.

'Then all is over!' muttered I. 'Matters have taken a dreadful turn.'

'What do you mean?' cried he.

'My lord,' said I, 'are you quite, quite certain that you have lost them?'

'See yourself,' cried he, lifting his lip. 'They are gone, gone for ever!'

'They are indeed,' said I. 'And now you may be gone too.'

'Ha! what mean you?' cried he.

'My lord,' said I, 'of this you must be conscious, that a complete set of teeth are absolutely indispensible to a hero.'

'Well?' cried he, starting.

'Well,' said I, 'having lost two of your's, you must be conscious that you are no longer a hero.'

'You stretch my heart-strings!' cried he. 'Speak! what hideous whim is this?'

'No whim, my lord,' answered I; 'but principle, and founded on law heroic; founded on that law, which rejects as heroes, the maimed, the blind, the deformed, and the crippled. Trust me, my good lord, teeth are just as necessary in the formation of a hero as a comb.'

'By Heaven!' cried he; 'I can get other teeth at a dentist's; a composition of paste that would amaze you. I can by all that is just.'

'That you may, my lord,' said I, 'and be happy with them; for never can you be happy with me.'

'I am wilder than madness itself!' cried he; 'I am more desperate than despair! I will fly to the ends of the earth, hide in a cavern, and throw my ideas into a sonnet. On a fine summer's evening, when you walk towards the mountains, sometimes think of me.'

'Never as a lover, my lord,' said I: 'so put that out of your head at once. Oh! it shocks me to think I should ever have received you as one!'

He began a tremendous imprecation; but was interrupted by the sudden arrival of a gentleman on horseback with a servant after him. The gentleman stopped, alighted, approached.

'Mr. Betterton!' cried I; 'can it be possible?'

'Nothing is impossible,' said he, with his obsequious bow and confirmed smile, 'when the charming Cherubina prompts our efforts. You remember you left me in a ridiculous dilemma, which your friend Stuart contrived;—masterpiece of ingenuity, faith, and for which I freely forgive him: he's an excellent young fellow; excellent, 'pon my soul; and I have made my friends so merry with an account of that affair. Well, I remained in limbo till the sessions, when none appearing to prosecute, the judge discharged me; so the first use I made of my liberty was to visit Lady Gwyn, who told me that I should find you here; here therefore I am to pay you my devoirs.'

I thanked him, and then bade Jerry run towards the village, and hurry my vassals; as the castle lost much of its pomp without them.

Jerry went: my visitors recognized each other; and already their hostile feelings and opposite interests had began to manifest themselves, when, to my great surprise, three men turned short round the western tower, and stood before me.

'That is she!' cried one of them.

I looked at the speaker, and recognized in him the postilion who had brought down the barouche.

'Your name is Cherry Wilkinson,' said another of them to me.

'Sir,' said I, haughtily: 'my name is Lady Cherubina de Willoughby.'

'That is your *travelling* name,' rejoined he: 'but your real name I discovered at your lodgings in Drury-Lane; which lodgings I found out from the wife of one Jerry Sullivan, the man that conspired with you to swindle Mr. Perrot, the coach-maker, out of the barouche yonder. You see, I have the whole story; so you need not deny it; and now, Miss, look at this warrant. I arrest you, in the king's name, for the most audacious piece of swindling that ever came in my way to know.'

With these words he seized me, and was dragging me from the castle, while I screamed for help.

'A rescue! a rescue!' cried Betterton, and collared the man who held me. Montmorenci laid hold of the other, and the servant felled the postilion to the ground. And now a furious fight began. The man whom Betterton had seized drew a pistol and fired it: at this moment, down came the minstrel from the turret; I got loose and ran into the castle, nor ventured to look again, till, after much uproar, I heard a shout of victory from my friends: then venturing to the gateway, I saw the three wretches limping from the place, in piteous plight.

It now appeared that the ball aimed at Betterton had just grazed the fleshy part of his servant's arm, which was bleeding a good deal. I felt much shocked, and assisted him in binding the wound. This matter employed some minutes, and during that time, I could perceive Betterton and Montmorenci whispering earnestly together.

At last Betterton addressed me thus:

'Now, Lady Cherubina, should we remain here much longer, we shall certainly be seized and imprisoned for having assaulted his majesty's officers in the discharge of their duty. We have, therefore, nothing for it but flight. My house is but a few miles distant, and as these officers could not have known me, we shall be perfectly safe there. What says your ladyship? Shall we repair thither?'

'Sir,' answered I; 'as I was not concerned in that assault, and as I am innocent of the crime for which they came to take me, nothing shall induce me to quit my castle: if they chuse to make another attempt, I shall go with them, establish my innocence, and return triumphant. But if I am to act on the skulking system, how can I reside here at all?'

Montmorenci now joined his entreaties, but I remained immoveable. Again they retired to consult, and again came forward.

'Lady Cherubina,' said Betterton, 'you must excuse me when I say that both Lord Montmorenci (for his lordship has just disclosed to me his noble lineage) and myself conceive ourselves fully warranted in compelling, if we cannot persuade your ladyship, to leave this castle (where we cannot remain to protect you), and in conveying you to my mansion, where you will be safe.'

'Compel me?' cried I. 'Compel me? But I disdain to hold farther parley with you. Farewell for ever. Minstrel, follow me to the Black Chamber.'

'Stop them!' cried Betterton.

His lordship placed himself between us and the gateway: the minstrel, brandishing his collected knuckles, struck him to the ground. Betterton assailed my brave defender behind, the servant before; but he fought with desperation, and his blow was like the kick of a horse. Still numbers appeared about to prevail; and now his breathing grew shorter, and his blow slower, when, transport to my sight! I beheld Jerry, with several of my vassals, come running towards us. They reached us: the tide of battle turns, and his lordship and the servant are well beaten with bludgeons; while Jerry himself does the honours to Betterton, in a kicking.

Nobody could bear it more gently than he did; and after it was over, he mounted his horse and vociferated:

'Now, by all that is sacred, I will go this moment, raise the neighbourhood, and have you driven from your nest, you set of vipers;—you common nuisances, you! Lady Gwyn's castle shall no longer be made the receptacle of ragged and marauding Irishmen.'

So saying, off he gallopped on one horse, and his lordship on another; while the servant trudged on foot.

We now held a grand council of war, for affairs began to wear an alarming aspect. If Betterton should put his threat of raising the neighbourhood into execution, a most formidable force might be collected against us. After much deliberation, therefore, it was decided, that some of the vassals should be dispatched to collect more of their countrymen, who, they said, slept in several adjoining villages. I too wrote a note to Susan, begging that she would raise a counterposse in my favour, and rescue me from an implacable enemy, as I had rescued her from a criminal and fatal attachment. This note I sent to her cottage by one of my vassals.

During this awful interval, the remainder of those who had been with me yesterday arrived. I planted sentinels and outposts, and employed the rest in filling up the windows with stones, repairing the breaches, and searching amidst the rubbish for the mouth of some subterranean cavern, where I might conceal myself in the last emergency.

As I had not a white and azure standard, like Beatrice, I directed Jerry to stain a large piece of muslin with the blood of the wounded servant, which still besprinkled the grass; then to fasten it on a long pole, and hoist it, as my banner, at an angle of the eastern turret.

Susan's cottage being only half a mile from the castle, the messenger soon returned with an answer, that she would certainly assemble her friends, and come to me. Just as he had announced these happy tidings, another came back, with a fresh accession of ten Irishmen; and in a short time more arrived; till at length we mustered to the amount of fifty.

I stood, and gloried in my strength. Already I beheld the foundation of a feudal settlement. Already I considered myself the restorer of that chivalric age, when neighbouring barons were deadly foes, and their sons and daughters clandestine lovers. Ah! what times for a heroine! it was then that the Lady Buccleugh and the Duchess of Cleves flourished.

'And these,' cried I, in an ecstasy of enthusiasm, 'these shall again revive in the person of Lady Cherubina De Willoughby!'

As I spoke, Jerry came to tell me that one of the scouts had just returned with information of his having seen a large party of Lady Gwyn's tenants assembling about a quarter of a mile off; in order, as he found on inquiry, to drive us from the castle.

Now then was approaching the most important moment of my life, and I resolved to support my part with dignity. As the first step, I dressed myself in a style of magnificence suited to the occasion. Having flung the drapery of embroidered gauze over my white muslin, I next (in imitation of ancient heroines, who wore armour in the day of battle), put Montmorenci's helmet on my head; then, with his shield in the one hand, and his spear in the other, never did I look so lovely.

I now called up the warden, and constituted him commander of the forces; then ordered him to send six picked men, and the minstrel, as my body-guards, up to the Black Chamber.

They came; I equipped them in black cloaks and feathers, and made them mount to the top of the tower. In a few minutes afterwards I myself ascended with a beating heart. There I found the preparations for battle almost completed. The bloody standard was streaming to the gale; the body-guards were collecting a heap of stones from the broken parapet; while beneath the turret I beheld the whole of my troops, with oaken staffs, marshalled in awful array. The spectacle was grand and imposing. Lightly I leaned on my spear; and while my feathered casque pressed my ringlets, and my purfled drapery floated and glistened in the sun, I stood on the battlements, mildly sublime, sweetly stern, amiable in arms, and adorned with all the terrible graces of beauty belligerent.

I now resolved to harangue my men for the purpose of encouraging them, and of attaching them to my person; but as I knew nothing of political orations, I had nothing for it but to copy the speech of Beatrice in the Knights of the Swan; and those that I had read in the daily prints.

A profound silence prevailed; I waved my spear, and thus began.

'My brave associates, partners of my toil, my feelings and my fame! Two days have I now been sovereign of this castle, and I hope I may flatter myself that I have added to its prosperity. Young, and without experience, I merely claim the merit of blameless sentiments and intentions.

'Threatened with a barbarous incursion from my deadliest enemies, I have deemed it indispensible to collect a faithful band of vassals for my defence. They have come at my call, and I thank them.

'I promise to them all such laws and institutions as shall secure their happiness. I will acknowledge the majesty of the people. (*Applause.*) I will give to them a full, fair, and free representation. (*Applause.*) And I will grant to them a radical reform; or in other words, a revival of the feudal system. (*Shouts of applause.*) I will assume no monarchial prerogatives that are unjust; if I should, do not forget that the people have always the power and the right to depose a tyrant.

'I promise that there shall be no dilapidated hopes and resources; no army of mercenaries, no army of spies, no inquisition of private property, no degraded aristocracy, no oppressed people, no confiding parliament, no irresponsible minister. (*Acclamation.*) In short, I promise every thing. (*Thunders of acclamation.*)

'Each man shall have an acre of ground, a cottage, and an annual salary. (*Long life to you! cried the troops. That is the best thing you have said!*) Such is the constitution, such are the privileges that I propound to you. Now then, my brave fellows, will you consent on these conditions to rally round my standard, to live in my service, and to die in my defence? (*We will! we will! cried they.*)

'Thank you, my generous followers; and the crisis is just approaching when I shall have occasion for your most strenuous exertions. Already my mortal foe prepares to storm my castle, and drive me from my hereditary domain. Already he has excited my own tenantry to sedition against me. Should he succeed in his atrocious object, I must return to my tears, and you to your sickles. But should we repel him, my government will be secured, my territory perhaps enlarged, my castle rebuilt; and the cause of liberty will triumph. What heart but throbs, what voice but shouts, at the name of liberty? (*Huzza!*) Is there a man amongst you who would refuse to lay down his life for liberty? (*Huzza!*) And if, on an important occasion like the present, I might take the liberty—(*Huzza!*) to dictate, I would demand of you this day to sacrifice every earthly consideration in her sacred cause. I do demand it of you, my friends. I call upon your feelings, your principles, and your policy, to discard family, property, and life, in a cause so just, so wise, and so glorious. Let eye, foot, heart, hand, be firm, be stern, be valiant, be invincible!'

I ceased, the soldiery tore the blue air with acclamations, and the ravens overhead flew swifter at the sound.

I now found that it was not difficult to make a popular speech; and I judged that the same qualities which have made me so good a heroine, would, if I were a man, have made me just as illustrious a patriot.

After much entreaty, I persuaded the minstrel to deliver an address; as he, being learned, might expound constitutions and political economy better than I. He therefore leaned over the battlements, and began.

'Gentlemen,

'Unaccustomed as I am to public speaking, I feel that words are inadequate to express my high sense of the honour you have conferred upon us. Gentlemen, I will institute an apt comparison between the foundation of this little settlement, and that of the ancient Romans; in order to prove, that this, though small at present, may, like that, terminate in an extensive empire. Gentlemen, Rome took its rise from a set of the greatest beggars and reprobates that ever crawled upon earth——'

'Throw him over, throw him over!' burst from the troops.

The minstrel shrunk back in consternation.

'Silence, lads,' cried Jerry, 'and I will make a bit of a speech for you; but instead of sending you to Rome, I will send you no farther than Ballinasloe. (*Laughter and bravo!*) Eh, my boys, don't you remember the good old fun at the fair there? To be sure, how we used to break each other's heads, without the least anger or mercy; and to be sure, 'tis the finest feel in the world, when one gives a fellow a neat, clean, bothering blow over the skull, and down he drops like a sack; then rises, and shakes himself like a wet dog, and begins again. (*Much laughter.*) Ay, my boys, fighting may be an Englishman's or a Frenchman's business, but by the Lord Harry, 'tis an Irishman's amusement! (*Shouts.*) So now, hearties, all you have to do is to club your sticks, and fancy yourselves at Ballinasloe; and never heed me if we havn't a nice comfortable fight of it.'

Rude as was this rhetoric, it touched the domestic spring of their hearts, and my patriotic promises did not produce half such a roar of delight as followed it.

Silence was but just restored, when I beheld, from my turret, our enemies advancing in vast numbers across the common. I confess my heart sank at the sight; but I soon called to mind the courage of the feudal heroines, and recollected that I was in no personal danger myself. Then, the greatness of the cause animating me with ardour, I exclaimed:

'Lo! yonder come our enemies. To arms, to arms! Sound the tocsin; blow, blow the horn!'

A vassal blew the horn.

The warden then stationed his men in front of the gate-way, which was the only vulnerable entrance into the castle; and my body-guards, holding huge stones, stood forward on the battlements. All was ready. I trembled with agitation.

And now the foe, having approached within fifty paces, halted to reconnoitre. The traitor Montmorenci, divested of his armour, commanded them in person. Betterton was seen on horseback at a distance; and the troops themselves, about sixty in number, stood brandishing stakes, bludgeons, and poles. As my men were not more than fifty in all, I looked round, with anxious expectation, for the succours promised by Susan; but no sign of them appeared.

Montmorenci now began to form his troops into a compact phalanx, with the poles and stakes in front; evidently for the purpose of piercing our line, and forcing the gateway. Jerry, therefore, called in his wings, and strengthened the centre. He then desired those in the turret to direct all their stones against the foremost rank of the foe.

'Soldiers,' cried I, 'listen to my last commands. The moment you shall hear the horn sound again, whether in the midst of conquest, or of defeat, hurry back to the gateway, and draw up just as you stand at present; for while you are fighting at a distance, my castle may be taken by surprise, unless I secure prompt assistance. And now, my brave fellows, success attend your arms!'

As I spoke, the foe began advancing at a rapid rate: my troops awaited them with firmness; and when they had approached within fifteen paces of the castle, I gave the word to my body-guards, who hurled several vollies of stones in quick succession. Some of the foremost rank were staggered by them; two behind fell, and amidst the confusion, in rushed my troops with a tremendous shout. Thick pressed the throng of waving heads, and loud grew the clamour of voices, and the clatter of staffs; while the wielded weapons appeared and disappeared, like fragments of a wreck on the tossing surges. For some moments both armies fought in one unbroken mass; those struggling to gain the gateway, these to prevent them. But soon, as two streams rushing from opposite mountains, and meeting in the valley, broaden into a lake, and run off in little rivulets; so the contending ranks, after the first encounter, began to spread by degrees, and scatter over the plain. And now they were seen intermingled with each other, and fighting man to man. Here a small wing of my brave troops, hemmed in on all sides, were defending themselves with incredible fury. There a larger division of them were maintaining a doubtful contest: while a few straggling vassals, engaged in single combat, at a distance, were driving their antagonists before them.

At this juncture, Montmorenci, with a chosen band that he kept round his person, had attacked the warden, and a few who fought by his side. These performed prodigies of valour; but at last, overpowered by numbers, they were beginning to retire, covered with glory, when I dispatched four of my body-guards, as a corps of reserve, to their assistance. They rushed upon the chosen band, and checked its career. It soon received

121

reinforcements, and again pressed forward. I sent out the minstrel and another vassal; and again its progress was checked.

But now my castle had but a single defender: our foes were drawing frightfully near; and if they could once turn our flank, they would gain the turret, and make me their prisoner. This was the great crisis. A moment more, and all might be lost.

'Blow, blow the horn!' cried I.

The vassal blew the horn.

At the signal, I see my dispersed troops come pouring from all quarters towards the castle. They reach the gateway, halt, and form a front before it. The foe, who had followed them in a confused manner, seeing them on a sudden so formidable, stop short.

'Let the body-guards come into the castle!' cried I.

The body-guards obeyed.

'Now, soldiers,' cried I to the rest, 'if you rush upon the foe before they can collect again, and keep in a body with your captain, the day is our own.' 'Spring on them like lions! Away, away!'

The whole army shouted, and burst forward in a mass. Jerry led the van. Montmorenci with his sacred squadron fled before them. They pursued, overtook the fugitives, and after a short skirmish, made the whole detachment prisoners; while the remainder, scattered in all directions, stood at a distance, and dared not advance. Never was a more decisive victory. My brave veterans marched back in triumph with eight captives; and then halting at the gateway, gave three cheers.

Palpitating with transport, I commanded that the prisoners' hands should be tied behind their backs, and that they should be confined in the northern tower, with sentinels over them.

As for Lord Montmorenci, his rank entitled him to more respect; so I ordered the warden to conduct him up to the Black Chamber.

I stood in the midst of my guards to receive him; and if ever grandeur and suavity were blended in one countenance, it was in mine, at that glorious moment.

'My lord,' said I, 'victory, which so long hovered over the field with doubtful wing, has at last descended on my legions, and crowned the scale of justice with the laurel of triumph. But though it has also put the person and the fate of the hostile chieftain in my hands, think not I mean to use my power with harshness. Within these walls your lordship shall experience the kindest treatment; but beyond them you must not be permitted to go, till my rights are re-established and my rebellious vassals restored to their allegiance.'

'Fal lal la, lal lal la,' said his lordship, stepping a minuet.

'Pinion him hand and foot!' cried I, quite disgusted and enraged. 'I will have no minuets in this castle.'

'That I will do,' cried Jerry, 'for his feet are nimble enough at making off. Though he talks big, he runs fast. The creature is all voice and legs, like a grasshopper.'

Just as the minstrel and warden had secured his wrists and ankles with a handkerchief, a vassal came to tell me that a number of men, and a girl at their head, were running towards the castle.

'I thought she would not disappoint me!' cried I, as I hastened down to meet her. It was, indeed, Susan herself, and a train of youths. I stood at the gateway ready to receive her, and trembling with terror, lest Betterton and the routed remains of his army, who were now consulting together at some distance, should intercept her.

These fears were not at all lessened when I saw her stop, as she arrived amongst them, and converse with them some time. I made my men hold themselves in readiness to support her, and we shouted to her with all our might. But just judge of my consternation, when I beheld her and her party enrolling themselves in the hostile ranks, and the whole allied force preparing to pour down upon us! I stood horror-struck. Her ingratitude, her perfidy, were incredible.

But I had no time for moral reflection. My own glory and the interests of my people demanded all my thoughts. What was I to do? We had taken but eight prisoners, and these too would require a strong guard; while the traiterous Susan had brought a reinforcement of twenty men to the foe; so that to contend against such superior numbers in the field would be madness.

I determined therefore to draw all my troops and all my prisoners into the eastern turret, and to stand a regular siege; for, as we had a large stock of provisions, we might hold out several days. In the mean time our enemies, tired of such a protracted mode of warfare, and having other occupations of more importance, would probably retire and leave us in quiet possession.

This plan was put into instant execution. I had the prisoners placed in the Black Chamber, with a numerous guard; and I made the remainder of my soldiery man the battlements.

These arrangements were but just completed, when I beheld our formidable opponents advancing in line, with Betterton, on horseback, at their head. Again my men armed themselves with stones; again the horn was sounded; again three cheers were given.

When the besiegers had arrived within forty paces of us, they halted. Then Betterton, waving a white handkerchief, advanced under the walls, and spoke thus:

'Lady Cherubina De Willoughby, I demand of you to surrender at discretion. Refuse, and I pledge myself that in five minutes I will drive the leopard into the sea, and plant my standard on the towers of Monkton.'

'Sir, I both refuse, and defy you. My castle is impregnable.'

'Not to hunger, at least,' cried Betterton; 'for we will turn the siege into a blockade.'

'Yes, to hunger!' exclaimed the minstrel, flinging down half a loaf of bread, that had remained since breakfast. 'There, Sir, is a proof of it, deduced from the Roman history!'

'As I perceive that war is inevitable,' said Betterton, 'I shall stand acquitted both here and hereafter for all its consequences by my now just going through the form of proposing a general pacification.'

'Pacific Ocean!' cried Jerry. 'No, thank you; I have got a surfeit of that word already.'

'Nay, my honest fellow——'

'Never honest-fellow me,' cried Jerry: 'it won't take, old boy. So bad manners to you, and that is worse than bad luck, go boil your tongue hard, like a calve's, and then it won't wag so glib and smooth;—ay, and go boil your nose white like veal too. But this I can tell you, that you will neither beat us out, nor starve us out; for we have sticks and stones, and meat and good liquor; and we will eat together, and drink together, and——'

'And sleep together, I suppose,' cried Betterton: 'for of course, her ladyship will think nothing of sleeping in the same apartment with twenty or thirty men.'

The fatal words fell upon me like a thunderbolt! It was, indeed, too true, that a large portion of my troops must remain all night in the Black Chamber, as there would be no room for them elsewhere: so how in the name of wonder could I contrive to sleep? Certain it is, that Ellena Di Rosalba travelled a whole day and night in a carriage with two ruffians, who never left her for a moment; and it was not till after Luxima and the missionary had journeyed together several entire days, that (to quote the very words) *for the first time since the commencement of their pilgrimage she was hidden from his view.* How these heroines managed I know not; but this I know, that I could not abide the idea of sleeping in the presence of men. And yet, to surrender my sweet, my beloved, my venerable castle, the hereditary seat of my proud progenitors, at the moment of an immortal victory, ere the laurel was yet warmed on the throbbings of my forehead;—and all for what? For the most pitiful and unclassical reason that ever disgraced a human creature. Why, I should be pointed at, scouted at. 'Look, look, there is the heroine who surrendered her castle, because——' and then a whisper and a titter, and a "Tis fact 'pon my honour.' Oh, my friend, my friend, the thought was madness!

I considered, and reconsidered, but every moment only strengthened me more and more in the conviction that there was no remedy.

'Jerry,' said I, 'dear Jerry, we must surrender.'

'Surrender!' exclaimed Jerry, 'Why then, death alive, for what?'

'Because,' answered I, 'my modesty would prevent me from sleeping before so many men.'

'Poo,' cried he, 'do as I do. Have too much modesty to shew your modesty. Sleep? By my soul you shall sleep, and snore too, if you have a mind. Sleep? Sure, can't you pin the curtains round, so that we shan't see you? Sleep? Sure, how did the ladies manage on board the packet that I came over in? Sleep—sleep—sleep? O murder. I believe we must surrender, sure enough. O murder, murder, 'tis all over with us? For now that I think of it, we shan't have even room to lie down you know.'

'This is a sad affair,' said I to the minstrel. 'Can you devise no remedy?'

'None,' said the minstrel, blushing through his very eyeballs.

'Well,' cried Betterton, 'is the council of war over?'

'Yes, Sir,' said I, 'and I consent to conclude a peace.'

'I thought you would,' cried Betterton; 'so now for the terms.'

After much altercation, these articles (written by Betterton, with his pencil, and signed by him and the warden, who went down for the purpose) were agreed upon by the contending powers.

Art. 1.

All the prisoners, at present in the castle, shall be forthwith released.

Art. 2.

The troops of the contending powers shall consign their arms into the hands of the respective leaders.

Art. 3.

The commandant of the besieged army shall evacuate the castle, at the head of his men, and take a northerly direction; and at the same moment the commandant of the besieging army shall lead his forces in a southerly direction.

Art. 4.

The Lady Cherubina De Willoughby shall depart from the castle as soon as both armies are out of sight; and she shall not hold communication, direct or indirect, with the warden, for the space of twenty-four hours.

Art. 5.

The minstrel, Higginson, shall be permitted to remain with the Lady Cherubina, as her escort.

(Signed) Betterton.
Sullivan.

While Betterton returned to his army, for the purpose of announcing the peace, I fixed with Jerry to meet him in London at the expiration of twenty-four hours.

I now perceived Susan running towards the castle, with all her men; and as soon as she got under the walls, she cried:

'No peace; no peace; but bloody, bloody war! Come down here, you wretch with the steel bonnet, till I tear your eyes out;—you special babe of hell, that robbed me of the only friend I had on earth!' And she ran on with the most horrible imprecations, and vows of vengeance.

'Arrah, and is that Susy?' cried one of my men, leaning over the battlements.

'Patrick O'Brien!' exclaimed she. 'Oh! Patrick, Patrick, are you so faithless as to be taking part with my mortal enemy?'

'I am taking part with my countrymen,' cried Patrick; 'and we have just made a peace; so by gog, if you break it, 'tis yourself will be my mortual innimy!'

'Dear, dear Patrick!' said she, 'don't let that vile woman decoy you from me, and I will do whatever you desire.'

'Then I desires you to go back this moment,' said Patrick.

Susan retired to the main body, without uttering a word.

The several articles were then executed in due form. The prisoners were liberated: the soldiers on both sides laid down their arms. I distributed all my remaining money amongst my men: they thanked me with a shout; and then, headed by the warden, issued from the castle. At the same time, Betterton and his party marched off the field.

When Jerry had got almost out of sight, he halted his men, faced them towards the castle, and all gave three last cheers. I waved my handkerchief, and cried like a child.

I then took a tender leave of my dear Black Chamber; and with a heavy heart, and a tardy step, departed from my castle, till better days should enable me to revisit it. I proceeded with the minstrel to the poor woman's cottage, whence I now write; and I have just dispatched him for a chaise, as I shall return to London immediately.

My heart is almost broken.

Adieu.

LETTER XL

MS.

O YE, WHOEVER YE ARE, WHOM CHANCE OR MISFORTUNE MAY HEREAFTER CONDUCT TO THIS SPOT, TO YOU I SPEAK, TO YOU REVEAL THE STORY OF MY WRONGS, AND ASK YOU TO REVENGE THEM. VAIN HOPE! YET IT IMPARTS SOME COMFORT TO BELIEVE, THAT WHAT I NOW WRITE MAY ONE DAY MEET THE EYE OF A FELLOW-CREATURE; THAT THE WORDS WHICH TELL MY SUFFERINGS MAY ONE DAY DRAW PITY FROM THE FEELING HEART.

KNOW THEN, THAT ON THE NIGHT OF THE FATAL DAY WHICH SAW ME DRIVEN FROM MY CASTLE, BY RUTHLESS FOES, FOUR MEN IN BLACK VISAGES, RUSHED INTO THE COTTAGE WHERE I HAD TAKEN SHELTER, BORE ME FROM IT, AND FORCED ME AND MY MINSTREL INTO A CARRIAGE. WE TRAVELLED MILES IN IMPENETRABLE SILENCE. AT LENGTH THEY STOPPED, CAST A CLOAK OVER MY FACE, AND CARRIED ME IN MY ARMS, ALONG WINDING PASSAGES, AND UP AND DOWN FLIGHTS OF STEPS. THEY THEN TOOK OFF THE CLOAK, AND I

FOUND MYSELF IN AN ANTIQUE AND GOTHIC APARTMENT. MY CONDUCTORS LAID DOWN A LAMP, AND DISAPPEARED. I HEARD THE DOOR BARRED UPON ME. O SOUND OF DESPAIR! O MOMENT OF UNUTTERABLE ANGUISH! SHUT OUT FROM DAY, FROM FRIENDS, FROM LIFE—IN THE PRIME OF MY YEARS, IN THE HEIGHT OF MY TRANSGRESSIONS,—I SINK UNDER THE——

ALMOST AN HOUR HAS NOW PASSED IN SOLITUDE AND SILENCE. WHY AM I BROUGHT HITHER? WHY CONFINED THUS RIGOROUSLY? THE HORRORS OF DEATH ARE BEFORE MY EYES. O DIRE EXTREMITY! O STATE OF LIVING DEATH! IS THIS A VISION? ARE THESE THINGS REAL? ALAS, I AM BEWILDERED.

Such, Biddy, was the manuscript that I scribbled last night, after the mysterious event which it relates. You shall now hear the particulars of all that has occurred to me since.

After the ruffians had departed, and I had rallied my spirits, I took up the lamp, and began examining the chamber. It was spacious, and the feeble light that I carried could but just penetrate it. Part of the walls were hidden with historical arras, worked in colourless and rotten worsted, which depicted scenes from the Provençal Romances; the deeds of Charlemagne and his twelve peers; the Crusaders, Troubadours, and Saracens; and the Necromantic feats of the Magician Jurl. The walls were wainscotted with black larchwood; and over the painted and escutcheoned windows hung iron visors, tattered pennons, and broken shields. An antique bed of decayed damask, with a lofty tester, stood in a corner; and a few grand moth-eaten chairs, tissued and fringed with threads of tarnished gold, were round the room. At the farther end, a picture of a soldier on horseback, darting his spear upon a man, who held up his hands in a supplicating attitude, was enclosed in a frame of uncommon size, that reached down to the ground. An old harp, which occupied one corner, proved imprisonment, and some clots of blood upon the floor proved murder.

I gazed with delight at this admirable apartment. It was a perfect treasure: nothing could be more complete: all was in the best style of horror; and now, for the first time, I felt the full consciousness of being as real a heroine as ever existed.

I then indulged myself with imagining the frightful scenes I should undergo here. Such attempts to murder me, such ghosts, such mysteries! figures flitting in the dusty perspective, quick steps along the corridor, groans, and an ill-minded lord of the castle.

In the midst of this pleasing reverie, methought I heard a step approaching. It stopped at the door, the bolts were undrawn, and an antiquated waiting-woman, in fardingale, ruffles, flounces, and flowered silk, bustled into the room.

'My lord,' said she, 'desires me to let your ladyship know that he will do himself the honour of waiting on you in half-an-hour.'

'Tell your lord,' said I, 'that I shall be ready to receive him: but pray, my good woman,' said I, 'what is the name of your lord?'

'Good woman!' cried she, bridling up; 'no more good woman than yourself: Dame Ursulina, if you please.'

'Well then, Dame Ursulina, what is his name?'

'The Baron Hildebrand,' answered she. 'The only feudal chieftain left in England.'

'And what is the name of his castle?'

'Gogmagog,' answered she: 'and it is situated in the Black Forest of Grodolphon, whose oaks are coeval with the reign of Brute.'

'And, alas!' cried I, 'why have I been seized? Why thus imprisoned? Why——'

The Dame laid her finger across her lips, and grinned volumes of mystery.

'At least, tell me,' said I, with a searching look, 'how comes that blood on the floor; for it appears but just spilt?'

'Lauk!' cried she, 'that blood is there these fifty years. Sure your ladyship has often read in romances of blood on floors, and daggers, that looked as fresh as a daisy at the end of centuries. But, alas-o-day! modern blood won't keep like the good old blood. Ay, ay, ay; the times have degenerated in every thing;—even in harps. Look at that harp yonder: I warrant 'tis in excellent tune at this moment, albeit no human finger has touched it these ten years: and your ladyship must remember reading of other cobwebbed harps in old castles, that required no tuning-hammer, after lying by whole ages. But, indeed, they do say, that the ghost keeps this harp in order, by playing on it o' nights.'

'The ghost!' exclaimed I.

'Ay, by my fackins,' said she; 'sure this is the haunted chamber of the northern tower; and such sights and noises—Santa Catharina of Sienna, and St. Bridget, and San Pietro, and Santa Benedicta, and St. Radagunda, defend me!'

Then, aspirating an ejaculation, she hastily hobbled out of the room, and locked the door after her, without giving me farther satisfaction.

However, the visit from Baron Hildebrand occupied my mind more than the ghost; and I sat expecting it with great anxiety. At last, I heard a heavy tread along the corridor: the door was unbarred, and a huge, but majestic figure, strode into the chamber. The black plume towering on his cap, the armorial coat, Persian sash, and Spanish cloak, conspiring with the most muscular frown imaginable, made him look truly tremendous.

As he flung himself into a chair, he cast a Schedoniac scowl at me; while I felt, that one glance from the corner of a villain's eye is worth twenty straight-forward looks from an honest man. My heart throbbed audible, my bosom heaved like billows: I threw into my features a conventual smile, and stood before him, in all the silence of despair, something between Niobe, patience, and a broken lily.

'Lady!' cried he, with a voice that vibrated through my brain; 'I am the Baron Hildebrand, that celebrated ruffian. My plans are terrible and unsearchable. Hear me.

'My daughter, the Lady Sympathina, though long betrothed to the Marquis De Furioso, has long been enamoured of the Lord Montmorenci. In vain have I tried entreaties and imprecations: nothing will induce her to relinquish him; even though he has himself confessed to her that you reign sole tormentress of his heart.

'While doubtful what course to take, I heard, from my vassals, of your having seized on a neighbouring castle, and of Montmorenci's being there with you. The moment was too precious to be lost. I planted armed spies about the castle, with orders to make you and him prisoners the first opportunity. These orders are executed, and his lordship is a captive in the western turret.

'Now, Madam, you must already guess my motive for having taken this step. It is to secure your immediate marriage with his lordship, and thus to terminate for ever my daughter's hopes, and my own inquietude. In two days, therefore, be prepared to give him your hand, or to suffer imprisonment for life.'

'My lord,' said I, 'I am a poor, weak, timid girl, but yet not unmindful of my noble lineage. I cannot consent to disgrace it. My lord, I will not wed Montmorenci.'

'You will not?' cried he, starting from his seat.

'I will not,' said I, in a tone of the sweetest obstinacy.

'Insolent!' exclaimed he, and began to pace the chamber with prodigious strides. Conceive the scene;—the tall figure of Hildebrand passing along, with folded arms; the hideous desolation of the room, and my shrinking figure. It was great, very great. It resembled a Pandemonium, where an angel of light was tormented by a fiend. Yet insult and oppression had but added to my charms, as the rose throws forth fresh fragrance by being mutilated.

On a sudden he stopped short before me.

'What is your reason for refusing to marry him?' said he.

'My lord,' answered I, 'I do not feel for his lordship the passion of love.'

'Love!' cried he, with yells of laughter. 'Why this is Sympathina's silly rhodomontade. Love! There is no such passion. But mark me, Madam: soon shall you learn that there is such a passion as revenge!' And with these words he rushed out of the chamber.

Nothing could be better than my conduct on this occasion. I was delighted with it, and with the castle, and with every thing. I therefore knelt and chaunted a vesper hymn, so soft, and so solemn; while my eyes, like a magdalen's, were cast to the planets.

Adieu.

LETTER XLI

I had flung myself on the bed: my lamp was extinguished; and now sleep began to pour its opiate over me, when, (terrible to tell!) methought I heard steps stealing through my very chamber.

'She sleeps,' whispered a voice.

'Then poniard her at once,' said another.

'Remember, I must have five ducats,' said the first.

'Four,' said the second: 'Grufflan, the tormentor of innocents, would charge but two.'

'Then I will betray the murder.'

126

'I will take good care you shall not.'

'How so?'

'I will assassinate you after it.'

'Diavolo! 'Tis prudent, however. But by St. Jago, I will not consent to be assassinated under a ducat a-piece to my children.'

'Well, you shall have them.'

'Then, Maestro mio illustrissimo, the Bravo Abellino is your povero devotissimo!'

The next instant my strained eyeballs saw a figure half starting from behind the tattered arras, in a long cloak, and flat cap. His right hand held a dagger, and his left a dark lantern, that cast a yellow glare on the ruffianly sculpture of his visage.

I screamed;—but sorry am I to say, less like a heroine than a sea-gull;—and the bravo advanced. On a sudden, the door of the chamber was burst open, and Montmorenci rushed forward, with a brandished sword. At the same moment, Baron Hildebrand sprang from behind the tapestry.

'Turn, villain!' cried Montmorenci; and a desperate battle began.

My life was the stake. I hung upon every blow, winced as the steel descended on Montmorenci, and moved as he moved, with agonised mimicry.

At length, victory declared in his favour. The bandit lay lifeless, and the baron was disarmed; but escaped out of the chamber.

'Let us fly!' cried my preserver, snatching me to his heart. 'I have bribed a domestic.—A horse is in waiting.—Let us fly!'

'Let us, let us!' said I, disengaging myself.

'Yet hold!' cried he. 'I have saved your life. Save mine, by consenting to an immediate union.'

'Ay, my lord——'

'What?'

'I cannot.'

'Cannot!'

'Come, my lord; do come!'

'On my knees, lady——'

'Seize the villain, and immure him in the deepest dungeon!' exclaimed the baron, rushing into the room with his domestics.

Some of them laid hold on Montmorenci, the rest bore off the body of the bandit. The baron and I were left alone.

'My lord,' said I, flinging myself at his feet (for alas, I had now lost all my magnanimity), 'that man is my horror and detestation. But only promise to spare my life for one day more, and indeed, indeed, I will try if I can make up my mind to marry him.'

''Tis well,' said the baron. 'To-night you sleep secure: to-morrow decides your fate.'

He spoke, and stalked out of the chamber.

This horrid castle—would I had never set foot in it. I will escape if I can, I am resolved. I have already tried the walls, for a sliding pannel or a concealed door; but nothing of the kind can I discover. And yet something of the kind there must be, else how could the baron and bravo have entered my chamber? I protest this facility of intrusion in antique apartments is extremely distressing. For besides its exposing one to be murdered, just think how it exposes one to be peeped at. I declare I dare not even undress, lest some menial should be leering through a secret crevice. Oh, that I were once more in the mud cottage! I am sick of castles.

Adieu.

LETTER XLII

This morning, after a maid had cleaned out the room, Dame Ursulina brought breakfast.

'Graciousnessosity!' cried she, 'here is the whole castle in such a fluster; hammering and clamouring, and paddling at all manner of possets, to make much of the fine company that is coming down to the baron to-day.'

'Heavens!' exclaimed I, 'when will my troubles cease? Doubtless they are a most dissolute set. An amorous Verezzi, an insinuating Cavigni, and an abandoned Orsino; besides some lovely voluptuary, some fascinating desperado, who plays the harp, and poisons by the hour.'

'La, not at all,' said the dame. 'We shall have none but old Sir Charles Grandison, and his lady, Miss Harriet Byron, that was;—old Mr. Mortimer Delville, and his lady, Miss Cecilia, that was;—and old Lord Mortimer, and his lady, Miss Amanda, that was.'

'Can it be possible?' cried I. 'Why these are all heroes and heroines!'

'Pon my conversation, and by my fig, and as I am a true maiden, so they are,' said she; 'for my lord scorns any other sort of varment. And we shall have such tickling and pinching; and fircumdandying, and cherrybrandying, and the genteel poison of bad wine; and the warder blowing his horn, and the baron in his scowered armour, and I in a coif plaited high with ribbons all about it, and in the most rustling silk I have. And Philip, the butler, meets me in the dark. "Oddsboddikins," says he (for that is his pet oath), "mayhap I should know the voice of that silk?" "Oddspittikins," says I, "peradventure thou should'st;" and then he catches me round the neck, and——'

'There, there!' cried I, 'you distract me.'

'Marry come up!' muttered she. 'Some people think some people—Marry come up, quotha!' And she flounced out of the room.

I sat down to breakfast, astonished at what I had just heard. Harriet Byron, Cecilia, Amanda, and their respective consorts, all alive and well! Oh, could I get but one glimpse of them, speak ten words with them, I should die content. I pictured them to myself, adorned with all the venerable loveliness of a virtuous old age,—even in greyness engaging, even in wrinkles interesting. Hand in hand they walk down the gentle slope of life, and often pause to look back upon the scenes that they have passed—the happy vale of their childhood, the turretted castle, the cloistered monastery.

This reverie was interrupted by the return of Dame Ursulina.

'The baron,' said she, 'has just gone off to London; we think either for the purpose of consulting physicians about his periodical madness, or of advising government to propose a peace with France. So my young mistress, the Lady Sympathina, is anxious to visit you during his absence,—as he prohibited her;—and she has sent me to request that you will honor her with your permission.'

'Tell her I shall be most happy to see and to solace a lady of her miseries,' answered I. 'And I trust we shall swear an eternal friendship when we meet.'

'Friendship,' said the dame, 'is the soft soother of human cares. O, to see two fair females sobbing respondent, while their blue eyes shine through their tears like hyacinths bathed in the dews of the morning!'

'Why, dame,' cried I, 'how did you manage to pick up such a charming sentiment, and such elegant language?'

'Marry come up!' said she, 'I havn't lived, not I, not with heroines, not for nothing. Marry come up, quotha!' And this frumpish old woman sailed out of the chamber in a great fume.

I now prepared for an interview of congenial souls; not was I long kept in suspense. Hardly had the dame disappeared, when the door opened again, and a tall, thin, lovely girl, flew into the room. She stopped opposite me. Her yellow ringlets hung round her pale face like a mist round the moon. Again she advanced, took both my hands, and stood gazing on my features.

'Ah, what wonder,' said she, 'that Montmorenci should be captivated by these charms! No, I will not, cannot take him from you. He is your's, my friend. Marry him, and leave me to the solitude of a cloister.'

'Never!' cried I. 'Ah, madam, ah, Sympathina, your magnanimity amazes, transports me. No, my friend; your's he shall, he must be; for you love him, and I hate him.'

'Hate him!' cried she; 'and wherefore? Ah, what a form is his, and ah, what a face! Locks like the spicy cinnamon; eyes half dew, half lightning; lips like a casket of jewels, loveliest when open——'

'And teeth like the Sybil's books,' said I; 'for two of them are wanting.'

'Ah,' cried she, 'this I am informed is your reason for not marrying him; as if his charms lay in his teeth, like Sampson's strength in his hair.'

'Upon my honor,' said I, 'I would not marry him, if he had five hundred teeth. But you, my friend, you shall marry him, in spite of his teeth.'

'Ah,' cried she, 'and see my father torture you to death?'

'It were not torture,' said I, 'to save you from it.'

'It were double torture,' cried she, 'to be saved by your's.'

'Justice,' said I, 'demands the sacrifice.'

'Generosity,' said she, 'would spare the victim.'

'Is it generosity,' said I, 'to wed me with one I hate?'

'Is it justice,' said she, 'to wed me with one who hates me?'

'Ah, my friend,' cried I, 'you may vanquish me in Antithetical and Gallican repartee, but never shall you conquer me in sentimental magnanimity.'

'Let us then swear an eternal friendship,' cried she.

'I swear!' said I.

'I swear!' said she.

We rushed into each other's arms.

'And now,' cried she, when the first transports had subsided, 'how do you like being a heroine?'

'Above all things in the world,' said I.

'And how do you get on at the profession?' asked she.

'It is not for me to say,' replied I. 'Only this, that ardor and assiduity are not wanting on my part.'

'Of course then,' said she, 'you shine in all the requisite qualities. Do you blush well?'

'As well as can be expected,' said I.

'Because,' said she, 'blushing is my chief beauty. I blush one tint and three-fourths with joy; two tints, including forehead and bosom, with modesty; and four with love, to the points of my fingers. My father once blushed me against the dawn for a tattered banner to a rusty poniard.'

'And who won?' said I.

'It was play or pay,' replied she; 'and the morning happened to be misty, so there was no sport in that way; but I fainted, which was just as good, if not better. Are you much addicted to fainting?'

'A little,' said I.

"Pon honor?'

'Well, ma'am, to be honest with you, I am afraid I have never fainted yet; but at a proper opportunity I flatter myself——'

'Nay, love,' said she, 'do not be distressed about the matter. If you weep well, 'tis a good substitute. Do you weep well?'

'Extremely well, indeed,' said I.

'Come then,' cried she, 'we will weep on each other's necks.' And she flung her arms about me. We remained some moments in motionless endearment.

'Are you weeping?' said she, at length.

'No, ma'am,' answered I.

'Ah, why don't you?' said she.

'I can't, ma'am,' said I; 'I can't.'

'Ah, do,' said she.

'Upon my word, I can't,' said I: 'sure I am trying all I can. But, bless me, how desperately you are crying. Your tears are running down my bosom like a torrent, and boiling hot too. Excuse me, ma'am, but you will give me my death of cold.'

'Ah, my fondling,' said she, raising herself from my neck; 'tears are my sole consolation. Ofttimes I sit and weep, I know not why; and then I weep to find myself weeping. Then, when I can weep, I weep at having nothing to weep at; and then, when I have something to weep at, I weep that I cannot weep at it. This very morning I bumpered a tulip with my tears, while reading a dainty ditty that I must now repeat to you.

'*The moon had just risen, as a maid parted from her lover. A sylph was pursuing her sigh through the deserts of air, bathing in its warmth, and enhaling its odours. As he flew over the ocean, he saw a sea-nymph sitting on the shore, and singing the fate of a shipwreck, that appeared at a distance, with broken masts, and floating rudder. Her instrument was her own long and blue tresses, which she had strung across rocks of coral. The sparkling spray struck them, and made sweet music. He saw, he loved, he hovered over her. But invisible, how could he attract her eyes? Incorporeal, how could he touch her? Even his voice could not be heard by her amidst the dashing of the waves, and the melody of her ringlets. The sylphs, pitying his miserable state, exiled him to a bower of woodbine. There he sits, dips his pen of moonshine in the subtle dew ere it falls, and writes his love on the bell of a silver lily.*'

This charming tale led us to talk of moonshine. We moralized on the uncertainty of it, and of life; discussed sighs, and agreed that they were charming things; enumerated the various kinds of tresses—flaxen, golden, chesnut, amber, sunny, jetty, carroty; and I suggested two new epithets,—sorrel hair and narcissine hair. Such a flow of soul never was.

At last she rose to depart.

'Now, my love,' said she, 'I am in momentary expectation of Sir Charles Grandison, Mortimer Delville, and Lord Mortimer, with their amiable wives. Will you permit them, during the baron's absence, to spend an hour with you this evening? They will not betray us. I shall be proud of showing you to them, and you will receive much delight and edification from their society.'

I grasped at the proposal with eagerness; she flitted out of the chamber with a promissory smile; and I was so charmed, that I began frisking about, and snapping my fingers, in a most indecorous manner.

What an angel is this Sympathina! Her face has the contour of a Madona, with the sensibility of a Magdalen. Her voice is soft as the last accents of a dying maid. Her language is engaging, her oh is sublime, and her ah is beautiful.

Adieu.

LETTER XLIII

Towards night I heard the sound of several steps approaching the chamber. The bolts were undrawn, and Lady Sympathina, at the head of the company, entered, and announced their names.

'Bless me!' said I, involuntarily; for such a set of objects never were seen.

Sir Charles Grandison came forward the first. He was an emaciated old oddity in flannels and a flowing wig. He bowed over my hand, and kissed it—his old custom, you know.

Lady Grandison leaned on his arm, bursting with fat and laughter, and so unlike what I had conceived of Harriet Byron, that I turned from her in disgust.

Mortimer Delville came next; and my disappointment at finding him a plain, sturdy, hard-featured fellow, was soon absorbed in my still greater regret at seeing his Cecilia,—once the blue-eyed, sun-tressed Cecilia,—now flaunting in all the reverend graces of a painted grandmother, and leering most roguishly.

After them, Lord Mortimer and his Amanda advanced; but he had fallen into flesh; and she, with a face like scorched parchment, appeared both broken-hearted and broken-winded; such a perpetual sighing and wheezing did she keep.

I was too much shocked and disappointed to speak; but Sir Charles soon broke silence; and after the most tedious sentence of compliment that I had ever heard, he thus continued:

'Your ladyship may recollect I have always been celebrated for giving advice. Let me then advise you to relieve yourself from your present embarrassment, by marrying Lord Montmorenci. It seems you do not love him. For that very reason marry him. Trust me, love before marriage is the surest preventive of love after it. Heroes and heroines exemplify the proposition. Why do their biographers always conclude the book just at their wedding? Simply because all beyond it is unhappiness and hatred.'

'Surely, Sir Charles,' said I, 'you must be mistaken. Their biographers (who have such admirable information, that they can even tell the thoughts and actions of dying personages, when not a soul is near them), these always end the book with declaring that the connubial lives of their heroes and heroines are like unclouded skies, or unruffled streams, or summer all the year through, or some gentle simile or other.'

'That is all irony,' replied Sir Charles. 'But I know most of these heroes and heroines myself; and I know that nothing can equal their misery.'

'Do you know Lord Orville and his Evelina?' said I; 'and are not they happy?'

'Happy!' cried he, laughing. 'Have you really never heard of their notorious miffs? Why it was but yesterday that she flogged him with a boiled leg of mutton, because he had sent home no turnips.'

'Astonishment!' exclaimed I. 'And she, when a girl, so meek.'

'Ay, there it is,' said he. 'One has never seen a white foal or a cross girl; but often white horses and cross wives. Let me advise you against white horses.'

'But pray,' said I, addressing Amanda, 'is not your brother Oscar happy with his Adela?'

'Alas, no,' cried she. 'Oscar became infatuated with the charms of Evelina's old governess, Madam Duval; so poor Adela absconded; and she, who was once the soul of mirth, has now grown a confirmed methodist; curls a sacred sneer at gaiety, loves canting and decanting, piety and *eau de vie*. In short, the devil is very busy about her, though she sometimes drives him away with a thump of the Bible.'

'Well, Rosa, the gentle beggar-girl,—what of her?' said I.

'Eloped with one Corporal Trim,' answered Sir Charles.

'How shocking!' cried I. 'But Pamela, the virtuous Pamela?'——

'Made somewhat a better choice,' said Sir Charles; 'for she ran off with Rasselas, Prince of Abyssinia, when he returned to the happy valley.'

'Dreadful accounts, indeed!' said I.

'So dreadful,' said Sir Charles, bowing over my hand, 'that I trust they will determine you to marry Montmorenci. 'Tis true, he has lost two teeth, and you do not love him; but was not Walstein a cripple? And did not Caroline of Lichfield fall in love with him after their marriage, though she had hated him before it?'

'Recollect,' cried Cecilia, 'what perils environ you here. The baron is the first murderer of the age.'

'Look at yonder blood,' cried old Mortimer Delville.

'Remember the bandit last night,' cried old Lord Mortimer.

'Think of the tremendous spectre that haunts this apartment,' cried Lady Grandison.

'And above all,' cried the Lady Sympathina, 'bear in mind that this chamber may be the means of your waking some morning with a face like a pumpkin.'

'Heavens!' exclaimed I, 'what do you mean? My face like a pumpkin?'

'Yes,' said she. 'The dampness of the room would swell it up like a pumpkin in a single night.'

'Oh! ladies and gentlemen,' cried I, dropping on my knees, 'you see what shocking horrors surround me here. Oh! let me beseech of you to pity and to rescue me. Surely, surely you might aid me in escaping!'

'It is out of the nature of possibilities,' said Lady Sympathina.

'At least, then,' cried I, 'you might use your influence to have me removed from this vile room, that feels like a well.'

'Fly!' cried Dame Ursulina, running in breathless. 'The baron has just returned, and is searching for you all. And he has already been through the chapel, and armoury, and gallery; and the west tower, and east tower, and south tower; and the cedar chamber, and oaken chamber, and black chamber, and grey, brown, yellow, green, pale pink, sky blue; and every shade, tinge, and tint of chamber in the whole castle. Benedicite, Santa Maria; how the times have degenerated! Come, come, come.'

The guests vanished, the door was barred, and I remained alone.

I sat ruminating in sad earnest, on the necessity for my consenting to this hateful match; when (and I protest to you, I had not thought it was more than nine o'clock), a terrible bell, which I never heard before, tolled, with an appalling reverberation, that rang through my whole frame, the frightful hour of One!

At the same moment I heard a noise; and looking towards the opposite end of the chamber, I beheld the great picture on a sudden disappear; and, standing in its stead, a tall figure, cased in blood-stained steel, and with a spectral visage, the perfect counterpart of the baron's.

I sat gasping. It uttered these sepulchral intonations.

'*I am the spirit of the murdered Alphonso. Lord Montmorenci deserves thee. Wed him, or in two days thou liest a corpse. To-morrow night I come again.*'

The superhuman appearance spoke; and (oh, soothing sound) uttered a human sneeze!

'Damnation!' it muttered. 'All is blown!' And immediately the picture flew back to its place.

Well, I had never heard of a ghost's sneezing before: so you may judge I soon got rid of my terror, and felt pretty certain that this was no bloodless and marrowless apparition, but the baron himself, who had adopted the ghosting system, so common in romances, for the purpose of frightening me into his schemes.

However, I had now discovered a concealed door, and with it a chance of escape. I must tell you, that escape by the public door is utterly impracticable, as a maid always opens it for those that enter, and remains outside till they return. However, I have a plan about the private door; which, if the ghost should appear again, as it promised, is likely to succeed.

I was pondering upon this plan, when in came Dame Ursulina, taking snuff, and sneezing at a furious rate.

'By the mass,' said she, 'it rejoiceth the old cockles of my heart to see your ladyship safe; for as I passed your door just now, methought I heard the ghost.'

'You might well have heard it,' said I, pretending infinite faintness, 'for I have seen it; and it entered through yonder picture.'

'Benedicite!' cried she, 'but it was a true spectre!'

'A real, downright apparition,' said I, 'uncontaminated with the smallest mixture of mortality.'

'And didn't your ladyship hear me sneeze at the door?' said she.

'I was too much alarmed to hear anything,' answered I. 'But pray have the goodness to lend me that snuff-box, as a pinch or two may revive me from my faintness.' I had my reasons for this request.

'A heroine take snuff!' cried she, laying the box on the table. 'Lack-a-daisy, how the times are changed! But now, my lady, don't be trying to move or cut that great picture; for though the ghost comes into the chamber through it, no mortal can. I know better than to let you give me the slip; and I will tell a story to prove my knowledge of bolts and bars. When I was a girl, a young man lodged in the house; and one night he stole the stick that I used to fasten the hasp and staple of my door with. Well, my mother bade me put a carrot (as there was nothing else) in its place. So I put in a carrot—for I was a dutiful daughter; but I put in a boiled carrot—for I was a love-sick maiden. Eh, don't I understand the doctrine of bolts and bars?'

'You understand a great deal too much,' said I, as the withered wanton went chuckling out of the chamber.

I must now retire to rest. I do not fear being disturbed by a bravo to-night; but I am uneasy, lest I should wake in the morning with a face like a pumpkin.

Adieu.

LETTER XLIV

About noon the Baron Hildebrand paid me a visit, to hear, as he said, my final determination respecting my marriage with Montmorenci. I had prepared my lesson, and I told him that my mind was not yet entirely reconciled to such an event; but that it was much swayed by a most extraordinary circumstance which had occurred the night before. He desired me to relate it; and I then, with apparent agitation, recounted the particulars of the apparition, and declared that if it should come again I would endeavour to preserve my presence of mind, and enter into conversation with it; in order (as it appeared quite well informed of the picture) to learn whether my marriage with his lordship would prove fortunate or otherwise. I then added, that if its answer should be favourable, I would not hesitate another moment to give him my hand.

The baron, while he could not suppress a smile, protested himself highly delighted with my determination of speaking to the spectre, and encouraged me not to fear it, as it was the most harmless creature of its kind ever known.

He then took his leave. I spent the remainder of the day reflecting on the desperate enterprise that I had planned for the night, and fortifying my mind by recalling all the hazardous escapes of other heroines.

At last the momentous hour was at hand. The lamp and snuff-box lay on the table. I sat anxious, and kept a watchful eye upon the picture.

The bell tolled one, again the picture vanished, and again the spectre stood there. Its left thumb rested upon its hip, and its right hand was held to the heavens. I sent forth a well-executed shriek, and hid my face in my hands, while it spoke these words:

'*I come to thee for the last time. Wilt thou wed Montmorenci, or wilt thou not?—Speak.*'

'Oh!' cried I, 'if you would only promise not to do me a mischief, I have something particular to ask of you.'

'A spirit cannot harm a mortal,' drawled out the spectre.

'Well then,' said I, faltering and trembling.—'Perhaps—pardon me—perhaps you would first have the goodness to walk in.'

The spectre advanced a few paces, and paused.

'This is so kind, so condescending,' said I, 'that really—do take a chair.'

The spectre shook its head mournfully.

'Pray do,' said I, 'you will oblige me.'

The spectre seated itself in a chair; but atoned for the mortal act by an immortal majesty of manner.

'As you are of another world,' said I, "tis but fair to do the honours of this; and in truth, I am not at all astonished that you apparitions should speak so harshly as you usually do, we mortals always shew such evident aversion and horror at your appearance.'

'There is a prejudice gone forth against us,' said the spectre, with a hollow voice, 'in consequence of our coming at night, like thieves.'

'Yes,' said I, 'at one precisely. And it has often struck me how well the clocks of old castles were kept, for they regularly struck just as the ghost appeared. Indeed, ghosts keep such late hours, that 'tis no wonder they look pale and thin. I do not recollect ever to have heard or read of a fat or a fresh-coloured phantom.'

'Nor of a ghost wanting a limb or an eye,' said the spectre.

'Nor of an ugly ghost,' said I bowing.

The spectre took the compliment, and bowed in return.

'And therefore,' said the spectre, 'as spirits are always accurate resemblances of the bodies that they once inhabited, none but thin and pale persons can ever become ghosts.'

'And by the same rule,' said I, 'none but blue-eyed and golden-haired persons can go to heaven; for our painters always represent angels so. I have never heard of a hazel-eyed angel, or a black-haired cherub.'

'I know,' said the spectre, 'if angels are, as painters depict them, always sitting naked on cold clouds, I would rather live the life of a ghost, to the end of the chapter.'

'And pray,' cried I, 'where, and how do ghosts live?'

'Within this very globe,' said the spectre. 'For this globe is not, as most mortals imagine, a solid body, but a round crust about ten miles thick; and the concave inside is furnished just like the convex outside, with wood, water, vale and mountain. In the centre stands a nice little golden sun, about the size of a pippin, and lights our internal world; where, whatever enjoyments we loved as men, we retain as ghosts. We banquet on visionary turtle, or play at aërial marbles, or drive a phantasmagoric four in hand. The young renew their amours, and the more aged sit yawning for the day of judgment.—But I scent the rosy air of dawn. Speak, lady; what question art thou anxious that I should expound?'

'Whether,' said I, 'if I marry Lord Montmorenci, I shall be happy with him or not?'

'Blissful as Eden,' replied the spectre. 'Your lives will be congenial, and your deaths simultaneous.'

'And now,' said I, walking closer to it, 'will you do me the favour to take a pinch of snuff?'

'Avant!' it cried, motioning me from it with its hand.

But quick as thought, I flung the whole contents of the box full into its eyes.

'Blood and thunder!' exclaimed the astonished apparition.

I snatched the lamp, sprang through the frame of the picture, shut the concealed door, bolted it; while all the time I heard the phantom within, dancing in agony at its eyes, and sending mine to as many devils as could well be called together on so short a notice.

Thus far my venturous enterprise had prospered. I now found myself in a narrow passage, with another door at the farther end of it; and I prepared to traverse winding stairs, subterranean passages, and suites of tapestried apartments. I therefore advanced, and opened the door; but in an instant started back; for I had beheld a lighted hall, of modern architecture, with gilded balustrades, ceiling painted in fresco, Etruscan lamps, and stucco-work! Yes, it was a villa, or a casino, or a pallazo, or any thing you please but a castello. Amazement! Horror! What should I do? whither turn? delay would be fatal. Again I peeped. The hall was empty; so, putting down my lamp, I stole across it to an open door, and looked through the chink. I had just time to see a Persian saloon, and in the centre a table laid for supper, when I heard several steps entering the hall. It was too late to retreat, so I sprang into the room; and recollecting that a curtain had befriended me once before, I ran behind one which I saw there.

Instantly afterwards the persons entered. They were spruce footmen, bringing in supper. Not a scowl, not a mustachio amongst them.

As soon as the covers were laid, a crowd of company came laughing into the room; but, friend of my bosom, fancy, just fancy my revulsion of soul, my dismay, my disgust, my bitter indignation—oh! how shall I describe to you half what I felt, when I recognised these wretches, as they entered one by one, to be the identical gang who had visited me the day before, as heroes and heroines! I knew them instantly, though they looked twice as young; and in the midst of them all, as blithe as larks, came Betterton himself and Lord Altamont Mortimer Montmorenci! My heart died at the sight.

After they had seated themselves, Betterton (who sat at the head, and therefore was master) desired one of the servants to bring in 'the crazed poet.' And now two footmen appeared, carrying between them a large meal-bag, filled with Higginson; which they placed to the table, on a vacant seat. The bag was fastened at the top, and a slit was on the side of it.

The wretches then began to banter him, and bade him put forth his head; but he would neither move nor speak. At last they turned the conversation to me.

'I wonder can he be ghosting her all this time?' said Betterton.

'Well,' cried the fellow who had personated Sir Charles Grandison, 'I ought to have played the ghost, I am so much taller than he.'

'Not unless you could act it better than you did Grandison,' said the late Lady Sympathina. 'No, no, I was the person who performed my part well;—pouring a vial of hot water down her neck, by way of tears; and frightening her out of her senses by talking of a face like a pumpkin!'

133

'Nay,' cried my Lord Montmorenci, 'the best piece of acting you ever saw was when I first met her at the theatre, and persuaded her that Abraham Grundy was Lord Altamont Mortimer Montmorenci.'

'Except,' said Betterton, 'when I played old Whylome Eftsoones, at the masquerade, and made her believe that Cherry Wilkinson was Lady Cherubina De Willoughby.'

I turned quite sick; but I had no time for thought, the thunderclaps came so thick upon me.

'She had some mad notion of the kind before,' said Grundy (I have done with calling him Montmorenci), 'for she fancied that an old piece of parchment, part of a lease of lives, was an irrefragable proof of her being Lady De Willoughby.'

'Ay,' cried Betterton, 'and of poor Wilkinson's being her persecutor, instead of her father; on the strength of which vagary he lies at this moment in a madhouse.'

'But,' said Grundy, 'her setting up for a heroine, and her affectation while imitating the manners and language that authors chuse to give their heroines, would make a tiger laugh. I vow and protest, our amorous interview, where she first told her love, was the most burlesque exhibition in nature. I am thine, and thou art mine! whimpered the silly girl, sinking on my bosom. She now says she does not love me. Don't believe a syllable of it. Why, the poor creature could not even bridle her passion in my presence. Such hugging and kissing as she went on with, that, as I hope to be saved, I sometimes thought she would suffocate me outright.'

"Tis false as hell!' cried I, bursting into tears, and running from behind the curtain. 'Upon my sacred honour, ladies and gentlemen, 'tis every word of it a vile, malicious, execrable falsehood! Oh, what shall I do? what shall I do?' and I wrung my hands with agony.

The guests had risen from their seats in amaze; and I now made a spring towards the door, but was intercepted by Betterton, who held me fast.

'In the name of wonder,' cried he, 'how came you here?'

'No matter,' cried I, struggling. 'I know all. What have I ever done to you, you base, you cruel people?'

'Keep yourself cool, my little lady,' said he.

'I won't, I can't!' cried I. 'To use me so. You vile set; you horrid, horrid set!'

'Go for another meal-bag,' said he, to the servant. 'Now, madam, you shall keep company with the bagged poet.'

'Mercy, mercy!' cried I, 'What, will no one help me?'

'I will if I can!' exclaimed Higginson, with his head thrust out of the bag, like a snail; and down he slided from his seat, and began rolling, and tumbling, and struggling on the floor, till he got upon his feet; and then he came jumping towards me, now falling now rising, while his face and bald forehead were all over meal, his eyes blaring, and his mouth wide open. The company, wherever he moved, kept in a circle round him, and clapped their hands and shouted.

As I stood, with Betterton still holding me fast, he was suddenly flung from me by some one, and my hand seized. I turned, and beheld—Stuart. 'Oh! bless you, bless you!' cried I, catching his arm, 'for you have come to save me from destruction!'

He pressed my hand, and pointing to Betterton and Grundy, who stood thunderstruck, cried, 'There are your men!'

A large posse of constables immediately rushed forward, and arrested them.

'Heydey! what is all this?' cried Betterton.

"Tis for the beating you gave us when we were doing our duty,' said a man, and I recognised in the speaker one of the police-men who had arrested me about the barouche.

'This is government all over,' cried Betterton. 'This is the minister. This is the law!'

'And let me tell you, Sir,' said Stuart, 'that nothing but my respect for the law deters me at this moment from chastising you as you deserve.'

'What do you mean, sirrah?' cried Betterton.

'That you are a ruffian,' said Stuart, 'and the same cowardice which made you offer insult to a woman will make you bear it from a man. Now, Sir, I leave you to your fate.' And we were quitting the room.

'What thing is that?' said Stuart, stopping short before the poet; who, with one arm and his face out of the bag, lay on his back, gasping and unable to stir.

'Cut it, cut it!' cried the poor man, in choaking accents.

'Higginson I protest!' exclaimed Stuart, as he snatched a knife from the table, and laid open the bag. Up rose the poet, resurrectionary from his hempen coffin, and was beginning to clench his fist; but Stuart caught his arm, and hurried him and me out of the room.

Stuart, with great eagerness, now began asking me the particulars of all that had occurred at Betterton's; and his rage, as I related it, was extreme.

He then proceeded to tell me how he had discovered my being there. After his departure from Lady Gwyn's, he set off for London, to prosecute his inquiries about my father; and spent some days in this way, to no purpose. At length he returned to Lady Gwyn's, but was much shocked at learning from her that I had robbed her, and absconded; and had afterwards made an assault on her house, at the head of a set of Irishmen. By the description she gave, he judged that Jerry Sullivan was one of them; and not finding us at Monkton Castle, whither she directed him, he posted back to London, in order to make inquiries at Jerry's house. Jerry, who had just returned, related the whole history of the castle; adding that I was to call upon him the moment I should arrive in Town. Stuart, therefore, waited some time; but as I did not appear, he began to suspect that Betterton had entrapped me; so he hastened to the coachmaker, and having explained to him that I was no swindler, and having paid him for the barouche, he told him (as he learned from Jerry) that Betterton was one of those who had assaulted the postilion and constables. The coachmaker, therefore, applied at the police-office; and a party was dispatched to apprehend Betterton. Stuart accompanied them, and thus gained admission (which he could not otherwise have done) into the house.

Higginson now told a lamentable tale of the pranks that Betterton had played on him; and amongst the rest, mentioned, that a servant had seduced him into the bag, by pretending to be his friend, and to smuggle him out of the house, in the character of meal.

He could gather, from several things said while the company were tormenting him, that Grundy had agreed to marry me; and then, for a stipulated sum, to give Betterton opportunities of prosecuting his infamous designs. Thus both of them would escape the penalties of the law.

He likewise informed me, that the female guests were (to use his own words) ladies whom the male guests loved better than they ought to do; and he then explained that the several rooms were furnished according to the fashions of different countries; Grecian, Persian, Chinese, Italian; and that mine was the Gothic chamber.

By this time, having reached the village, and stopped at an inn, where we meant to sleep, I desired a room, and bade Stuart a hasty good night.

Shocked, astonished, and ashamed at all that had passed, I threw myself on the bed, and unburdened my full heart in a bitter fit of crying. What! thought I, not the Lady Cherubina De Willoughby after all;—the tale fabricated by Betterton himself;—the parchment that I had built the hope of my noble birth upon a mere lease of lives;—could these things be? Alas, there was no doubt of the fatal fact! I had overheard the wretches boasting of it, and I had discovered their other impositions with my own eyes. To be thus upset in my favourite speculation, in the business of my whole life; to have to begin all over again,—to have to search the wide world anew for my real name, my real family—or was Wilkinson indeed my father? Oh! if so, what a fall! and how horridly had I treated him! But I would not suffer myself to think of it. Then to be laughed at, despised, insulted by dissolute creatures calling themselves lords and barons, and bravos, and heroes and heroines; and I declared to be no heroine! am I a heroine? I caught myself constantly repeating; and then I walked about wildly, then sat on the bed, then cast my body across it. Once I fell into a doze, and dreamed frightful dreams of monsters pursuing me swifter than the wind, while my bending limbs could only creep; and my voice, calling for help, could not rise above a whisper. Then I woke, repeating, am I a heroine? I believe I was quite delirious; for notwithstanding all that I could do to prevent myself, I ran on rapidly, am I a heroine? am I? am I? am I? till my brain reeled from its poise, and my hands were clenched with perturbation.

Thus passed the night, and towards morning I fell into a slumber.

Adieu.

LETTER XLV

This morning my head felt rather better, and I appeared before Stuart with the sprightliest air imaginable; not that my mind was at ease;—far from it;—but that I could not endure to betray my mortification at having proved such a dupe to buffoons and villains.

After breakfast, we began arranging our plans, and decided on proceeding to London; but did not determine on my place of residence there. I had my own projects, however.

As Higginson had assisted in rescuing me from the police, Stuart advised him to remain concealed somewhere, till after the trials of Betterton and Grundy; for though the poor man did not know that they were officers of justice whom he was assaulting (he having been in the turret when the fray commenced), yet this fact might be difficult to prove. Stuart, therefore, gave him some money, and I a letter; and he set off, in extreme tribulation, for the cottage of the poor woman; there to stay till the business should be decided.

135

Stuart and I then took our departure in a chaise. Unable to counterfeit gaiety long, I relapsed into languor; nor could my companion, by any effort, withdraw me from the contemplation of my late disgrace.

As we drew near Lady Gwyn's, he represented the propriety of my restoring her portrait, lest she should have recourse to an arrest. Disheartened by the past, and terrified for the future, I soon consented; and on our arriving at the avenue of the gentleman who had the portrait in his possession, Stuart, by my desire, went to the house without me. He was absent some time, but at last came back with it in his hand.

We then drove to Lady Gwyn's; and while I remained at the gate, he proceeded to execute the commission for me. Presently, however, I saw him return accompanied by Lady Gwyn herself, who welcomed me with much kindness, begged I would forget the past, and prevailed on me to go into the house.

But it was only to suffer new mortifications. For now, at the instance of Stuart, she began to relate all the pranks which she had practised upon me while I was with her. She confessed that the crowning ceremony was merely to amuse her guests at my expence; and that my great mother was her own nephew! Think of that, Biddy! She said that Stuart, who had known her for some years, begged of her when I paid her my first visit to let me remain under her care, till his return from Town; and to humour my pretty caprices, as she called them. But he did not desire her to go so far with the jest; and she had now just begun an apology for her conduct, when I rose, overwhelmed with shame and indignation, dropped a hasty courtesy, and fairly ran out of the house.

We proceeded some miles silent and uncomfortable. My heart was bursting, and my head felt as if billows were tossing through it.

At last I found myself in sight of the village where William, whom I had separated from his mistress a few weeks before, used to live. As this was a favourable opportunity for reconciling the lovers, I now made Stuart acquainted with the real origin of their quarrel, which I had concealed from him at the time it happened, lest he should mar it. He shook his head at the recital, and desired the driver to find out William's house, and stop there. This was done, and in a few moments William made his appearance. He betrayed some agitation at seeing me, but saluted me with respect.

'Well, William,' said I, sportively, 'how goes on your little quarrel with Mary? Is it made up?'

'No, Ma'am,' answered he, with a doleful look, 'and I fear never will.'

'Yes, William,' cried I, with an assuring nod, 'I have the happiness to tell you that it will.'

'Ah, Ma'am,' said he, 'I suppose you do not know what a sad calamity has fallen upon her since you were here. The poor creature has quite lost her senses.'

'For shame!' cried I, 'What are you saying? Lost her senses! Well, I am sure it was not my fault, however.'

'Your's?' said he. 'Oh, no, Ma'am. But she has never been in her reason since the day you left her.'

'Let us be gone,' whispered I to Stuart, as I sank back in the carriage. 'Surely not,' said he. 'Tis at least your duty to repair the mischief you have done.'

'I should die before I could disclose it!' cried I.

'Then I will disclose it for you,' said he, leaping out of the chaise.

He went with William into the house, and I remained in such a state of mind, that I was several times on the point of quitting the chaise, and escaping I knew not whither; but any where from the horrid scene awaiting me. At last, Stuart appeared without William; and getting in, gave the driver directions to Mary's cottage.

I wanted him to go without me: but he declared that no effectual explanation could take place, unless from myself. He then said every thing to re-assure me. He told me that the poor girl was quite harmless, and had only temporary fits of wandering; and that, were the circumstances of the fatal letter once explained to her, and a reconciliation effected, she might eventually recover from her derangement; for William, it seems, had never divulged the contents of that letter, as it enjoined him not; but now Stuart brought it with him.

Having arrived near the cottage, we got out, and walked towards it. With a faltering step I crossed the threshold, and found the father in the parlour.

'Dear Miss,' said he, 'welcome here once more. I suppose you have come to see poor Mary. Oh! 'tis a piteous, piteous sight. There she does nothing but walk about, and sigh, and talk so wild; and nobody can tell the cause but that William; and he will not, for he says she forbade him.'

'Come with me,' said Stuart, 'and I will tell you the cause.'

He then led the miserable old man out of the room, and I remained at the window weeping.

But in a few minutes I heard a step; and on turning round, saw the father, running towards me with a face haggard and ghastly; and crying out, 'Cruel, cruel, cruel!' then grasping my shoulder, and lifting his tremulous hand to heaven: 'Now,' said he, 'may the lightning of a just and good Providence——'

'Oh! pray,' cried I, snatching down his hand—'oh! pray do not curse me! Do not curse a poor, silly, mad creature. It was a horrid affair; very horrid; but, indeed, indeed, I meant no harm.'

'Be calm, my good man,' said Stuart, 'and let us go to the garden where your daughter is walking. I am sure this young lady will not refuse to accompany us, and do her utmost in this critical moment.'

'I will do any thing,' cried I, 'come along.'

We now passed into the garden; and I shuddered as I beheld the beautiful wreck at a distance. She had just stopt short in a stepping posture: her cloak had half fallen from her shoulders, and as her head hung down, her forefinger was lightly laid on her lip.

Panting to tell her all, I flew towards her, and caught her hand.

'Do you remember me, Mary?' said I softly.

She looked at me some moments with a faint smile; and at last she coloured.

'Ah! yes, I remember you,' said she. 'You were with us that very evening when I was so wretched. But I don't care about him now;—I don't indeed; and if I could only see him once more, I would tell him so. And then I would frown and turn from him; and then he would follow, so sad and so pale: don't you think he would? And I am keeping his presents to give back to him, as he did mine; and see how I have my hair parted on my forehead, just as he used to like it, ready the moment I see him to rumple it all about; and then he will cry so. Don't you think he will? And then I will run, run, run away like the wind, and never see him again; never, never again.'

'My dear Mary,' said I, 'you shall see him again, and be friends with him too. Your William is still faithful to you;—most faithful, and still loves you better than his life. I have seen him myself this moment.'

'You have?' cried she, reddening. 'Oh! and what did he say? But hush, not a word before my father and that man:' and she put one hand upon my mouth, and with the other round my waist, hurried me into a little arbour, where we sat down.

'And now,' whispered she, stealing her arms about my neck, and looking earnestly into my eyes, while her whole frame shook, 'and now what did he say?'

'Mary,' said I, with a serious tone and aspect, 'you must collect your ideas, and listen attentively, for I have much to disclose. Do you recollect a letter that I got you to write for me when I was here last?'

'Letter—' muttered she. 'Letter.—Yes, I believe I do. Oh! yes, I recollect it well; for it was a sad letter to your sweetheart, telling him that you had married another; and your sweetheart's name was William; and I thought, at the time, I would never write such a letter to my own William.'

'And yet, Mary,' said I, 'your own William got that letter, by some mistake,' (for I could not bear to tell the real fact) 'that very evening; and seeing it in your hand-writing, and addressed to William, he thought it was from you to him; and so he gave you back your presents, and——'

'What is all that?' cried Mary, starting up. 'Merciful powers! say all that over again!'

I made her sit down, and I shewed her the letter. As she read it, her colour changed, her lip quivered, her hand shook; and at the conclusion, she dropped it with a dreadful groan, and remained quite motionless.

'Mary!' cried I, 'dear Mary, do not look so. Speak, Mary,' and I stirred her shoulder; but she still sat motionless with a fixed smile.

'I shall, I will see her!' cried the voice of William at a distance; and the next instant he was seated breathless by her side.

'Mary, my Mary!' cried he in the most touching accents.

At the well-known voice, she started, and turned towards him; but in a moment averted her face, and rose as pale as ashes. Then drawing some letters and baubles from her bosom, she threw them into his lap, and began gently disarranging her hair, all the time looking sideways at him, with an air of pretty dignity.

'Come,' said she, taking my hand, and leading me out of the arbour. 'Well, was not that glorious? Now I shall die content.'

'Yes,' said I, 'after having first killed your William. Have I not explained all about the letter; and how can you now treat him so cruelly?'

'The letter,' said she. 'Ay, true, the letter. Let me consider a moment. He thought it was mine, do you say?'

'He did indeed, Mary; and yet you will not be friends with him.'

'But you see he won't follow me.' said she. 'He would have followed me once. Is he following me?'

'He cannot,' answered I. 'The poor young man is lying on the ground, and sobbing ready to break his heart.'

Mary stopped.

'Shall I call him?' said I.

'Why now,' said she, 'how can I prevent you?'

'William!' cried I. 'Mary calls you.'

William came flying towards her. At the sound of his steps she turned, stretched forth her hands, uttered a long and piercing cry;—and they were locked in each other's arms.

But the poor girl, quite overpowered by the sudden change, fell back insensible; while William, kissing her, and weeping over her, bore her into the house, and laid her on a bed.

It was so long before she shewed any symptoms of animation, that we began to feel serious alarm; and William ran to the village for an apothecary. By degrees she came to herself, and appeared somewhat more composed; but still wandering. At last, with her hand clasped in her lover's, she fell asleep; and then, as our presence could be no farther useful, we took leave of the venerable peasant; who, generous with recent hope, freely gave me his forgiveness and his blessing.

In my first transports of anguish at this scene, I disclosed to Stuart, what I had all day determined, but dreaded to tell—the situation of my father in the madhouse. At the horrid account, the good young man turned pale, but said not a word. I saw that I was undone, and I burst into tears.

'Be comforted, my dear girl,' said he, laying his hand on mine. 'You have long been acting under the delusion of a dreadful dream, but this confession, and these tears, are, I trust, the prognostics of a total renunciation of error. So now let us hasten to your father and release him. He shall forgive you; past follies shall be forgotten, past pleasures renewed; you shall return to your real home, and Cherry Wilkinson shall again be the daughter of an honest squire.'

'Mr. Stuart,' said I, 'as to my past follies, I know of none but two;—Mary's and my father's matters. And as to that father, he may not be what you suppose him. I fancy, Sir, there are such things as men who begin life with plain names, and end it with the most Italian in the world.'

'Well?' cried Stuart.

'Well,' said I, 'that honest squire, as you call him, may yet come out to be a marquis.'

Stuart groaned, and put his head out at the window.

We have reached London, and I take the opportunity to write while Stuart is procuring from Grundy, who now lies in prison, such a statement as cannot fail to make the Doctor release my poor father without hesitation.

How shall I support this approaching interview? I shall sink, I shall die under it. Indeed I wish to die; and I feel an irresistible presentiment that my prayer will shortly be granted. All day long I have a horrid gloom hanging over me, besides a frequent wildness of ideas, and an unusual irritability. I have a chilliness, and yet a burning through my skin; and I am unwilling even to move. If I could lock myself up in a room, with heaps of romances, and shut out all the world, I sometimes fancy that I should be happy. But no, my friend; the grave will soon be my chamber, the worms my books; and if ever I write again, I shall write from the bed of death. I know it; I feel it. I shall be reconciled to my dear parent, acknowledge my follies, and die.

Adieu.

LETTER XLVI

Agitated beyond measure, I found myself at the madhouse, without well knowing how I had got there; and Stuart, after a long altercation with the Doctor, supported me to the room where my father was confined. He had to push me gently before him, and as I stopped breathless inside the door, I saw by the dusky twilight a miserable object, shivering, and sitting on a bed. A few rags and a blanket were cast about it: the face was haggard, and the chin overgrown with a grisly beard. Yet, amidst all this disfigurement, I could not mistake my father. I ran, prostrated myself at his feet, and clasping his knees, exclaimed, 'Father, dear father!'

He started, and gazed at me for a moment; then flung me from him, and threw himself with his face downward on the bed. I cast my body across his, and endeavoured, with both my hands, to turn round his head, that I might embrace him; but he resisted every effort.

'Father!' cried I, clasping his neck, 'will you break my heart? Will you drive me to distraction? Speak, father! Oh! one word, one little word, to save me from death!'

Still he lay mute and immoveable.

'You are cold, father,' said I. 'You shiver. Shall I put something about you? shall I, father? Ah! I can be so kind and so tender when I love one; and I love you dearly—Heaven knows I do.'

I stole my hand on one of his, and lay caressing his forehead, and murmuring words of fondness in his ear. But nothing could avail. He withdrew his hand by degrees, and buried his forehead deeper in the cloaths. And now half frantic, I began to wring my hands, and beat the pillow, and moan, and utter the most deplorable lamentations.

At last I thought I saw him a little convulsed, as if with smothered tears.

'Ah,' cried I, 'you are relenting, you are weeping. Bless you for that. Dear, dear father, look up, and see with what joy a daughter can embrace you.'

'My child, my child!' cried he, turning, and throwing himself upon my bosom. 'A heart of stone could not withstand this! There, there, there, I forgive you all!'

Fast and fondly did we cling round each other, and sweet were the sighs that we breathed, and the tears that we shed.

But I suffered too much: the disorder which had some time been engendering in my frame now burst forth with alarming vehemence, and I was conveyed raving into a carriage. On our arrival at the hotel, they sent for a physician, who pronounced me in a violent fever of a nervous nature. For a fortnight I was not expected to recover; and I myself felt so convinced of my speedy dissolution, that I requested the presence of a clergyman. He came; and his conversations, by composing my mind, contributed in a great degree to my recovery. At my request, he paid me daily visits. Our subject was religion,—not those theological controversies which excite so much irreligious feeling, and teach men to hate each other for the love of God; but those plain and simple truths which convince without confounding, and which avoid the bigotry that would worship error, because it is hereditary; and the fanaticism that would lay rash hands on the holy temple, because some of its smaller pillars appear unsound.

After several days of discussion on this important topic, he led me, by degrees, to give him an account of my late adventures; and as I related, he made comments.

Affected by his previous precepts, and by my own awful approach to eternity, which had suppressed in my heart the passions of ambition and pride, I now became as desirous of conviction as I had heretofore been sophistical in support of my folly. To be predisposed is to be half converted; and soon this exemplary pastor convinced my understanding of the impious and immoral tendency of my past life. He shewed me, that to the inordinate gratification of a particular caprice, I had sacrificed my duty towards my natural protectors, myself, and my God. That my ruling passion, though harmless in its nature, was injurious in its effects; that it gave me a distaste for all sober occupations, perverted my judgment, and even threatened me with the deprivation of my reason. Religion itself, he said, if indulged with immoderate enthusiasm, at last degenerates into zealotry, and leaves the poor devotee too rapturous to be rational, and too virulent to be religious.

In a word, I have risen from my bed, an altered being; and I now look back on my past delusions with abhorrence and disgust. Though the new principles of conduct which I have adopted are not yet rooted or methodized in my mind, and though the prejudices of a whole life are not (and indeed could not be) entirely eradicated in a few days; still, as I am resolved on endeavouring to get rid of them, I trust that my reason will second my desire, and that the final consequence of my perceiving what is erroneous will be my learning what is correct.

Adieu.

LETTER XLVII

My health is now so far re-established, that I am no longer confined to my room. Stuart pays us constant visits, and his lively advice and witty reasoning, more complimentary than reproachful, and more insinuated than expressed, have tended to perfect my reformation.

He had put Don Quixote (a work which I never read before) into my hands; and on my returning it to him, with a confession of the benefit that I derived from it, the conversation naturally ran upon romances in general. He thus delivered his sentiments.

'I do not protest against the perusal of fictitious biography altogether; for many works of this kind may be read without injury, and some with profit. Novels such as the Vicar of Wakefield, The Fashionable Tales, and Cœlebs, which draw man as he is, imperfect, instead of man as he cannot be, superhuman, are both instructive and entertaining. Romances such as the Mysteries of Udolpho, the Italian, and the Bravo of Venice, which address themselves to the imagination alone, are often captivating, and seldom detrimental. But unfortunately so seductive are the latter class of composition, that one is apt to neglect more useful books for them; besides, when indulged in extreme, they tend to incapacitate us from encountering the turmoils of active life. They present us with incidents and characters which we can never meet in the world; and act upon the mind like intoxicating stimulants; first elevate, and at last enervate it. They teach us to revel in ideal scenes of transport and distraction; and harden our hearts against living misery, by making us so refined as to feel disgust at its unpoetical accompaniments.

'In a country where morals are on the decline, novels always fall several degrees below the standard of national virtue: and the contrary holds in an opposite state of things. For as these works are an exaggerated picture of the times, they represent the prevalent opinions and manners with a gigantic pencil. Thus, since France became depraved, her novels have become dissolute; and since her social system arrived at its extreme of vicious refinement, they too have adopted that last master-stroke of refined vice, which wins the heart by the chastest aphorisms, and then corrupts it by the most alluring pictures of villainy. Take Rousseau for instance. What St. Preux is to Heloise, the book is to the reader. The lover so fascinates his mistress by his honourable sentiments, that she cannot resist his criminal advances. The book infatuates the reader, till, in his admiration of its morality, he loses all recollection of its licentiousness; for as virtue is more captivating, so vice is less disgusting when adorned with the Graces. It may be said that an author ought to portray vice in its seductive colours, for the purpose of unmasking its arts, and thus warning the young and inexperienced. But let it be recollected, that though familiarity with enchanting descriptions of vice may add to prudence, it must diminish virtue; and that while it teaches the reason to resist, it entices the passions to yield. It was Rousseau's system, however, to paint the scenes of a brothel, in order to speak the cant of a monastery; and thus has he undone many an imitating miss or wife, who began by listening to the language of love, that she might talk sentiment, and act virtue; and ended by falling a victim to it, because her heart had become entangled, her head bewildered, and her principles depraved.

'Now, though we seldom see such publications in this country, yet there is a strain of well-meaning, but false morality prevalent in some. I will add (for why should I conceal it from you?) that your principles, which have hitherto been formed upon such books alone, appear, at times, a little perverted by their influence. It should now, therefore, be your object to counteract these bad effects by some more rational line of reading; and, as your ideas of real life are drawn from novels; and as even your manners and language are vitiated by them, I would recommend to you to mix in the world, to copy living instead of imaginary beings, and to study the customs of actual, not ideal society.'

With this opinion my father perfectly coincided: the system has already been begun, and I now pass my time in an alternation of instruction and amusement. Morality, history, languages, and music, occupy my mornings; and my evenings are sometimes enlivened by balls, operas, and familiar parties. As, therefore, we shall remain some time in town, my father has taken a house.

Stuart, my counsellor and my companion, sits by my side, directs my studies, re-assures my timidity, and corrects my mistakes. Indeed he has to correct them often; for I still retain some taints of my former follies and affectations. My postures are sometimes too picturesque, my phrases too flowery, and my sentiments too sublime.

This having been the day fixed for the trials of Betterton and Grundy, the prisoners were brought to the bar, and the names of the prosecutors called. But these did not appear, and of consequence the culprits were discharged. It is supposed that Betterton, the great declaimer against bribery and corruption, had tampered with the postilion and the police, and thus escaped the fate which awaited him.

Adieu.

LETTER XLVIII

In ridding ourselves of a particular fault, we are apt, at first, to run too far into its opposite virtue. I had poured forth my tender feelings to you with such sentimental absurdity, when I fancied myself enamoured of one man, that as soon as I began to reform, and found myself actually attached to another, I determined on concealing my fondness from you, with the most scrupulous discretion of pen. Perhaps, therefore, I should beg your forgiveness for never having hinted to you before, what I am now about disclosing to you without any reserve.

Even at the very time when I thought I was bound in duty to be devotedly in love with the hateful Grundy, I felt an unconscious partiality for Stuart. But after my reformation, that partiality became too decisive to be misinterpreted or concealed. And indeed he was so constantly with me, and so kind a comforter and friend; and then so fascinating are his manners, and so good his disposition; for I am certain there is no such young man at all—you see in his eyes what he is; you see instantly that his heart is all gentleness and benevolence, and yet he has a fire in them, a fire that would delight you: and I could tell you a thousand anecdotes of him that would astonish you.—But what have I done with my sentence? Go back, good pen, and restore it to the grammar it deserves: or rather leave it as it is—a cripple for life, and hasten to the happy catastrophe.

With a secret transport which I cannot describe, I began of late to perceive that Stuart had become more assiduous than usual in his visits to me; that his manners betrayed more tenderness, and his language more regard. These attentions increased daily; nor did he omit opportunities of hinting his passion, in terms which I could not mistake.

This morning, however, put the matter beyond a doubt. I was alone when he came to pay his accustomed visit. At first he made some faint attempts at conversing upon indifferent topics; but all the time I could perceive an uneasiness and perturbation in his manner that surprised me.

'Pray,' said I, at length, 'what makes you so dull and absent to-day?'

'You,' replied he, with a smile.

'And what have I done?' said I.

"Tis not what you have done,' answered he; 'but what you will do.'

'And what is that?' said I.

He changed to a nearer chair, and looked at me with much agitation. I guessed what was coming; I had expected it some time; but now, when the moment arrived, I felt my heart fail; so I suddenly moved towards the door, saying that I was sure I heard my father call. Stuart sprang after me, and led me back by the hand.

'When I tell you,' said he, 'that on the possession of this hand depends my happiness, may I flatter myself with the hope that my happiness would not contribute to your misery?'

'As I am no longer a heroine,' said I, smiling, 'I do not intend to get up a scene. You happen to have my hand now; and I am afraid—very much afraid, that——'

'That what?' cried he, holding it faster.

'That it is not worth withdrawing,' said I.

But in this effort to shun a romance eclaircissement, I had, I feared, run into the contrary extreme, and betrayed an undue boldness; so I got sentimental in good earnest, and burst into tears. Stuart led me to my chair, and soon dissipated my uneasiness by his eloquent expressions of gratitude and delight, and his glowing pictures of our future happiness. I told him, that I wondered how he, who knew my failings so well, would venture to stake his happiness upon me.

'It was by my knowledge of your failings,' said he, 'that I discovered your perfections. Those embarrassments of your life which I witnessed have enabled me to judge of you more justly in a few months, than had I been acquainted with you whole years, in the common routine of intercourse. They have shewn me, that if you had weakness enough to court danger, you had firmness enough to withstand temptation; and that while the faulty part of your character was factitious and superinduced, all the pure and generous impulses came from your heart.'

Our conversation was interrupted by the sudden entrance of my father; and on his hearing from Stuart (who, it seems had made him a confidant) the favourable issue of our interview, the good old man hugged both of us in his arms.

To detain you no longer, a week hence is fixed for our wedding.

I have just received a letter from Mary, mentioning her perfect restoration to health, and her union with William. I shall offer no observation on your late marriage with the butler; but I must remark, that your reason for having never given me advice, during my follies—namely, because my father had deprived you of the right to do so, evinced more anger towards him than love for me. However, I shall always be happy to hear of your welfare.

Adieu.

LETTER XLIX

I have just time to tell you, before I leave town, that my fate was sealed this morning, and that I am a wife.

On my return to the house, after the ceremony, I found an epithalamium, addressed to me by poor Higginson; but it was more filled with hints at his own misery than congratulations upon my happiness.

Honest Jerry Sullivan met me at the door, and shook my hand, and danced round me in a fury of outrageous joy.

'Well,' cried he, 'often and often I thought your freaks would get you hanged; but may I be hanged if ever I thought they would get you married!'

'You see,' said I to Stuart, 'after all your pains to prevent me from imitating romances, you have made me terminate my adventures like a true romance—in a wedding. Pray with what moral will you now conclude the book?'

'I will say,' returned he, 'that virtue—no. That calamity—no. That fortitude and resignation—oh, no! I will say, then, that Tommy Horner was a bad boy, and would not get plumcake; and that King Pepin was a good boy, and rode in a golden coach.'

Adieu.